The Nine Unknown

The Nine Unknown
Talbot Mundy

MINT EDITIONS

The Nine Unknown was first published in 1923.

This edition published by Mint Editions 2021.

ISBN 9781513280790 | E-ISBN 9781513285818

Published by Mint Editions®

 MINT
EDITIONS

minteditionbooks.com

Publishing Director: Jennifer Newens
Design & Production: Rachel Lopez Metzger
Project Manager: Micaela Clark
Typesetting: Westchester Publishing Services

Contents

I

"I cut throats with an outward thrust!"

I had this story from a dozen people, or thirteen if you count Chullunder Ghose, whose accuracy is frequently perverted. One grain of salt is never enough to add to the fat babu's misstatements, although anyone who for that reason elected to disbelieve him altogether would be just as wide of the mark as the credulous who take what he says at face value. Chullunder Ghose should he accepted warily. But the others are above suspicion, as for instance King, Grim, Ramsden, the Reverend Father Cyprian, and Jeremy Ross, all of whom regard the truth from various points of view as economical.

Chullunder Ghose considers all truth merely relative at best—likes to be thought a liar, since under that cloak he can tell diluted truth unblushing. Consequently he is the only one whose real motive for taking part in this magnificent adventure is not discoverable; he scratches his stomach and gives a different reason every time he is asked, of which the likeliest is this:

"You see, *sahib*, bad luck being habitual is bad enough, but better than absolutely no luck. Consequently I took chances, trembling much, stirring innate sluggishness of disposition with galvanic batteries of optimism, including desire to keep wolf from door of underfed family and dependents."

He certainly took chances, and he appears to have survived them, for I had a letter from him only a week ago begging the favor of a character reference and offering in return to betray trade secrets in the event of his securing the desired employment.

Then there is Leonardo da Gama the Portuguese, who is dead and tells no tales; but his death corroborates some part of what he said to me, for one, and to others as will presently appear. His motive seems to have been mercenary, with the added zest of the scientist in search of a key to secrets, whose existence he can prove but whose solution has baffled men for generations.

The Reverend Father Cyprian, past eighty and custodian of a library not open to the public, aimed and still aims only at Hindu occultism. He regards it as the machinery of Satan, to be destroyed accordingly, and it was for that reason he gave King, Grim, Ramsden and some others access to books no human eye should otherwise have seen. For Father Cyprian collects books to be burned, not piecemeal but in one eventual holocaust.

Some lay brother peculiarly conscious of a sin appointed Father Cyprian by will, sole trustee of a purchasing fund, hoping thus to rid the world of the key to such evil as the Witch of Endor practised. For half a century Father Cyprian has been acquiring volumes supposed long ago to be extinct, and it was possibly the last phase of his beleaguered pride that he hoped instead of burning them piecemeal to make one bonfire of the lot and go to his Maker directly afterward.

In that case even pride may serve appropriate ends; for if he had burned the books as fast as acquired, King could never have studied them and drawn conclusions. He took King, Grim, Ramsden and certain others into confidence subject to a stipulation; there were and are still said to be nine super-books whose contents total tip the almost absolute of evil. King and his friends might use what Cyprian already had, and might count on his counsel and assistance; but if they should come on any of the nine books, those were to be Cyprian's to be burned along with all the others.

They were not to study the nine books, if obtained, and above all they were not to reveal their contents to any outsider; for Cyprian's purpose was, and is, to abolish the very memory of those books' existence and the deviltry they teach, or are supposed to teach. (For some say they teach wisdom.) But they might make what use they cared to of information picked up on the side, and they were free to deal with individuals as circumstances and their own discretion might dictate. Father Cyprian, in fact, cared and cares not much for consequences. He believes in cutting off the cause, and he is sure those nine books are the key which, if thrown away, Will leave the cause of necromancy impossible to rediscover. So much for him.

Jeremy Ross came laughing on the scene, laughed with gay irreverence all through the piece, and still laughs, no more inclined to take life seriously than when he faced the Turks in the three-day fight at Gaza, sharing one torn blanket with a wounded Turk and destroying his chance of promotion by calling a British colonel "Algy" to his face. On the other hand, he is as unconquerably opportunist as when he tramped Arabia, lost, and survived by means of a reputation for performing miracles.

Jeremy's admitted motive was desire to learn more tricks and their underlying principles. He is convinced that even the "rope trick, so often told of and so invariably unconfirmed, in which a Hindu is supposed to climb a rope into the air and disappear, is simply the result of well-trained ingenuity.

"A chap who knows how can do anything," says Jeremy, and he proposed to learn how all the Indian tricks are done.

The motives he did not confess, but which were just as obvious as the laugh on his lips and the sunburn on his handsome face, were loyalty to Athelstan King and Grim and Ramsden, a kind of irresponsibility that makes him plunge for amusement into every game he sees, and a bedrock willingness to fight every combination of men and circumstances for the right to be his own master. He has no use whatever for orders from "higher up," for swank, eyewash, stilts, inherited nobility, or what is known as statecraft.

"A diplomat's like me," says Jeremy, "only I call mine tricks and he calls his statesmanship."

It was enough that King and Grim had winded the stronghold of secret tyranny. Instantly Jeremy was game to make a pitched fight and a picnic of the business of destroying it; and he was quicker than either of them at penetrating the outer screen of commonplace deception. He got along remarkably well with Father Cyprian, in fact, astonishingly well, all things considered.

James Schuyler Grim is the protagonist of peace where there is no peace. His passion is to introduce two pauses in the strife of men where only one was formerly, and so little by little to give some sort of new millennium a chance. Arch-pragmatist is Grim. He holds men's lives, his own included, as worthless unless at work, and his highest expression of friendship is to pile task on task almost to the breaking point. He, too, resists interference from "higher up," but without Jeremy's turbulence and with much more wisdom—nearly satanic at times; which is one reason why Jeremy does not always mock him to his face.

Jeremy does mock Athelstan King, because King is of the seventh generation in the British army and respects accordingly the little odds and ends of precedent and custom that to the Australian resemble idol-worship. Jeremy was a trooper. King was a colonel but is now employed by the same multi-millionaire who furnishes supplies for Grim and Ramsden; in fact, he took Jeremy's place, for Jeremy cannot abide the power of purse-strings and would rather juggle by the roadside for his daily bread than yield to any man on the ground of surplus cash.

Jeff Ramsden is another independent, who rather prides himself on being slow of wit and heavy on his feet, whereas he is really a solid thinker, building argument on argument until he is convinced, and setting one foot down before he prospects with the other. He is stronger physically than almost any two normally developed athletes, but it would probably break Jeff Ramsden's heart to lose his comfortable savings, whereas Jeremy loses his last cent as cheerfully as he would win the other man's.

Then there are Narayan Singh, and Ali ben Ali of Siktinderam, soldiers of fortune both, the one a Sikh with pantheistic tendencies and the other a Pathan with seven sons. At any rate, Ali ben Ali is pleased to admit they are his sons, and none denies that he fought and slew the indignant legal owners of the mothers, although there are cynics in the crag-top villages who vow that Ali flatters himself. The mothers' statements (there were seven) made for the most part under duress shortly before death were not considered trustworthy evidence in the land that Ali comes from.

Ali has enemies, but is a man, whatever else; and perhaps the highest compliment ever paid Narayan Singh is that Ali ben Ali of Sikunderam respects him and would think three times before challenging the Sikh to fight, even if a mutual regard for Grim and King did not put quarreling out of the question. They are awfully disrespectful of each other's gods, but came to an early understanding on the basis propounded by Narayan Singh after a night-long argument:

"If your ridiculous Allah objects to my opinions why doesn't he smite me? I challenge him! As for thyself, Ali ben Ali of Sikunderam, thou art worth a dozen Allahs, being less cowardly, more generous, and not afraid to stand up and be seen!"

"It is a pity about you, Narayan Singh," Ali ben Ali answered nodding tolerantly. "I shall make a friend of you in this world only to see you torn by devils in the next. However, that is Allah's business, who is Lord of Mercies."

"Who is a big joke!" Narayan Singh corrected. "He will turn thee into worms!" warned he of Sikunderam.

"Then I will gnaw the big thing's belly!" said the Sikh.

They agreed to postpone the debate until the next world and to be stout allies in this—a plan which if followed universally would abolish a deal of waste of time.

"For if I slew you, or you slew me," said Ali ben Ali, "there would only be half our manhood left!"

And that was a point on which they could agree at once, for neither of them had a poor opinion of himself, any more than either cared a rap for Grin's and King's idealism. What they chose to follow were the men, they being men, and like attracting if not like at least its tribute.

Burt they were also attracted as much as Chullunder Ghose was by the glamour of the unknown quantity and the lure of fabled treasure; the babu being all acute imagination and alarm, they all adventurous.

Surely ancient sciences meant nothing to them; yet it was pursuit of ancient science and of nothing else that brought the twelve together, and that might have added the thirteenth if the number thirteen had not justified its reputation by proving fatal to da Gama the Portuguese. And that was no pity, but for scientific reasons.

He drank too frequently and inexpensively, and washed too sparingly to be good company. His appetite in all ways was a glutton's, drink included, and he took his erudition as he did champagne or beer or curried anchovies, in gulps.

Nor was he nice to look at—saffron, under shiny black hair, with a pair of coal-black eyes whose whites were yellow and red with long debauch—short—stout—asthmatic—dressed always in rusty black broadcloth and occasionally white drill pants, with black boots tied with broken laces. His face was seamed and lined with tales untenable and knowledge unfit to be known. His finger-ends were swollen and his nails close-bitten. His shirt, which might have been a petticoat for stripe and color, bulged through the gap between his pants and vest, increasingly untidy as the day progressed, and he hitched his pants at intervals. He had a little, black imperial beard that only half-concealed a chin cloven not by nature but by some man's weapon. The cleft had the effect of making him look good-humored for a second when he smiled. The smile began with a sneer malignantly, passed with a peculiar melting moment through an actually pathetic phase, and ended cynically, showing yellow eye-teeth. He had no idea whatever of making himself pleasant—would have scorned himself, in fact, for the attempt if he had ever tried it—and yet he blamed the world and did the world all the injury he could for refusing to love him. He always wore a round black hat like an English clergyman's, and never took it off, even indoors, until he was seated, when he held it rolled up as if he kept his thoughts in it and was afraid of spilling them.

It was Chullunder Ghose who decoyed him into the office in the side-street off the Chandni Chowk, which is the famous Street of the Silversmiths in Delhi, and a good street if you know what goodness in a street consists of. Men—all manner of men—go by.

They had an office in a side-street, one flight up over a Maharatta drug-store, with the name "Grim, Ramsden and Ross" on a brass plate on the door. The next-door building was a warehouse for hides, hair, tallow, gum, turmeric and vicious politics, through the midst of which they had access to a back stairs by arrangement. But the front stairway by which you reached their office was a narrow, steep affair between two buildings, littered with fruit-peel and cigarette ends, and always crowded with folk who used it as a sort of covered grandstand from which to watch the street or merely to sit and think, supposing that anybody *could* think in all that noise.

You had to pick your way up-stairs gingerly, but going down was easier, because if you placed your foot flat against the back of a man's head, and shoved suddenly, he would topple forward and carry a whole row down with him, due to the fact that they sat cross-legged and not with their feet on the step below as Europeans would.

Existence there would have been precarious, but for Narayan Singh, Ali ben Ali and Chullunder Ghose—the first two truculent and the third a diplomat. It is fashionable nowadays to show contempt for Westerners by pushing them off the sidewalk and making remarks in babu English that challenge reprisals; so that, even though King, Grim and Ramsden can disguise themselves and pass for natives of the East, and Jeremy in plain clothes can make an Arab think he is an Aras in disguise, the firm's name on the brass plate would have been enough to start trouble, if it had not been so obvious that trouble would include a Sikh dagger, an Afghan *tulwar*, and the adder's tongue of the least compunctious babu in all India.

It was the babu's tongue that drew da Gama past the door. He was afraid of it, in the same way that some politicians are afraid of newspapers, and it may be that he hoped to murder the babu as the simplest road to silence. All are agreed he was surprised and angry when Narayan Singh; swaggering down the narrow passage, bunted into him as he stood hesitating and, picking a quarrel on the instant, shoved him backward through the office door. Inside he found himself confronted by the whole party, for Narayan Singh followed him through and locked the door at his back.

He stood at bay, in silence, for a minute, showing his yellow teeth, his hands making the beginnings of a move toward his pockets and repeatedly refraining. So Ali ben Ali strode up to him and, taking him in one prodigious left arm, searched him for weapons. He pulled out a long knife and a black-jack, exposed them, grinning hugely, in the palm of his right hand and returned them to their owner. There was no pistol. Then he pushed the Portuguese toward the office stool, which was the only seat unoccupied. Da Gama sat on it, putting his heels on the rungs, with his toes turned outward, whereafter he removed his round, black hat and rolled it.

The others sat around the wall on bentwood chairs, or otherwise as temperament dictated, all except Father Cyprian, who had been accorded the desk and revolving chair in deference to age. Cyprian held the desk-lid raised, but lowered it suddenly, and at the noise da Gama started, stared a second, and then swore in Portuguese between his teeth. None in the room understood Portuguese, unless possibly the priest.

"You recognize me, I believe?" piped Cyprian, almost falsetto, his little bright eyes gleaming through the wrinkles and his mobile lips spreading and spreading away into a smile that advertised amusement and was certainly a mask.

He has a face like a friendly gargoyle, full of human understanding and a sort of merry disdain that goes with it.

"Keep to your trade of mumbling Mass! What do these others want?" the Portuguese demanded rudely. "I have nothing to do with priests!"

His low-pitched asthmatic voice was an absolute contrast to the other's. So was his surliness. There was no connecting link between them but that one, swift, momentary cloven lapse from hardness as the Portuguese's face changed from one scowl to the next. But Cyprian recognized that and was swift, before the human feeling faded:

"My friend," he said, "it was you who tried to steal my library, and I have never sought to have you punished, for I know the strength of the temptation—"

"You are a miser with your books—a dog in a manger!" the Portuguese retorted. "You break your own law, which says you shall not hide light under a bushel!"

"It is darkness that hides!" the priest answered with another of his expansive smiles. "It was you, my friend, who tried to murder me—a sin from which I only saved you by being one inch to the eastward of your bullet's course."

"You lie like any other priest!" da Gama growled.

"No, no. Not all of us are rash. In fact, we—we all of us are—are occasionally careful. Is this not the pistol that you tried to shoot me with?"

He raised the lid of the desk again and drew out a surprising thing born of the law against carrying firearms. It was a pistol built of springs and teak-wood, nearly as clumsy as the old museum holster pieces but as able as a cobra to do murder at close range. Da Gama was silent.

"My friend, I have not even blamed you," the priest went on, his thin voice squeaking with the rust of years. "I have pitied you, and as for me you are forgiven. But there are consequences."

"What?" the Portuguese demanded, betraying, between scorn and anger, once again that moment of human feeling.

"Something is required of him to whom so much has been forgiven," the priest answered firmly.

"What?" the Portuguese repeated.

Jeremy reached for the pistol and began fooling with the thing, as pleased with its mechanism as he was impatient of preliminaries. Ali ben Ali of Sikunderam drew out his own long knife and thumbed its cutting edge suggestively.

"You for twenty-five, and I for fifty years have sought the same thing," the priest said, speaking slowly. "You have taken one line, I the other. Mine is best, and now you must follow mine, my friend—"

"For I cut throats with an outward thrust," Ali ben Ali interrupted. "The point goes in across the wind-pipe and the knife's heel separates the neck-bones."

It was horribly well spoken. Ali ben Ali failed in his youth for a Bachelor's Degree but passed in rhetoric. Da Gama shuddered.

"Peace!" commanded Cyprian.

"For the present," assented he of Sikunderam, stowing the knife away with its hilt projecting. For religious reasons he was careful not to show the alien priest too much respect.

"What do you want?" da Gama asked.

Father Cyprian reached into his desk and produced a little chamois-leather bag. Opening that he poured about thirty gold coins into his hand and held it out toward the Portuguese, whose eyes changed expression suddenly.

"The balance of those," said Cyprian, "and the nine books. You may have as much of the money as you can use, my friend, and you may have my share too, for I need none of it. But the books must be mine to do as I choose with."

Da Gama went through all the motions of his smile and ended on the usual sneer. "No doubt! If you have the books you will need no money."

"I shall do as I please," the priest answered, not choosing to argue that point. "Do you know whence these came? Look at them."

He poured the coins into da Gama's open hand, and the Portuguese's dark eyes seemed to take fire from behind. None was of more recent date than a thousand years B.C., and one or two were of such soft gold that all the impression had been rubbed and squeezed away.

"The little bag—you know the little bag?" the priest asked, handing him that too. "You recognize it? Yes? You left that, you remember, with the money in it when you tried to shoot me, and my servant pulled your coat off. He would have captured you, but—"

Da Gama smiled again, beginning and ending meanly, on a note of insolence, but passing inevitably through that momentary human stage.

"But never mind," Cyprian went on. "You may have them back, except the gun. My servant shall bring your coat. You have been forgiven. But where did you get that money? I must know."

"Yes, we must all know that," agreed Ali ben Ali's deep voice, and the Northerner drew his knife again, thumbing its edge with a kind of professorial appreciation.

Grim, dressed as a Punjabi, had sat watching da Gama's face. Now he saw fit to betray that really it was he who was in charge of the proceedings.

"You understand?" he asked. "All that Father Cyprian asks for is the books."

"And you?" da Gama demanded, sneering again. It seemed to be his policy to get on terms with strangers by provoking. "You care only for money?"

Grim dug into the folds of his loose upper garment and produced a telegram from his employer in New York.

INVESTIGATE AND REPORT ON PERPETUAL DISAPPEARANCE OF SPECIE IN INDIA. MELDRUM STRANGE.

He passed it to da Gama, who read it and cocked one eyebrow:

"Your alibi?" he suggested, pronouncing the word as if it were Portuguese, which for undiscoverable reasons made it more offensive.

Grim ignored that.

"We want to discover what has happened to the billions of dollars worth of gold and silver that has been won from the earth during the thousands of years since mining was first commenced. The cash in circulation doesn't account for one per cent. of it. Where is the rest?" he explained.

"What if you find it?" asked da Gama.

"If you help, you may have as much of it as you can use," Cyprian interposed.

"Father Cyprian wants the nine books," Grim repeated. "He wants to destroy the knowledge that has enabled certain unknown men for thousands of years to drain the world of its supply of gold and silver. I wish to discover where the gold and silver is. You may have enough of it if your help amounts to anything."

"I also desire to know where the gold and silver is!" remarked Ali ben Ali, from his seat on a cushion in a corner. "I, too, desire enough of it!" he added, sticking his long-knife point-downward in the floor and laying the palm of his hand on the hilt to stop its trembling. "My heart quivers as the knife does!"

It was easy to believe him. At that moment his gray-shot beard framed avarice and not much else, except the ruthlessness that gave it energy. His eyes contained the glint of morning on the Himalayan crags. Ali ben Ali of Sikunderam saw many visions at the mention of the magic name of gold and silver.

"I cut throats with an outward thrust!" he added meaningly, pulling up the knife again and glancing at the Portuguese.

Then Athelstan King took a hand.

"The same men who own those nine books keep the secret of the gold and silver coin," he said, speaking downright as his way is.

"How do you know?" da Gama sneered.

"Because like you I have devoted years to the pursuit," King answered; and in his eyes there was the sort of steely gray strength of the hunter who looks up-wind and into sunlight.

"Pursuit?" Da Gama was at his usual occupation, sneering. "Did you catch much?"

"You, at any rate!" King answered; and Chullunder Chose observed the opportunity for self-advertisement.

"His honor having given orders to this babu—said babu having followed same," he smirked, wiping sweat from his hairy chest with a handkerchief, perhaps to call attention to the diligence with which he had labored.

Then he chose to emphasize and illustrate dexterity by throwing down the handkerchief and catching it between his toes.

"You're simply a prisoner," said King, looking straight at the Portuguese.

"This," said Narayan Singh, on the floor beside Ali of Sikunderam, "is the writing of one Dilji Leep Singh, who swears that he helped you steal books out of a temple, but was never paid for it. He will be a witness if required."

Narayan Singh laid a paper on the floor just within range of da Gama's eye, and it was that that really turned the trick. He had imagination. He could see defeat.

"You may have a fair share of the money, if we find it with your assistance," Grim reminded.

"And I have forgiven you," added Cyprian.

"But I cut throats with an outward thrust," said Ali ben Ali of Sikunderam.

"Oh, what is it you want?" the Portuguese exclaimed, throwing up his clenched fists suddenly—theatrically. "Am I briganded and held to ransom after twenty-five years? All right! I surrender! Write down your promises, and I will tell!"

II

"Produce but the gold, thou Portuguese!"

But they wrote no promises. It was da Gama, desperate to the point of daring them to take his life and never sure that Ali ben Ali or the Sikh would not accept the challenge, who wrote down terms on a half-sheet of paper.

"Hell! There! My minimum! Without you sign that there is not a torture in the universe severe enough to make me talk!"

"Same being Portuguese opinion, anarchistic possibly! This babu risking personal humiliation volunteers advice—be skeptical!" remarked Chullunder Ghose, rolling off-center so as to reach the door of a small cupboard.

He pulled out a gallon jar of whisky and shoved it along the floor sufficiently noisily to attract da Gama's notice. Father Cyprian walked out, saying nothing, and Narayan Singh relocked the office door behind him.

"Advice not being asked, same tendered deferentially, which is—" said the babu, pausing—"give him one drink, subsequently withholding remainder of contents of gallon jar pending answers to questions. No water on any account!" he added, pursing up his lips.

The sweat broke out on da Gama's forehead. He was no hero, but was gifted with imagination. As long as the priest stayed he had banked on that unbegged forgiveness, calculating, too, that the priest would tolerate no illegal violence in his presence. But Cyprian was gone, and he looked around the room. They all knew, and he knew they knew, what the whisky torture meant to a man of his disposition. He shoved the crumpled half-sheet into his pocket and capitulated.

"What do you want to know?" he demanded hoarsely.

"Give him one drink," ordered King, and then, when the Portuguese had tossed that down his throat—"Where did you find those coins?"

"In the ruins of a temple. I cannot describe the place."

"Why not?"

"It has no name."

"You can lead us to it."

Da Gama nodded.

"Yes," he said. "I can lead, but you will find nothing. That is, I removed the gold—you see it. You may search a thousand years. I brought it all. I am intelligent—me. You have not the intellectual requirements. Yet I tell you, I know nothing—nothing! Only Cyprian the priest is capable, for he has books. But the fool thinks they are wicked, and he won't tell! He is a dog in a manger—a miser—a—"

"Never mind him. Tell us what *you* know," King interrupted.

"I know that none of you will live unless you cease from interference with the Nine Unknown!"

"Put that whisky back into the cupboard!" Grim ordered.

Chullunder Ghose obeyed. It was stifling in the office and for the second time the Portuguese capitulated.

"There is only one course worth trying," he said, trying to moisten his lips, which had grown dry at the mere mention of the whisky jar. His tongue looked a size too large. "You must subsidize me—support me. You must get those books from Cyprian and let me read them. You will all fail otherwise. I am the only man who ever lived who carried the search for the Nine Unknown the little way that even I have gone. I am the only one who found *anything*. They have made several attempts on *my* life. What chance would *you* have to escape them? Whisky please."

Grim shook his head.

"Then water!"

"Earn your drink," Grim answered.

"*Tshaa!* Well—it doesn't matter what I tell you! You will be useless without me. You lack the required intelligence. The problem is vertical, not horizontal. All the clues are cut off—blind from underneath. There—you do not understand that. What is the use of telling you? The Nine Unknown are at the top. That is a simple statement. Nine individuals, each independent, collectively forming a self-perpetuating board—each known to all the other eight but to no other individual on earth—not known, that is to say, to any other person in the world as being a member of the Nine. You understand that?

"Each of the Nine, then, appoints nine others known only to him, and each of whom supposes his principal to be merely a servant of the Nine. They think the orders they receive from him are second-hand orders, passed along. Thus, there are eighty-one first lieutenants, as it were, who think themselves to be second-lieutenants. And each of those eighty-one employs nine others, in turn known only to himself, making seven hundred and twenty-nine third lieutenants, each of whom knows only eight, at most, of his associates, but all whom are at the service of the Nine, whom they know neither by sight nor name. You follow me?

"Every one of the seven hundred and twenty-nine third lieutenants has nine men under him, of his own choosing, each of whom again has nine more. So the chain is endless. There are no clues. If you discover, say, a fourth lieutenant, all he knows is the identity of the individual who gives him orders and, perhaps in addition to his own nine subordinates the names of eight associates, none of whom knows more than he.

"When one of the Nine Unknown dies, the other eight elect an individual to take his place. None but they even guesses that a vacancy was filled. None, except the Nine, knows who the Nine are. Each first, second, third, fourth, fifth, sixth, seventh, eighth lieutenant is responsible for nine; and they to him. Nothing is written. No muster-roll."

"How old is this organization?" King demanded.

"How old is India?" the Portuguese retorted. "How many dynasties have thought they ruled? They levied taxes and they all paid tribute to the Nine! If the money the Nine have received during all those ages had been invested at compound interest the whole world would be so awfully in debt that people would understand what has been happening and might possibly wake up. But there is wisdom in the books the Nine make use of—one book to a man, each book dealing with a branch of wisdom. They have simply hoarded money, letting the nations use gold as it is won from mines and only taking tribute of principal, not interest. Do you believe that?"

King, Grim, Ramsden and Jeremy nodded. Ramsden read aloud from a memorandum book:

"Last year the production of silver alone amounted to more than a hundred and sixty million ounces. The East absorbed more than a quarter of that—"

"And is howling for silver again!" said King. "Where did forty million ounces disappear to? There is some in circulation—not much; ornaments account for some of it; a little has been hoarded by the peasants, but it's less in these days of high prices and taxes; where is the balance?"

"I have none of it, Lord knows!" exclaimed Chullunder Ghose, holding up both hands with pious resignation.

"Where did it disappear?" said the Portuguese. "Here is some"—he shook the chamois-leather bag—"but all I found was leavings in a crack of a temple cellar, where they stored the tribute a thousand years ago."

"Nevertheless," remarked Chullunder Ghose, "India continues swallowing gold and silver in measures of *crores*, that which is swallowed not reappearing in any discernible shape, contrary to teachings of political economy, which being religion of West is probably poppycock possessing priests with check-books and top-hats. Where is gold and silver? That is whole point."

"Babylon had gold and silver," said the Portuguese. "Where is it?"

Jeremy took twenty sovereigns from his belt. (He always carries them, they constituting his uttermost reserve, never to be spent, but to be bluffed with.) He jingled them from band to hand as if their music inspired him. Da Gama went on talking:

"*Always* India has imported gold and silver—always! But where is it? Some jewelry, but not much; the bracelets of one generation are melted by the next. A very small percentage disappears from wear. Of course, there is a little lost. A little more is buried and forgotten. But the balance—the accumulated surplus of at least six thousand years—I estimate it as a heap as great as the pyramid of Gizeh! And. where is it?"

Chullunder Ghose blinked. Ali ben Ali drew his knife and stuck it quivering in the floor again. Narayan Singh breathed sibilantly through set teeth. Jeremy palmed his twenty sovereigns in a pile, and they all disappeared except one, which was fascinating; he did it again and again, and you couldn't tell where the nineteen were until he caught them out of air in his left hand.

"What became of the gold of Solomon?" da Gama asked. "He had so much of it. The records say men thought nothing of gold and silver during his reign. He died, and the gold went—where? Some say Solomon himself was one of the Nine Unknown—"

"Who says that?" King demanded.

"I for one!" da Gama answered. "But there are books. Ask Cyprian the priest. He has them. Where is the gold the Spaniards and the Portuguese shipped home from South America and Mexico? Where is all the product of the Rand and of Australia? They took seven billions of dollars worth of gold and silver from the Comstock—just one reef in Nevada—yet tell me: how much gold and silver is there in the world to-day? The greatest hoard—greater than all other known hoards put together—is in the United States Treasury, and it doesn't amount to a hat-full compared to the total that is known to have been mined in the course of history! Where has the rest disappeared?"

"That's what we're asking *you*," Grim warned him; and Ali ben Ali drew the handle of his knife back and let go so that it hummed like a thing thrown.

"I must see the books that Cyprian the priest has," da Gama answered, looking at the knife and shuddering.

"They give no clue to the treasure," King answered.

Da Gama actually laughed, a thing he hardly ever did. It sounded like something breaking. Jeremy laughed too, like breaking water, and palmed all twenty sovereigns with one sweep, instantly showing the same hand empty.

"The hand deceives the eye!" said Jeremy. "And I've seen written stuff that fooled a banker's clerk!"

"No book can fool me!" said da Gama, slapping his forehead and showing the cloven weakness as he smiled. "I know Sanskrit as Max Müller never dreamed of knowing it! Show me the books of Cyprian the priest and I will tell you where the treasure is!"

"You're talking rot!" said Jeremy. "If Father Cyprian has the books and they contain the secret, why can't he go straight and find the treasure? Eh? We wouldn't waste whisky on you!"

"Pardon me, but it is little whisky that you waste," da Gama answered. "As for Cyprian, the man is blinded by fanaticism. He knows a little Sanskrit—just perhaps enough to pass for erudition among ignoramuses—brut he will not read what he sees. He is purblind."

"I read what I saw, and I know more than a little Sanskrit," King retorted quietly, but da Gama was more than ever cock-sure and sneered back at him.

"If Cyprian the priest were not a fool," he said, "he would have set his communicants to stealing books from me! For I have the keys to his books, and he cannot read his without mine. And all my keys are good for is to fit the locks that he guards like a miser! Get me his books, and I will unlock their secrets for you in a week. In ten days I will show you such a heap of gold and silver as will make you mad! I wish to see you mad! Have no fear that I will disappoint you!"

Nevertheless, there was not one man in the room who would have dared place Father Cyprian's books in the hands of da Gama.

"Let's see; you have escaped the vengeance of the Nine how many years?" asked Grim, and da Gana laughed again. He saw the point.

"Bring us your books, and you shall compare them with Father Cyprian's," said King. "Thereafter, the books are his, but you shall have as much as you can use of any gold and silver found."

Da Gama hesitated. He had intellect, and worked it—prided himself on that. Few of the human passions, except drink and avarice and infidelity, had any influence with him, so he reviewed the situation on its merits, being candid with himself. Like Grim, he sought no solace but results, and he would have wondered why Grim despised him, had he been aware of it.

"I cannot bring my books," he said. "They weigh too much."

"We'll carry them," offered Jeremy.

"Give me a drink," da Gama answered, nodding. It was obvious he agreed, with a proviso.

The babu poured forth whisky into the office tumbler and presented it. Da Gama drank.

"We should have an understanding," he said, smacking his lips. "There was wisdom in the accumulation of gold and silver by the Nine. Don't disregard that. It all has to do with the *Kali Yug** and its end that was prophesied six thousand years ago. The purpose is to cheapen money by the squandrous abundance of it—"

"Krishna!" gasped Chullunder Ghose.

"—to abolish capitalism—do you see?" da Gama went on. "That will be the end of the *Kali Yug*. Capitalism is the age of darkness. To put in place of money—brains—intellect, that is the idea. To cheapen money by abundance, not of promises to pay, but of veritable gold and silver. Money being worthless, brains will count—intellect—you understand me? Have you intellect? No! Just habits! Have I intellect? Oh yes! But have I the reforming zeal? By no means! I am lazy. Let the world remain material and money-drunk; it suits me better! Can you accomplish anything without my intellect? No indeed. You cannot understand the Sanskrit, which is a language of conundrums. You would turn the floods of money loose and create a havoc. Money would be worthless, and you no better off. In the books the Nine Unknown possess is the only secret of how to prevent the havoc. It means high thinking, and that is hard work—too hard. I say, let us take advantage of the money, and not turn it loose. Let the *Kali Yug* persist! Let us be rich—wealthy—affluent beyond the dreams—"

---

* The age of darkness referred to in Sanskrit writings.

"Nay, nay! There is no affluence beyond my dreams!" said Ali, plucking at his knife. "I could use a million *crores* of gold and silver! I would buy the North—and build a city—and raise a *lashkar** such as Iskander's†—and—and speak not of millenniums! The world will burn my day out! Produce but the gold, thou Portuguese!"

"Produce the books!" said Grim.

The Portuguese got down from the high stool and leaned his back against it.

"Are we agreed about the money?" he asked, looking from eye to eye for disagreement.

His was that disposition. He would promise anything to men in whom the seed of disagreement lay, knowing that the future would hold opportunity. But his wandering eye was fascinated by Jeff Ramsden's clenched, enormous fist. It seemed to symbolize. It was a totem. It did not stand for intellect, but it was heartbreakingly honest, neither Latin in its attitude toward a problem, nor cynical, nor unjust—not too credulous—just aboveboard, and direct, and faithful.

"Produce the books!" repeated Grim.

But he was dealing with the Latin temperament, which is not frank, reserving always little secret back-ways out from its commitments.

"I will go and arrange it," da Gama answered. Whereat Jeremy did three tricks in succession with a coin, as if by way of illustration.

"I'll go with you," Ramsden volunteered. "I can carry quite a lot of books."

"No!" said the Portuguese, contriving to look scandalized in the way the Latin nations do when anyone suggests a view of their back-yard. "There are my personalities. I mean, I am not a pip-show. I go alone. I will arrange. You may meet me. You shall have the books."

"I have seven sons," announced Ali ben Ali of Sikunderam, with his steel eyes focused on infinity, as if he were dreaming of his distant hills.

"Well—they would, no doubt, do to carry books," said the Portuguese, not understanding him.

Whereat Ali ben Ali got up and left the room, Narayan Singh locking the door again when he was gone. The others understood that perfectly.

"Go and make your arrangements. Where will you meet us?" Grim demanded.

---

* Army.
† Alexander the Great.

"Do you know my quarters? There then," said the Portuguese. "In an hour? No, that is too soon. I have books in one place and another. They must be collected. Come to-night."

"Leave one of those coins with me," said Jeremy. "You shall have it back."

Da Gama made a gesture of magnificence and passed the chamois-leather bag. Jeremy tipped the contents into his hand, and chose, holding up a coin between his fingers.

"What's it worth?" he asked. "You can have it when you like, but—"

"Write me a receipt for it."

Da Gama took a crumpled sheet of paper from his pocket and straightened it out, smoothing the reverse side.

"This babu advising skepticism, as aforesaid! Safety first!" advised Chullunder Ghose, squirming nervously. "Same being ancient adage!"

"I get you," laughed Jeremy, and he waved aside the proffered sheet of paper, which da Gama pocketed again with an air of impudent indifference.

Jeremy produced an English five-pound note from his pocketbook and wrote his name on it.[*]

"Take it. I'll trade back whenever you say."

The Portuguese looked disappointed but folded the five-pound note on second thought and slipped it in the lining of his hat.

"So," he said tartly, "I cannot make use of that one, since it is offered as security. If your excellency had another of the same denomination, to be lent me pending—"

King pulled out his wallet at once and produced the equivalent of five pounds in Indian currency notes. The Portuguese accepted them, and they needed no signature.

"*Gracas.* To be repaid, *señor.* Then we meet tonight—at my—ah—hotel."

He bowed magnificently, wholly unaware that the gesture made him look ridiculous. Narayan Singh unlocked the office door, and he backed out, continuing to bow, ignoring nobody, treating Chullunder Ghose to equal deference, the sneer on his yellow face giving the lie offensive and direct to his politeness, and he unconscious of it. He believed he made a most impressive exit.

---

[*] A formality usually required before any responsible party, will cash a stranger's bank-note.

"He is thirsty—very thirsty. And he has five pounds," remarked Chullunder Ghose, as apropos of nothing as the Northerner's remark had been about his seven sons.

"Let's look at the coin," said Grim, and Jeremy passed it.

Grim is a numismatist, if a job in a museum at the age of eighteen can make a man that. They sent him to the Near East subsequently on the strength of what he knew. He shook his head.

"It's the same one Cyprian showed us. I've never seen one, nor a reproduction of one like it. I believe it's older than Cyrene. It's not Indian—at least, that isn't Sanskrit lettering—and it's better made than any of the earliest coins we know about. That might be a coin from lost Atlantis!"

"Pre-Adamite!" suggested Jeremy, but Grim was serious.

"I tell you," he answered as the door burst open and Ali of Sikunderam strode in, "we're in touch with the riddle of all history—the riddle of the Sphinx perhaps! Oh Lord, if we can only keep in touch!"

"By Allah, there are worse responsibilities than seven sons!" said Ali ben Ali, grinning. His grin sat crosswise of a black beard like sea-foam in the night. "If keeping touch is all your honor asks, then count it done!"

"Does a watched pot boil? Or a watched thief steal? Or a watched door open? Your sons will interfere with him!" remarked Chullunder Ghose, scratching his nose with an action suggestive of thumbing it.

"Bellyful of forebodings! They have orders not to interfere with him," the Northerner retorted.

"Simply to watch?" asked King.

"Simply to watch him."

"Watch me!" said Jeremy. "Come close if you like."

He palmed the prehistoric coin in half-a-dozen ways in swift succession, making it move from hand to hand unseen, and plucking it at last from mid-air, said:

"I'll bet a fiver the Don steals a march on us."

"He will steal nothing!"

Ali ben Ali of Sikunderam held up a hand as if declaiming in the mosque.

"My seven sons are the cleverest thieves that live! A thief can fool a non-thief, but not a professional. They are seven to one!"

But Jeremy laughed. Whereat Ramsden, bearded like the bust of Anthony, unclenched his fist and let go the burden of his thoughts. He was a prospector by profession, used to figuring in terms of residue.

"Forty million ounces!" he exclaimed. "Do you know what only one million ounces a year, say, for six thousand years would mean—how many trains of box-cars it would take to move it? It would need a fleet of ocean liners! Talk of secrecy's a joke!"

"Nine Unknown having kept said secret for six thousand years!" Chullunder Ghose retorted.

"And whose is the money by right?" asked Grim; that being the kind of poser you could count on him for.

"The fighter's—the finder's!" shouted Ali of Sikunderam, and Narayan Singh agreed, nodding, saying nothing, permitting his brown eyes to glow. And at that Chullunder Ghose looked owlish, knowing that the soldier wins but never keeps; sacrifices, serves, eats promises, and dies in vain. He did not tell all he knew, being a rather wise civilian. He sighed—Chullunder Ghose did.

"There possibly may be enough for all of us!" he said, rolling his eyes upward meekly.

Then Cyprian returned from strolling in the Chandni Chowk with that incurious consent of crowds conferred on priests and all old men—between the hours of indignation.

"You didn't hurt him? Children, you didn't hurt him?" he demanded. "Did he drink a little too much? Did he talk?"

King and Grim repeated what had happened, Cyprian smiling, shaking his head slowly—possibly because of old-age, yet perhaps not. At eighty years a man knows how to take advantage of infirmity.

"The long spoon!" he said. "The long spoon! It only gives the devil leverage! You should have kept him here."

Ali ben Ali flared up at that, Koran in mind along with many other scriptures that assail the alien priest. "My sons—" he began.

"Are children, too," said Cyprian. "I credit them with good intentions."

"They are men!" said Ali, and turned his back.

Then Jeremy, who has no reverence for anyone or anything, but two men's share of natural affection, took Cyprian by the arm and coaxed him away to lunch at a commercial club, promising him a nap on a sofa in a corner of the empty cloakroom afterwards. The ostensible bait he used was an offer to introduce a man who owned an ancient roll of Sanskrit *mantras*; but it was Jeremy's own company that tempted; Cyprian leans on him, and seems to replenish his aging strength from the Australian's superabundant store—a strange enough condition, for as religion goes, or its observances, they are wider than the poles apart.

"All things to all men, ain't you, Pop!" said Jeremy. "Come and eat curried quail. The wine's on ice."

"And there you are!" remarked Chullunder Ghose, as the two went out, illustrating the "thereness" of the "areness" by catching a fly on the wing with his thumb and forefinger and releasing it through the open window, presumably unharmed. "Matters of mystery still lack elucidation, but 'the wine's on ice!' How Anglo-Saxon! Wonderful! United States now holding greater part of world's supply of gold, and India holding total invisible ditto, same are as plus and minus—so we go to lunch! I dishonestly propose to issue bills of exchange against undiscovered empyrean equity, but shall be voted down undoubtedly—*verb. sap.* as saying is—brow-beaten, sat upon—yet only wise man of the aggregation. Sell stock, that is my advice! Issue gilt-edge scrip at premium, and pocket consequences! Sell in U. S. A. undoubtedly, residing subsequently in Brazil. But there you are! Combination of Christian priest, Sikh, fanatical Moslem, freethinker, agnostic, Methodist minister's son and cynicalist, is too overwhelming for shrewdness to prevail. Myself, am cynicalist, same being syndicalist with opportunist tendencies. I go to tiffin. Appetite—a good digestion—a siesta. *Sahibs*—humbly wishing you the same—*salaam!*"

Chullunder Ghose, too, bowed himself out backward, almost as politely as the Portuguese had done—indubitably mocking—giving no offense, because, unlike the Portuguese, he did not sneer.

III

"Light and longer weapons"

In their day the Portuguese produced more half-breeds per capita than any other nation in the world; there are stories about a bonus once paid for half-breed babies. Their descendants advertise the Portuguese of Goa without exactly cherishing the institutions of the land that gave them origin. They have become a race, not black nor white, nor even yellow, but all three; possessed of resounding names and of virtues that offset some peculiarities; not loving Goa, they have scattered. A few have grown very rich, and all exist in a no-man's land between the rival castes and races, where some continue to be very poor indeed. Others are cooks, stewards, servants; and a few, like Fernandez de Mendoza de Sousa Diomed Braganza, keep hotels.

His was the Star of India, an amazing place with a bar and a license to sell drinks, but with a separate entrance for people ridden by compunctions. It was an ancient building, timbered with teak but added to with sheets of corrugated iron, whitewashed. Some of the upper rooms were connected with the cellar by cheap iron piping of large diameter, up which those customers who had a reputation to preserve might pull their drink in bottles by a string. Still other pipes were used for whispering purposes. In fact the "Star of India Hostelry" was "known to the police," and was never raided, it being safer to leave villains a place where they thought themselves safe from observation.

As happens in such cases, the Star of India had a respectable reputation. Thieves only haunt the known thieves' dens in story books. It was no place for a white man who insisted on his whiteness, nor for Delhi residents, nor for social lions. Nevertheless, it was crowded from cellar to roof with guests belonging by actual count to nineteen major castes, including more or less concealed and wholly miserable women-folk. The women in such a place who keep themselves from contact and defilement suffer worse than souls in the seventh pit of Dante's hell.

Nine out of ten of the guests were litigants in from the country, waiting their turn in the choked courts, tolerating Diomed's hospitality because it was cheap. The farce of caste-restrictions could be more or less observed. Intrigue was easy. You could "see" the lawyer of the other side. And as for thieves and risks, where are there none? The tenth in every instance was undoubtedly a thief—or worse.

There lived da Gama, pure blooded Portuguese, greatly honoring the half-breed by his presence. Like the caste-women, da Gama kept within the stifling walls by day as a general rule. But, again as in the women's case, his nights were otherwise. *They* went to the roof then, where such little breeze as moved was hampered by curtains hung on clothes-lines to make privacy. *He* went to the streets, and was absent very likely all night long, none knowing what became of him, and none succeeding in entering his locked, large, corner room.

That night King, Grim, Ramsden and Jeremy went to Diomed's hotel to keep their tryst with da Gama. They were dressed, except Jeremy, as Jats—a race with a reputation for taking care of itself, and consequently seldom interfered with; surly, moreover, and not given to answering strangers' questions. Jeremy wore Arab clothes, that being the easiest part he plays; plenty of Arabs go to Delhi, because of the agitation about the Khalifate, so he excited no, more comment than the other three.

Mainly, in India, the religions keep apart. But that is where the Goanese comes in. He acts as flux in a sort of unacknowledged way, currying favor and abuse from all sides. There were in Diomed's Star of India hotel not only Sikhs and Hindus, but bearded gentry, too, from up Peshawar way, immensely anxious for the fate of women-folk they left behind them, but not so respectful of a Hindu's matrimonial prejudices.

So the roof was parceled into sanctuaries marked by lines of sheeting, each stifling square in which a lantern glowed—a seraglio, crossing of whose threshold might lead to mayhem; for nerves were on end those murderous hot nights, and lawsuits had not sweetened dispositions.

To the Northerners the quartering of that roof by night was pure sport, risk adding zest. They were artists at making dove-cotes flutter—past grand masters of the lodge whose secret is the trick of making women coo and blush before their husbands' eyes. And not even an angry Hindu husband takes chances, if he can help it, with the Khyber knife that licks out like summer lightning in its owner's fist. So there were doings, and a deal of wrath.

King, Grim, Ramsden and Jeremy found da Gama's room and drew it blank. There was a key-hole, but it was screened on the inside by a leather flap that yielded when pushed with a wire without giving a view of the room. Some one—there was always someone lurking in a corner in the Star of India, possibly a watchman and perhaps not—volunteered the information that the "excellency *sahib*" might be on the roof.

Fernandez de Mendoza de Sousa Diomed Braganza, sent for, denied having a pass-key to the room or any knowledge of its occupant's movements. He, too, deliberately non-committal, suggested the roof and, deciding there was no money to be made, began to be rude. So Grim offered him fifty rupees for one look at the inside of da Gama's room.

"There is nothing in there," Diomed insisted.

Grim raised the offer to a hundred and then pretended to lose interest, starting away; whereat the Goanese chased all possible informers out of the passage, produced an enormous key, and pushed wide the two-inch teak door that was supposed to keep da Gama's secrets.

"I told you there was nothing in there!" he said, pocketing Grim's money.

He was right to all intents and purposes. There were a bed, one chair, a little table, half-a-dozen empty shelves, and a cheap old-fashioned wardrobe, from which such garments as da Gama owned had been thrown out on the floor. For the rest, a dirty tumbler, two empty bottles, a carafe, pens, ink, paper, a dilapidated dictionary and some odds and ends.

"Where are his books?" Grim asked.

"Gone!" said the Goanese unguardedly.

"Then there *were* books!"

"That is to say your excellency, *sahib*—how should I know? Are you spies for the police? If so—" Grim showed him another hundred-rupee note.

"I am a poor man," said Diomed. "I would like your honor's money. But I know nothing."

The eyes of a Goanese are like a dog's, mild, meek, incalculably faithful; but to what they are faithful is his own affair. He is likely not faithful to the world, which has broken trust with the half-breed too often for the shattered bits to be repaired. He was afraid of something—some one—and too faithful to the fear to take any liberties.

Nevertheless, the room was dumbly eloquent. It had been raided recently by men who were at no pains to conceal the fact. Even the pockets of the clothes were inside out.

"How many men came?" Grim demanded.

"*Sahib—bahadur*—your excellency's honor—I do not know! Are you spies for the police?" he asked again, and then smiled suddenly at the absurdity of that, for the police don't argue with hundred-rupee notes. "I will die rather than say a word!" he continued, and crossed himself.

"You know Father Cyprian?" asked Jeremy in English, so unexpectedly that the Goanese stampeded.

"You must all come out! I must lock the door! You must go away at once!" he urged. "Yes, oh yes, I know Father Cyprian—an old man— veree estimable—oh, yes. Go away!"

"Take my tip. Confess to Father Cyprian! Let's try the roof," said Jeremy; and as it was no use staying where they were the others followed him.

"You see," said Jeremy over his shoulder, pausing on the narrow wooden stairs, with one hand on the rail, "if he goes and confesses to Cyprian, Cyprian won't tell us, but he'll know, and what's in a man's head governs him. Better have Cyprian know than none of us."

They emerged on the roof into new bewilderment, for there were sheets—sheets everywhere, and shadows on them, but no explanation— only a pantomime in black and white, exaggerated by the flapping and the leaping lights. Somewhere a man sang a Hindu love-song, and an Afghan was trying to sing him out of countenance, wailing his own dirge of what the Afghan thinks is love—all about infidelity and mayhem.

"That's one of Ali's seven sons," said King, so Grim cried out, and the man came, swaggering between the sheets and breaking down a few as his elbows came in contact with the string, leaving a chattering rage in his wake that pleased him beyond measure. Nor was it one of the sons at all, but Ali of Sikunderam himself.

"Where is the Portuguese?" King asked him.

"My sons have him in view. I don't know just now where he is."

"Where are they?"

"That's just it. I don't know. They were to report here one by one, as each watched him for a distance and then turned him over to another."

"And none has returned."

"No, none yet."

"What have you been doing?"

"By Allah! Quarreling with Hindus. If you *sahibs* had not come there is one who might have found his manhood presently and made sport—"

"Have you watched da Gama's room?" demanded King.

"Nay, why should I? Who should watch a bat's nest! I have held the roof, where my sons may find me."

"Then you don't know who, or how many men went to the Portuguese's room?" Ramsden asked him.

"Ask the Prophet! How should I know! You heard me say I kept roof," he retorted. He had a notion that Ramsden was a subordinate who might be snubbed, because he said less than the others.

"Are your sons as wide-awake as you are?" Ramsden asked; and Jeremy, seeing his friend's fist, drew deductions; he whistled softly and stood aside.

"My sons are—"

"The Seven Sleepers!" Jeff suggested, finishing the sentence for him; which was cartel and defiance in the raw code of Sikunderam, although Ramsden hardly knew that yet.

He learned it then. Ali whipped his knife out and sprang, being due some education too.

The knife went whinnying through the air and pierced a sheet, where it knocked a Hindu lantern out and was recovered presently. Before a hand could interfere or a word restrain them Ali and Ramsden were at grips. The hairy Northerner within the space of ten grunts lost his footing and began to know the feel of helplessness; for Ramsden's strength is as prodigious as his calmness in emergency.

As easily as he had wrenched the knife away Jeff whirled the Afghan off his feet and shook him, the way a terrier shakes a rat, making his teeth rattle and a couple of hidden knives, some cartridges and a little money go scattering along the roof—shook him until all the kick was out of him—shook him until his backbone ached and even his desperate fingers, weakening, ceased from clawing for a hold.

Then, holding him with one hand by the throat so that he gurgled, Jeff set him on his feet, reserving his other fist for such necessity as might arise.

"This had to come," he said. "Now—you know English—are we friends or enemies?"

He let go with a laugh and shoved Ali back on to his heels, ready to grip again if the other should choose enmity.

"By Allah! Wait until my sons learn this!" gasped Ali, rubbing the throat under his beard where Jeff's thumb had inserted itself.

"I will lick them two at a time when their turn comes. Now's your turn. What's *your* answer?"

Ali looked in vain for a hint of sympathy. The others stood back, giving the man of their own race full opportunity. There was nothing for Ali ben Ali to do but capitulate or fight. He did not stomach either course contentedly.

"If I say friend you will think I am a coward," he retorted.

"If you say enemy, I will know you are a fool!" said Ramsden, laughing; and that was additional cause for offense, for whatever you do you must not laugh when you speak of weighty issues with Sikunderam.

"You laugh at me? By—"

Ramsden realized his error in the nick of time. Sikunderam would submit to being thrown off the roof rather than be laughed at.

"I jested with the thought that you could be a fool," Jeff answered.

It was lame, but it just limped. It gave the Northerner his chance to back down gracefully.

"By Allah, I am friend or enemy! Nothing by halves with me!" said Ali. "I am not afraid of life or death, so take your choice!"

"No, *your* choice," Jeff answered.

"Mine? Well, I have enemies and by Allah a friend is as scarce as an honest woman! Let these be witnesses. I call you friend!"

"Shake hands," said Ramsden, and Ali shook, a little warily because of the strength of the grip he had felt.

"You have the best of the bargain," he said, striving to grin, not finding it too easy, for he passed in his own land for a man who brooked no insult. "You are one man and I eight, for I have seven sons!"

"If they're included," answered Jeff, "that saves my thrashing them!"

"They *are* included, for the sake of thy great thews," said Ali. "Now they are yours as well as mine. Your honor is theirs, and theirs yours. We become nine!"

"Nine again!" laughed Jeremy. "If anyone were superstitious—!"

Jeff thought of a superstition, and of Ali's knife that had gone slithering through the sheet and smashed a lamp. The Northern knife is more than weapon. It is emblem, sacrificial tool, insignia of manhood, keeper of the faith, in one. Jeff set out to find the knife and give it back, doing the handsome thing rather more effectively because of clumsiness.

Seizing a handful of the Hindu's. slit sheet, he tore the whole thing down, disclosing two inquisitively angry women and a man. The man was stout, and could not speak for indignation, but was not so bereft of his senses that he did not know the value of a silver-inlaid Khyber knife.

Jeff threw the sheet over the women, solving that part of the problem with accustomed common sense, and solved the other with his toe, inserting it under the indignant Hindu, who was exactly wide enough of beam to hover the whole weapon under him diagonally as he sat still with his legs crossed. Jeff seized the long knife, picked up a corner of the bobbing sheet, pushed the Hindu under it to join his women-folk, and offered the knife to Ali, hilt-first.

"Thou art my brother!" exclaimed Ali, minded to grow eloquent. Emotion urged him to express his fundamental creed, and the easiest thing in the world that minute would have been to start him slitting Hindu throats. "Together thou and I will beard the Nine Unknown!" he boasted. "We nine will show the rest the way! By Allah—"

He was working himself up to prodigies of boasting, to be followed certainly by equally prodigious feats, for that is how swashbuckling propagates itself; and no mistake is greater than to think swashbuckling is unimportant; the world's red history has been written with its sword-points.

"Thou and I—"

But there came interruption. One of his sons arrived, striding like a Hillman up the stairs and touching nothing with his garments, as a cat can go through undergrowth. A young man, with his beard not more than quilling out.

"Now we shall know!" said Ali, and King took the youngster's elbow, swinging him into the midst, where he stood self-consciously.

"Where is the Portuguese?" King asked him. "The Portuguese?"

Ali of Sikunderam, magnificently posing, scratched his beard and grew increasingly aware of anti-climax as the meaning of the question was explained. The youngest of the seven sons with his spurs to win and no more than a murder yet to his credit seemed to be lagging behind opportunity—forgot—was stupid.

"Oh! Ah! Yes. That little yellow man—him with the little black beard and the black coat—da Gama—him you mean? How should I know where he is? Oh yes, I followed him a little way. But there were others, who left this roost with him, carrying books and rolls and things like that. One beckoned me and ordered me to carry books. Hah! He was a Hindu by the look of him, a man in a yellow smock. Having received my answer, which was a good one, he acknowledged his mistake and paid me a compliment. He said he had not understood. He had been told that porters and dependable guards would come, and had mistaken me for a porter. He asked my forgiveness, standing in mid-street with his arms full of musty books—what sort of books? Allah! How should I know! Not a Koran among them, you may be sure of that!—I wasn't interested in his books—He said that men would soon come from a house in the next street, who would seek to kill him, so would I go to that house—he described it to me, and an evil place it is—and obstruct the men who came out, quarreling if need be? Well—that was a man's work, and I went. I have just come from there."

"What of da Gama? What happened? Did you see the Portuguese?"

The questions came like pistol-shots in several languages—English, Punjabi, Pushtu, Hindustanee.

"No. I don't know what became of the Portuguese. There was a woman there—inside. I followed her in. Men came later, and I hamstrung one of them! When I can find my brothers we will all go to that house, and there will be happenings!"

There was nothing to be said. Not even Ali spoke a word. The youngster went rambling on, inventing things he might have said and deeds he might have done if he had thought of them at the time, until it slowly dawned on him that there was something lacking of enthusiasm in his audience. Ali did not even trust himself to utter a rebuke, and none else cared to. The vibrations of bitter disappointment—if that is what they are—made themselves felt at last, and the young man backed away, explaining—to himself—to the night at large:

"How should I have known? The man said *he* would carry books, and would I do the dangerous work? Am I a coward? How could I refuse him? And besides—"

There came two others of the seven—older men—hard breathing, breaking out in sweat, and anxious for news of Abdullah the youngest. They had seen nothing of the Portuguese at all. In accordance with a plan—a "perfect" plan as they explained it—they had waited in the appointed shadows to see the Portuguese go by. There were only six streets he could take, and they had watched each one, leaving the youngest to tag along behind the Portuguese and act as communicating link. Whichever way the Portuguese should take, the brother whom he passed would follow; and Abdullah, the youngest, would run to inform the others. The plan was perfect. The Prophet himself could not have devised a better one.

But Abdullah had not come. And another man *had* come, who said Abdullah was lying belly-upward of a knife-thrust in another street. So. They went to see, Suliman first finding Ahmed, so as to have company and help in case of a brawl. Not finding Abdullah they had come back.

"There is Abdullah," remarked Ali dryly. "Beat him!"

Which they did. Like the immortal Six Hundred at Balaclava, theirs not to reason why. They beat him to the scandal of a whole community that bivouacked on one roof, and rival roofs with no such violence to entertain them cat-called comment to and fro, casting aspersions on the house and good name of Fernandez de Mendoza de Sousa Diomed Braganza, who could not endure that in silence, naturally. He came up on the roof to investigate.

Running into King and cannoning into Grim off Ramsden, Diomed recognized the strangers who had invaded his hotel, paying money for unprofitable answers, and undoubtedly not sent by the police. That was enough. The stranger is the man to turn on, because the crowd is sure to back you up. Besides, he had their hundred rupees, which probably exhausted that source of revenue—and the dry cow to the butcher, every time!

Striking an attitude that would have cheapened Hector on the walls of Troy with his straight black hair abristle like a parokeet's crest, Diomed Braganza called on the "honorable guests of his hotel" to "come and throw robbers off the roof,"—a dangerous summons on a hot night in a land where passion lies about skin deep and nearly all folk have a bone to pick with Providence.

There had been enough North country horse-play, and enough meek tolerance for once. The women's voices chattered like a hennery aroused at night, and the men responded, from instinct and emotion, which combine into the swiftness and the fury of a typhoon.

"I am your servant! I have tried to make you comfortable! These ruffians are too many for me!" shouted Diomed. "Come and help me, noblemen—my guests!"

They came with a rush, the nearest hesitating under cover of the flapping sheets until they saw and felt pressure behind them and the dam went down, not in a tide of courage but of anger with the racial rage on top, which is the swiftest of all, and the fiercest.

That was no time to argue. Ramsden took Diomed by thigh and shoulder, raised him overhead, and hurled him screaming and kicking into the thick of the assault, to create a diversion if the half-breed had it in him. And he hadn't! He had shot his bolt and served his minute. Three or four went down under his impact, but the rest ignored him as the spate screams past an obstacle. And there were knives—clubs—things thrown. Over and through and under all the noise there was a penetrating voice that prodded at the seat of anger:

"They are spies! They are government agents! *Bande Materam!*"*

Ramsden held the stairhead for the others to back down one by one, King dragging Ali ben Ali by wrist and neck to keep him from using his Khyber knife that according to his own account of it had leaped from the sheath unbidden. (Ali was not the first, at that, to blame his true reactions on to untrue circumstance.) And even so, King only held him as you hold a hound in leash, until the moment—which occurred when Grim and Jeremy fell backward down the stairs together, struck by a bed hurled at random; wooden frame and loose, complaining springs that whirred like the devil in action. King dodged to avoid the thing, and Ali cut loose to uphold the testy honor of Sikunderam.

So there was a scrimmage for a minute at the stairhead that beat football, Grim and Jeremy returning, forcing their way upward to stand with their friends, and the others all in one another's way as each insisted on retreating last and all except Ali helped to plug the narrow exit. They had Ali's sons in the midst of them, for precaution, but that arrangement did not last long. Ali's Khyber knife was whickering and working in the dark a stride or two ahead, and someone reached Ali with a long stick, drawing blood. Ali yelled— not a call for help exactly, yet the same thing, *"Akbar! Allaho akbar!"* the challenging, unanswerable battle-yell of Islam, naming two truths, one implied—that "God is great" and that the witness of it means to die there fighting.

Might as well have tried to hold a typhoon then as Ali's three sons. There was one who had been beaten, with his pride, all raw, aspiring to be comforted in anybody's blood. He broke first, but the other two were only a fraction of a second after him, and there was a fight joined in the dark a dozen feet ahead, where men hurled broken lanterns, bed-legs, copper cooking-pots, friend hitting friend—where a fool with a whistling chain lashed right and left—and answering the *"Akbar! Akbar! Allaho akbar!"* of Sikunderam there rose and fell the *"Bande Materam!"* of someone prodding Sikh and Hindu passion.

"Hail motherland!" You can stir the lees of almost any crowd with that cry. Thought of retreat had to go to the winds as King, Grim, Ramsden and Jeremy hurled themselves into the fray to disentangle Ali and his illegitimates, if possible—as all things, of course, are possible to men whose guts are in the right place.

---

* Hail Motherland!—the slogan of the Indian nationalist.

TALBOT MUNDY

Possible, but not so easy! It was dark, for one thing; all the lamps were smashed that had not been extinguished by the women, and Ali had deliberately struck to kill at least a dozen times, using the quick, upturning thrust that lets a victim's bowels out. There was blood in quantity that made the foot slip on the roof and, though it was impossible to see how many he had hit—and his own count of a hundred was ridiculous—there was no doubt of the rage for retaliation. The men in front were yelling to the men behind for light and longer weapons, and three or four came running with a pole like a phalanx-spear, while shouts from below announced that some had fallen off the roof.

Another shout, worse, wilder, turned that shambles into panic in which women fought men with their long pins for a footing on the stair.

"Fire!" And the acrid, stringing smell of it before the cry had died away and left one man—Grim—aware that he who had started the "*Bande Materam*" and he who had cried "Fire!" were the same! It was the note of cynicism—the mechanical, methodical, exactly timed note—the note of near-contemptuous understanding that informed Grin.

Not that information did him any good, just then. There was a rush of panic-stricken brutes, plunging deathward in the lust for mere life, screaming, stripping, scrambling, striking, tearing at the clothing of the ranks ahead; and the half-inch iron pipe that did for stairhead railing went down like a straw before it, so that men, women, children poured into the opening like meat into a hopper and there jammed, filling the jaws of death too fast! Others leaped on top of that, hoping to unplug the opening by impact, or perhaps beyond hope, crazed. There wasn't anything to do that could be done. No seven men in all the earth could tame that rush—not even Ramsden, who fought like old Horatius on the bridge across the Tiber, and was borne hack on his heels until he swayed above the street and saved himself by a side leap along the low parapet.

Then the smoke came, billowing upward all around the roof, and a scream arose from the people jammed in the stairhead—song of a charnel-house!—hymn of the worst death!—and an obbligato made of crackling. Then the smell, as human flesh took fire, worse even than the Screaming and the roar of flames!

Through all that ran a bellowing—incessant—everlastingly repeated—on another note than the mob-yell from the street and the brazen gong of the arriving firemen—penetrating through the scream and the increasing crash of timbers—giving a direction through the choking smoke as a fog-horn does at sea.

"Jimgrim! Oh, J-i-m-g-r-i-m! Oh, J-i-m-g-r-i-m! It is I—Narayan Singh! Come this way, J-i-m-g-r-i-m!"

Over and over again, unvarying, on one note, nasal, recognizable at last as bellowed through the brass horn of a phonograph—the summons of a sane man in a sea of fear!

Grim gathered the others. There was light now and a man could see, for the flames had burst the roof. Thirty or forty more of Diomed Braganza's guests swooped this and that way in a herd like mercury on a tipping plate, and one cried that the bellowing through the trumpet was the voice of God! That was the end, of course. Fatalism multiplied itself with fear and they leaped, hand-in-hand some of them, some dead before they reached the street and others killing those they fell on. Sixty feet from coping down to pavement—plenty for the Providence that governs such things!

"Jimgrim! Oh, J-i-m-g-r-i-m! Oh, J-i-m-g-r-i-m! It is I—Narayan Singh! Come this way, J-i-m-g-r-i-m!"

Grim took to his heels and the others after him, running along the two-foot parapet because the roof was hot and smoking through—leaping the right-angle corner to avoid a flame that licked like a long tongue—making for the middle of the rear end, where the smoke blew back, away from them, and they saw a man like the spirit of the black night shouting through a brass phonograph horn thirty feet away from a roof across the narrow street.

"Jimgrim! Oh, J-i-m-g-r-i-m!"

"Here we all are! What now, Narayan Singh!"

"*Sahib*, there is a ladder below you! Reach for it!"

Too low! Too late! The ladder lay dimly visible along a ledge ten feet below. They saw it as the roof gave in and a gust of flame scorched upward like the breath of a titanic cannon, illuminating acres. All the secret tubes for conveying drinks and information in the "Star of India" were carrying draft now. The core of the inferno was white-hot. King's and Ali's clothes began to burn; the others were singeing. Narayan Singh's voice through the brass horn bellowed everlastingly, emphasizing one idea, over and over:

"For the love of God, *sahib*, reach that ladder!"

The ladder was out of reach.

"I don't cook good!" laughed Jeremy, amused with life even in the face of that death. "I'd sooner die raw! Anybody strong enough to hold my feet? Not you, Jeff—you take his—it calls for two of us. Hurry, some one!"

Jeremy leaned on his stomach over the parapet. King seized the long Arab girdle, knotted that around his own shoulders so that the two of them were lashed together in one risk, and laid bold of Jeremy's heels.

"Over you go, Australia! You belong down-under!"

Jeremy laughed and scrambled over. Ramsden laid hold of King's ankles, setting his own knees against the parapet; and to the tune of crackling flame and crashing masonry the living rope went down—not slowly, for there wasn't time—so fast that to the straining eyes in the street it almost looked as if they fell, and a scream of delighted dread arose to greet them.

Jeremy reached the ladder, grabbed it, and it came away, adding its weight and awkwardness to the strain on Ramsden.

"Haul away!" yelled Jeremy—not laughing now.

The turn-table motion of the ladder in mid-air was swinging him and King.

Jeff Ramsden's loins and back and arms cracked as he strained to the load. The others, obeying Grim, held him by the waist and thighs to lend him leverage, Grim holding his feet, in the post of greatest danger at the rear, where the flame roared closer every second.

"Quick, *sahib*! Quick!" came the voice of the Sikh through the brass horn.

Ramsden strove like Samson in Philistia, the muscles of his broad back lumped up as his knees sought leverage against the parapet and King's heels rose in air. (His legs would have broken if Jeff hadn't lifted him high before hauling him in.) Grim, unable to endure the heat behind, put an arm around Jeff's waist and threw his own weight back at the instant when Jeff put forth his full reserve—that unknown quantity that a man keeps for emergency. The ladder and the living rope came upward. And the parapet gave way!

It was Grim's arm around Jeff's waist that saved them all, for Jeff hung over by the thighs; the Afghans' hold was mainly of Jeff's garments, and they tore. The broken stone hit King and Jeremy, but glanced off, harming no one until it crushed some upturned faces in the crowd. And Jeff's task was easier after all without the stone to lean on. He did not have to lift so high. He could pull more. King, Jeremy and ladder came in, hand over hand.

"Quick! Quick! Oh quickly, *sahibs*!" came the Sikh's voice through the horn.

But the heat provided impulse. There was only one way to get that ladder across from roof to roof. They had to up-end it and let it fall, trusting the gods of accident, who are capricious folk, to keep the thing from breaking—they clinging to the butt to prevent its bouncing over. And it fell straight with four spare rungs at either end. But it cracked with the weight of its fall, and by the light of the belching flame behind them they could see the wide split in the left-hand side-piece. Someone said that Jeff should cross first, because his weight was greatest and the frail bridge would endure the strain better first than last.

Jeff did not argue, but lay on the ladder and crawled out to where the break was, mid-way. Across the midway rung he laid his belly—then set his toes on the last rung he could reach behind him—passed his arms through the ladder—and seized with his hands the rung next-but-one in front. Then he tightened himself and the ladder stiffened.

"Come on! Hurry!" he shouted.

They had to come two at a time, for the last of the roof was going and they stood on a shriveling small peninsular beleaguered by a tide of flame. The Afghans came afoot, for they were used to precipices and the knife-edge trails that skirt Himalayan peaks, treading along Ramsden's back as surely as they trod the rungs. But King and Grim crawled, King last. And it was when Grim's hand was almost on the farther coping, and King's weight was added to Jeff's midway, that the ladder broke.

Narayan Singh had turbans and loin-cloths twisted through the rungs at his end long ago, and had a purchase around a piece of masonry. So only the rear end of the ladder fell to the street. King clung to Jeff's waist while the other half swung downward against the opposing wall, and the thrilled mob screamed again. Jeff, King and ladder weighed hardly less than five hundred pounds between them. They went like a battering ram down the segment of an arc, spinning as the turbans up above, that held them, twisted.

It was the spin that saved them—that and the madness of Narayan Singh, who snatched at the ladder and tried to break its fall with one hand! Both circumstances added to the fact that the ladder broke unevenly, caused it to swing leftward. It crashed into the wall, but broke again above Jeff's hands, and catapulted both men through the glass of a warehouse window, where Narayan Singh discovered them presently laughing among bales of merchandise. They shouldn't have laughed. There were more than a hundred human beings roasted in the building they had left. Maybe they laughed at the unsportsmanship of Providence.

Narayan Singh was deadly serious, though unexpectedly.

"I watched the Portuguese! *Sahibs*. I *thought* these seven sons are not the princes of perfection they are said to be! They made a plan in that whispering gallery that you just left! But I kept my own counsel. I followed the Portuguese. I know where he went. The Portuguese has talked. The Nine Unknown are aware of danger! You are spied on. They knew you would come to this place. Someone in their pay set fire to the hotel, and said you did it! Their agents now are telling the mob to tear you in pieces! They say you are secret agents of the Raj, who set fire to the place because a few conspirators have met there once or twice! *Sahibs*, if you are caught there will be short argument! They saw you from the street. Listen! They come now! What shall we do?"

"Do? Track the Portuguese!" said King. "How's that, Jeff?"

"Sure!" said Ramsden, something like a big dog in his readiness to follow men he liked anywhere, at any time, without the slightest argument.

IV

"Here's your Portuguese!"

They escaped by way of the roof by means of the oldest trick in Asia, which is the home of all the artifices known to man. All thieves know it, and some honest men. You join in the pursuit. You call to the human wolves to hurry. You have seen the fugitive. You wave them on, answering questions with a gesture, saving breath to follow too, glaring with indignant eyes, impatient of delay, but overtaken—passed. So, falling to the rear, you face about at last and, while the wolves yelp; on a hot trail in the wrong direction, you walk quietly in the right one—yours—the opposite—away.

They found a stair down to the street through the house of a seller of burlap, who was edified to learn that they were authorized inspectors. He obeyed their recommendation to shut his roof-door tight. They took some samples of his goods to prove, as they said, by laboratory tests that the fire risk in his house was nothing serious, which made him feel immensely friendly. And out in the street they became customers of the burlap-merchant, hurrying home after a belated bargain—bearing samples—an excuse that let them through the fireline formed of regiments just arrived, whose business seemed to be to drive every one the way he did not want to go.

So presently, behind the drawn-up regiments, they threaded a thinning crowd toward the north, leaving the tumult and the honking motor-horns behind. The streets grew dimly lighted and mysterious, to Jeremy's enormous joy. His passion is pursuit of everything unconventional. They strode down echoing alleys where no European ever goes, unless there is a murder or a riot too high-tensioned for the regular police. They stopped and ate awful food in a place where sunlight never penetrated, drinking alongside surly ruffians, who sat on their knives in order to keep conscious of them all the time.

The way they took led by taverns out of which the stink of most abominable liquor oozed—raw, reeking ullage with the King of England's portrait on a label on the bottle—where women screamed obscenities and yelled in mockery of their own jokes—places where the Portuguese had led his night-life, and had not been loved. Time and again Narayan Singh, with a sheepskin coat hung loosely on his shoulder as a shield, peered into a den—sometimes opium, sometimes drink was the reek that greeted him—to inquire whether the Portuguese had headed back that way by any chance. Invariably he was cursed, and certain gods were thanked, by way of answer. One could gather that da Gama was not liked even relatively in the places he frequented.

Narayan Singh, full of his office of guide, and proud of his accomplishment in having found and blazed da Gama's trail, visited every haunt the Portuguese frequented, talking between-whiles.

"It was here they sat, *sahib*—he and the man who gave orders to the others who carried the books. And the Portuguese told all about our meeting in the office, I listening, pretending to be drunk—so drunk along the floor they all but trod on me! Da Gama desired to play you on a hook, saying he needed money from you. Therefore the other said— nay, *sahib*, I never saw him before, and don't know who he is, but he wore yellow—the other said the Nine will give da Gama money, if he will go to a place he knows of, where he will discover it left in a bag for him. The Portuguese asked how should he believe that? And the other answered that neither the Nine nor any agents of the Nine tell lies for any reason; moreover, the other added that all you *sahibs* and your servants—by whom he meant Ali and his sons and me—will be roasted to death within an hour or two. So I rolled out of this *kana*[*] into the gutter, which is cleaner, and as soon as I had watched da Gama to another place I ran to warn you. Let us only hope he has not escaped us between then and now."

"Can't!" laughed Jeremy. "He's no more than a shilling up a conjurer's sleeve! Process of elimination gives the answer."

So they harked along da Gama's trail into a rather better quarter of the city, where the ladies of undoubtful reputation ply the oldest trade without severely straining any caste laws. Priests live fatly thereabouts. Whoever entertains a Sikh, for instance, or Mohammedan, or Hindu of a lower caste than hers, may regain purity for payment—which is very shocking to the civilized, who only buy seats in the senate, or perhaps a title, or who "use their pull with the press" to hush up things the public shouldn't know.

There, in a rather wider street, in a house that had gilded shutters, they sat cross-legged on embroidered cushions vis-à-vis to a lady

---

[*] A word meaning almost any kind of place.

sometimes known as Gauri, which is a heavenly name. She was pretty besides inquisitive, and the turquois stud in the curve of one side of her nose contributed a piquancy that offset petulance. Her vials of vituperation were about full, and she outpoured almost at the mention of da Gama's name.

Know him? Know that slime of adders stuffed into a yellow skin? She wished she did not! But who were the gentlemen, first, who wished to know about him? Men whom he had robbed? Amazing! What a mystery, that such a *pashu** as that Portuguese could win the confidence of anyone and steal as much as one rupee! Yet he had robbed her—truly! Her! A lady of no little experience—He had robbed her of a thousand rupees as lately as yesterday. He had laughed at her to-day! The beast had spent her fortune! Practically all her savings, except for a jewel or two.

And he had robbed others! Although it served the others right! Vowing fidelity to her—the brute—he had intrigued elsewhere, as she had only just discovered, coaxing other women's savings from them. What did he use the money for? To bribe the priests' servants to bring him old books out of temples—smelly old books full of magic and ancient history! *He* said that if he can get the right book he can find so much money in one place that all the rest of the wealth in the world wouldn't be a candle to it! She was to have a tenth of all that. She supposed he made the other women equally tempting offers.

As a rajah on his throne might feel toward a dead dog on a dung-heap; so she felt toward da Gama! She wished the Lords of Death no evil, but she hoped they might have the Portuguese, nevertheless! He had come that afternoon and laughed at her! She had asked him for a little of her money back, and he had mocked her to her face! He had boasted flatly that she would never see one *anna* of her money back, and had then gone, mocking her even from the street!

Whereat Jeremy, adept at following the disappearing shilling, hinted to King in a whisper. So King made a suggestion, and the priestess of delight blew cigarette smoke through her nose in two straight, illustrative snorts.

She—hide that *pashu* in her house—now—after all that had happened? There *was* a day when she had hidden him—a day born in

---

* Unmitigated brute having neither soul nor conscience—a very comprehensive Hindi word.

the womb of bitterness, begotten of regret! How vastly wiser she would have been to leave him to the knives of the men he had robbed! He was always a thief. She knew that now, although then she had thought he was persecuted.

King made another suggestion, launching innuendo deftly on the ways of jest as he accepted sherbet from the Gauri's maid. She looked as if she wished the drink were poisoned, and retorted without any button on her rapier:

"Thug! You would like to search my house to steal the Portuguese's leavings! There is nothing! He took all! And it would cost me three hundred rupees to the priest to repurify the place if I let such as you go through it!"

Now a fool would have taken her statement at face value, believing or disbelieving as the case might be, and learning nothing. A clever fool would have paid three hundred for the privilege to search, learning that the Portuguese was not there, but otherwise no wiser after it. Wisdom, yoked up with experience, paid attention to the price she quoted and, not liking to be cheated, doubled the price and made a game of it. For, although *all* cheat him who buys, and *some* cheat the gambler, the odds against the gambler are so raised already by the gods that some folk let it go at that.

"Three hundred for the priest? I'll bet six hundred you don't know where the Portuguese is now!" said King.

Her eyes snapped.

"Tell for less than a thousand?" she retorted scornfully. "I am not a spy!"

"But I am a gambler," King answered. "I offered to bet. I will bet you five hundred you don't know where da Gama is this minute."

"You said six hundred!"

"Now I bet five. In a minute I reduce my stake to four. Next minute three—"

"I have no money to bet with," she answered. "Da Gama has it all!"

"Yet, if you were betting on a certainty you wouldn't lose, so you could afford to stake your jewelry," King answered. "I will bet five hundred rupees against that necklace of pearls that you can't tell me where the Portuguese is!"

"Who would hold the stakes?" she asked hesitating.

That was a poser, but Ali of Sikunderam was ready for it. He drew forth his silver-hilted knife and made the blade ring on the floor.

"You hold them!" he said, looking hard at her—upwind, the way he was used to viewing the peaks of Sikunderam. "If my friend wins, I come to claim the stakes. I am old in the ways of women, and I come with this in my right hand! Only if you win you keep the stakes."

She judged his eyes, and understood, and nodded. King laid on the carpet five one-hundred rupee notes. She laid her necklace opposite. Ali of Sikunderam raked all the lot together with the point of his weapon and then pushed them toward her. She put on the necklace and folded the notes.

"I could send my maid," she said. "The place is indescribable."

But the maid of any such mistress as Gauri is more untrustworthy than treachery itself. Having nothing to lose, and the world before her, her eccentric trickery is guaranteed.

"I deal with principals. I bet with you," said King.

"I cannot go there! I am afraid to go there! It is too far!" exclaimed Gauri. "It was my maid, not I who followed him. She knows the way. I—"

Ali of Sikunderam ran a thumb-nail down the keen edge of his knife, and Gauri shuddered, but it was Narayan Singh who voiced the right solution. He leaned over and touched the nearest of Ali's sons, who was day-dreaming over the maid's delightfulness—perhaps imagining her likeness in the Moslem paradise.

"Two horses!" he commanded. "Instantly!"

The youngster came to with a start and glanced at his sire, who nodded. King produced money. Gauri claimed it.

"Let the owner of the horses send his bill to me!" she insisted, and nearly enough to have bought two horses disappeared into a silken mystery between her breasts.

So Ali's youngest went on an errand he could run without much risk of tripping up, but "instantly" is a word of random application and he was gone an hour before the horses stood incuriously at the door perceived by half a hundred very curious eyes; for the doings of a lady such as Gauri are of deeper interest than chronicles of courts.

It was not until Ramsden came forth, bulking like a rajah's bully, and the others formed up like the riff-raff hirelings who attended, to the unprintable pursuits of aristocracy, that the crowd went its way to imagine the rest and discuss it over betel-nut or water-pipes.

Gauri ceased expostulating when it dawned on her that she would ride escorted by nine assorted footmen. That is an honor and a novelty that comes to few of her position on the stairs of disrepute. And then, there was intrigue, that was meat and drink to her. There was the possibility—the probability of venomous revenge; and a bet to win, if no chance of her money back from the Portuguese.

She began to try to stipulate before the hour was up.

"If I find him for you, you must kill him!" she insisted.

"If you don't find him, you lose your necklace," King retorted.

"What if he tells you his secrets?" she said suddenly. "The *pashu* will be afraid. He will tell the secret of the treasure! He has had ten thousand rupees of my money! You must tell me what he tells you—"

She grew silent—looking—reading men and faces, as the third of her profession was. King's eyes had met Grim's and the glance passed all around the circle—not of understanding, but unanimous. They recognized a chance, and without speaking all accepted it. So King conceded terms:

"Daughter of Delight," he said, "if in obedience to us you help find treasure, you shall have your share of it.

"How much?" she demanded.

But it is wiser, if you want to shorten argument, to let East's daughters bear the market for themselves.

"How much do you want?" King asked and she named the highest figure she could think of that conveyed a meaning. (*Crores* look nice on paper but are over ambition's head.)

"A *lakh!*" she said, laughing at her own exorbitance.

"Good! If your help is worth an anna you shall have a *lakh* of rupees!" King answered.

She demanded, naturally, two *lakhs* after that, but Ali of Sikunderam declaimed on the subject of unfaithfulness. A *lakh* she had said; a *lakh* she should have; his Khyber knife was there to prove it! He was as vehement as if they had the treasure in the room with no more to do than divide it, and she capitulated, more fearful of Ali's Northern knife than of all other possible contingencies. She understood the glint in those eyes that were the color of the breeding weather.

"A *lakh*," she agreed; and then the horses came, and fiscal whispers had to be exchanged between the owner of the horses and the maid, who indubitably swindled everybody, though she had to part with a "reward" to Ali's son, that being India—specifically Delhi and the seat of government, where extortion is the one art that survives. The horses were an illustration—crow's meat, hungry, made to labor for a last rapacious overcharge.

But nothing more was required of the horses than a walking pace. The two veiled women rode them in the midst of men who were in no haste, because to seem to hasten is to draw attention. It was better to swagger and invite attention, which has a way of producing the opposite effect.

They headed as straight as winding ways permitted toward the northern outer fringe of Delhi, where the ruins of the ancient city lie buried amid centuries' growth of jungle. Not a tiger has been seen in that jungle for more than thirty years, but few care to wander at night there, for everything else that is dangerous abides in that impenetrable maze, including fever and fugitives from justice.

As they left the last of the modern streets the moon rose and they followed a track that wound like the course of a hunted jackal between ancient trees whose roots were in much more ancient masonry. The "servant of delight," as she preferred to call herself since her mistress was what she was, led with King's hand on her bridle-rein, recognizing the route by things she was afraid of—ruins shaped like a human skull that drew a scream from her—roots like pythons sprawling in the way—a hole in a broken wall that might be a robber's entrance—terrified, and yet employing terror consciously—enjoying it, as some folk like to sit in a rocking boat and scream. Life to amuse her had to raise the gooseflesh and offend the law, both of which are accomplishments of night in northern Delhi; so her faculties were working where another's would have turned numb.

They came at last to the world's end, where a shadow blacker than a coal mine's throat declared that life left off, and might have been believed except for moonlight that glistened beyond it along the ragged outline of a broken wall. There, under the bough of an enormous tree, whose tendrils looked like hanged men swinging in the wind, they turned into a space once paved so heavily that no trees grew and only bushes strangled themselves, stunted, between masonry. On the far side was a building, still a building, though the upper part had fallen and the front looked like the broken face of a pyramid.

Once it had been magnificent. The outside and the upper portions had collapsed, from earthquake probably, in such way as to preserve the middle part like the heart of an ant-heap. Partly concealed by bushes was an opening indubitably dug by men through the débris. That they entered, into a tunnel that was once a corridor open on one side to the air. And at the end of fifty dark yards, guided by matches struck two at a time, they turned to the left into a hall, whose marble sides had been quarried off long ago, but whose columns were still standing like rows of twisted Titans holding up the world's foundation.

There was a platform at one end, on which had stood a throne. But on it now were a canvas camp-bed, an old black hand-bag with a dirty shirt in it, a couple of pairs of filthy blankets, and a lantern. Someone lighted the lantern, and about a million bats took wing; the air was alive with them, and the women hugged their heads, screaming.

A few opened tin cans tossed into a corner showed how someone had contrived his meals; and one meal at any rate was recent, for there was unspoiled soup remaining in a can beside the bed. But no sign of the Portuguese. Not a hint of where he might be. Only the certainty that he had been there that day! There, on the bed, turned inside out and empty, lay the chamois-leather bag that Cyprian had given back to him; but there was no more trace of the coins that had been in it than of da Gama.

Narayan Singh was the first to speak:

"Da Gama came for money, *sahibs*. I heard the boast made that the Nine never lie." He seemed afraid his own word might be doubted since they hadn't found da Gama. "Nevertheless—the money that we know he had is missing—gone—where?"

He picked up the chamois-leather bag and shook it. "Up somebody's sleeve!" chuckled Jeremy. "Look for the Don and I'll bet you—"

He spoke English, and the women's exclamations stopped him.

Ramsden went looking, not so talkative but bashfully aware, as big men sometimes are, of strength and an impulse to apply it. It was foolish to go looking in an empty hall, but men who don't pride themselves on intellect occasionally are better served by intuition. He stooped over where a solitary section of a broken marble column lay on top of débris in a corner of the floor, and they heard his joints crack as he shoved the marble off the heap.

"Here's your Portuguese!" he said quietly.

He might have found a golf-ball. But he, too, spoke English and the women exclaimed at it. The maid seized hold of Jeremy's hand and began to examine his fingernails, which inform the practised eye infallibly; but Jeremy snatched his hand away and hurried to hold the lantern and look with the rest at what Ramsden had discovered.

The yellow rays shone on the body of the Portuguese laid dead and hardly cold in a shallow trench hoed in the rubble. The marble column had closed it without crushing what was in there, and the corpse was smiling with the funny, human, easy-natured look that the man had worn in life for fragments of a second as he passed from sneer to sneer. He had died in mid-emotion, and the women vowed the gods had done it. They promised the gods largesse to save them from a like fate.

There was no other explanation than theirs of how he died, nor of who else than the gods had killed him. They searched the body. There was no wound—bruise—no smell of acid poison—no snake-bite—nothing, but a corpse with a scarred chin, smiling! And no hat!

V

"The nine's spies are everywhere!"

For those who sacrifice themselves upon the altar of her needs—whether supposititious needs or otherwise—India holds recompense, as such quarters for instance as Father Cyprian's, wedged between two gardens in a sleepy street, with the chimney of a long-disused pottery kiln casting a shadow like that of a temple-dome on the sidewalk in the afternoon. From India's view-point Cyprian was all the more entitled to consideration in that he had never openly conducted any siege against her serried gods. He had saved the face of many a pretending pagan, holding in the privacy of his own conscience that the damned were more in need of comfort than an extra curse. So pagan gratitude had comforted his old bones, unpretending pagans not objecting.

He was housed ascetically; but there is a deal more repose and contentment to be had in quiet cloisters than in the palaces of viceroys, princes, bishops. Tongue in cheek, he had pretended to the arch-pretenders that he thought their magic formulas bewildering, doing it repeatedly for fifty years until it was second nature, and men, whose minds were rummage shops of all the secondhand old-wives' tales, not only used their influence to repay flattery but labored, too, to unearth facts for him beyond their understanding. India, surviving Anglo-Saxon worship of the playing fields and all unnecessary sweat, takes her amusement mentally. It was "entertainment exquisite" to bring to Father Cyprian, the alien albeit courteous priest, new facts and revel in his intellectual amazement. (For in fifty years a man learns how to play parts, and, as Jeremy had noticed, Cyprian was "all things" to a host of various men.)

He could discuss the metaphysical, remote, aloof though omnipresent All of Parabrahman just as easily as listen to the galloping confession of a Goanese in haste to unburden conscience and, as it were, dump burdens at the padre's feet. Shapely, dignified old feet, well cased in patent-leather slippers, resting on a folded Afghan *chudder* to keep them off the tiled floor.

Fernandez de Mendoza de Sousa Diomed Braganza watched them, as he knelt and searched the very lees of his imagination. He was very proud indeed to confess to Father Cyprian, a rare enough privilege, that of itself, if boasted of sufficiently, would raise him twenty notches in the estimation of the envious world he knew. All he could see below the screen were those old aristocratic-looking slippered feet, but they were reassuring, and he longed to touch them.

"And so, father, that Arab, speaking English veree excellentlee, so that in fact I was awfulee taken by astonishment and made suspeecious—yes indeed—recommended me to come to you for confession!"

"Why did you obey an Arab?" wondered Cyprian.

"Oh, I think he, was the devil! How else should he speak English and laugh so light-heartedly? I saw his head against the night sky and I think he had horns—oh yes, certainlee!"

Cyprian cautioned him.

"If *he* was not thee devil, that one, then the other was—the great brute dressed as a Jat who seized me as if I were trash to be thrown away and hurled me against my customers! Father, I assure you I was like a cannonball! He hurled me and I upset many men—oh yes, decidedlee! And though the whole hotel was subsequently burned, and from below I saw those veree selfsame individuals burning in the flames, I have seen them since! If they are not the devil, they are salamanders—"

"It is not for you to say who the devil is," warned Cyprian, aware of how the Goanese mind leaps from one conclusion to another. "How is it you escaped?"

"Oh, veree simplee. I have been most faithful in the matter of the candles for the altar of Our Lady of Goa, so when that—I am sure he was thee devil!—hurled me into the ranks of my customers I was assured in my conscience that that is enough, and I fled first, before there was a stampede, which I foresaw infalliblee. So when the stampede began I was on the stairs, and there I smelt the smoke and went to see as Moses went to see the burning bush, and seeing flame I ran to thee street and was saved. But my whole hotel and my fortune are up in flame—oh pity me!"

So Father Cyprian pitied him with due restraint, and dismissed him after a priceless homily in which he pointed out how profitably Diomed might have given all that property to the Church, instead of keeping it for the devil to make a bonfire of. Whereafter he told his servant to open the slats of the jalousies and admit sufficient of the morning sun to make the place look cheerful.

And a plain, cool, white, stone room with an ancient tiled floor and vaulted ceiling is a great deal easier to make cheerful than any sumptuously furnished boudoir in the world. The delights of mild asceticism are immensely keener than the pleasures of the epicure. The sun came in, obedient, and the light and shadow alternated in long triangles on floor and wall, leaving the rear of the room in shadowed mystery.

There was no sign of the library—merely a breviary, and one or two books liberally marked with penciled slips on a table against the wall. In addition to the chair that Cyprian used there were six others, equally simple and equally almost impossibly perfect in design and workmanship—each chair as old as the Taj Mahal and no two chairs alike, yet all one unity because of excellence.

A man may be ascetic without craving ugliness—an anchorite, in moderation, without shutting out his friends. A bronze bell from a vanished Buddhist temple announced visitors.

The servant—Manoel—another Goanese—soft-footed as a cat and armed with pots of fuchsias came in to announce what he regarded as too many visitors at that hour of the morning.

"They are *not* elegant. Not in the least—oh, no."

"Their names?" asked Cyprian.

Manoel mispronounced them, was reproved, set the pots down, and departed to admit the visitors, changing his mood like a chameleon, only much more swiftly and with rather less success. For instance, it did not convince Cullender Ghose, who entered first, as impresario.

"Hitherto not having poisoned padre *sahib*, said sacred person being vigilant, you therefore impel malevolent influence of evil eye on these unholy *sahibs* who are honoring this babu with employment? Stand back, son of miscegenation! Cease from smiling!"

Who *would* smile if addressed in those terms by an arrogantly fat babu? Not a *bishop's* butler. Still less Manoel. He scowled and—so tradition says—a man must smile before he can blast with that dreadful bane called Evil Eye in which the whole of the Orient and most of the newer world believes implicitly. Under the protecting scowl Chullunder Ghose, with his back to Manoel for extra safety's sake, marshaled the party in—Grim, Jeremy, King, Ramsden, Ali of Sikunderam, Narayan Singh, and one of Ali's sons who was beckoned in by Chullunder Ghose for "keyhole prophylaxis," as the babu explained in an aside. The other sons remained squatting in the dust in the patterned shadow of a great tree opposite. Falstaff never had a raggeder, less royal following as far as mere appearance went—inside or outside the priest's house.

They all looked like men who trod the long leagues rather than the pavement.

For though in the new, raw world, where twenty centuries have not sufficed to give the sons of men a true sense of proportion, he who would be listened to must masquerade and mountebank in new clothes of the newest cut, India knows better—looks deeper—and is more wise. So in vain that net is laid in sight of her. Viceroys, kings and all their pomp are side-shows, and the noise they make is a nuisance to be tolerated only for the sake of more or less peace. They are heard in the land and not listened to—seen, and appraised like shadows on the sands of time. The men who go in rags out-influence them all.

Manoel the Goanese, for instance, with all European error multiplied within him by miscegenation, scorned that ragged bodyguard beneath the tree for servants of men of no intellect or influence; and even so, a passing constable, with native vision warped by too much European drill, but with all his other faculties and fondnesses alert, paused over the way to meditate how innocence might be made to pay tribute to worldly wisdom—paused, scratching his chin with the butt of a turned wooden truncheon and both eyes roving for a safe accomplice.

"That constabeel is a Hindu pig with hair on his liver, who designs an inconvenience to us—by Allah!" said one Hill brother to the next.

And all six nodded, in a circle, resembling bears because of sheepskin coats hung loosely on their shoulders.

So within; the padre's servant Manoel approached the seventh, who stood guard by the door of Cyprian's sitting room, offering cakes to Cerberus.

"Taste it," he suggested. "Veree excellent—from oversea—the land of my ancestors—it came in a great flagon. Onlee veree distinguished people have been given any."

A hand like a plucked bear's paw closed tight on the long glass, and with both eyes on the Goanese the Hillman poured a pint of sweet, strong liquid down his throat, not pausing, not even coughing. The glass was back in the hand of the Goanese before the other had finished his gasp of astonishment.

"Tee-hee! You like it, eh? Come, then, into the pantry, where is plentee more. You shall have your fill."

"No, for I don't drink wine," said Rahman, wiping his lips on a sleeve. "Such dogs as thou know nothing of the Koran, but to drink wine is forbidden."

In vain the Goanese brought more, in a glass jug, tempting scent and vision. Rahman stood with his back to the keyhole, just sufficiently inflamed by one pint of Oporto to have split the Goanese's stomach open at the first excuse, and not quite sure that he hadn't already excuse enough for it. So Manoel kept his distance, and the conference within proceeded safely.

Cyprian began it, naturally, beaming on them with his loose, old lips and eyes that never betrayed secrets.

"So you failed? I see you failed," he said, glancing from face to face. "He gave you the slip, that Portuguese?"

"They killed him," Grim answered simply.

"Ah! A longer spoon than ever! Too bad! But his hat—you found his hat of course?"

"No. Missing!" answered Jeremy. "He had a five-pun' note inside the band, with my signature."

Cyprian's lips moved, but he said nothing audible.

"Worse than that!" King added. "In his pocket should have been a paper on which he had jotted down terms he was prepared to make with us. We wouldn't sign it, but the terns were down and an enemy would draw conclusions."

"Gone too?" asked Cyprian.

"Yes. Taken," King answered. "Pocket was inside-out."

"Worse yet!" put in Ramsden. "All those ancient coins have disappeared. Here's the bag—empty!"

"All except this one!"

Jeremy held up the one he had given pledge for. Cyprian took it, turning it over and over in a hand as soft and smoothly wrinkled as a royal grandmother's.

"Coins gone? Hat gone? Eh?" said Cyprian. "That hat—he kept his memoranda on a strip of parchment inside the sweat-band. If we had the hat—well—if we had the hat, I might have fitted his key into my lock, as it were. Well—so we are worse off than before!"

"Much worse!" remarked Chullunder Ghose. "Flesh creeping, holy one! This baba, consumed by elementary anxiety, calls attention to arresting key of situation, which is: Enemy lurking in ambush, is now aware of opponents' identity. Opponents being us! Alarming—very! Unseen, and selecting opportunity with exquisite precision, will sneak forth and smite us shrewdly, wasting no time! *Verb. sap.*! Your obedient servant, *sahibs*!"

"He knows," said Cyprian nodding. "He knows."

Ramsden half-unconsciously clenched two enormous fists, and Cyprian laughed.

"If we could deal with them in that way their secret would have been the world's five thousand years ago—wouldn't it?" he said whimsically. "No, my friends. They may do violence to us; we must admit that possibility. But it behooves us to use other means. We are lost if we try violence—babes in the wood, eh? No whit safer then than Sennacherib's Assyrians. We might as well walk barefoot into a cavern full of snakes! But the Lord slew the Assyrians. The Lord, too, fought against Sisera. Wisdom! We must be wise! You understand me?"

He was trying to be all things at the same time to seven men of differing creeds, not one of which was his, and he was much too wise to venture on the freehold of religion, although that, and no other motive, was the impulse that had kept him laboring for fifty years. He knew that Jeremy, for one, would openly rebel at the first suggestion of creed or dogma, to say nothing of Narayan Singh and Ali of Sikunderam, who perhaps were not so important, although quite as unwilling to be compromised.

"Nobody understands a damned thing!" answered Jeremy. "I know what we saw—a dead Don minus hat, and his pockets inside-out. We all know what the woman said. I've heard you. It all amounts to nothing, plus one gold coin—"

"Perhaps I'd better hear about the woman," Cyprian suggested.

Jeremy told him, reproducing the whole scene and Gauri's conversation, down to the last remark of Gauri when she saw da Gama lying dead.

"'See? See? They fooled him, and the fool tricked me! I am a greater fool! I tell you, none but a *fakir* has the better of a *fakir!* Men say of me, and such as me, that I learn secrets. *Phagh!* Go and be *fakirs*, all of you! That's what Gauri thought of it," said Jeremy.

"And she was right. She was right," said Cyprian.

Whereat Jeremy whistled. He smelt adventure coining down wind—unexpected—just the way he likes it best. Chullunder Ghose, who loves to feel his own flesh creep, made a noise like a stifled squeal and shivered.

"Padre *sahib*, be advised by me!" he interrupted. "Being far from affluent baba perspiring much for underdone emolument, am nevertheless like package of Autolichus containing products of experience! That Mister Ross can be a *fakir*, yes. He is so clever, he can even imitate himself, same being most difficult of all cynicisms. But he is Australian. His deity is Nth power of Irreverence, same if brought in contact with high-church parties lacking sense of humor, being much more dangerous than dynamite with fuse and caps! I speak with feeling! Mister Ross will make conjuring tricks with seven-knotted bamboo rod of holiest mahatma, and we are all dead men—families at mercy of the rising generation—oh, my aunt!"

Jeremy smiled, pleased; he likes applause. Head suddenly on one side like a terrier's who hears the word cat, he watched Cyprian's face, alert.

"There is truth in what Chullunder Ghose says—truth, and exaggeration," Cyprian announced. "There is always danger in attacking deviltry. But exaggeration in such cases is"—he was going to say a sin, but checked himself—"a serious mistake because it terrifies."

Every man in the room except Chullunder Ghose smiled broadly at that. Cyprian smiled too, and none of them, except perhaps the babu, realized that he had chosen that means of eliminating any shade of terror from the argument.

"You!" he said suddenly, pointing a finger at Jeremy. "You! Are you able to govern yourself? Can you understand that if you play this part, one laugh at the wrong minute may mean death?"

"I hope I'll die laughing—in my boots," responded Jeremy.

"Your death—and others!"

"Whose, for instance?" Jeremy came back at him. "I've seen men in India I'd kill for sixpence each!"

"These—your friends," said Cyprian.

"That's different. All right. I don't laugh. I make up as the lousiest-looking holy man you ever saw. What after that?" demanded Jeremy.

Cyprian looked hard at him. In one soft palm lay the gold coin, and he tapped it with a forefinger.

"This is our only point of contact," he began. "You must take it and do tricks. You must challenge the Nine in public! It is dangerous, and others must go with you to prevent abduction. Are you willing?"

"Bet your life!" said Jeremy. "Who comes?"

"Oh, my God!" remarked Chullunder Ghose, aware of the wheels of Destiny.

"My young friend Jeremy, do you command sufficient self-control to let yourself be disciplined by our babu?" asked Cyprian.

The padre's lips moved pursily, as if he were masticating something, and his face was toward Jeremy, who grinned, but his mind was already far away considering something else. Grim noticed it and grew aware that Cyprian had made his mind up without waiting for the answer. Quick work! But Grim is constitutionally cautious.

"How about the babu?" he objected. "Can Chullunder Ghose—"

Cyprian banished the objection with a gesture.

"You must be dumb, friend Jeremy—dumb!" he went on, forcing deep thought to the surface through a sieve that strained out all unnecessary words—particularly all unnecessary argument. "Chullunder Ghose must talk."

"My God! You see me shudder?" exclaimed the babu, not exaggerating.

His fat shoulders heaved as if an earthquake underlay them, and a kind of grayness settled on his face. Nevertheless, none doubted his intention. A century or two ago he would have braved the Holy Inquisition out of curiosity.

"Whatever is said, Chullunder Ghose must say," repeated Cyprian.

"Hear me say it now, then! Caesar, *moriturus te saluto*! Speech, committing me, silence absolves actual offender! My belly shakes, yet family must eat. *Sahibs*, increase my microscopical emolument!"

Never was a man more serious. Chullunder Ghose, all clammy with anxiety, rolled his handkerchief into a ball and caught it with his naked toes repeatedly; but King moved over, and sat on a cushion on the floor beside him.

"You and I have tackled worse than this together," he said.

"Ah! Yes. *You* and I! But this Australian! He would tie a knot in the tail of Hanuman* himself, and trust to irreverence to get him out of it! He will cry, Cooee!—and pretend to a Brahman that such is colloquial *lingua franca* of the gods!"

"It is!" laughed Jeremy. "Australia's God's country. If I can't talk the dialect, who can?"

"Peace, peace!" said Cyprian, smiling. "Let us joke afterward. Colonel King, may I trust you to instruct friend Jeremy—drill him, that is? We cannot afford mistakes."

King nodded. In all India there was none else who had traveled, as King had done, from end to end of India in different disguises, penetrating the reputedly impenetrable. If King had but possessed a tithe of Jeremy's gift of doing marvels with his hands, he would have been the man to send. But you don't discover jealousy in men of King's

---

* The monkey-god.

attainments. A trace of that would have made them fail a hundred times. Both he and Grim were safer men than Jeremy, and knew it; but they were also much less brilliant, and knew that too. As far as courage went there was nothing to choose, although they would all have picked on Ramsden if asked who was least amenable to fear; and Ramsden, knowing too well what it cost him to control those thews of his, would have picked Narayan Singh.

"You know there is a Hindu festival at Benares very soon?" said Cyprian. "I am old, or I would go with you. I know those ceremonies. I could guard against mistakes. Now, understand: the danger is abduction! There will be a million men and women in Benares—more! You—disguised—unknown—you could vanish as easily as seven pebbles from the beach! So you must all go, each to watch the others. Be two parties. Jeremy, Chullunder Ghose, Ramsden—one. The other, all the rest of you, pretending to be strangers to the first. But all Hindus, mind—able to claim acquaintance if you must."

"We shall be in next world very presently!" remarked Chullunder Ghose. "What is object of this impropriety?"

Cyprian made a noise with his tongue. He did not like the word impropriety. He answered looking anywhere but at the babu.

"The Nine Unknown must keep themselves constantly informed. In order to know they must observe. To observe they must go, or send their representatives. To be in touch with the mind of the mass—which their purpose must be certainly—they will take care to attend the festivals, in person or by proxy. If one of their number should go to Benares—as is possible—extra precautions will be taken of course to preserve incognito. But in any case there will be at least one of their principal lieutenants there to bring dependable reports. You understand that? Now—"

The old man was warming up. He moved in his chair restlessly and kept wiping his lips on a lawn handkerchief. His gestures, losing the indeterminate, painstakingly tactful quality, were becoming imperative.

"In cryptographic books in my possession it is laid down as inviolable rule that one of the Nine *always* visits Benares at this season of the year. They receive money—gold and silver—that accumulation never ceases. And the East changes slowly; without a doubt a great deal of the money even in these days of banks goes to Benares, Hardwar, Prayag and such places by porter at the times of pilgrimage. Someone is there to receive it. You understand?"

Ramsden opened his mouth at last. Economy—constructive, pioneer economy was his long suit.

"It would take a freight-train to haul the money. The amount that disappears in one year—"

"Could be carried among a million pilgrims without attracting notice," Cyprian retorted. "Do you realize your opportunity? Contact is our problem! If, by challenging attention, you can once make contact with the Nine Unknown, you may leave the rest to me! We will presently find the books! Then you may have the money—anyone may have it! The books—those nine books—they are the true goal."

"If the cash really goes to Benares, it would take a train to haul it out!" Ramsden insisted. "In that case we need only watch the railway—"

"Who said the money is hauled out again?" Cyprian retorted testily. "For all you know there is a hole under a temple in Benares—"

He checked himself, aware that for the first time he had awakened incredulity. Even Chullunder Ghose allowed an expression of mockery to light his face up suddenly. Ali of Sikunderam exploded:

"Allah! If the Hindus had that much money in a hole beneath a temple, the Hills would have smelt it years ago! Moreover would the English not have learned of it? They smell gold as a thirsty horse smells water in the plains. And if the English were afraid to take it on a pretext, would the Hills refrain? Would that bait not have brought the *lashkars*[*] yelling down the Khyber? And would guns have held them back in smell of all that loot? Allah! Show me but one sack of gold, and I will show you how hillmen plunder—I and my sons!"

But Ali of Sikunderam was wax in Cyprian's hands. Swift, subtle flattery turned his indignation into boasting, out of which net there was no retreat.

"You and your sons—invaluable! Splendid! You should have a part, but oh, the pity of it! You are Moslems."

"Aye! The pity of it!" answered Ali. "When the *sirkar* needed men to go to Lhassa who should not upset the heathen bellies of Thibetians with a true religion, was I chosen with three sons to make that journey because we could not act Hindu? Doubtless! Bring me a thousand Hindus, and if one of them can pick me out of a crowd as not being a Hindu of the Chattrya caste, I will go back to my Hills and hold my peace!"

"But not in Benares. You would not dare in Benares," suggested Cyprian.

---

[*] Hillman armies.

TALBOT MUNDY

"By Allah, in Benares they shall think me a double-holy Brahman born in paradise! I will have the sadhus kissing feet within the hour!"

"So. Excellent!" said Cyprian. "That is, if you dare."

"I would like to see the thing I dare not do—I and my sons!" answered Ali.

"You speak of them as yours. I would rather heat them pledge themselves," said Cyprian.

"By Allah, they will swear to what I bid them swear to!" answered Ali. "If I say a hill is flat, they prove it! If I say a Hindu wears his belly inside out, they demonstrate that, too, on the nearest unbeliever! If I bid them be Hindus, they will even shave themselves and look that part. Wait and see! I will bring them in."

He strode to the door to tell Rahman, who was standing guard, to go and summon them. Rahman went off to obey and the door was closed again, but opened a minute later by Chullunder Ghose, who leaned his whole weight on the knob and used it suddenly. Manoel, the butler, entered on his knees and fell face-downward, saying nothing, amid silence.

"Eavesdropping!" exclaimed Cyprian at last.

The Goanese did not answer—too afraid, or too wise. He lay with his face between his hands in an attitude of abject supplication.

"Put him outside for the present," ordered Cyprian; and Ramsden took Manoel by the waistband, tossing him into the pantry as you throw a stick into the fire.

"I tell you," said Cyprian, "we war with powers! The Nine's spies are everywhere. More than once I have suspected Manoel, but—"

The door burst open again. It was like a thunderclap in that quiet sanctuary. Rahman stood with a hand laid flat on either door-post, leaning in, his eyes screwed tip and glinting like the heart of flint.

"They are gone!" he said.

"Allah! My sons gone?"

Ali leaped up and drew his knife, though none, not even he, knew why.

"All gone!" answered Rahman. "There was no fight, for there is no blood. I think they went of their own will."

"By Allah, then they saw the prospect of a fight!" swore Ali.

He stood on feudal right that instant—claimed Ramsden's help, they two having plighted troth over a restored knife, and there is no pledge more inviolable.

"Brother, I need thy strength," he said with dignity.

And Ramsden did not hesitate. Believing that his wits are slow and that strength is all he has, he volunteers for all the odds and ends and heavy work, the others conceding the point to avoid discussion, but setting far too high a value on him to risk him unnecessarily. (You may discuss a man's thews to his face, but not his spirit.) So they trooped out behind Jeff, Jeremy leading, leaving only Grim alone in the room with Cyprian.

It had occurred to Grim, as intuitions do come to a thoughtful man in a flash sometimes, that if the guard left in the street had gone so suddenly there was a chance that someone hoped to gain advantage by their absence.

If so, then Cyprian was the obvious objective. If not, even so it would do no harm for one of the party to stay and protect the old man.

He offered no excuse, no explanation; simply stayed.

VI

"They fled before me!"

Having eased his mind concerning the requirements of another world, Fernandez de Mendoza de Sousa Diomed Braganza began to speculate on the improbabilities of this one—improbability of credit in the first place. None had been so foolish as to underwrite the fire risk on his hotel. It was a dead loss. It was equally improbable that any of his erstwhile guests would pay their bills, since the books were burned; they would blame him for the loss of their effects, and probably bring suit against him.

He knew equally well that the police would be in search of him that minute to arrest him on a charge of criminal responsibility. He knew his wisest course would be to go to the police and surrender himself because Father Cyprian, the next-door-to-infallible, had said so, and, deciding to do that, he hurriedly reviewed another long list of improbabilities—acquaintances, who had been friends before the fire, who might be asked, but probably would not consent to furnish bail.

So he turned to the left when the padre's front door shut behind him, minded to call on one acquaintance on his way to the police. That circumstance prevented him from seeing the arrival of Grim, Ramsden, Jeremy, King and all the others, who approached Cyprian's from the opposite direction. They were within before Diomed turned and retraced his steps. So all he saw were Ali's sons in the dust under the tree—them and the constable opposite, who was rubbing at his jaw-bone with the end of a yellow truncheon to assist the processes of thought.

What brought him back was nothing more concrete than one of those changes of mind, like the action of a ship in irons in a light wind; in India they call them disembodied spirits that govern men in their extremity. He had vacillated—thought of another acquaintance, who might be less difficult to pin to than the first. Noticing the constable he chose the other sidewalk, naturally. And with both eyes on the law's hired man from under the sheltering brim of his soft felt hat he just as naturally stepped by accident on the skirts of the sheepskin coat of one of Ali's sons.

The men of Sikunderam don't fancy being stepped on. It is even likely they would choose a Goanese last if obliged to name the individual to be permitted some such liberty. Nevertheless, the act was obviously unintentional and nothing more than a mild curse would have followed if Diomed had not, tripping and trying to recover, kicked the hilt of a yard-long northern knife. And that is sacrilege. A Hillman would not kick his own knife.

So the curse that leaped from the lips of one of Ali's sons was like the hissing and explosion when you plunge a hot iron into oil. Diomed sprang back as if a snake had bitten him, and even the constable across street awoke out of speculative meditation, for it looked as if the gods had come to life to solve his problem for him. It is good to be alert and on hand when the gods arrange the play.

And as he sprang back Diomed knew the face of his antagonist for one that had cursed him previously—on the roof before the fight and the fire began. He recognized him as a man who had been held back by the others lest he use steel prematurely. And thought in the mind of a Goanese confronted by predicament is as swift and spiteful as an asp's. It recoils automatically on the person who aroused it.

Now he could surrender to advantage! Now he need not go empty-handed to the mills of the police that grind so small, and so impartially, so be that they get their grist! This came of confessing his sins to Father Cyprian! Now bail was unimportant. There were dozens who would hurry to his aid if it were known he had scapegoats, locked up in the next cell, ready to be sacrificed.

All of that passed through his mind with the speed of starlight, in between the opening and closing of the Hillman's angry teeth. He beckoned the constable, who came, standing warily a good yard from the sidewalk, not enamored of the chances yet, for they were six to one and the gods not finished shuffling. It is the privilege of the gods to make things easy for a man.

"Arrest all these!" commanded Diomed, in English for the sake of extra emphasis. "They are the villains who set fire to my hotel! I warn you they are dangerous! Arrest them instantlee!"

The constable could recognize the danger without help. He was perfectly aware of six long knives—not yet free of their scabbards, but poised between earth and air like Mohammed's coffin. Moreover, the fire was news to him.

"Brothers, I *said* that constabeel designed an inconvenience to us! Stand back-to-back!"

The "brothers" stood so, around the tree-trunk, inoffensive as a third rail.

"In case you reefuse to arrest them I will reeport you! This is a highlee important case—veree!" said Diomed, pulling out a pencil to write down the constable's number. "I saw these men set fire to my hotel!" he added.

But the constable, preferring life to an eulogium in the Gazette, demurred.

"Where are your witnesses?" he countered, grinning.

Diomed flew into a rage immediately. He knew the law, or said he did, and threatened to invoke the whole of it, including dark and lawless influence, on the constable's unrighteous head. He named names. He cited instances. He mentioned the policeman's ancestry. Raising his voice indignantly he summoned all the neighborhood to witness cowardice—corruption—a policeman in receipt of bribes refusing to arrest six murderers!

The neighborhood had no will to associate itself with outside scandal, having plenty of its own, and the few who had been in the street departed—all but one. A man in an orange-yellow smock, with a big, red caste-mark in the middle of his forehead, a twisted orange-yellow turban, and no other visible garment, property or distinction, stood where another great tree marked a narrow cross-street and beckoned, holding his forefinger close up to his eye as if in some way that lent long range to the invitation.

And the constable by now was more enraged than Diomed, with this addition, that his rage was based on absolute injustice; for the things that Diomed had said of his female relatives were not to be borne by a man of spirit and some authority. They had reached the stage of snapping fingers, and Diomed's two arms were waving like semaphores as he leaned forward, showing simian teeth, to spit denunciation in the constable's indignant face.

"One beckons," said a voice beside the tree.

"And you are corrupt—corrupt—everybodee knows it—son of an evil mother—you accept bribes from all and sundree and—"

"He wears a yellow garment, brothers, such as the *sadhus** wear, but yellower. He is only one. We could beat him if he lied to us. He beckons, and he signals silence—"

"All together—run, then!"

---

* Wandering holy men.

They were gone like leopards flushed from cover, down-street, each with a hand on the hilt of a Khyber knife, as good to stand in way of as the torrents of Sikunderam in spate. They swooped on the man in yellow as if he were foe, not friend, meaning to seize him and whirl him along between them; but he knew the. . .

(The next paragraph was partially unreadable in the book.)

. . . he had evoked, and he stepped down. . . had vanished when they reached the. . . lasted half a minute casting this and. . . of hounds before one of them saw. . . and the six went full-pelt at a. . . course, hardly thinking now, but. . . and three purposes: to outrun the con. . . to overtake the man in yellow, to keep together.

"There!" exclaimed Diomed, pausing in a torrent of abuse. "Now all thee world can see how you let criminals escape!"

And the abuse had got its work in. There is poison in the stuff, that breeds miscalculation. It is like a smoke-screen thrown off by a human skunk to mortify whoever has weak sensibilities. The constable was angry and aware of duty to be done—someone to be arrested. Six criminals, accused of arson, had escaped under cover of the seventh's volleys of abuse, and so the seventh must be guiltier than all! He raised his truncheon—actually to hammer out a signal on the side-walk—but, in Diomed's excited imagination, to attack. And Diomed struck him—twice, in the face, with the flat of his hand, hysterically—struck an officer of the law in execution of his duty!

So the truncheon went to work in earnest, and poor Diomed was beaten over collar-bone and forearm until he wouldn't have dared move them for the agony. Then he was handcuffed ignominiously, swearing, beseeching, praying, and marched away, followed by inevitable small boys as free from the vials of compassion as the monkeys are that some say are their ancestors. They said things that excited Diomed to wilder imprecations yet.

And among the boys there was a dwarf—a man in orange-yellow, taller by half a head than the tallest youngster, and as stocky as two of them, but gifted with the same free movement, so that he passed in the crowd unnoticed. He edged his way closer and closer to the constable, who glanced about him nervously, aware that in these "higher education days" the riots and the rescuing are done by school boys while their elders do the propaganding in the rear. He hurried, driving his prisoner in front of him with thumps from the truncheon on the backbone just above the trousers-band. It was several minutes before the dwarf could edge close enough to speak low and yet be heard.

"You are fortunate!" he said at last. "Surely you have promotion in your grasp! You have taken the infamous Braganza, who is charged with burning his hotel and murdering a hundred guests!"

"I knew it! Come and give your evidence!" the constable retorted, for the East lies glibly or not at all. He tried to seize the dwarf as a material witness, but missed him in the crowd, and had to hurry on for fear of losing Diomed, whom he charged presently with arson and with employing six Afridis to preserve him from arrest. "I fought them all, and they fled before me," he asserted.

Meanwhile, there was a strange assortment of individuals in more or less pursuit of Ali's sons, with Ali in the lead, of course, since the "sons" were his valuable property, and with Chullunder Ghose as naturally in the rear, as utterly indifferent to the sons' fate as the noon is to the netting of fish at ebb tide, but on the job and anxious notwithstanding.

"For if an earthquake had emptied Bedlam, releasing affinities of swine of Gadarenes, and if government officials plus editors of daily press were in charge of whole proceedings, *that* would be diamond-edged sanity compared to *this!* This is worse than acting on advice of experts! This is—oh, my aunt!"

He was not far wide of the mark; for as he waddled, wiping sweat from his fat face, he could see the whole long-drawn line extending down-street, each in his own way calling curious attention. Jeremy, for instance, reveling in being taken for an Arab, looking ready to go mad and do a whirling dervish dance at the first excuse, with the long, loose sleeves of his black coat spread like wings, in full flight after Ali.

Then Ramsden angrily, annoyed with Jeremy for making such a public exhibition of himself yet unable to overtake him and remonstrate, striding along like Samson who slew the Philistines.

King next, side by side with Narayan Singh, neither of them even fractionally off-key, and therefore about as noticeable as two true notes in a flat and sharp piano scale.

"Man that is born of a woman is like ginger-pop!" remarked Chullunder Ghose, pausing to consider. "Cut string—cork flies—and he spills himself! Step one on the path of wisdom is to *be* wise—*ergo*—by the waters of this Babylon I sit me down and weep—thus—tree, I greet you, weeping sweat, not tears! Great tree, what a world of men and women you have mocked! Mock me a while, your shade is comforting and your shafts of wit pass overhead! Now let us see—King *sahib* is remarkable for sanity. *Ergo*, he will notice me in rear. Observing emulation of Fabius Cunctator by this babu, King *sahib* will suppress inborn proclivities of Anglo-Saxon and pattern his thought accordingly.

"He will follow down that street to next corner, where he will park himself broodily, sending Narayan Singh forward to repeat process. Thus, whenever I proceed as far as corner and become conspicuous, King *sahib* will observe me and will signal to Narayan Singh. We shall thus be in touch. And the others will behave as the sparks that fly upward, which can't be helped. That is my guess. Being heirs of all the ages, I shall sit in shade and see the world go by. Suspicious? Very!"

Chullunder Ghose was right. King did turn the corner in pursuit, and at the next one did sit down on the veranda of a boarding-house for Sikhs, where Narayan Singh, who kept up the pursuit along another street, could find him and whence he himself might see Chullunder Ghose if the babu should see fit to come to the corner and signal. The others, following Ali of Sikunderam, who shouted inquiries a hundred yards ahead, stuck to the pursuit like people in a motion-picture comedy.

"Item one, a fool is very foolish," said Chullunder Ghose to himself, leaning his fat back against the tree and flapping flies with an enormous handkerchief. "Therefore congenital deficiencies of Ali's sons comply with formula. *Verb. sap.* If they had been attacked said idiots would have stood at bay by door of padre's house, in accordance with law that nature abhors a vacuum—doubtless. Empty heads apply, at spigot of authority to be filled with instructions. They would have focussed attention on padre's house inevitably. *Quad erat—nicht wahr? Ergo*, they were not attacked.

"What then? A woman? Much too early in the morning. And again— no fight! If six such idiots pursued a woman, or women, through the streets of Delhi, there would be bad blood spilt as certainly as there are speeches when a politician pursues office. Therefore not a woman. This time not the sex that bringeth forth in sorrow and regretteth same.

"Then a man! The unproductive sex! At least as sorrowful but less opaque! Motives more easily discernible. The six translucent jewels of Sikunderam have been decoyed—and by a man, or men—therefore for profit! Whose? Why? I lift a stone. Why do I lift a stone? Because I need the space it sits on—or I wish to throw it—or—if he—they— needed the space on which the sons of Ali sat—or the street in which they sat—I see—I get you—'Steve, I get you!' as Jimgrim says—behold,

I see through mystery! Let us hope actions are not so loud as words. Thou tree—thou solid, dumb, obtruding tree, farewell!"

There came a *tikka-gharri**** drawn by one horse on the way home from assisting at the *Rishis*[†] only knew what all-night revelry. Chullunder Ghose signaled the driver, who declined a fare sleepily, without success. The babu waddled to mid-street and had climbed in before the protesting Jehu could whallop his nag to a trot.

"Give her gas!" said Chullunder Ghose, translating slang learned from Grim into opprobrious vernacular.

So the weary cabman whacked the wearier horse and, better to call attention to himself, the babu stood up screaming that he had a gall-stone and would die unless in hospital within the minute. He was seen, heard, contemplated.

But he only drove two blocks, around a corner, and then paid the astonished cabman the exact fare. If he had overpaid him he would only have multiplied suspicion. Then he walked back three blocks, parallel to the street in which was Cyprian's house, and turning the corner suddenly was just in time to see three men in orange-yellow smocks approach Cyprian's door and ring the bell. He stood there long enough to watch them enter and see the door shut again behind them.

"Kali!" he exclaimed then. "Let us hope Jimgrim is appreciative! Dogs of the Wife of Siva the Destroyer! Oh, my aunt!"

He had been in time to see Ali of Sikunderam charge up the steps and plunge into the building—for the men he hurled his questions at had misdirected Ali and he had covered an unnecessary mile before learning that his precious sons were foul of the law.

He ran like an articulated jellyfish until he reached a corner whence he could see King perched on the boarding-house veranda. There, ignoring all discretion, he pulled his rose-pink turban off and threw the thirty yards of silk in air, whirling it until King raised a hand in answer.

Promptly King leaned out over the veranda-rail at the corner of two streets and made a gesture that Narayan Singh saw from a quarter of a mile away. And the Sikh, not optimistic, having seen too much, but understanding that the gang was wanted back at Cyprian's, went at the double to retrieve as many of the gang as possible from a building in front of which two square lamps advertised—POLICE.

---

* Hired cab.

[†] Spirits.

Narayan Singh had seen Rahman follow Ali, and then Jeremy, then Ramsden. None had come back down the steps, so he was in no doubt what to do, although he did not know yet how absurdly simple the strategy of the man in orange-yellow had been, nor how simpler and more finished would be that of Jeremy.

Like will-o'-the wisp in orange livery he had simply led those six North-country swashbucklers a dance along street after street—up the stairs of the police station—and there had accused the lot of them of theft! There was nothing whatever for the police to do but hold them.

When Ali got there pandemonium was loose, for the six sons' weapons had been taken and they were resisting further search as desperately as hell's imps would object to baptism—teeth—talons—imprecation—horizontal mostly, with a couple of policemen laboring at each limb and each lot expanding and contracting soddenly in spasms. One policeman—he who had recently arrested Diomed the Goanese—went from lot to lot using a truncheon unapplauded, aiming at the heads of Afghans but oftener hitting his friends. He said nothing about recognizing them, having already claimed to have defeated them in mortal combat. The obvious solution was to stun them lest they recognize himself, but it was extremely difficult to hit their heads.

And into that confusion Ali leaped like a firecracker, knife and all, to be brought to a stand by the officer's revolver. The officer was in his place, in charge, behind the desk. There might have been murder done, Ali was in no mood for compliance, with his darlings being whacked and twisted under his eyes. The fact that the police were bleeding, and his sons not more than warming up for a morning's work, added to his zeal, and instinct warned him that the man in yellow was the "father" of the rumpus. Therefore, Ali was for springing at the man in yellow's throat when Jeremy strode in smiling like an illustration from the Book of Ruth, with Rahman yelping like a wolf a step behind him.

"*Salaam aleikoum*! Peace! Let there be peace!" boomed Jeremy in a voice with a ventriloquial note that fills a room. He sounded, as he looked, like a man from the Old Testament. Ali detected magic in the wind and yelled a word that his sons obeyed on the instant. Even so, the police were human and eager for revenge, but Ramsden walked in.

Baring his forearms, he offered to kill with his hands the first three constables who struck a prisoner. So there was peace as Jeremy requested, and the man in yellow took advantage of it, going close to two of Ali's sons, who were held fast, with a policeman on each wrist. He said he wanted to identify them. Jeremy observed, and Ramsden observed Jeremy. The officer observed all three, but Jeremy's hand is swifter than any eye.

"They are the men who stole from me!" said the man in yellow. "I had a gold coin similar to this one in each hand. Rushing at me, they seized my wrists and took the money, which you will find on their persons. Search them!" He drew from a pocket in his smock and displayed one ancient coin that Jeremy and Ramsden identified as having belonged to the Portuguese da Gama.

"Search them!" ordered the officer, tapping his revolver on the desk.

"Wait! First let me also identify!" said Jeremy; and he, too, went close to the same two of Ali's sons.

He removed and palmed a coin that the man in yellow had secreted in the nearest man's sash.

Not satisfied with that, he walked tip to the police officer and whispered to him. Then, from him, to the man in orange-yellow who was beginning to look less pleased—a mite impatient.

"Have I ever seen you anywhere?" asked Jeremy. "Were you ever in Jerusalem? Jaffa? Alexandria?"

"No!"

"He lies!" said Jeremy. "I know him well! This was a trick by the Hindu to steal a gold watch from your honor," he went on, smiling at the officer as if butter hardly ever melted in his mouth. "However, as the Prophet saith, on whom be peace, 'Let not words and emptiness of speech suffice!' Search all three men!"

Now Ali's sons stood still, submitting, for they had felt what Jeremy's nimble fingers did. And Jeremy, with his back to Ramsden, passed to him two gold coins for safety's sake, stepping forward again instantly. The jaw of the man in orange-yellow dropped.

"He—that Arab—" he began.

But the searchers had stripped Ali's sons in vain, and it was his turn. The first hand thrust into his pocket drew out the officer's gold watch and chain.

"Magic!" exclaimed the officer. "He never once came near me!"

"Lock him up then! Such as he are dangerous!" said Jeremy not turning a hair, and the officer accepted the advice, insisting, too, however, on holding three of Ali's sons as witnesses.

It was then, as the door of one cell slammed on all four and a fifth already in there, that Narayan Singh strode in, appraised the situation, and strode out again, leaving as many to follow him as could or would.

VII

"Shakespearean homeopathic remedy!"

Grim and Cyprian sat face to face in silence with a shaft of sunlight streaming through the space between them. Infinitely tiny specks of dust—for Cyprian was a martinet and Manoel used cloth and broom incessantly—danced tarantella-fashion, more or less as gnats do, in the golden fairway.

"You observe them?" said Cyprian presently. "Each one of those moving specks is itself made of billions of infinitely tiny specks all in motion. That is the way the universe is made. All atoms—all in motion—in an all-pervading essence known as ether. You know that? It is in the books—the oldest of all books as well as the newest. The ancients knew about it seven thousand years ago, if we accept their heretical chronology. I have their books to prove it. These Nine Unknown are the inheritors of scientific secrets that used to form the basis of the Ancient Mysteries. Yes, that's so. That's so. There isn't any doubt of it. Not religious secrets, understand me—no, no, they are enemies of all religion! They use scientific truths to stir superstition by pretending their phenomena are miracles! Devils' work! They know—the rascals! They have knowledge! Compared to them our modern scientists are just as Julius Cesar would have been if somebody confronted him with Paine's fireworks or an eighteen-inch gun or the radio. Clever fellow, Csar. Bright as a button. He would have tried to explain it away; tried—but there would be the phenomena—effect—result of cause; you have to know the cause to understand effect. No use repudiating it. Our moderns fail exactly as Julius Caesar would have done. And the Nine Unknown laugh. Devils!

"Nothing suits them better than to have the scientists, the newspapers, the governments, the secret service, the police, all vow that no such knowledge as theirs exists—no such organization. Above all they chuckle because the church denies them. Missionaries are their best friends. To declare they are non-existent without proving it leaves the rascals free to do as they please, without lessening the superstition of the crowd. You understand?"

Grim did not. He has the pragmatist-adventurer's view of life, dissatisfied with all veils hung between himself and noumenon, and studying each phenomenon from the angle of "what's the use of it?"

"Why deny what you can't prove? Why not discover their science and employ it properly?"

Cyprian interrupted him with a frown and a flash of temper that betrayed volcanic will unweakened by his age and only curbed by discipline.

"*Tchut!* Wiser minds than yours decided about that long ago. Beware of the sin of presumption! These people have been branded as magicians—tricksters! Their pretensions, magic—tricks! Humbugs!—evil-workers!—liars!—cheats! They have imposed on superstition. Take the consequences. Banned by the Church. Outlawed. Burn their books! Who shall say then that they have, or ever had, a scrap of scientific knowledge? That is my task—fifty—two-and-fifty years of effort. Burn the books! The nine books! Burn them! They have defied the Church—*sed prevalabit!*"

"I don't get you," answered Grim. "Knowledge ought to be known. Those books—"

"Are mine! To do as I see fit! Did you not agree?" demanded Cyprian.

Grins had agreed, but that did not admit the whole contention. Grim, because he keeps an open mind, has been accused by missionaries of belonging to nearly every heathen cult in turn, but his name stands written on no muster-roll. He is under no vows of obedience. He countered:

"King and I have talked this over—lots. King has been on the trail of it twenty years you know. Are you sure the Nine aren't honorable men, who know more than is safe to teach the public?"

Cyprian smiled at that like a martyr prepared to die for his convictions.

"Only, someone killed the Portuguese," Grim went on. "Why? If they know so much, why kill a drunken crook you can afford to pity?"

"I have told you. They are devils," answered Cyprian.

"And while the hotel burned there was a voice urging the crowd to attack us," Grim continued. "The same voice shouted, 'Fire!'—deliberated creating panic. Someone had searched the Don's room—carried his books away. Same man—same men more likely—returned to burn their tracks. That hardly seems like men who, as you put it, have inherited the knowledge of the Ancient Mysteries."

The expression of Cyprian's face changed. He drew on his mask of patience that at eighty a man has learned to use consummately or not at all. It was quite clear that if he gave discussion rein these colts of other creeds would gallop away with him, Grim particularly. Discipline was out of the question. Whip he had none. Argument was useless. It would do no good to tell a man like Grim to let speculation alone.

"Would you go and find my servant Manoel?" he asked; for helplessness is like a weapon, in a wise man's hand.

Grim left the room.

Manoel sat cross-legged on a blanket in the corner of the pantry, hardly having moved from the spot where Ramsden dumped him down. The sin of speculation—if it is a sin—could not be laid to him, for he was dumb—determined—obstinate—like a clog that has hidden to escape a thrashing and will neither run away nor come to heel. He did not even shake his head when Grim ordered him into the padre's presence; so Grim went back and reported the state of affairs, having more than one purpose in mind.

And it seemed good to Cyprian just then to supply Grim with the wherewithal to take his mind off the subject they had been discussing. Helplessness was put to work again.

"I am old. It tires me to undertake these—do you think Mr. Ramsden frightened him too much—I wonder—would you mind, eh? See what you can do with him—persuade him to come in here—yes? Such a rascal as he has been!—no, by no means always honest—but a servant— he has been a comfort. Will you talk to him?"

That was tantamount to *carte blanche*. Grim, incapable of nosing into the domestic secrets of his host, could, would and did crowd every limit to the edge when given leave. He squatted down, cross-legged too, in front of Manoel and waited until the shifty brown eyes had to come to a rest at last and meet his gray ones. (The passport says they are gray, which makes it legal, but no two agree as to their real color. Possibly they change, although his zeal is fixed.)

"You're in luck. You've one chance!" Grim said speaking in Punjabi.

Manoel did not answer; but the word luck probed the very heart of inborn passion.

"Da Gama and Braganza had no luck at all," said Grim, and Manoel lowered his eyes, not straight downward but along the arc of an ellipse because of certain racial peculiarities.

"Da Gama died. Braganza's house was burned. Do you feel brave?" Grim asked him.

Manoel looked up—suddenly.

"Who are *you?*" he asked.

His lips parted loosely. The corners of his mouth dropped, and he shifted his eyes to left and right, showing more than was wholesome of the bloodshot whites.

Dread, unexpected and acute, was unmistakable; it acted like a solvent on the sullenness of fear. Grim saw his chance—almost too long to be called chance; he had nothing to go on but conjecture.

"Who do you *think* I am?" he retorted. "Look into my eyes! Who am I?"

Manoel hesitated, with the expression of self-conscious innocence facing a firing squad. Having double-crossed friend and enemy alike there was nothing to fall back on but his conscience, obviously! Grim bored in, wishing he knew something definite to base assault on.

"Didn't you expect me?" he demanded.

"Yes, but—"

The million-to-one shot landed! Grim's face hardly changed expression, but his eyes had laughter in them that the Goanese was far too scared to recognize.

"—but I didn't look for a Punjabi. He who told me wore a yellow smock—a *sadhu*. I have not had time—"

"Time!" Grim retorted, forcing the note of indignation.

"I have not had time, and I have not been paid," said Manoel, shifting his eyes again, and then himself, so that Grim, who was all alert suspicion, jumped to a conclusion.

"Do you know they killed da Gama?" he asked, setting his face like brass, and Manoel shuddered. "Do you mean to tell me you have not been paid?" he went on, fixing his eyes on the Goanese and speaking slowly.

And whether or not Manoel had pocketed his price, imagination warned him he was helpless, at the mercy of someone who would harvest whether he had sown or not. Admission that he had been paid was no proof of it at all, he being what he was.

"But now he knows I was at the keyhole. He will dismiss me. And first he will investigate. So he will find out, and I do not dare! I will give the money back!"

That, too, was no proof that he had been paid. But it *was* proof that he had taken more than one step on the path of treason. Grim turned and swiped at a fly. Again the unhappy Manoel shifted—not so much his eyes this time as his whole person, although his eyes did move. It was because his eyes moved that he did not see Grim looking in the little kitchen mirror.

"Give it here!" said Grim.

"The money? I—I—"

"No. Give *it* here—or—"

"Let me go then! I must run! I do not dare stay and face his anger!"

But Grim knew now, and he is one of those who use knowledge, patiently or promptly as the case may be. He leaned forward. Manoel screamed, as a chicken does when a housewife has her by the legs. Grim seized him by the collar-band, and all ten chocolate fingers closed on the iron wrist. Grim jerked him forward, threw him on his face and sat on him, proceeding then to raise the blanket.

"Thought so! Yow! You little scorpion!"

He seized his victim's wrist and twisted it until a knife dropped—kicked the knife across the floor—glanced at the back of his thigh to observe that it was hardly bleeding—laid the folded blanket on the Goanese's head and sat on that—then lifted what had been beneath the blanket, carefully.

It needed care. It was an old book bound in vellum, crackled with age. Within, in sepia, beautifully written in the Maharatta tongue, with diagrams, on paper yellowed with age and thumbing, was what purported to be a literal translation of a very ancient roll.

The first page, on which the translator's name had very likely been, was missing. On the second was a pentagram within the dodeahedron—the geometrical figure on which alchemists assert the universe was built. Beneath that was a diagram of the Hindu cosmogony side by side with the Chaldean. On the third page, in Maharathi at the top, as if continuing a paragraph from page one, was the following:

Whereafter, being certain that the roll would not be missed until (here a name was illegible) should come again, I hid in the cave with the hag who made provision for my needs, and by the light of the unextinguishable lamp I labored at the construing, with haste, that the whole might be accomplished, yet with diligence, lest errors enter in.

This finished volume witnesseth.

Which being done, this shall be hidden in a place known only to the hag. Whereafter, I will endeavor to return the roll lest (the undecipherable name again) should fall under suspicion and stiffer for infidelity. That risk is great, for it is hard to come at the place where the rolls are kept.

But death is no more than the gates of life.

The hag has her instructions. So this fruit of my long husbandry shall fall into the right hands. He who guided hitherto being All-wise to accomplishment.

Then here begins:

On the next page, at the top, in bold Maharathi characters, was the first law of the Cabalists, and of all alchemists and true magicians since the world began.

As Above, So Below.

Grim read no further, for the stuff absorbed him to the point where near-unconsciousness of every other circumstance prevailed. His whole being yearned to the lure of that musty volume and its secrets. He craved it as some unfortunates crave opium. The merely physical appeal of drugs, prodigious though it is, monopolizes no more than the intellectual attraction of the unknown does a man of Grim's temperament. If he had read another page he would have read a dozen, and a dozen would have only whetted appetite. He closed the book with a slap that brought the pungent dust out, and removed himself from Manoel's head.

"You insect! If you had the original of this I'd trade you my right hand for it!"

"Let me go!" sputtered Manoel. "Oh, sir; I am afraid to face him! Take the book and let us both go!"

But Grim took book and Manoel, each by the back, and shoved the Goanese along in front of him into the padre's presence.

"He seems to have been keeping this for you," he said and laid the volume on Cyprian's knees.

"Had he read it?" demanded Cyprian.

"Oh, no! Oh, no, sir! Oh, father, oh, no, no! It is black magic and forbidden. I would never read it!"

"What odds? He wouldn't understand a word," said Grim, and Cyprian nodded.

"Let him go," said Cyprian. "Drive him from the house!"

But Grim had spoken English, and the fear that gnawed Manoel's bowels multiplied. It dawned on him that he had been tricked. Grim, then, was Father Cyprian's friend, and not—

"No, no, no!" he shouted. "No! You must be merciful! This is my sanctuaree! I may not be driven forth! I tell you I did it to save you from murder because you are old! You are ungrateful! You commit a great sin if you drive me forth!"

He wanted to throw himself down in the attitude of supplication, but Grim had him by the neck.

"He expected somebody," said Grim. "Shall we see this through now?"

"Face the adversary!" Cyprian answered.

But age gave way to youth. He waited for Grim to make the next decision. And Grim held his arm out, helping—almost lifting the old man from his chair.

"You'd better be seen at the door," he said. "We'll let them see Manoel go empty-handed."

He turned on the Goanese and shook him.

"Listen, asp! Get your belongings. Oh! Only a blanket, eh? Preparations all made—everything out of the house but that?"

He followed him to the pantry, watched him through the door, and seized him by the neck again as he emerged.

"Now, you've another chance. Don't speak in the street! Show you haven't got the book—look scared—walk! You understand me? If you disobey I'll—"

"Oh, oh! Onlee let me not go! I will—"

Grim stood back. It was Cyprian, trembling with age rather than emotion, who stood in the doorway and sped the errant Goanese with his left hand raised palm-outward and a look of pursed-up horror.

"I tell you, father, I did it to preevent murder!" sobbed Manoel with great tears running down into his whiskers. "Give me benediction then, I—"

Cyprian did not deny him that. It possibly accomplished more than Grim's threat. Manoel departed down-street with his head hung, and the blanket draped over one arm, avoiding all encounters; and a man in orange-yellow by the great tree opposite—where Ali's sons had sat—drew such deductions as he saw fit. Grim standing in shadow within saw the man make a signal.

"Good!" he said. "Shut the door now," and Cyprian obeyed as if learning lessons. It was hard, maybe, at eighty to learn to dispense with even a dishonest servant.

They returned to the sitting-room, whence the cloistered peace had gone, although the sunlight still streamed through the spaced jalousies.

"Pity the first page is missing," said Grim by way of making conversation.

"It isn't!" snapped Cyprian, and looked to see.

Confronted by the fact, his last strength seemed to vanish and he sat down, knocking the book to the floor. Grim rescued it.

"On the first page, at the top, was the finest cosmogony ever drafted," said Cyprian, "and underneath it an explanation of the terns used."

He spoke as if hope were dead forever. Grim changed the subject, or tried to—

"Let's hope our crowd don't return too soon!"

"I should have searched that blanket," Cyprian grumbled. "He had the first page wrapped in it. I know he had!"

Grim tried again. "Tell me what the 'unextinguishable lamp' means on page two," he demanded.

"Mind your own business!" Cyprian snapped back, struggling to be calm. "If I will burn books, shall you rifle their secrets first? Phoenix from the ashes, eh? No, no! Hear no evil—see no evil—know no evil—that is my advice to you, my son! What I burn need not trouble you!"

"Are your books in this house?" Grim asked, suddenly alarmed at a random notion.

But Cyprian chose to be amused at that, shaking his head sidewise with the palsied humor of old age.

"Do you think I am in my dotage?"

Grim had no time to reply. There came a long peal on the bronze bell, that clanged on its coiled spring as if the temples of all Thibet were in alarm. Grim went to the front door, opened suddenly, and stood back.

Three men entered, all in yellow smocks. They came in swiftly, almost on the run—stopped suddenly—and hesitated. They were surprised to see Grim.

"I am the padre *sahib's* new servant," he said in the dialect, smiling.

Then he turned the key and threw it out through the little round peep-hole that exists somewhere or other in most Indian front-doors.

"Father Cyprian is in there," he said, with a jerk of his head in the direction of the sitting-room.

They eyed Grim curiously, saying nothing. Bigger, stronger than Grim as far as appearance went, they wore the impudent expression of men who have been taught from infancy that they are better than the crowd, of other clay—bold, yet with a sort of sly air underlying impudence, and an abominably well-fed look, although they wore the simple smock of the ascetic. Finally they all three smiled at Grim, and one of them motioned him to lead the way into the sitting-room. The man next to him who motioned had a long silk handkerchief in one hand, and on his forehead the crimson signet of the goddess Kali. Grim stepped back instead of forward—ducked—stepped back again—and stood in the pantry entrance with blood chilled and the gooseflesh rising.

"My hour is not yet!" he assured them.

Except for Grim's activity there had hardly been a motion visible, and yet—the handkerchief was in the other hand. The executioner had missed. And if there had been a score of witnesses they would likely all have sworn there had been no attempt made, for the pride of the Thug* is in his swiftness. None sees the strangling when it happens, it is so quick.

All three men smiled with the coppery, cast expression of determination that can bide its time. Grim motioned them again toward the sitting-room, and they went in one by one, the man with the handkerchief first, and the last man turning on the threshold to assure himself that Grim was not bent on reprisal. But no effort was made to exclude him. The door was left open until he walked in after them and closed it—having his own reasons.

Cyprian was very near collapse. The apparition of the three in orange-yellow came like an almost mechanical dénouement, to which Manoel's misconduct had been overture—warning perhaps. His old hands clutched and clutched again the carved ends of the chair-arms. But he said nothing. He was fighting for self-mastery. His lips were moving, probably in prayer; and repeatedly his eyes sought Grim's, although Grim refused him any answering signal. Grim knew he held the winning hand, and he who knows that is a fool if he fails to play it carefully.

His cue was to make believe he had no weapon—to postpone violence—to unmask purposes—to ascertain facts—before admitting the possession of a forty-five. Even when the orange-yellow exquisite tried thuggery he had not so much as made a gesture to reach his weapon, and the three were fairly satisfied that he was unarmed. They sat down in a row on the long strip of yak-hair rug that covered half the floor, facing the shuttered window, at an angle of forty-five to Cyprian.

Grim went and sat in the corner facing Cyprian, whence he could watch them at an angle athwart the flowing lines of light. They were

---

* Thuggee, as far as its practise by wandering bands is concerned, was stamped out by the Government long ago; but its methods, and the skill of its practitioners, survive.

TALBOT MUNDY

nearer to the door than he was, but had no forty-fives, which made a difference. They produced what they did have—two old-fashioned muzzle-loading pistols between three of them—cocked, and fitted with percussion caps. Grim looked afraid, and Cyprian *was* afraid.

"You want what?" Cyprian demanded, speaking English for no other reason than that those words trembled out first.

"Books!" replied the middle of the three men, using the same language with a readiness and absence of foreign accent, that astonished because of his bronzeness and the orange-yellow smock. There was no reason why he should not know English, except that he looked like one of those who pride themselves on their refusal to learn it.

"What books?" asked Cyprian feebly.

But only his voice failed. There was no suggestion in his eye that he dreamed of yielding. Rather, he was recovering self-command as the effect of shock receded.

"All the books you have, including that one," the same man answered, pointing at the volume Grim had saved from Manoel's clutches.

Cyprian took his own time about answering that, moving his lips and jaws as if first he had to masticate the words and glancing down at Grim repeatedly to see whether Grim had any signals for him.

But Grim sat still, the way a *chela* sits by the feet of his *guru*, unpresuming, waiting for the wisdom to come dropping word by word from the privileged lips of age. When the time should come for Grim to give a signal he was minded to make it abrupt and unmistakable.

"Who are you men?" demanded Cyprian at last; and the three in yellow looked amused. Either they disbelieved that he did not know, or they thought it amusing he should dare to ask; it was not clear which.

"We are they who demand the books," answered he with the handkerchief, and his companions nodded.

"And if the books are not here?" Cyprian asked.

"We will take that one, and you with it! Later you will show us where the others are."

Grim heard the noise he was waiting for, but did not move, for the sound was vague as if, on the sidewalk, thought was producing words, not action yet. He hoped the bell would not ring—hoped the key dropped through the hole would be interpreted—hoped Cyprian would not have apoplexy at his next remark. For it was time and he was ready.

"Holy one," he said in the dialect, playing the part of the *chela* still, "would it not be wiser if I tell them where a *few* books are?"

He allowed his eyes to wander furtively in the direction of the far wall, where the room was in shadow.

"And I win!" he exclaimed in English suddenly.

They had turned their heads to follow the direction of his glance. They looked back along the barrel of a forty-five. And of all things in the world that are difficult, the hardest is to tell which of three of you sitting side-by-side will be first in the path of a bullet.

"They are hollow-nosed bullets," Grin assured them. "Put your hands up, please!"

They held their hands up, palms to the front, suggesting Siva's image.

"We are not afraid," said the man in the middle. "We are watched for. Others come."

"Yes, others come," said Grim, aware of noises penetrating through the thick door and thicker walls.

"Bet you they're in here! What'll you bet?" demanded Jeremy's voice as the door flew open and the whole crowd poured in, Jeremy leading— all the crowd, that is, who had been in the room before and two besides.

Ali of Sikunderam came last, volcanically angry, muttering Islamic blasphemy into his ruffled beard that either he had tugged at or some other man had pulled.

Narayan Singh went straight for the two pistols and kicked them away from their owners. One went off. A lead ball as large as a pigeon's egg was flattened on the stone wall close to Cyprian and the smell of cheap black powder filled the room. Using that as an excuse the three in orange-yellow put the ends of their turbans across their mouths and nostrils, moistening them thoroughly with spittle.

"Being very holy men no doubt, oh yes!" remarked Chullunder Ghose, picking up both pistols as his own perquisite. "Spirits of the cess-pool! Who invoked them? That is the worst-smelling powder! Are infernal regions advertised by Christian missionary actual? My aunt! Shall I open window, holy one?"

But Cyprian was losing consciousness. King went at a bound for the door and was in time to stop the three strange visitors with three blows. (India, who knew almost all human knowledge long before the West was born, has yet to learn to use her fists.) He bade Ali and his sons hold them, and returned to discover what the source of the reeking smoke was. He suspected a grenade with some new sort of fuse. But there was only the assassin's long silk handkerchief, dropped on the carpet as if by accident. He kicked it and nothing happened, though the smoke did not cease.

Meanwhile, Grim was holding Cyprian's head while Ramsden lifted him and Jeremy forced a window. Between them they got the old man's head into the fresh air. He showed signs of recovery. But the three coughed so violently that they could hardly hold him up, and the open window seemed to make no difference inside the room; there was no telling where the smoke came from.

Nor was it actually smoke; rather a thin mist, with a hint of pearliness and green in it. There was a faint suggestion of sweetness and a little ether. It was a compound undoubtedly, and there was lots of it, but neither King nor yet Chullunder Ghose exploring on hands and knees could find its source nor any container that might have held it.

Outside the room, where the gas or whatever it was spread swiftly but not so densely into the hall, Ali and his sons were taking law into their own hands. There was a cellar door—a trap with big strap-hinges— and the weight of the door, with rust and friction added, was as much as two men striving mightily could move. That appealed, and the sons of Ali raised it. Down below was a stonewalled cellar twelve by twelve or so, empty of everything except some builders' trash.

Ali with his drawn knife drove the prisoners one at a time until they jumped down in there.

"If they break their legs, may Allah mortify the stumps!" he requested piously.

Meanwhile, tearing about the room, upsetting things and vowing there were devils loose, Narayan Singh lost equilibrium, fell over Chullunder Ghose, and collapsed with his head near the silken handkerchief. King seized him to drag him from the room, and noticed a burn where his face had touched the silk. Chullunder Ghose picked up the handkerchief and dropped it with a yell.

Ramsden, Jeremy and Grim picked Cyprian up between them and ran for the door with him, meaning to make for the street. They met King dragging the Sikh, and for a second there was a tight jam, into which Chullunder Ghose came headlong.

"Oh go! All go! Only go!" he shouted. "Now I know it! Manicheean magic!* It is death! It is unquenchable!"

---

* The Manichees were Persians, whose teaching was a form of dualism. But they also celebrated mysteries and were said to practise magic and theurgy.

Cyprian heard him.

"Poison—from the ancient books!" he gasped. "Come away!"

They had reeled through the door in front of the babu's impact.

"Where are those prisoners?" King shouted.

Ali and his sons began to labor at the trap-door, but it had jammed in place and was difficult to start again. Chullunder Ghose, purple with effort and choking, sized the situation up and charged back into the sitting-room.

He came back like a "soccer" forward, shouting and kicking the handkerchief along in front of him.

"Out of my way! Out of house! Quick!"

They fled before him—all but Ali and his sons. The men of Sikunderam considered dignity and flight before a babu, at his order, incompatible. They went on working at the trap, and raised it about six inches.

"So! Good! Now down again!"

The babu kicked the handkerchief through the opening and, as Sikunderam showed no symptoms of obedience, jumped on the trap, forcing it out of their fingers and down into its bed with a report like an explosion. There he squatted, looking like a big bronze temple image.

"Now is good!" he said. "Keep open house until gas shall evanesce! Practitioners of Manicheean deviltry will now be hoist like engineers with own petard! Shakespearean homeopathic remedy! *Verb* very *sap!* Oh yes! Tell *sahibs*, no more danger now!"

And saying that, Chullunder Ghose himself keeled over.

VIII

"He is very dead!"

I n one hot brick cell, closed by an iron door with a peep-hole in it, there were three of the sons of Sikunderam, one Hindu in orange-yellow with a crimson caste-mark on his forehead, who had refused his name, and Fernandez de Mendoza de Sousa Diomed Braganza, whose name and occupation were as well known as his temper was notorious and his predicament acute.

None of the others seemed to worry much. The "sons" were aware that father Ali and his patrons knew their whereabouts, and it is Law in the North, whence they came, that the feudal claims are first. There would either be a rescue, or a use of influence, or possibly raw bribery this side of midnight. They were sure of that, whether rightly or wrongly.

And he in orange-yellow, having had the trick turned back on him by Jeremy, was none the less apparently at ease. He wore the would-like-to-be-dangerous smile of the hanger-on of priests not subtle, rather threatening—the smile of a man who holds himself superior to others as rule number one of policy. There is nothing in the world more sure than that the priests and politicians *always* abandon their clients when convenient; nor anything more fixed than the assurance of the due-to-be-abandoned until the miserable fact confronts them.

Diomed, on the other hand, was neither full of faith nor hope; and he never did pin much to charity. Having counted on forgiveness of his sins, he found that there was fortune still to reckon with; and he did not believe that fortune ever favored Goanese much. He supposed he must sin some more.

"We are five in one predicament. Shall we compare notes?" he suggested.

Being first man in that cell he felt almost *in loco parentis*, a guise that any innkeeper assumes without much difficulty. That son of Ali whom he had recognized in the street was not one of those detained, so he was unaware of facing men whose enmity he had already, and could not lose without suitable compensation, of which they, and they only, would be judges.

The sons of Ali held their peace. Their knives had been taken from them. Talk is no equivalent for steel. Lacking the one, in the North's opinion, it is unheroic and incontinent to substitute the other.

"Wait!" says Sikunderam. "The hour of God's appointing cometh! Wait, saying nothing!"

But the man in orange-yellow, regarding Allah as a myth, served an even more destroying goddess, whose devotees are encouraged to seek opportunity, not wait. He spoke, and his voice was strangely reminiscent, so that Diomed stared open-mouthed at him.

"Someone set fire to a hotel in the night," he said.

"Mine! My hotel!"

"So there are three," said he in orange-yellow: "he who knows the secret, they who wish the secret kept, and he or they who wish to know who did it."

"Do you know who did it?" demanded Diomed, thrusting his little black-bearded face forward so as to read the other's expression better.

But there was no expression, except that cast-copper smile betokening superiority. He in yellow was returning the compliment by watching Diomed, so neither of them saw the rapt attention displayed on the faces of Ali's sons. But the men of the North, who are fools, as all India knows, were born with their ears to the whimpering wind. They are easy to deceive, but as to voices and the memory of voices never. Six eyes from Sikunderam, more used to lean, long distances, met in the cell gloom and three heads nodded almost imperceptibly.

"They who wish the secret not known may bid first," said the orange-yellow man. "Nothing for nothing and from nothing. The key that opens is the key that fits. My necessities are a lock that holds me. Has anyone the key?" He stared into the eyes of Sikunderam, impudently, challenging. In the dark of the cell they looked like three young startled animals.

"Whoever would take on himself the theft of that policeman's watch would have my friendship," said he in orange-yellow.

"You know!" exclaimed Diomed. "You know who burned my hotel!"

"I know!" he confessed, with another of his bronze smiles, glancing surreptitiously, at Ali's sons.

His need was to make *them* understand him. Diomed might shout to heaven that he had stolen the watch, and the world would only vote him mad; but if one of those Hillmen should confess, and the other two should confirm it, what court could help believe?

"I will say who set fire to the hotel unless—"

"It was they! It was they! They did it!" Diomed interrupted. "Now I know them! They are the devils who fought on the roof! They are the sons of evil mothers who—"

He was silenced by a slap across the mouth, backhanded, that made his lips bleed and cut the knuckles of the smiter. But not one word was said to him. Nor did he who had struck the blow speak at all, for economy is the essence of good teamwork.

It was the second of three self-styled brothers who pointed a lean fore-finger; and the third who gave tongue to what all three had in mind.

"Aye! Thou knowest! And we know! We know the voice of him who cried *'Bande Materam!'* That same voice—thy voice—cried 'Fire!' before the fire was set!"

"Ye were there then?" the Hindu answered mockingly; and Diomed, with a half-breed's instinct for coming violence, drew his knees up to his chin on the bench. He screwed himself into the corner to be able to jump either way.

"Aye, we were there, seven of us and the father of the seven, a Sikh too, and a Jat and some *sahibs*, who will swear to that voice of thine, thou raven croaking in a cave! We are not men who can be imposed on! We—"

The man in orange-yellow interrupted. Like all who pride themselves on their intelligence he underrated that of his would-be victims. He threatened them. Whereas, two things are sure: if you threaten the men of Sikunderam you must be able to make good, and prove it; and if you plead to them, you must prove you are empty-handed—a true supplicant for charity. Between those two poles all earth lies belly-upward to be bargained over. They are poles like light-houses that no man possessed of open eyes could miss. But pride is like box-blinkers.

"You Moslems don't like to be hanged. I can call witnesses. Better make terms with me!"

The Indian courts of justice war with a system of perjury that is older and more popular than law. The consequent precautions and delays, and the system, that if ten men swear to a thing and twenty swear against it, the twenty win, may lend itself to obvious abuses that, according to Sikunderam, are avoided easiest with cold steel.

The sons of Ali had no steel. Tradition would have counseled patience and dissimulation. But the heat in the cell was growing insufferable for men born where the clean air whistles off everlasting snow-peaks, and stuffiness—being kin to strangulation—breeds hysteria, which in turn brings all innate proclivities to the surface and upsets any calculation based on intellect. He in orange-yellow was an intellectual. He knew the rules. The sons of Ali were no psychologists.

"Let him die before he does us injury! Be quick, my brothers!"

That was a call for action, understood and never argued, over. He in orange-yellow gave a shout blended of agony and unbelief as fingers like hairy spider-legs closed on his throat. Other parts of his anatomy grew palsied with pain, in a grip that he had no more chance of breaking than a sheep has of breaking the butcher's hold. Noise ceased.

It was at that stage of proceedings that the cell-guard, whose ear had been to the peep-hole, hurried to summon his officer. He ached with ill-will, because his sinews had been twisted when the sons of Ali objected to arrest. He wanted to see them dragged out one by one and beaten. But exactly at the same moment there entered from the street three men in orange-yellow, with the caste-mark of Kali on their foreheads, who approached the desk and made signs to the bewildered officer. The bewilderment was all too obvious.

He was as displeased as a magistrate might be to whom an arrested violator of the law made masonic signals; nevertheless, not nearly so certain what to do, since there was no appeal in this case to his honor and the dictates of conscience. He was bluffed before they said a word to him.

"This is a day of reckoning," announced the leader of the three. "One of ours is in your keeping. He is part of the price. We demand him."

The Moslem officer hardly hesitated. Saying nothing, but livid under the impress of that fatalistic fear which is the only force blackmail has, he started toward the cells and disappeared through a door into the corridor, followed by the cell-guard. The door slammed, but opened again a minute later. The officer stood there beckoning. The three followed him in, and the door, slammed shut a second time.

"Look!"

The officer flung the cell-door open and the cell-guard brought his carbine to the charge, showing his teeth for extra argument. The three in yellow, self-controlled, peered in like visitors being shown the sights, their bronze faces showing no more emotion than the image on copper coins; but the police-officer was trembling with anxiety.

"I ask you to believe—" he stammered in Punjabi.

One of the three interrupted him, touching his sleeve, not wasting any words.

The three were interested—neither more nor less. There was possibly as much trace of amusement on their lips as you may see on the granite monument of one of the old Pharaohs—semi-humorous acceptance of the iron rule of destiny, observed without surprise. The officer tried speech again.

"Beware, most honorables! They are dangerous!"

The same quiet hand on his sleeve requested silence. The three had seen all there was to see, but continued looking; for the processes of thought are said to be accomplished best with all eyes on the object.

In front of the door, as if laid there for inspection, was the body of the individual in orange-yellow who had threatened the sons of Sikunderam. Most of his throat had been torn out by human fingers, and the back of his head lay flat against the shoulder-blades in proof of a broken neck. Both arms were twisted so that the hands were around again to where they should be, backs to the floor. The feet were toe to toe, after describing three quarters of an outward circle, and a leg was obviously broken.

"He is very dead!" remarked the one voice of Sikunderam, speaking for three minds.

The sons of Ali sat back on the bench, backs to the wall, in an attitude that gave them leverage in case one indivisible impulse should decide them to attack. They could launch themselves from the wall like tigers out of ambush. One hint of reprisals and no cell-door on earth would be able to slam quick enough to keep them in.

But unaccountably there grew an atmosphere of calm, as if Allah, Lord of Kismet, had imposed an armistice. The electric tension eased, as it were, and muscles with it. Someone in yellow smiled, and Sikunderam answered in kind through a gap in a black beard. All three men in yellow strode into the cell, stepping over their co-religionist, and one of them turned to beckon in the officer, who, at their suggestion, sent the cell-guard to the office out of sight and hearing.

"Is it lawful to imprison these five, of three languages, three races, three religions, in one cell?" was the first question. There was only one answer possible:

"No, but—"

The same quiet finger on the same sleeve banished the explanation. Without a word said it was made clear that the legal, or rather the illegal fact was all-sufficient.

"Most honorables, that is how your co-religionist in yellow met his death!" piped Diomed, emerging out of a catalepsy. "Most worthy followers of Kali, these three savages attacked him without excuse and butchered him brutally. I offer to give evidence!"

Miscegenated intuition—perverted, that is—told Diomed that his chance lay in taking sides against the man in uniform. The three he addressed were obviously visitors, not prisoners, and the officer's fear of them was plain enough.

"This policeman threw us into one cell in the face of protests. *He* is responsible."

He pointed at the officer, who scowled but the three ignored both of them. Instead, the one who acted spokesman launched a question at the sons of Ali that was half-proposal, half-riddle, and breath-taking regarded either way.

"You understand, that if you escape from this cell illegally, you are guilty of that in addition to the charge of murdering this man?"

"And other charges—other charges, *señores*! They burned my hotel! Arson! That is what the judges call it—an indictable offense!"

One of the sons of Ali smote Diomed over the mouth again, and nobody objected. There was a little something after all in his thought that fortune hardly favors Goanese. The sons of Ali fell back on the code of Sikunderam, which calls for incredulity at all times, but particularly when a Hindu makes a proposition. They looked what they were exactly—men from out of town. The smiter rubbed his knuckles.

"Ye speak riddles," said the spokesman.

"You understand, that they who might set you at liberty, ignoring authority, would have the power to overtake and kill?" asked the man in yellow.

It began to dawn on Sikunderam that these were overtures for a bargain. All three faces closed down in accordance with the code that decrees a bargain shall be interminable and he who can endure the longest shall have the best of it. But the men in yellow were in haste. One of them drew a long silk handkerchief from hand to hand with a peculiar, suggestive flick.

"You understand that for all advantages there is a price? Go free!"

"But—but—" said the officer.

The finger on his sleeve commanded silence. He obeyed.

"Go free, in the fear of Kali, Wife of Siva, the Destroyer! Go free, until a day of reckoning! When Kali asks the price—observe!"

As if one thought functioned in the minds of all three, one of the men in yellow stepped toward the Goanese and taking him by the shoulders jerked him to his feet. The Goanese was too astonished to defend himself.

"Have I not offered—" he began; but the second of the three in yellow pushed him sidewise, so that he reeled backward on his heels toward the third.

There was a motion of the handkerchief, as quick as lightning but less visible, and Diomed fell unpicturesquely—dead—a heap of something in a soiled check shirt and crumpled collar—so dead that not a muscle twitched or sigh escaped him.

"For a death there must be a death," said one of the men in yellow.

The teeth of Sikunderam flashed white in a grin of pleased bewilderment.

"Hee-hee! He didn't slay your yellow man. We did it!" chuckled the spokesman.

The Thug was at no pains to explain his beastly creed. It was better to leave the three less cultivated savages to speculate on what the sacrifice had meant. His point was won. He had impressed them. They had seen the swiftness of the silken death. Undoubtedly they would soon begin to ponder on the fact that Diomed was slain in the presence of an officer of police, and to couple that with another mystery.

"Go! Let them go!" ordered one of the three, and the officer began to fumble with the lock.

He flung the door open with an air of petulant impotence, and it struck the cell-guard, who had crept back to listen. The door hit his heel as he ran and one of the three in orange-yellow stepped out into the corridor without the least suggestion of surprise. He beckoned him. Not a word was said. The second—not he with the handkerchief—held out a hand to warn the sons of Ali that freedom was postponed. The first man continued beckoning, and the cell-guard kept on coming, carbine at the charge, as if he intended violence. But he stepped into the cell with his eyes fixed in a stony stare, as if he had been hypnotized. It was the second man's turn to beckon; and as the "wretched, rash, intruding fool" obeyed the unspoken call of nemesis, the third man used the handkerchief. The cell-guard fell in a heap on Diomed. The officer picked up the carbine mechanically and laid it on the bench.

"Now go!" said the spokesman, motioning the Hillmen out with a gesture worthy of the angel of creation bidding the aeons begin. "Kali is all-seeing. Ye cannot hide. Kali is all-hearing. Ye may not tell. Kali is unforgetful. Therefore, when a price is set pay swiftly—even as ye saw this man pay!" He laid a finger on the officer's sleeve, who trembled violently. "For if not, ye will pay as these did!" He signified the corpses with a gesture. "Go!"

So the three went, wondering, not troubled as to what the official explanation would be, of three murders in a cell and three lost prisoners. The newspapers next day might call that mystery. To them another mystery was paramount, and all-absorbing:

Who were the men who had released them? Where had they learned that skill with a handkerchief? Why had they slain Diomed? And why had they three been released? Moreover, what would the price be that was mentioned, and would they—three Moslems—be justified in paying it, suppose they could, to the priests, of a Hindu goddess? How much would they dare tell to Ali, their ferocious sire, considering the silence that was laid on them? And if they should tell Ali, and he should tell Jimgrim, for instance, and Jimgrim should consult the others, would the priests of Kali visit vengeance on themselves as the fountainheads of disobedience?

There was more to it besides:

If Kali was all-seeing, as the Three had warned them, did that simply mean that they were being followed?

He in the middle faced about suddenly and walked backwards with his arms in his brothers'; but he could see no Hindus in pursuit. They tried a score of tricks that Hillmen use when the stones are lifted in the valleys and the "shooting-one-another-season" has begun—tricks that the hunted leopard tries, to assure himself that he has left the hunter guessing wild. But though they hid, and strode forth suddenly from doorways, so that passersby jumped like shying horses in fear of highway robbery, they detected no pursuit.

"The man in yellow lied to us," said one of them at last. "They let us go, and that is all about it."

"But why?"

"They were afraid."

"But of what? They could have killed us easily."

"Nay! None slays me with a handkerchief! By the Bones of Allah's Prophet—"

"They could have slain the cell-guard in the passage, and could then have shot us with his carbine through the hole in the iron door. They were not afraid of us!"

"Nevertheless, we three are afraid of them!" announced the brother who had spoken first. The other two did not dispute the fact. "I say—if we are wise—we will—hold our peace—a little while—and wait—and see—and consider—and if perhaps—there should seem to be a need—and an advantage—then later we might tell. What say you?"

"Allah! Who put wisdom into *thy* mouth?"

"It is wisdom! Let us consider it!"

They agreed to use their own term, to leave the proposition "belly-upward" for a while.

IX

"SILENCE IS SILENT"

Cyprian was not in a quandary. He would have known what to do, but his eighty-year-old lungs were too full of a sickly-tasting gas for him to function physically. That which is born of the spirit is spirit, but the brain must wait on material processes. He was just then in Jeremy's keeping—held in the Australian's arms—being thought for by Jeremy.

And as the stars in their courses once warred against Sisera, circumstances and his reputation combined to trick Cyprian. Never would it have entered Jeremy's head that dignity, discipline, responsibility to some one higher tip were necessary ingredients of Cyprian's code. Having saved the padre's life the only other thing that Jeremy considered was "the game."

Then there were the neighbors. Right and left were locked godowns stored with merchandise. Opposite, behind shade trees and a wall were Goanese, who would not have thought it moral, expedient, polite or safe to interfere in the padre's doings uninvited, even supposing they had seen what was going on. And the heat prevented their seeing anything, for May was merging into June and none who could afford to stay indoors dreamed of venturing forth.

The remainder of the street's inhabitants were Moslems with a sprinkling of Hindus at the lower end; and every one of those knew Cyprian by reputation as a student, and perhaps a practitioner of black magic—a man to be feared, if not respected; moreover, a man with influence. Nine out of any ten of them would have looked the other way if Cyprian's house were burning down. The tenth in nearly every instance would have run as far away as legs or a bicycle could take him.

The constable, whose duty it was to patrol that street, having quitted himself well with one arrest that morning, retired to a basement cellar to brag of his doings and gamble on fighting quails.

On top of all that there undoubtedly had been some deliberate clearing of the street by influences never named but referred to, when spoken of at all, as "they." The street was as peculiarly empty as it sometimes is when a royal personage is due for assassination.

The obvious course for a man in Cyprian's position, with three would-be assassins in his cellar and his whole house full of anesthetic, was to report at once to the authorities, leaving subsequent developments to take their course. But Cyprian was in no condition to give orders; and none of the others, King included, cared to invoke official skepticism. No man, who confesses to himself that he is searching for a heap of gold as heavy as the Pyramid, and for the books that explain how the heap was accumulated, is exactly unselfconscious when official investigation looms among the possibilities.

There was furthermore Narayan Singh, unconscious—in itself an almost incredible circumstance; for that doughty Sikh is a drinker of notorious attainment and less likely than any of them to succumb to fumes. He had keeled over like a gassed canary. King and Grim were giving him first aid, considering his recovery of vastly more importance than any debatable obligation to call in the police. They knew the police for mere bunglers at best and sheer obstructionists as far as true inquiry was concerned. They knelt on the sidewalk one each side of the Sikh, who breathed like a cow with its throat cut; and Jeremy, holding Cyprian like a baby in his arms, came and watched.

"If you can make him vomit, he's yours!" he advised. "Get something functioning—no matter what. One natural process encourages the next. Knead him in the solar plexus."

King and Grim, having tried all other methods, experimented with Jeremy's.

"Damn it! There's an antidote if only we could lay our hands on it," said King. "I've heard about this stuff—saw its effects before. It's a capsule as big as a rupee. They puncture it under a handkerchief. The minute the air gets to it the contents turn to gas. Beastly stuff burns the skin as it emerges, but changes again as it spreads and becomes anesthetic. The thieves who use the stuff carry the antidote with them. It's all in one of Cyprian's books."

"If pop 'ud wake," suggested Jeremy. But Cyprian only sighed.

"Where are the three Hindus?" Grim demanded.

"In the cellar. Ali pitched 'em in there—first-class job. Chullunder Ghose is sitting on the hatch to keep 'em out of further mischief," Jeremy announced.

"Ramsden—where's Rammy?" Grim demanded.

"Here."

Jeff, with a cloth about his face well drenched in water, had been exploring the floor of the sitting-room on hands and knees for evidence that would explain the enemy's method. He emerged through the front door, panting.

"Gas is disappearing," he gasped.

"Rammy! Narayan Singh is going West! Get a move on! Get those three Hindus. *Make* 'em produce their antidote! Stop at nothing!" That was Grim with the mask off—dealer in fundamentals.

So the purple patch that was the shadow of Jeff Ramsden ceased from existence on the white wall—simply ceased. He can be swift when occasion calls for it. Within, where more or less silence had been, was a great noise, as Jeff's weight landed on the trap and that of Chullunder Ghose, capsized, complaining.

"Off the trap! Lively!"

Ali of Sikunderam and his sons had been lying belly-downward listening in vain for noises from below. Imagination yearned for cries of pain and half-invented them. But the door was too thick, and sat too tightly in its bed for even their fond wish to get itself believed.

"By Allah I swear I broke the legs of all three!" boasted Ali, face to the wood.

But he said no more, for Ramsden seized him by arm and leg and threw him clear, the sons scampering away on hands and knees before the like indignity could happen to themselves. Then Ramsden got his fingers into the only crevice, strained, grunted, strove and gave it up. The door and frame were jammed hermetically.

"Crowbar!"

Ali Sikunderam—to employ their estimate—scattered in search of cold iron, while Jeff continued torturing his fingers vainly. One of the sons came in from the street on a run with loot from a Moslem godown. Blood on his forearm told the story—view of a crowbar through a window—action—acquisition.

"Good!" said Ramsden, and the woodwork began splintering forthwith—old teak, as dry and hard as temple timber, ripping apart with a cry as if it lived, and desired to live.

"Get a rope—or a ladder!" Ramsden grunted.

Out on the sidewalk, under Jeremy's running fire of comment and advice, Narayan Singh had vomited and was showing other signs of resuming the burden of life, as Jeremy had prophesied. Cyprian, on the contrary, had fallen into the easy sleep that overtakes old folk and infants, so that Jeremy, sniffing to make sure the gas was all gone, carried him inside presently and up the narrow stone stairs to the first-floor bedroom—clean, simple, severe as a monastery, yet comfortable, since only the needless things were missing.

The head of the bed was backed against an iron door that was papered over, white like the rest of the walls, with an overlapping fringe to hide the tell-tale crack.

The legs of the bed were set tight against wooden blocks screwed down to the floor, with the obvious purpose of re-enforcing the lock that was low enough down on the door to be hidden by the bed-frame. Jeremy noticed how tightly the casters were jammed against the blocks, as if they had been subjected to tremendous pressure, and it was that, as he laid Cyprian down, that caused him to scrutinize the door more curiously.

He is sure of his senses, having trained them. Too used to deceiving others' eyes he disciplines his own. He could have sworn that the door moved—inward—by a fraction of an inch; that is to say toward the wall and away from the head of the bed. He tested it, after making sure again that Cyprian was sleeping, and discovered he could get the fingers of one hand in between the bedpost and the door. And there was a long mark on the wide paper covering the iron door, in proof that it had recently pressed outward against the bed.

So either the lock was unlocked, or it did not function, or else it had been locked again since he entered the room.

Curiosity eats Jeremy like acid. He must know or be miserable. Mystery merely whets appetite. With an, other glance to make sure Cyprian was sleeping, he cautiously pulled the bed clear of the wooden blocks and rolled it a yard along the floor. Then he stooped to examine the keyhole. There was no key in it, and there had not been, for it was still stuffed with soap, and a piece of white paper rubbed on to the soap was in place—Cyprian's modest effort at constructive camouflage. On the floor lay an irregularly oblong sliver of white stone—two inches by an inch. The door had been forced from the inside, recently.

Jeremy tore back the paper from door and wall in two considerable strips. The tongue of the old-fashioned lock projected not more than an inch into unprotected stonework and was merely resting now in a neat groove that the fallen sliver fitted. Nothing—on Jeremy's side, that is—prevented the door from swinging open. He tested it with his fingers. It refused to yield.

And he could swear he had seen it move when he first laid Cyprian on the bed.

He glanced at Cyprian, half-inclined to wake him—glanced at the iron door again and speculated.

"Probably the old boy keeps his books in there. Shock might kill, if he wakes and learns thieves are in the coop. Sleep on, Melchizedek!"

Knowing the danger to himself of using firearms, in a country in more or less perennial rebellion, where the carrying of modern weapons is forbidden except for sport, Jeremy looked about him for an implement less compromising to himself. In a corner, behind a cretonne curtain under which the padre's garments hung, he found an Irish blackthorn walking stick—a souvenir of Ballyshannon days, where Cyprian once did temporary duty. The stick was as strong as a professional shillalah with twice the length—a deadlier weapon than gun or sword in given circumstances.

Down-stairs Ramsden broke up the trap-door section by section—layer by layer. It was so thick and so well carpentered that nothing less than absolute destruction laid the hinges bare. By the time it was possible to reach the bolt, that swung in place across the whole width of the trap and bit into twelve-inch beams, there was no more sense in fooling with it, for the door was totally destroyed. Jeff used the bolt for a purchase for his rope, the sons of Ali having failed to find a ladder, and went down band over hand into the dark.

Not even the eyes of Sikunderam could see more than an unexpected red light, and trash heaped in a mess below; but there seemed to be less of the trash than when Ali had flung the three into the pit. Where a pile of boxes had been, that should have lessened Jeff's descent, there was nothing to meet his exploring feet and he had to drop the last yard, for the rope was short.

The next they all knew was a roar like a bull's as Jeff joined battle with an unseen foe; and that was followed by an increase of the crimson glow and the indrawn roar of a furnace. It was like a glimpse into the bowels of a great ship, or into Tophet.

"Come on! Help, you fellows!" was all the explanation Jeff had time for—English at that—a sure enough sign he was excited.

King left Narayan Singh in Grim's hands—came on the run—and swung down the rope like a sailor. And Chullunder Ghose was next, "so curious" as he explained it afterward, resembling a seaman less than any other being in the world, first jammed in the broken trap like a cork in the neck of a bottle—breaking the hold of the wood-work by sheer weight and strength—then suddenly descending with the rope like red hot wire between his hands, to fall the last yard and be met—as it seemed to him—by an ascending floor constructed of upturned splinters.

And down on Chullunder Ghose in that unfortunate predicament there dropped Sikunderam in swift succession, sire and sons, grateful for the cushion—but to Allah, not the babu—and stepping off without pausing to pass compliments.

At the cellar's farther end there was a door down, and the whole of Cyprian's arrangements for the eventual holocaust of black books were plain to see in the light of a galloping fire. The holocaust was prematurely born. The three had set the match that was to have been Cyprian's torch on his last pilgrimage. The books, stacked hundreds in a pile inside an ancient pottery kiln, were all alight and the glue in the backs of some of the more modern ones was priming for the rest.

Cyprian had stacked ample fuel under them in readiness, but to that the three had added trash. There was no fire-door to be shut to exclude a draft; the furnace-jaws gaped wide. The chimney at the junction of Cyprian's house and the godown was serving its ancient purpose, and the trap-door that Ramsden broke was letting enough draft to feed the ravening fires of Eblis. Out on the sidewalk Grim saw the shadow of sulphur-and-black smoke belching from the summit of the old quiescent kiln; Narayan Singh was left to do his own recovering, and Grim, guided by instinct, took the stairs four at a stride instead of plunging like an *ifrit* into Ramsden's broken hole.

He was just in time to see Jeremy swing the blackthorn down two-handed on the back of a head that emerged for reconnoitering purposes through the cautiously opened iron door. The blow would have cut the head clean off if the weapon had only been an ax. A man in yellow fell face-forward and his shoulders prevented the door from shutting, although someone tried to pull him back in by the feet. Simultaneously Grim and Jeremy seized the iron door and wrenched it wide open, and a stab like a fork of lightning missed Grim by the thickness of a moonbeam—missed and was not quick enough, for Jeremy brought the blackthorn down on a long knife with a serpent handle, disarming a yellow, invisible someone, who dropped whatever else he held and retreated into deeper gloom.

Cyprian slept on, moving his lips and old fingers as if dreaming. Jeremy, all-trusting in his own luck, signaled, passed the blackthorn into Grim's hand and reached for matches. Grim agreed with him. With their feet they shoved the victim of Jeremy's weapon back whence he had come and stepped through over him, closing the iron door at their backs. Then Jeremy struck a match—in time—exactly in the middle of the nick of shaven time. The blackthorn came in use again—crack on a wrist that thrust upward with another such knife as the first man had tried to sting with. The blow broke the wrist. Someone smothered an exclamation.

"Curse these matches!" exclaimed Jeremy, and struck another.

On the floor of a closet about ten by ten lay two of the Three. The man whom Jeremy had first struck was dead undoubtedly. The other's leg was broken—Ali's work—and now the wrist was added to his inconveniences. He was writhing in pain, though making no noise, and all mixed up with the dead man. Evidently two of them had been carrying the fellow with the broken leg, and the third had run back through a door that faced the iron one—a rat in a stopped run, panicking this and that way.

Jeremy struck another match and Grim tried the inside door. As he laid his hand on it the fugitive, finding retreat cut off below, came charging back and Grim recoiled against the wall, guarding with the blackthorn like a single stick. The man in yellow lunged at him with a knife such as the other two had used, but as he lurched forward with his weight behind the thrust the point of another knife knocked his upper front-teeth out and cut through his upper lip, emerging an inch or two, then turning crimson in the flow of blood. Through the opened inner door came red light glowing and diminishing—glowing and diminishing—silhouetting Ali of Sikunderam.

"It is all in the trick of the thrust, *sahibs*," announced Ali, stooping over the victim to withdraw his beloved weapon. "See—the neck is broken—thus—the point of the knife goes in between two vertebrae, and Allah does the rest!"

"What's that fire below there?" Grim demanded.

"The old kiln. Rammy sahib—"

"What's burning?"

"All the priest's books, praise Allah!"

Grim's face looked ghastly in the waning red light. In that moment he saw all his hopes go up in smoke and flame.

"There'll be a blaze through the top of the chimney by now that'll bring the whole fire brigade!" he announced with resignation.

"Not a bit. Trust Ramsden," said another voice.

Athelstan King came up like a stoker from a ship's inferno, more than a little singed and sucking burned finger-ends.

"Ramsden found an old sheet of corrugated iron underneath the litter and bent it to fit the fire-door. The draft's in control. It was hot work."

"And the books?" Grim asked him.

"Napoo! No more books! Where's the padre?"

"Fast asleep."

"When he learns this it'll kill him," said King with conviction, unconsciously confirming Jeremy's first guess.

Ramsden came up the narrow stairway and demanded light. The glow behind him was so low that his bulk in the door obscured it altogether. Grim cautioned him and opened the door into Cyprian's room. The light fell on Ramsden's singed beard and his clothes all charred in patches.

"All red ash now," he whispered. "No more smoke." Jeremy tiptoed into the bedroom and stood looking down at Cyprian. Presently he felt his pulse.

"Fever!" he whispered. "He's unconscious."

Ramsdell gathered tip the man with the broken wrist and leg and laid him on the floor in Cyprian's room. They all trooped in, followed by Ali and his sons, Chullunder Ghose last. The babu was the only one who showed any symptoms of contentment, although he, too, was singed, and burned about the hands.

"Expensive consideration for man with family on microscopic stipend!" he remarked, removing a burned silk turban and readjusting it. "What shall do next?"

None answered. None knew exactly what to do. One of Ali's sons—the youngest—succumbed to the weak man's impulse to invoke the Blessing of the Platitudes.

"Silence is golden," he announced sententiously.

"Oh excellent advice! O god out of a Greecian box! O oracle!" Chullunder Ghose exclaimed. "All the wisdom of all those wicked books is incarnated into this fool! Silence is not only golden, it is silent! Silence is as silence does! *Verb* very *sap!* O *sahibs*, let us muzzle all these men! Shut up this shop until darkness intervenes, then beat it, in jargon of Jimgrim sahib—same expressive—very! Beat all concerned, this prisoner included unless the gives us every information, plus!"

"Plus what?" asked Ramsden.

"Plus obedience—not like these sons of Himalayan mothers, whose only virtue is that they economize by sleeping mostly in the jail!"

Ali was over by the window, looking out into the street.

"My sons are here," he announced grandiloquently, trying to hide a grin.

"Where? Outside? Call them in!" King snapped. "We don't want more publicity."

Ali threw the window open and beckoned. The sons came lumbering up-stairs like half-trained animals.

"Tell the *sahibs*: how did you leave the jail?" demanded Ali. Maybe intuition warned him that they had a splendid lie all cooked and ready to serve.

"We fought our way out! See—we left our knives in the guts of the police! Each of us slew three men!"

"Allah! My boys! My sons!" exclaimed Ali.

The others all looked down at Cyprian. Jeremy took a towel and put water on the old man's parched lips. None—not even Ali—as much as half-believed the story of the fight with the police, but all knew it was based on lawlessness of some sort that would not add to Cyprian's peace of mind when he should recover consciousness.

"If he pulls through this, the worry and disappointment will kill him anyhow," said Ramsden, rather ignoring the circumstance that for upward of eighty years Cyprian had been training himself to withstand the slings of fortune.

"We might give the old boy a chance," suggested Jeremy. And in his eye there gleamed antipodean mischief.

Ali was still at the window.

"Lo, a constabeel!" he announced. "He observes smoke issuing from the chimney without a tikut.* Lo, he speaks with Narayan Singh, who lies to him. A child can tell you when a Sikh lies. Lo, he writes a reeport in his parketbuk.† There will be a summons before municipal magistrates. I know the custom."

Narayan Singh, a little weak yet as to equilibrium, came up-stairs and thrust his head cautiously through the bedroom doorway.

"There will be a summons for smoke-nuisance against a Hindu, name of Murgamdass," he announced with a grin.

---

* Ticket. The English word is used to mean any kind of pointed and numbered permit.
† Pocketbook.

Grim caught all eyes, glancing from face to face, as a captain measures up his team in an emergency.

"Did the policeman appear suspicious?" he asked quietly.

"Very!" Narayan Singh answered. "He suspected a Hindu of seeking to avoid payment of fee for necessary permit to use furnace within municipality. I confirmed his plausible suspicion, hoping—"

"Anything else?" Grim asked him.

"No, *sahib*. Nothing else."

"You fellows game?"

Grim caught all eyes again. If they were not game, none are. There were all the brands and all the elements of that geist that is all-conquering because it simply cannot understand defeat.

"Two courses," Grim announced. "We can call in the police, and quit."

Chullunder Ghose sighed like a grampus coming up for air.

"Or we can carry on and face the consequences. Vote please. Those in favor—"

Chullunder Ghose raised both hands; all the others one.

"Ayes have it. Very well. Then after dark we'll take these two dead yellow-boys and plant them where their friends put da Gama. Meanwhile, take Cyprian somewhere and get a good doctor for him. Don't say who he is. Ali, you and your sons guard the prisoner while we find a good place to hide him in."

X

"Can't hatch a chicken from a glass egg"

That night there stood in front of Cyprian's an ox-cart, tented and painted to resemble the equipage of old-fashioned country gentry's womenfolk. Chullunder Ghose had conjured the thing from somewhere, magnificent Guzerati bullocks included, selecting the form of conveyance least likely to be interfered with by police.

But to make assurance on that ground doubly sure there was Narayan Singh as driver, naked of leg and otherwise garbed as a Hindu, reenforced by Ramsden and two of Ali's sons, the latter shaven, and so angry at having to adopt Hindu disguise that it would have called for a whole squad of "constabeels" to arrest them.

Directed by Ramsden the corpses of the two followers of Kali were laboriously trundled by the oxen as far as possible in the direction of the scene of da Gama's death, and thence carried by Ali's protesting sons, who dumped them naked into the débris where the Portuguese had lain, and rolled the same broken pillar over both of them that once had helped to hide da Gama's remains.

Judged as corpses they would have looked more edifying in the orange-yellow smocks they wore in life, but smocks, dyed just that color, are not purchasable in the open market. Thrift is thrift—the careful use of opportunity.

In another part of Delhi a more dangerous negotiation was proceeding, rendered no easier by the almost unconquerable yearning to fall asleep that was the natural consequence of two nights' wakefulness in Punjab heat.

It was Jeremy's proposal. Grim had seconded. King demurred. Chullunder Ghose had so squealed and chuckled with approval, vowing the whole proposal a stroke of genius "better than the gods could think of," that King gave in.

They drove the still unconscious Cyprian, wrapped in a blanket, to Gauri's house and lodged him there—a member of an order of strict celibates, in the house of a lady of Rahab's trade!

"What's the odds? He doesn't know it," argued Jeremy.

The lady was over ears and eyes in delicious responsibility—intrigued until her fat ribs shook with giggling—unaware of the patient's identity, for they had put him into a nightshirt, but as sure as that the stars were shining, that life—her life as she loved it—was being lived.

"If you hold your tongue you shall have for yourself one full share, equal to that of each of us, in whatever we discover," Grim explained to her.

"But let one hint drop, and you eat my knife!" said Ali. And Gauri believed both of them.

In all lands where the laws are written for the benefit of privilege there are smugglers—not only of contraband jewels and rum, but of contraband knowledge and skill. There are men, who belong to no certified profession, who can do as well for you in the way of experience, and at half the price, as any blockade runner can in the matter of lace or tobacco. No license confers skill, any more than payment of the duty improves art. Many a doctor, barricaded from or pitched out neck and crop from his profession knows more than the exclusive orthodox. But he has to follow Aesculapius and Galen in peril of imprisonment and fine. That is the point. He must not talk.

None knew, and none cared, why Doctor Cornelius MacBarron might not any longer use the title legally that his patients conferred on him gratefully, whether the law approved or not. For one thing he was an Eurasian—fifty-fifty—Caledonian Light Infantry on one side, and a dark mama—no sinecure to go through life with. So he might not choose. What people said to or concerning him he had to tolerate, extracting now and then advertisement, more profitable than solacing, from the scandalous—even if merited—slanders of the regular professionals.

It was bruited abroad in Delhi—behind the drugstore counters, and in mess-rooms, and elsewhere—that at absurdly reasonable prices Cornelius MacBarron would cure anything—and what's more, hold his peace. He was said to have quite a wide following, and to know more secrets than a banker.

Whatever he knew, and whomever he recognized, he said nothing when brought in a cab in broad daylight to the Gauri's scandalous abode. With the long, lantern jaws and raw bones of a Scotsman, sad brown eyes, an unenthusiastic presence and a sallow skin, he did not seem to invite conversation or curiosity. Rather he repelled both.

"There's your man," said Jeremy, showing him Cyprian in Gauri's scented bed. "Cure him if you can."

MacBarron did not ask, "Who is he?" but "Is he hurt?"

"No. Sick. Old. That's all," answered Jeremy.

"My fee will be fifty rupees—per visit," MacBarron announced, as if saying his prayers.

Jeremy produced the money. MacBarron folded it, and spoke again—"Leave me alone with him, please."

Whereat Jeremy demurred, but was overruled by the others, who conceded, under the inspiration of Chullunder Ghose, that it was reasonable. A man without the right to practise has excuse for dispensing with witnesses.

MacBarron emerged from the bedroom about fifteen minutes later and announced, like a verger opening pews, that in his opinion the patient would recover.

"He must lie still. Here is a prescription. Let him drink it as often as he will. You may pay me now for a second visit; that is wiser."

So they paid him, and he was on his way to the waiting cab when King detained him.

"Not so swiftly! We've another job. Do you mind walking?"

MacBarron minded nothing if he was paid. King led him through narrow streets to a place where three alleys came together on the right-hand side and a high wall on the left with a narrow door in it concealed the lower story of a minaret, whose mosque had long since succumbed to the ravages of time.

The door opened when King struck three blows on it, and Ali's dark face appeared in a challenging scrutiny.

"He groans much, but says nothing at all," Ali announced abruptly, and turned his back to lead them in.

The minaret was Ali's good provision. *Wakf*, the system of Moslem endowments for charitable purposes, is as liable to abuse as any other human scheme for standing off the evil day. Ali's blood-brother, having lent his sword in a blood-feud to which a wealthy merchant in the Chandni Chowk was party, was now in receipt of a comfortable income and the job of muezzin to a minaret without a mosque. In theory he was supposed to cry the summons to prayer at the appointed times, but in practise he was neither seen nor heard, lest busybodies should inquire into the source of his revenue.

Naturally, no man with a sinecure like that would be willing to share it for nothing. He demanded hotel prices, and was indignant when Ali withheld ten per cent. as his own commission. But the virtue of him was that he was just as much bent on secrecy as anyone, and the watch he kept in consequence was priceless. Even after Ali had admitted King and MacBarron within the wall Ali's brother examined them and grumbled at having to entertain half Delhi.

"Is this a *Salleevayshun-armee-khana*?" he demanded.

King led MacBarron by the winding inner stair to a room at the top of the minaret, where the muezzin was supposed to sleep, and whence the now decrepit gallery was reached by a narrow door in the masonry. The door was closed, and such light as was available came through a six-inch slit in the wall, for Ali's brother would permit no artificial light for fear of attracting attention.

On a truck bed in the darkest part of the round room lay the sole survivor of the three who had burned Cyprian's books. The whites of his eyes gleamed in darkness, but the rest of him was nearly invisible, for they had taken his yellow robe away, and his coppery, dry skin was of a shade that nearly matched the gloom. It was too hot to endure blankets.

MacBarron glanced at him, and then at King without visible emotion.

"My fee will be a thousand rupees," he announced.

"Check do?"

"Cash."

King was obliged to return and obtain the money from Grim. That took time, because Grim had to send a messenger to cash his check. When King reached the minaret again the prisoner's leg was already in plaster of Paris brought by Ali from a Goanese apothecary's, and the wrist was being manipulated in spite of the Hindu's protests. They had tied him to the bed; there was no other way of controlling him. The only thing he had not done to make trouble for them was to cry aloud.

"That arm must come off," announced MacBarron five minutes after King's return. "The reason is this—"

He went into details, deeply technical, displaying the same fearlessness in diagnosis that an engineer does when ordering parts of a locomotive scrapped. His objection to witnesses had vanished, for it was obvious that none of this secretive batch of clients would dare to expose him; and he had sufficient sense for situations not to ask the prisoner's permission. The whole conversation was in English until he bent over the bed at last and, looking straight into the victim's eyes, said curtly in Punjabi—

"Your arm must come off at the elbow."

That produced speech at last—coppery, resonant argument all mixed with threats intended to convey one point of principle: Anything—anything went; they might burn him living; he would not resist. But he would enter whole into the next world, with his right wrist fit for Kali's service! If they sought to take his arm off he would work a vengeance on them! If they did not believe that, let them take the first step!

"Hocus-pocus!" said MacBarron, not particularly *sotto voce*.

"Is the leg all right?" King asked him.

"It is set. It will heal. He will limp."

"Good enough. Please come again this evening," said King.

"To cut the arm off? Very well. That is two visits in twenty-four hours. Two hundred rupees extra. In advance."

King paid him, and he went.

"By Allah, we of Sikunderam, who think we will plunder India when the British go, must first take lessons from that man!" remarked Ali.

"Go below and keep watch!" ordered King, and in a minute he and the prisoner were alone together, looking in each other's eyes.

"Want to lose your arm?"

The man grinned in agony. The grin was half-grimace, but there was defiance and even amusement there.

"The arm that knows the trick of the handkerchief—the killing arm?"

King put as much cruelty and mockery as he could summon into his voice.

But the trouble was that King knew well how far in the worst extremity he would be willing to go. And what was strength of character, too manly to take full advantage of helplessness even for any reward, the other could read but could not understand. He misinterpreted it as weakness—fear. Whereas about the only fear King has (and that unspoken—secret—sacred in his inner-being) is that he may not in some crisis quit himself as if all the decent fellows in the world were looking on.

"Will you amputate?" asked the Hindu, pointing to the injured wrist with his other hand and grinning again. He had feared MacBarron. He was no more afraid of King than a priest is of policemen. The worst of it was King knew well that, whatever power this fellow might have of summoning assistance without the use of obvious means, he would not use it except in dire necessity.

There is no rule more strict than that, probably because the penalty for breach of it is unimaginably awful. Radio is a joke, a mere clumsy subterfuge, compared to the gift some Indians have of communicating with one another across great distances. Every man who has the least acquaintance with the East knows that. But they don't give up their secret even in extremity, or use it without unquestionable reason.

It was possible that he might tell secrets under the torture and fear of amputation. But King was not morally capable of doing that. Instead he tried bribery—a bargain he would have said.

"Keep your arm and join us. You may have one full share in any discovery we make."

The man laughed genuinely—just as copper-voiced as he was copper-skinned. It was as if some devil in an unseen world had reached over and struck a gong in this one—three rising notes and then the overtones, all mockery.

King laughed too, on a descending scale. He appreciated—what few from the Western Hemisphere can realize—that money, a material reward, or any of the compensations that the West deems valuable have no weight whatever in the calculations of the thinking East. The politicians and a few of the bunnia class have swapped old lamps for new, but at the very mention of western money or wisdom the old East laughs. She can afford to.

"All right," King said. "Where are we then?" He turned his face away deliberately, as if discouraged. "If I can't overcome you, what do you propose to do with me?"

He gave the man time to consider that, then met his eyes again—objective-thinking Anglo-Saxon challenging the East that thinks subjectively or not at all. Neither could pierce the other's veil.

"You are no use," said the Hindu, letting his head fall back on the folded blanket that served for pillow. His eyes were alight with fever.

In spite of the intolerable heat King made sure that the door leading out to the gallery was locked, for whoever dares set limits to the capacity of esoteric India is likely to find himself surprised. Then he left him, giving orders below to keep on the *qui vive* and not to give the prisoner water or information. He would let the man torture himself a while and lift his veil in his own way.

And presently at Gauri's house, superintended and giggled over by Gauri and her maid, King, Grim and Jeremy put on the three orange-yellow smocks that had been the garb of the enemy, coppering their skins with some compound of vegetable greases that Gauri procured for them, and changing every expression of their faces until Gauri and the rest pronounced them perfect strangers. Then Grim and Jeremy submitted to King's drill, which was exasperating in insistence on minutest details, Gauri prompting him.

"Do you think you could manipulate a handkerchief the way you saw it done?" King asked, tossing one of Gauri's long silk scarfs to Jeremy.

He imitated perfectly the swift, apparently effortless pass from hand to hand. There is nothing that Jeremy can't imitate. Nothing was lacking except the will to kill by strangling the victim, and the secret of how it is done.

"Can't hatch a chicken from a glass egg," he said apologetically. "I'm safe until I thug somebody."

King was insatiable—drilling, drilling, making them repeat all manner of proposed behavior in emergency, until they struck at last from very weariness, and Gauri brought cooling drinks and comfort in the shape of flattery.

"Perfect!" she told them.

"Nevertheless, this deferential babu, like wholesale tiger smelling traps invariably, would better accompany this expedition," said Chullunder Ghose. "Obesity is only disadvantage—curiosity impelling—adipose impeding—striking happy medium at all times—"

"You be still!" commanded King.

"Certainly, *sahib*! I desist! Am silent! Sublime satisfaction in service of noblemen makes obedient babu dumb! Your humble servant. Mum's the word, like Yankee skirmisher in No Man's Land! Nevertheless—"

He paused, looking up under lowered eyelids like a meek, ridiculous, fat schoolgirl.

Grim recognized the reference to a Yankee skirmisher as an appeal to himself. "Spill it!" he ordered. "Be quick."

"Silence being self-imposed on all three *sahibs*, somebody should come along to scintillate with clever verbiage. Self being otherwise unoccupied—"

"Whatever you said would give the game away," Grim interrupted severely.

"Even secret hymn to goddess Kali?"

He intoned it, throwing out his chest and making a pig's snout of his fat lips around the lower bass notes, that rumble and roll like the voice of the underworld glorifying in destruction, making of cruelty, death and disease sweet satisfaction for the dreadful bride of Siva. Few ever heard that hymn who were not initiates of Kali's dreadful cult, or—

"Were you ever held for the sacrifice?" King asked him suddenly.

"*Sahib*, I am superstitious! Reference to secret details of risky past might cause repetition of same, which decency forbid! Am dumb!"

He would not tell how he had learned that hymn. He knew the value of it, and of silence. He was indispensable.

"No extra charge!" he announced with pursed lips.

"One break and you're fired!" said Grim.

"One break and we are all dead!" he retorted. "Awful! Yet—at my age—nevertheless—how many last chances I have had! Cat-o'-nine tails is rank outsider compared to most of us! Whoever boasted of dying daily had me in mind. *Verb. sap.*"

They waited until long after dark, when Ramsden reported the safe disposal of two corpses, and was detailed to take care of Cyprian.

"Tell him he's in the house of an Indian gentleman, whose wife can't very well interview him in her husband's absence," Grim advised. "Say his own place was full of gas, so we had to lock it up. If he asks any more questions, tell him the doctor says he must sleep."

Narayan Singh was told off to await the doctor. Then the three, Chullunder Ghose following, set forth on what was actually a forlorn hope.

"Pray, you men!" said King, half-laughing. "If we can't get an inside track to the Nine through this man, we may as well admit defeat. He's dry—full of fever—in pain—half-conscious. We can fool him now or never."

They could almost fool themselves. Their shadows on the street wall so resembled the parts they played that they had the sensation of being followed by assassins, the heavy footsteps of Chullunder assisting the suggestion.

They totally fooled Ali of Sikunderam and his suspicious brother. Ali thrust his long knife through the partly opened door in the wall and threatened to disembowel the lot of them unless they made themselves scarce.

"By Allah, shall a Hindu set foot on the sacred threshold of a mosque?" he demanded, as the rightful keeper of the place shifted a lantern this way and that behind him to expose the intruders better.

The voice of Chullunder Ghose was revelation—impiously making use of holy writ from the shadows in the rear:

"And they came unto their own, but their own received them not. Even in A. D. seventy they knew the nature of Sikunderam! Give sop to Cerberus, *sahibs*! Price of admission is payable in Beehive brandy!"

"I knew it all along!" said Ali with a curt laugh.

"Aye, any fool would know it;" his brother agreed.

"Open the door then, fools!"

Chullunder Ghose waddled in first, pushing aside the two custodians, bowing in his three employers, retiring again behind them to hold up both hands like the leader of an orchestra directing *pianissimo*. Thereafter not a word was said.

In creaking, bat-winged darkness they four mounted the minaret stairs, pausing each half-dozen steps to listen for sounds from above. Chullunder Ghose, holding a flask of water destined for the prisoner's use when he should acquire the right to it by bargain, stopped on the rickety floor below the upper room and sat, cross-legged, with his face toward the opening through which the other three must pass—a square hole at the stair-head. Low sounds—human speech assuredly—emerged through it, using some other than the ordinary language of the streets.

The words ceased as King in the lead reached midway up the last flight of stairs. A face appeared in the opening—coppery even in that dim gloom—a new face, not the prisoner's. King, never hesitating, took the next step and the others followed. A word would have betrayed them. But even the babu—he particularly—rose to the heights of instant self-command.

A stanza of the hymn to Kali rose from the babu's throat like a burst of faraway organ music, and the face in the opening withdrew. King went on up. He had not hesitated. He was not lost.

Keeping step, not harrying, not looking to the right or left but purposely moving like men in a dream, the other two followed him through and sat down along-side him in the attitude the three book-burners had taken on Cyprian's yak-hair carpet, Jeremy at one end.

The owner of the unexpected face thrust his hand against the door that led to the gallery, letting in sufficient star-light to reveal the orange-yellow of his long smock. Then he sat down facing them, with his back to the wall by the head of the bed.

He said something, using a language that is dead—extinct—that never did exist according to some authorities. Instead of attempting to answer, all three bowed low from the waist with their hands palms-outward, like temple images come to life. And again Chullunder Ghose's gorgeous barytone burst forth in praise of death.

There is this about ancient mysteries. Nine-tenths of them, if not more, are forgotten and the words a generation passes to the next one—"mouth to ear and the word at low breath"—if not a substitute are no more than a fragment of lost knowledge. He who had spoken in perhaps the mother-tongue of lost Atlantis was content to carry on in Punjabi.

"Ye heard his call, too? Brothers, ye were awake! I came up the outside and broke the lock with a chisel. Ye were cleverer! Ye did not slay, for I hear the voices of the guards down-stairs. Ye did well. Are there orders? Ye are not of my Nine, for ye make no answer to the signal."

Speech was impossible. Their one chance was to pretend to a vow of silence, such as *fakirs* often take. Instead of speaking Jeremy flicked the handkerchief from one hand to the other with the diabolical, suggestive swiftness of a past-practitioner of Thugee.

The man by the head of the bed betrayed astonishment—maybe disgust.

"By whose order should he die?" he demanded. "I have tested him according to rule. He has not betrayed. His failure is not complete. He—they—two of them are dead—burned all the books because they could take none. This one sent the Silent Call to give us information. He deserves life."

He paused for an answer. And the first sign having succeeded, Jeremy repeated it—as an executioner whose patience was exhaustible.

Promptly, as if they had rehearsed that very combination, Chullunder Ghose sang of the death that is Kali's life, and his voice boomed through the opening in praise of pain that is Kali's ease—and of want that is her affluence.

That tide in the affairs of men that Shakespeare sang was surely at flood that night! It brimmed the dyke. He by the head of the bed was aware of it, restlessly.

"The Nines are no longer interlocked as formerly," he grumbled. "One Nine has an order that another counteracts. There is confusion. There is too much slaying to hide clumsiness. Our plan was patterned on the true plan of the Nine Unknown, but we are a bad smell compared to their breath of roses! They know, and are Unknown. We do not know, and too many know of us."

A thrill that commenced with King and passed through Grim reached Jeremy, but none of them confessed to it. They sat still, expressionless, three bronze faces staring straight forward, only Jeremy's fingers moving in the overture to death. The long silk handkerchief flicked back and forth like a thread in the loom of the Fates.

The man on the bed groaned dismally, and as if that were a signal for the bursting of the dyke that stood between ignorance and understanding—for there always is a dyke between the two, and always a weak point where the dyke will yield if men can only find it—he by the head of the bed called up from his inner-man the lees of long-ago forgotten manliness. Then not in anger, but calmly as became a follower of the Destroyer's Wife, he cast his ultimatum at the three.

"I, who shall be slain for saying this, yet say this. Listen, ye! Dumb be the spirit in you as the lips your vow has sealed! This man, whom ye have come to kill because he failed, lest failure be a cause of danger to worse devils than ourselves—is my friend!"

He paused, appearing to expect some sign of astonishment. Friendship is treason to Kali. Comment was due, and Chullunder Ghose obliged, hymning new stanzas in praise of Her who annihilates.

"This man once spared me. I spare him. Ye shall not sacrifice him. Hear me! I came, not knowing who he was. Ye came, knowing. Your orders are to kill *him*. Mine are to go to Benares and slay one said to be a true Initiate of the Nine. But I am weary of all this. Ye *shall* not slay; I *will* not—unless—"

He paused again, making no motion with his hands. But he left no doubt there was a weapon within reach with which the argument might be continued if convenient to all concerned. Jeremy's hands moved, but only to manipulate the handkerchief. He, Grim and King all had pistols, so no need for hurry. King broke silence, sparing words like one who mistrusts speech—

"We three have grown so weary of it all that a watch was set on us, lest we fail."

Confirming that, Chullunder Ghose's barytone hymned one more stanza to the Queen of Death. The man on the bed groaned wearily. In the street the sound of revelry—the last verse of a drunkard's love-song—announced and disguised the news that Narayan Singh arrived on the scene with the doctor.

"If there is only one who watches you, is there any reason why we four should fear him?" asked the man by the head of the bed.

That sounded like a trap. In dealing with the secret brotherhoods it is safe to suspect that every other question is asked for precaution's sake. The wrong answer would be an astringent, drying up confidence at the source.

"So be *one* died—" said King, not daring yet to speak openly, because he did not know the key-phrases that identify man to man.

The other nodded.

"I am not an executioner," he said. "Let your brother use his skill."

And he nodded suggestively at Jeremy. The man on the bed groaned again. Chullunder Ghose was absolutely still. From below came Narayan Singh's carousal song and the voices of Ali and his brother commanding silence in the name of decency.

It began to be clear to King that his suspicion was accurate—that the members of one Nine did not know the members of any other Nine and had no means of challenging. Each Nine reported to its chief, who in turn was one of nine. That was what da Gama said, and though the Portuguese was not to be believed without deliberation, even deliberation must have limits. King took the chance.

"I have no means of testing you," he said. "You do not respond to my signs."

"Nor you to mine, brother! Let us then give pledges satisfactory to each."

"If we let this fellow live," King answered, and paused, observing that the man by the head of the bed pricked his ears.

He remembered that as Kali's follower he must not offer to deprive the goddess altogether of her prey. There must be a substitute.

"Will you betray the Initiate of the Nine to us in Benares in order that we may not fail to make Her a sacrifice?"

"No!" came the answer—abrupt and firm. "Substitute him who sings to Her below there!"

It was time for heroic measures. Insofar as reason applies to murder, he was reasonable. And besides, King was aware of a sound in the outer darkness that Chullunder Ghose heard too, for the babu sang to drown it.

"I believe you are an impostor! I believe you know nothing of Benares! I believe you are that faithless member of another Nine whom we were told to watch for! If there should be a substitute I think that thou—"

King pointed an accusing finger at him. Jeremy made the handkerchief perform like a living thing. It even looked hungry.

"Nay, nay!" said the other.

"Show me proofs!" said King.

The subtle noises in the night had ceased and there was now no cause for hurry. It was almost possible to see—as one could sense—the pallor on his face as the man by the head of the bed reached out to push the door a little wider open and admit more starlight. Whatever his weapon was, he had to see clearly to use it. As his wrist reached out across the opening a huge hand closed on it—from outside.

It was no use screaming, though the blood ran cold. The followers of Kali train themselves to self-control. It was no use moving, because two repeating pistols, King's and Grim's covered him.

He could not speak. Terror, the stronger for being suppressed, gripped him tighter than the unknown hand that held his wrist against the door-frame like material in a vise.

The door of the minaret below slammed suddenly, and one man was heard to enter. King felt the wheels of destiny turn once and drop the finished solution like a gift into his hand. Destiny had chosen the right man, and his assistants waited on him, saying nothing, offering no advice, not even glancing sidewise to observe him. It was apparent to the man by the head of the bed that they, all three acted on instructions in accordance with a pre-arranged plan, that which is obvious being untrue nine times out of ten.

"You are he whom we should watch for," King said slowly. "There is talk of your sedition. That is why they sent you to Benares. That is why you were picked to sacrifice that true Initiate of the Holy Nine."

King paused and took another long chance. Had not the others acted in threes? "You were ordered to Benares, where two others should join you. You, who cannot use the handkerchief, were to be decoy. We are they who should have met you in Benares! Yet you can no more tell which of us three are the two than you could escape from the task imposed on you!"

The man's jaw dropped. He believed himself taken in the toils of the relentless machine that owned him and a thousand others. There is no more paralyzing fear than that.

"You would have cheated HER!" said King.

He rose and made a sign to Grim and Jeremy that was not easy to mistake. They lifted the unconscious prisoner off the bed and, taking more care of his bandaged leg than was quite in keeping with the circumstances, carried him down through the opening in the floor. From below came the sound of one short strangling cry.

"Clumsy!" said King. "He lacks practise!"

Then there was whispering and the sound of a dead weight being carried down wooden stairs. The door below slammed. There was the noise of men's feet outside—then of wheels. First Grim returned, and then Jeremy. The expression on their faces was of great elation suppressed and crowded to the point of near-explosion.

"You will go to Benares. You will lead to the slaying him who was appointed for the sacrifice. You will be judged thereafter by the judges."

Some gesture that King made must have been visible from the outer-gallery, for the hand that held the wrist let go. The door was shut tight from without. In the ensuing darkness King descended, leaving Grim and Jeremy to guard the new prisoner, and Chullunder Ghose, holding both sides in silent laughter that made tears stream down his cheeks, motioned him toward the ground floor. Chullunder Ghose remained where he was, wallowing in exquisite emotion.

Narayan Singh, descending by broken masonry, groping for foothold, found his foot in King's hands and so reached *terra firma*.

"*Sahib*, it would seem the gods are with us! The doctor has a place where he can treat that patient better than in this tower. He and I brought a litter on wheels and men to push it. The babu signaled me that there were doings up-stairs, so I climbed by the broken masonry, knowing the value of surprise in an emergency! Shall the doctor amputate?"

"Tell him no," said King, "but keep him *incommunicado*."

XI

"Allah! Do I live, and see such sons?"

There was a cellar below the minaret—a mere enclosure in between foundations, but no less practicable as a dungeon on that account. Therein they cached the prisoner with Narayan Singh and three of Ali's sons on guard, instructed not to show themselves to the man they guarded but to be as rabid as wolves at bay toward all trespassers.

Then, because a good rule is to hold your conferences where not even friends expect you, King Grim and Jeremy went and sat like great owls in the shadow of a wall above a low roof several hundred yards away. There they could see one another and not be seen.

King met Grim's eyes. Grim met King's. The two spoke simultaneously—

"You were right!"

"Pop Cyprian won't believe it though!" laughed Jeremy, yawning. "Sleep under the stars, you blighters! Here goes then!"

He curled himself up, and was breathing like a kitten in a moment.

"There are two Nines!" King said with conviction.

"The real gang, and this Kali outfit!" Grim agreed.

"Right! But as Jeremy says, Cyprian won't believe it."

King faced toward Grim and as if playing cards they tossed deductions to and fro, each checking each. "One's good. The other's bad."

"The Kali outfit patterned their organization after the real Nine's, in the hope of stumbling on the secret."

"They've spotted a real Initiate of the Nine."

"Bet you! Maybe one of the Nine. Marked him down. Expect him in Benares."

"Told off this man-in-yellow to kill him."

"What for? *Qui bono*? Ring in one of their own thugs to pose as the dead man?"

"Probably. He might discover something before the remaining Eight get wise."

"But why pick a man who can't use the handkerchief, and whose loyalty must have been questionable?"

"Probably he's the only one who can identify the proposed victim."

"If so, they'll watch him."

"Which means they'll have watched him to-night!"

"Uh-huh. They must have seen him enter the minaret."

"Good thing we left Narayan Singh on guard."

"You bet—and those three sons of Ali's who were in trouble with the police. They'll fight like wolves."

"All nerves. Better than watch-dogs. What next?"

"Sleep!" said Grim.

And they did sleep—there on the roof, where none but the stars and the crescent moon could see them and only Chullunder Ghose knew where to track them down.

Chullunder Ghose slept too, hands over stomach and chin on breast, with the broad of his back set flat against a wall and his whole weight on the trap-door that provided access to the cellar—turban over one ear—so asleep that even minaret mice (hungrier than they who live in churches) nibbled the thick skin of his feet without awaking him.

The North—Sikunderam in particular—can sleep, too, when it has no guilty conscience; and it begins to measure guilt at about the deep degree, where squeamish folk leave off and lump the rest into one black category. None the less, although the sons of Ali yawned when Narayan Singh posted them around the iron-railed gallery, with orders to keep one another awake and summon him at the first sign of an intruder, yawning was as much as it amounted to. They sat like vultures on a ledge and listened to the Sikh's enormous snores that boomed in the waist of the minaret. (He calculated that the second floor, midway of either, was the key to the strategic situation.)

Nominally each of Ali's sons from where he sat could view a hemisphere, so that their vision actually overlapped. But in practise there was one whose outlook included a high, blank wall, over which it was humanly impossible for an enemy to approach, because there were spikes along the wall, and broken glass, and beyond it were the women's quarters of a much too married rajah.

So that one—Habibullah was his name—was more or less a free lance, able to reenforce the others or to spell them, without that extra loss of self-respect that might otherwise have attended desertion of a fixed post. Narayan Singh had said, "Sit here—and here—and here." Burt he had evidently meant "Divide the circle up between you." So

Habibullah construed it, the other two confirming; but it was an hour before anything happened. Then:

"One beckons," said Ormuzd—he facing due east. There was a roof in that direction on which the light from a half-shuttered upper window fell like a sheet of gold-leaf. "One sits like a frog in a pool and beckons. Come and see."

So Habibullah, having faced west long enough, changed his position and sat by Ormuzd.

"Huh! He beckons. Is his garment yellow, like that of him we slew in the jail, or does the light make it seem so?"

They watched with the infinite patience of Hillmen and all hunting animals, until the third brother came around to lend two eyes of flint—just one look and away again, back to his post.

"He beckons," he agreed.

"Does he beckon to us or—"

"To us!" said Habibullah. "Moreover, he is clothed in yellow. The light shows it. He is one of those who loosed us from the jail."

As if confirming Habibullah's words, the man on the roof in the pool of light raised up a Himalayan *tulwar*, shaped so exactly like the one that Ormuzd left in the police station that the two who saw it thrilled like women seeing a lost child. The northern knife is more than knife.

"What does he want with us, think you?"

"Go and see!"

"That drunken dog of a Sikh who snores within there will awake and—"

"Never mind him. Climb down by the broken edges of the stone. We have done worse many a time in our Hills."

But caution is as strong as curiosity in the mind of Sikunderam. No Highlander who followed Bonnie Charlie to his ruin was as hard to pin down to a course—or harder to turn from one, once on his way. Habibullah sat and weighed the pros and cons—including the likelihood that he in the pool of light might be a *shaitan*—until the other two cried shame on him. His reason in the end for going to investigate was fear that their loud arguing might wake Narayan Singh and that the Sikh might possibly claim all the credit for some discovery.

Hand over band at last he went down the broken side of the minaret—leaped like a goat on to the street wall above the heads of Ali and his brother, who were sleeping the sleep of innocence in the shadow of the gate—and gained the street.

But none came to meet him, as he had half-hoped. He was left to his own devices to find a way up to the roof the man had beckoned from—not nearly as easy a feat as threading the bat-infested ledges of eternal hills. In one street an unwise "constabeel" presumed to demand what his business might be; whereat Habibullah ran for half-a-mile in zig-zags, never losing direction; and finally, by way of a stable and the iron roof of a place where they sold chickens, he climbed to a point of vantage whence he could look down from darkness into the pool of light.

"*His-s-s-t!*" he remarked then to attract attention. And a second later his skin crawled like a sloughing snake's all up his spine and then down again.

The man in the pool of light took no notice, but another had leaned out of the darkness almost within arm's reach and, flashing a little electric torch, grinned straight into his face.

"You should go to him—go to him—he beckons, does he not? Go to him then!" he whispered.

The whisper was the worst part of it. If he had spoken out loud Habibullah would have tried a little bombast to reassure himself. As it was, the creepy sensation increased; nor was there any knowing how many other men there might be grinning at him from the darkness—grinning at him who had no knife! He could see one of his brothers—just a shadow motionless among the shadows of the minaret, and the sight made him lonelier than ever.

"Why wait for the handkerchief?" suggested the voice beside him; and that settled it; Habibullah leaped down on to the roof like a young bear, making all the noise he naturally could.

But the noise did not startle the man in yellow, who sat in the midst of the pool of light. It did not as much as annoy him. He smiled—a beastly, bronze, arrogant smile that chilled the blood of Habibullah worse than the other man's whisper had done.

"You beckoned?" said Habibullah, forgetting that he who speaks first most often has the worst of it.

The other shifted himself out of the patch of light suddenly, and left Habibullah standing there.

"Did I beckon a fool for the police to shoot at?" he asked from behind a chimney. "Their nets are laid. The order is to seize all strangers from Sikunderam. You and your brothers are as sure of death as the fat sheep in the butcher's hands, unless—step this way out of the light, fool!"

Habibullah obeyed, and was sorry he obeyed, on general principles.

"Who are *you*?" he asked. He tried to make his voice sound truculent, but it was only desperate. He wished he had not come.

"You left the jail without asking who I am. Why ask now? Better obey me."

"In what respect?"

"In all respects!"

Obedience is a hard pill to force down the throat of a Hillman. The fact that he thought himself helpless did not sweeten the dose for Habibullah. The other was a Hindu, which made it worse. So he said nothing, as the only way he knew of nursing his disgust, and perhaps the man in yellow believed that silence signified assent (although perhaps not. He was wise in some ways.) Nevertheless, he proceeded to display his ignorance.

"There are two men dressed like me in that minaret."

"*Two* men?" said Ali, looking hard at him.

"*Two*!" he answered positively. "One is injured. One is whole. The whole one is at fault and the injured one has failed. Both die to-night. It is your business to admit three of us into the minaret."

"Mine?"

"Yours and your brothers'."

"But—Bah! By Allah, what you ask is impossible! We are not alone there. There is a Sikh—"

"True. And a babu. Do they not sleep?"

"But there are others, who keep watch outside by the door in the wall."

"Aye, and *they* sleep, or how didst thou escape unseen? Kill them, too, and earn merit!"

Habibullah withdrew again into the silence, for emotion choked him. He could contemplate killing Narayan Singh and Chullunder Ghose with comparative calm, even while doubting that three of them could master the turbulent Sikh. But to murder in cold blood, without warning, Ali ben Ali of Sikunderam, sire, tutor, patron, paymaster, hero, bully and belligerent accomplice, was something that not even sons of the Hills could consider, say nothing of do. Hardly believing his ears he bridled speech, the slow, dour cunning of the mountains coming to his aid at last. The limit of amazement being reached—fear having worked its worst—he rose above both like a swimmer coming up for air.

"How much will you pay?" he demanded.

The man in yellow laughed—a conquering laugh all full of scorn and understanding.

"Rupees, a thousand!" he answered.

"Show me! Pay now!"

Habibullah stooped and held his hand out—mocking. He did not believe that man in yellow had a thousand rupees, certainly not that he would part with them. But the other produced a roll and counted the money out in hundreds:

"—eight, nine, ten!" he said, placing the lot in the Hillman's extended hand. "Blood-money! These are witnesses!"

He made a sound exactly like the hum of a bronze bell struck with a muted hammer. Instantly two faces, thrust forward into the light like disembodied phantoms, grinned at him.

"Go! Kill! And when you have killed set a lantern on the gallery of the minaret!"

Habibullah glanced down at the ten bank-notes that his fingers closed on, and all the Hillman's yearning for the hardest bargain ever driven surged in his ambitious breast.

"How shall we slay without weapons?" he demanded. "The police had our *tulwars*—"

The man in yellow interrupted him by passing hilt-first the *tulwar* that he had used to signal with. It was not Habibullah's own. He raised it—possibly to glory in its balance as it quivered like something golden in the window-light—yet even so perhaps not; for the North is quick to use the unsheathed argument.

He was aware of the click of an old-fashioned pistol in the dark not far behind him, so he lowered the *tulwar* again and thumbed the edge of it. Concession had bred appetite:

"We are three," he said. "We had three weapons—two more such as this."

"Aye," came the instant answer. "Thine and another's. That is not thine. That will be claimed by its owner. Thine and the other may be had for service rendered."

It was shrewd. No knight of the Middle Ages set a value on golden spurs one atom greater than the Hillman's superstitious reverence for his knife. With it he reckons himself a man; without it, something less, and so is reckoned.

Nevertheless, the greater the weight on one side of a bargain, the more determined should the haggling be. That is scripture.

Habibullah cast about for an alternative and landed a good one at the first attempt.

"You say two yonder must die? My brothers and I might kill those, saving trouble with the Sikh, who is a man of mighty wrath, to kill whom would offend his masters. Better bind him while he sleeps, and tell him afterwards that others did it. Then kill the babu, who is useless and has the tongues of ten women. Whereafter slay—we three could slay—the two men you say are due to die to-night."

That was a long speech for Habibullah. It produced a profound impression and he struck an attitude while the two disembodied faces appeared in the shaft of light again and conversed with number one. They spoke a language he knew nothing of, and displayed skill in the use of light and shade that was beyond his understanding, for although he screwed his eyes, and dodged, he failed to see anything but faces; and in the end he began to be afraid again, more than half-believing number one was speaking with spirits of the air.

"Only the spirits don't use pistols," he argued to himself. And twice he heard the click of a pistol hammer as if someone in the dark were testing it, not nervously but as a warning. "I would like to lay this blade just once where the neck of that face should be!" he thought.

And someone seemed to read his thought, for a pistol in a hand unconnected with any evident body emerged into the light and warned him pointblank.

"We should have to see bodies of the slain," said number one at last in plain Punjabi; and the two faces vanished.

"All Delhi may see them for ought I care!" Habibullab answered, forgetting for the moment that there was only one prisoner in the cellar.

"So we should have to enter the minaret."

"Lo, I make you a gift of the minaret!" laughed Habibullah, growing bolder as he realized his point was gained. These were not such dangerous people after all. How his brothers would wonder when he regaled them with the account of his skilful bargaining!

"You will need to arrange for us to enter," said the man in yellow.

Habibullah was silent, scratching his young beard, pondering what that proviso meant.

"The guard at the gate must be slain," his interlocutor went on. And Habibullah's beard continued to be scratched, a row of milk-white teeth appearing in a gap in the black hair as his lower lip descended thoughtfully.

Strange arguments appeal to savage minds. The rock on which Habibullah's wit was chafing itself keen just then was not the stipulation to kill Ali of Sikunderam (for that was excluded—imponderable—abstract—not to be reckoned with, and having no weight)—but the puzzling, protruding, concrete circumstance that he in yellow did not dream of entering the minaret by any other way than the front door.

Could he not climb? Was he lazy, or afraid, or proud? What was the matter with him? No man, having murder in his mind and able to command the very captain of the jail, was worth taking seriously if he only thought in terms of front-doors! Habibullah knew exactly what to do now.

"There is no other way than to kill those who guard the gate," said he in yellow.

"No other way," Habibullah agreed. "I will do it."

"How will you let us know when the work is done and the gate is unlocked?" the other demanded.

"We will light a lantern and carry it thrice in a circle around the gallery. Then come swiftly, for we will open the door and wait for you; and we will tell the Sikh afterwards that it was you who bound him," said Habibullah.

He was not sure yet what he meant to do. But he was sure he would outwit the man in yellow, whom he thoroughly despised now, not fearing him even a little, so mercurial, albeit simple are the workings of the Hillman intellect. He had the man's money. Why should he fear him? Who feared fools? Not Habibullah! Father Ali should have reason to boast of one son this night!

Something of his thought exuded—emanated—some vague aureole of ignorant conceit emerging under the cloak of pretended assent.

"Remember!" warned the man in yellow. "This is a part of the price to Kali, payable for your release from jail! There will be more to pay another time. And he who fails to pay Her the least particle of Her demand—is less to be envied than a woman dying as she bears a dead child!"

Habibullah shuddered, and recovered. He was not a woman, praise be Allah!

"It is time I go," he said abruptly, and in a moment he had swung himself down into the street along which he could see the "constabeel" vainly pursuing imaginary footsteps. He kept behind the "constabeel" and gained the minaret without accident. He was minded to beat on the door in the wall and swagger in triumphantly with all that story to relate and a thousand rupees to confirm it with. Only the suspicion that the man in yellow possibly could see him from the roof prevented.

He still did not know how the Hindu should be tricked. He knew that pocketing the money for a murder he had not the remotest intention of committing was only part of the business. They must be fooled to the full taste of Sikunderam, and none—no man on Allah's footstool—could do that half as well as Ali, father Ali, who was sleeping by his brother at the gate—father Ali, wiliness incarnate!

So he climbed the outer-wall like a bear in the hills, making much less noise than he normally did on level ground. And he dropped so lightly into shadow on the other side that Ali did not wake until the hot breath rustled in his ear.

"Look, father Ali! Look!"

He held the money—all that money!—most incautiously in the rays of the hooded candle that bode in a crevice of the wall against emergency. Ali—waking—seized the money—naturally—even before he rubbed his eyes. It was in the hidden pocket under two shirts, and with a sheepskin jacket double-buttoned over all, before poor Habibullah could protest.

And then, in the righteous wrath of an outraged sire, Ali ben Ali rose and cursed his son for daring to absent himself from post without permission!

"Allah! Do I live—and see such sons? The dung a pigeon drops on a ledge will stay there! Yet you leave! O less than ullage! Less than the stink of a debauch—for that clings! Son of all uncleanliness, get to thy perch again!"

So Habibullah went, for there was no gainsaying father Ali. He who had slain in seven duels the husbands of the mothers who had borne the sons he claimed, was not to be withstood by one son single-handed in the hour of rising wrath. The necessary element was speed, and Habibullah used it, shuddering as a new curse hounded his retreat.

Nor did he enter the minaret, for that would have been to awaken the babu and the Sikh too soon, before he—Habibullah—should have time to think. He climbed by the broken masonry again like a steeplejack, and swung himself up on the gallery between his wondering brothers.

"Mine!" said one of them, pouncing on the *tulwar*.

"You shall have it in exchange for mine!" said Habibullah, snatching it away. "Peace! Listen!" He had done his thinking. "Father Ali bade me say this: He will beat whichever of you leaves the gallery! He gave me other work to do."

Which untruth being loosed, and therefore off his conscience, Habibullah entered the minaret through the gallery door and descended the creaking stairs, after carefully fastening the door behind him lest his brothers overhear and make a hash of what should be a neat, nice piece of strategy.

He was angry with father Ali—not to the point of rebellion yet, but full of indignation and desirous of revenge. He was minded to take his information to a man who, all his faults considered, was a generous soldier of mettle and resource. The money was gone; but the chance for a creditable deed remained; and if his own brains were insufficient for the task, he knew where to find sufficient ones.

So he stooped over Narayan Singh and checked him in mid-snore. The Sikh seized his wrist and let go again.

"The foe?" he demanded. "Trespassers?" (Whoever is not friend comes into Narayan Singh's category of "foe," to be dealt with accordingly.)

"Hus-s-s-sh!" warned Habibullah. "Let the babu not hear!"

"No! Let the babu sleep!" Chullunder Ghose called up on his seat on the hatch. "There is first the thunder and then these whisperings! My God, for the gift of silence in these precincts! Oh, well, oh, very well, I come! Unfortunate babu is slave of circumstances in all things!"

He came waddling up the stairs, and struck a match so suddenly that Habibullah cursed him.

"Hillman's curse is Hindu's blessing!" said the babu piously. "Now spill the beans! Unleash the dogs of war and let speech coruscate! Give her gas!"

So Habibullah could not help himself. He was obliged to tell his tale to both men, neither of whom believed him because he could not show the thousand rupees that he boasted of having "lifted" from the man in yellow on the roof. In fact the whole tale was too fishy, coming on top, as it did, of that other yarn about fighting a way out from the police cells.

"That I should leave a virgin bed on a trap-door for this!" Chullunder Ghose sighed. "I lie, thou liest, he lies—what unregenerated Prussian calls *die Lust zum Fabulieren*! 'Gas!' I said, and he delivers hot air! Oh, deliver me!"

"If you could prove a word of it—" Narayan Singh suggested sleepily—"I might believe the next word; and if that one were true I would credit a third, and so further. As it is, if you are not back in your place on the gallery within—"

But Habibullah was desperate, and desperation has resources of her own.

"What if I bring the three in yellow to the front gate? Will you help me slay them?" he interrupted.

"I would *like* to slay them," said Narayan Singh. "Whoever promenades the streets in yellow with the mark of Kali on his forehead ought to be severed between skull and shoulders. Go back to the gallery and keep watch! In the morning I will tell your father Ali to discourage lying with a thick stick!"

"Lend me a lantern. I will prove it to you!" said Habibullah.

Chullunder Ghose arranged his turban sleepily.

"Observe a symptom of *in vino veritas*," he remarked, "wine being possibly imagination in this instance. The savage believes what he says, even supposing same is untrue."

Narayan Singh rose with a sigh and discovered a lantern he had hidden where none else would find and adopt it. He lit it with blasphemy, burning his fingers, ordered the babu back with his fat hind-quarters on the trap-door, looked disgustedly at Habibullah, shook himself to make sure the weights were there that told of hidden weapons, and yawned.

"Forward! Up-stairs! Prove it! If you fail to prove it, over with you!"

Habibullah led the way. With the lantern in the skirts of his sheep-skin coat, lest the enemy catch sight of it before the stage was ready, he stepped out on the gallery, with the Sikh peering over his shoulder suspicious of tricks. Then he ordered his brothers inside, they protesting volubly, making a show of disinclination to desert the post. Narayan Singh was deeply edified.

"Dogs on a dung-hill are as noisy and as timid!" he said pleasantly. "Better kneel in there and pray for good sense—if Allah is listening! Now, show thy proof!"

He shoved Habibullah outward to the railing and was close behind, but Habibullah begged him to stay in the open door and watch the light streaming from a window over a roof some way in front of them; and still suspecting trickery the Sikh obliged. He could not stand upright, but bent forward with a hand on either post.

Then Habibullah, holding the lantern in his left hand, turned to the right and made the circuit of the gallery three times, swinging the lantern constantly to call attention to it. And when he had made the third circuit, as it were of the walls of Jerico, the light streaming from the window that Narayan Singh watched went out suddenly—yet not so suddenly as when one switches off the current. Someone invisible had held an obstacle between the window and the minaret. He lowered it, and the light streamed forth again.

"They have seen. Now they will conic to the gate to be slain!" said Habibullah. "And if you, *sahib*, wish to have the credit for it all, take my advice and climb down this way, not waking father Ali!"

XII

"I AM DEAD, BUT THE SILVER CORD IS NOT YET CUT"

G rim nudged King. King jerked at Jeremy's flowing Arab headgear.
"Watch the minaret," Grim whispered.

The crescent moon had gone down. There was no light other than the glorious effulgence of the stars. The minaret—a phallic symbol posing as sublime—rose stately and quiet from a pool of purple darkness. Nothing moved. Not even a dog barked, for a wonder.

"Got the creeps?" asked Jeremy.

"Watch the minaret!"

A lantern appeared at the summit and disappeared—flashed for an instant, as it might be from the skirts of a protecting coat. Then, as whoever held it turned, its rays shone full on a man unmistakable—too tall for the door—bent forward in it, bearded and immense—Narayan Singh! The image was gone in an instant, but left no doubt. The Sikh was alert and moving.

"Something's wrong," said Grim.

"Wrong with your nut!" said Jeremy.

The lantern flashed again, and this time did not disappear. In someone's left hand—not Narayan Singh's, for they could see the legs beyond it and they did not move as the Sikh's would—it made the circuit of the gallery three times—then vanished.

"What do you suppose that means?"

"Sons of Ali fell asleep and off their perch. Narayan Singh looking for remains of 'em!" suggested Jeremy.

"It wasn't Narayan Singh who made the rounds," King answered. "That light to our right front disappeared and came on again after the signal."

"Signals, sure!" said Grim.

"Could the Sikh—"

"No!" Grim answered. "Narayan Singh is O.K."

"Trick-work nevertheless," said Jeremy. "There *were* three of Ali's sons on that gallery. They looked like great horned owls and we wondered before we all went to sleep what it was that resembled horns. Remember? Where are the three now?"

"I vote we investigate," said Grim.

"Seconded!"

"Unanimous!"

They reached a dark passage by way of neighboring roofs and dropped to street-level, nearly frightening to death the same policeman who had been disturbed by Habibullah. The servant of the public peace retreated at full speed and left them all that part of Delhi for experiments— assassination—robbery—what they willed. Since nationalism raised standard and voice the streets have not been safe for a lone policeman.

"If they've rescued our prisoner—" Grim began.

"More likely garroted him to keep him from talking," said King.

"Well, in either event—"

"We're flummoxed!"

King made no secret of his pessimism. He was all for action; all for reprisals; but he felt sure there had been disaster.

"If they've got him, we've lost our inside track. We'll never get another!" he said miserably.

There were no street sounds as they made their way cautiously along the shadows. Now and then a dog yelped in the distance, but as happens often when the moon has gone down all the neighborhood seemed hushed. Just once they heard—or thought they heard a cry and the *thump-thump-thump* of something falling. Then all was still again.

Suddenly a voice rose—high-pitched, eager, exultant:

"My son! Oh, Allah! Oh, my son!"

Another voice, low-growling, cursed the first one into silence. Then a door slammed. Voices again rose and fell in excited talk as it might be behind a wall; they were muted; the resonance was gone.

Grim, in the lead, began running. The others broke into a trot behind him. Grim stopped and drew his pistol. King came abreast feeling for his own weapon. Jeremy did the same on King's right. They were fifty paces from a man sitting in deepest shadow on a stone by the street-door of the minaret, who held his hand up, saying nothing.

"Narayan Singh!" said Grim at half-breath.

"Hurt?" (That was Jeremy.)

The Sikh seemed to be bending over something. He was holding up his hand for silence rather than to ward off an attack. He had recognized friends. They heard him growling in the general direction of the door, as if less talking behind him were what he craved. He rose as they approached, standing astride one fallen object, with another at his feet and a third behind him.

"It is good you came, *sahibs*. If you will drag these corpses in I will climb the wall and break the necks of Ali's sons! The sons of evil mothers shut the door on me, and are making more noise than stallions in a horse-camp!"

King laid his head to the door in the wall and gave tongue in the guttural speech of Sikunderam:

"Open, there, Ali! And silence!"

The door opened wide in a moment and Ali stood framed in the gloom:

"King sahib! *Sahibs*! Allah's blessing! Lo my boy! My Habibullah! Pride of my old heart! He slew three yellow ones with three blows of a *tulwar*! Three in three blows! There they lie! Lo! Look! The *tulwar*! See the blood on it! See the nick in the blade where it bit too deep and struck the wall beyond! A smites! Ho! A true son of Sikunderam!"

"Peace! Silence!" ordered King, and turned again to help drag in the corpses of three men in yellow smocks.

"He shall have a purse and fifty rupees in it!" Ali boasted.

But Narayan Singh cut that short, brushing by him, straight forward to essentials, discovering Chullunder Ghose recumbent on the trap-door, acting dead-weight.

"Back again, then?" said Narayan Singh—it might be scornfully.

"*In statu quo*," the babu answered, smirking. "Unless dead, in which case disembodied spirit might emerge unobserved, prisoner is in durance vile beneath me—among rats!"

"You weren't here five minutes ago," said the Sikh. "Get off. Let the *sahibs* see."

"I was certainly successful rogue in former incarnation," said the babu, rolling to his hands and knees and heading for the door. "*Karma*[*] now reversing rôle, I get away with nothing—absolutely!"

Narayan Singh raised the trap skeptically. Nevertheless, the prisoner was there. He blinked up at Grim, King and Jeremy. Smocked like himself in yellow they exactly fitted the only mental picture he had. Priest of a dreadful creed, dread was his portion. Likely he was only kept from suicide by the teaching that he who robs Kali of the joy

---

[*] Karma. The law by which sins of a former life are inevitably compensated for in this life or a future one, and good deeds in the same way are rewarded.

of killing in her own way is doomed to flicker in the astral gloom for aeons, useless and hopeless, until finally he ceases in darkness and never is.

"Others were less fortunate than thee. To them no opportunity to make amends and ease the pangs of afterlife! Behold them!" King said, speaking as if he himself were Karma, judging dead souls.

One by one—head in one hand, body in the other—Narayan Singh dumped the corpses of three followers of Kali down into the rat-infested dark; and Jeremy held the lantern so that he who had not lost his life yet might see and comprehend.

"Consider *them*," King warned him. "*They* died not by the handkerchief but by the sword, displeasing *Her* in death as well as life!"

And outside, just beyond the rays of the candle set in the niche of the outer wall, Chullunder Ghose held high dispute with Ali of Sikunderam.

"Shame?" said the babu. "I am utterly disreputable. Therefore appreciate value to others of what I lack. I assess shame of Habibullah at rupees a hundred. Ante up, as Jimgrim has it! Make it slippery and soon, as Jeremy *sahib* would say!"

"You have no honor!" Ali retorted hotly.

"None!" agreed the babu. "All dishonor me—including you! Insult me with rupees a hundred, or I will tell who slew those three! Habibullah will then resemble egg thoroughly sucked by grandmother—all hollow! The money please."

"May the curse of the Prophet of Allah, whose name none taketh in vain, wither and disintegrate thy bowels! May the worms that die not eat thee! May food be to thee like ashes and thy drink as bitter as a goat's gall! May thy—"

"Certainly!" said the babu. "Money please! Or else—"

So Ali of Sikunderam drew painfully from somewhere underneath his shirt—like a man pulling out a long thorn or a well barbed arrow-head—one bank-note for a hundred rupees, and the babu pouched it.

"Then it is agreed," said Ali, "that Habibullah slew those three with three strokes of his *tulwar*?"

"Agreed," said Chullunder Ghose. "Do you wish receipt in writing with stipulation black on white? Will sign same. No extra charge!"

"See this!" said Ali, showing his own knife. "The bargain is made. You have the money. Keep faith, or feel this!"

"My aunt!" said the babu, and shuddered. (But the shudder may have been the camouflaging movement under which he slipped the money into hiding.)

King, Grim and Jeremy emerged from within the minaret, listening to Narayan Singh, who wiped his hands on a piece of sacking and talked in low tones.

"Give Habibullah credit for it, *sahibs*. He was afraid of them, but what odds? He and I climbed down by the broken masonry and waited in the shadow of the wall. I would have used a pistol, but feared the police, so when the three came near I said to Habibullah 'Draw, and smite!' The fellow's hand was trembling so that he nicked the edge of the *tulwar* against the wall! And they came on, perhaps thinking we were waiting to welcome them. So I took the *tulwar* from him and struck three times. Then I gave the weapon back and said: 'Well smitten! Good sword, Habibullah!' And Ali heard, listening through the key-hole. He opened the door and called his bastard in, slamming it again on me. So I waited, hoping no police would come to see the bodies and start trouble."

Grim laughed silently. He had seen the Sikh's harvest before, and could have told his sword-cuts from among a hecatomb.

"Habibullah's head will swell, though, if we let him boast of what he didn't do," said King.

"Let it swell, *sahib*. It will fall the easier. These men in yellow are no Sadhus* blessing their enemies. They hold revenge more sweet than a hill-bear does wild honey. Let Habibullah boast of it!"

"Let's go!" said Jeremy suddenly. "I'm betting all I've got, those three were watched. For every one Narayan Singh killed there'll be ten on our track before morning!"

The eyes of all four met in the light of the match that Jeremy struck to light his cigarette. All four men nodded.

"Chullunder Ghose!"

The babu heard King's low call and came on the run, like a hippopotamus in flight for water.

"Quick now! Think!" King ordered. "Problem is to evacuate. Take away the prisoner—leave corpses here—all go somewhere safe, unseen. Do you think we can make the office in the Chandni Chowk?"

"Oh golly!" said the babu. You could feel him growing gray that instant. "Best imaginable is sane ox-cart used for general obsequies

---

* Holy men.

under direction of Ramsden *sahib*. Same is at Gauri's—probably—oxen asleep in gutter and—"

"Go get it!" ordered Grim. "Narayan Singh, go with him! Send Ramsden back, and wait at Gauri's, both of you!"

"For my emolument I take a manifold of risks!" Chullunder Ghose said. "Oh, fickle Fortune, I am undone this time! *Eimai, Ollola*, as Greeks would say! I vanish!"

And he did. His adiposity was no apparent handicap when sweet life was at stake. He had the gift of making even Ali's sullen brother open swiftly, and the door slammed shut behind babu and Sikh before King and Grim could light their cigarettes from Jeremy's. Thereafter he made no more noise than a parish clog would, slinking down dark alleys.

Followed conference. At best they would be a noticeable cortège marching in front and rear of an ox-cart drawn by such magnificent beasts as Chullunder Ghose would bring presently, if luck permitted. And at worst some one in yellow would tip off the police to interfere, perhaps accusing them of running contraband. Arrest, then, would be inevitable, and would mean the end of their investigation of the Nine Unknown.

Evidently more than one of the spurious Nines was linked against them, all guided by an unseen hand. There was no guessing whence the next assault would come, although it was fair to presume it would be surreptitious. Ali of Sikunderam, called into conference, turned Job's comforter:

"*They say* these followers of Kali have noiseless weapons, *sahibs*! Tubes that deliver a poisoned dart with accuracy as far as a revolver shoots! The poison is brewed from the venom of cobras and the blood of vampires—very quick stuff. A man struck by it falls conscious, yet stupefied, and in great pain sees himself decompose until the stink from his own body suffocates him in the end!"

"What do you advise?" King asked him.

"An exorcism! Let my brother hunt up a brewer of potions, and all the darts of Kali will never hurt us! A man known to my brother brewed me a potion before I returned to the Hills once on a time to establish Habibullah's parentage. Behold me: I live! He who disputed my claim was buried in more than one piece and in more than one place! Ho! I scattered him among the villages as Allah spreads the wind! I hewed him! I—"

"Good! Let your brother go," King interrupted.

There was virtue in the strange proposal. Ali's brother was a surly, ill-conditioned brute, too long possessed of a sinecure to be depended on. In a pinch he would be a positive handicap to whichever side he was on, and to be rid of him by any tolerable means was good use of opportunity. The brother himself provided all the absolution necessary.

"I should be paid!" he objected. "They ask to have their lives preserved. They could not find the magician without me. They should pay me rupees fifty!"

He could have had more, if he had only known. Grim paid him fifty and spoke him civilly, shoving him out through the gate. It was Jeremy, watching him curiously over the top of the wall where a broken stone provided a safe vantage point—just out of curiosity, to see which way he went, as he explained it afterward—who saw him shot down from behind by a dart that made no noise.

A part, then, of Ali's croaking had been accurate! His brother lay, if not dead, motionless. Jeremy, up at his niche in the wall, reported someone in what might be a yellow smock creeping up along the darkest shadows, searching the body, taking money and everything else he could find. Whereat Ali, using Habibullah's back for vaulting horse, leaped on the wall with the stone in his hands that had once sat in Jeremy's niche and, standing for better effect, hurled the stone down on the back of the head of the robber—and was gone down like a deep-sea diver in its wake before a voice could check hint. None knew—not even he—whether he had lost his footing or just followed to make sure.

They heard a skull crack under the impact of the stone, and Ali's voice, calling before his feet touched earth for the door to be opened for him. King opened and admitted someone else! A man in a yellow robe, exactly like those they three were wearing, strode in and stood with folded arms confronting them—producing the effect of ice on hot imagination! Habibullah raised the candle. Its light shone on beads of sweat on the cruellest face, as the handsomest, that any of the three had ever seen.

Bronze, as the other men had been. Smiling like the Sphinx—an incarnate enigma. Tall. Strong as a gorilla, judging by the heft and set of splendid shoulders. Standing with the air of absolute authority that only years of use of it can give. In majesty, in intellect, and in impressiveness, as far above those others who had hounded them as eagles are above the beasts they watch.

He stood in silence, and in due time with one finger pointed at the tell-tale cigarettes. Those contradicted the disguise of yellow robes and caste-mark. Surprise, or whatever it was that had numbed the minds of all three, now set King's wits moving again. He wondered why Ali had not taken advantage of the open door, and strode to shut it before any more of the enemy could enter. He with the bronze face touched him on the arm. King kicked the door shut with his foot, and as the spring-lock snapped he turned about to face a weapon he knew well.

He had cut his eye-teeth in the Indian Secret Service, and therefore knew the feel of hypnotism. He knew the only way to stand against it—switched his thought instantly to another object—anything—anything whatever, so be it served to concentrate his will and was outside the thought of the practitioner. Mathematics was King's formula. They vary. Each man acts on experience, and some withstand while others fail. He worked out in his head the cube of 77, and turned to swing for the jaw of the hypnotist.

His brain felt free but the blow failed. It glanced off as if guarded by a pugilist; and yet the newcomer had not moved. That was descent into subjection—step one! The others would follow swiftly. The man with the bronze face smiled at him, and King faced about—turned his back on him—worked with an ice-cold frenzy at the problem of the square of the hypotenuse—eliminating all else, visualizing the diagram—winning back to self-command and sanity.

The other two stood motionless. As they described it afterward, they thought they had been struck by one of Ali's fabled darts, making them inert while still aware of what was happening. They felt no pain, but there was a strange sensation in the ears and behind the eyes.

King was not more than half-in-command of himself. Habibullah and the other two of Ali's sons were stricken with superstitious awe. And on the door that King had kicked shut Ali of Sikunderam was now thundering with a fist and the hilt of his knife; it sounded like marriage tom-toms in the distance—somewhere away at the other side of Delhi—yesterday—last week—months ago—anywhere and any time but here and now.

"So it's up to me, is it?" said King to himself.

He sized up his antagonist, and fancied matching strength with him still less than he did the risk of attracting police to the scene. Suddenly he drew his automatic. And as suddenly the man in yellow moved a hand that touched the pistol. A shock like electricity went up King's arm and he dropped the pistol because he could not help it. The man in yellow, still smiling through his bronze mask, kicked it away into the shadows.

"Any more weapons?" he asked—in English! His voice was as magnificent as his stature—as surprising.

King knew he counted on the effect of it, for the hypnotist works by rule of thumb and uses one trick after another until the resisting victim yields. He hung on to his remaining self-command like a man over-board clinging to an oar, and was conscious of the sound of wheels advancing tip-street. He could hear bullocks' feet. He knew what that meant.

Ali's hammering ceased, and just as suddenly began again.

"What do you want?" King demanded—a very unsafe question to put to a skilful hypnotist, unless you happen to be just as skilful in defense. It was tantamount to lowering his guard by way of tempting an opponent. But he knew that all he had to do was gain time now and keep the man's attention. A hypnotist engaged in trying to master three strong men at once is as oblivious to other sounds and circumstances as his victims will be when he has control of them.

"You!" said the fellow with the bronze face. "Only you! These are not strong enough!"

He pushed Grim and Jeremy—brushed them aside with his left hand, and they fell to the ground as if he had pole-axed them. That of itself had almost been enough to overcome the last of King's resistance, only that King's face was toward the wall and the bronze man had his back to it. King saw something, the other did not even hear.

"You know so much, you shall be a Ninth, and later on perhaps a captain of a Nine!" He continued to speak English.

The bronze smile never varied, but the dark eyes changed; they were considering King's resistance, speculating as to the source of its strength, calculating which next trick to play. Slowly, the way a serpent moves advancing on a spell-bound bird, his right arm began to approach King's eyes, and every faculty the man owned was concentrated in one immense magnetic effort to induce a responding state of mind in King. King knew that if the finger touched him he would go down under it beaten—for the time at all events.

He stepped back—saw the wall—again saw something else— another, less inhuman hand—stepped back again and shouted to help break the spell:

"Rammy!"

Jeff boasts that eight of him would weigh a ton. If so, two hundredweight and a half of solid bone and muscle landed from the top of the wall feet-first on the shoulders of the hypnotist—as unexpected and as efficacious as a mine exploded in a crisis! The hypnotist was caught off-guard, and all his deviltry was no more good.

Slow to think and cautious as he always is, Ramsden had lain on the top of the wall to listen and look before jumping. He knew what to do. He had the whole plan mapped out in his mind. But he knew, too, that his only chance of executing it was to keep the bronze enemy engaged. Give him a minute's respite and he would be as dangerous as ever. The two had gone down on the stone flags hard enough to knock the senses out of any ordinary men. But the enemy recovered as swiftly as a snake recoiling for the strike, and Jeff had to wade in fist-first whether he wanted to or not, taking the fight to him, giving him no grace for concentration, forcing him on the defensive, barking his orders at King like irregular explosions from a motor-car's exhaust.

"Let Ali in! Out o' here! Leave this erne! Get Grim! Get Jeremy! Quick! Quick! Cyprian's! I'll fix this—"

Fixing consisted of catch-as-catch-can, no hold barred, all the fist-work thrown in there was time and room for. He of the bronze face knew his hour was come unless he could break the arms and legs of his heavy assailant. His occult powers were as contingent on environment and suitable conditions as are steam and electricity.

Jeff knew he could expect no quarter. Weight for weight they were a match, and strength for strength—a man who had kept fit by wrestling because he loved the last ounce of the grit and guts he drew from the Great Quartermaster's store—and another who had cultivated strength from a delight in mastery, and cruelty, and the ability to go unchallenged. The magic of good nature, slow to wrath, against black magic and relentlessness!

It was not easy to judge which way the odds were.

They tore, wrenched, struck and scrambled for holds like lions in the mating season when the lioness looks on. Once the man in yellow set his teeth into Jeff's collarbone and tried to tear it out; but that only offered Jeff a steady target for his fist; it was as good as a head in chancery; Jeff's fist went home into the other's jaw with a blow that put all hypnotism out of the question for the rest of that fight; it was like the thump of a pole-ax in the slaughter yards.

Every hold that either got was broken by fist-work or some other means that would be reckoned fouling in the ring. Again and again each crashed the other's head down on the stone flags. They fought beside the stones that had fallen from the summit of the minaret, striving to break each other's bones against sharp corners. Once, when the man in yellow drew a deep breath, Jeff got three fingers in under his ribs and all but tore them out. That was the only time when pain drew a cry from either of them. According to Ali, who was hectoring his sons, dragging out the prisoner, helping King to carry out Grim and Jeremy, and narrating his own adventure between breaths, they looked like a tiger battling with a python as they rolled, heaved, struck and snarled for breath under the torture of each other's holds. King said they looked like an illustration out of Dante's Hell.

They bled from collision with the masonry. They soon became so slippery with blood that no hold held, and that was when Jeff's advantage gradually told—(if gradually means much in a fight that was as swift as the whirling typhoon is from start to finish.) Ramsden had the other's arm bent backward around his head and was twisting it with one hand while he kept a scissors-hold and pounded the man's eyes with the other fist—when King at last got the prisoner and Grim and Jeremy, with Ali's sons for guard, into the covered ox-cart.

King came on the run then. He reached the spot as the bronze man broke the scissors-hold and writhed heels-over-head to untwist the tortured arm. And as King picked up a broken stone to brain the enemy, Jeff rose—swept tip his weakening man by neck and leg—lifted him—and with an effort born of twenty years' clean living and good will hurled him head-first on to the flags. His skull cracked like an egg.

"I *said* I'd fix him. Let him lie," said Jeff beginning to feel himself for damages.

"No, bring him," King answered.

Without waiting for the reason Jeff gathered up the still pulsating body and carried it outside to the already crowded bullock-cart. There Ali was holding forth to his sons, talking to them from the driver's seat through the embroidered curtains:

"Remember that, sons of forgetfulness! Bury my brother and bear it in mind against the day of revenge. He died like a fool, but I was wise. I felt the tingle of the magic and fell unresisting. Put him in the wagon gently. Lo, they took the rupees Jimgrim gave him! But I live! Hah! I lay considering how to attack that devil from behind! When the tingling left my bones I used my knife-hilt on the door, and if Rammy *sahib* had not come I—"

"One man make room for this corpse! Let the prisoner make its intimate acquaintance!" King interrupted.

So Ali's advice to his sons was cut short and one of the guards had to get out and follow the cart, in which were now two corpses, the prisoner, Ali and two sons, and Grim and Jeremy. Ramsden acted as driver, sticking his toes under the bullocks' tails in the fashion of Hindustan and steering with a tail in each hand, making noises to the patient brutes pretty closely resembling the cry of an angry parrot.

Ramsden could have passed for a hospital case without extra make-up. His late antagonist had used the losing desperado's recipe, disfiguring where he could not break, in the vain hope of destroying the superior man's morale. With hair torn from his black beard—raw seams where the Hindu's fingernails had grouted—blood in his hair, and turban gone—torn raiment, and great bruises showing through the rents—Ramsden looked more like a wild man from the Hills than any sort of civilized being. And that was no ill circumstance in itself, for it tended to prevent interference.

The same solitary constable who had run when Grim, Jeremy and King dropped down into the street like highwaymen, came close to regain his own self-respect by bullying these night-farers. But King walked in front in yellow garb, with that red caste-mark on his forehead; one of the sons of Ali with a *tulwar* walked behind, making the keen steel whistle and announcing that three heads with three blows was his average score. Worst of all, Ramsden sat perched above the shaft-tail, looking capable and willing to pull any man to pieces—growling like a big bear.

So the constable remarked it was a hot night, and Habibullah called him a liar, saying no heat was like that of Tophet, where the enemies all went whom he beheaded three at a time with three blows.

"Ho! I scatter their brains for the birds!" he shouted, until even father Ali—richer than he had been—considered it expedient to reprimand him.

"Have I wasted rupees fifty on an empty boaster?" he demanded acidly through the rear embroidered curtains; and thenceforward Habibullah marched sedately, thumbing the *tulwar* instead of swinging it, reflecting on life's little ironies no doubt.

Inside the ox-cart Grim and Jeremy recovered presently, not having once lost consciousness. The effect of the bronze man's hypnotism had been like that of the drug curare, paralyzing the nerve centers yet leaving them free to feel and to think as acutely as ever. The hypnosis lasted several minutes after the man's death.

"Proving," said Grim, "that we ourselves did it to us. All he did was to know how to make us do it."

But that did not help Jeremy. He was disconsolate. Shame ate his heart out that he, the deceiver of thousands, the ventriloquist, the conjurer, should have fallen captive of another's bow and spear.

"For it's as much a trick as palming 'em!" he grumbled. "I swear it's a trick! By crickey, I'll learn it, and by God I'll hypnotize the whole of India! You watch!"

Grim lit an oil lamp that hung in a bracket from the roof and, more with the notion, of quieting Jeremy than anything, began to introduce the prisoner to the corpse.

It was no use pretending any longer to the prisoner that they were Indian members of a different Nine; he had heard them speaking English.

But there was a chance that he knew no German, and an almost equally good one that superstition had eaten all his judgment long ago. Grim whispered a long while in German to Jeremy, who presently raised the battered corpse and propped it in the corner, where the feeble lamp-rays shone on the face and the open eyes. The jaw fell, and Grim, watching the prisoner's face, settled back into his own dark corner satisfied.

The corpse spoke!

"I am dead!" it announced in Punjabi through broken teeth that had left their mark indelibly on Ramsden's fist.

The prisoner gasped. Ali and his sons grew gray with fear. Their teeth chattered. Ali would have used the hilt of his long knife on the corpse to beat it into silence but for Grim's restraining arm. The atmosphere was perfect for any kind of illusion—stifling, electric, full of panic.

"I am dead, but the silver cord is not yet cut," said the corpse.

Even Grim felt a shiver pass through him. He reached up and turned the light out lest the illusion fail, for the jaw had dropped unseemly and betrayed no intention of closing again to frame the words that Jeremy put into it. Nevertheless, they had seen the blood and the broken teeth—enough to account for faults of pronunciation.

"I see dimly—only dimly," said the corpse. "Who sits against me?"

Two of the sons of Ali, deathly frightened, named their names. The corpse went on with sharper accent:

"Who else? I smell—"

The word smell may have had significance unknown to Jeremy. It made the prisoner toe the line. He sat up straight and answered:

"I sit in front of you. Why speak Punjabi? Talk in our tongue!"

"I? I? Who is I?" the corpse demanded angrily. "Nanak."

"Ah! I had looked for Nanak. I was seeking Nanak when the Karma overtook me.* Nanak—listen!"

"Speak the secret tongue!" said Nanak, trembling in his last effort to retain incredulity and self-control.

Grim struck a match and blew it out. The moment's flash lit up the dead face, making it seem to move—an accident—one of those accidents that do occur to men who strive persistently. All that Grim had intended was to guard against Nanak's escape.

"Nay. For I will not speak twice; and these must understand," said the corpse. "Hear thou me, Nanak. These are they of an alien race whom the gods have sent to unmask the Nine Unknown. Obey them, Nanak. For. the Nine Unknown are known to the gods, who have endured them long enough."

The prisoner had passed the point of incredulity and hesitated on the verge of full belief.

"If thou speakest truth," he said, "tell me, why art thou dead, and I living?"

A poser for the priests! But the answer was as prompt as the solution of any trick staged by Jeremy.

"Karma† overtook me. The tale of thy years, Nanak, has a while to run. Thy willingness to shield a friend at thy cost has obtained thee a privilege. Obey these men, Nanak, that the gods may love and recompense thee!"

The corpse ceased speaking. In the ensuing silence Nanak with a crackling throat sought to induce it to say more, wheedling, imploring, praying for answers to a score of doubts that tortured his bewildered mind.

But if Jeremy knows one thing it is this: Never repeat a miracle! If lightning never strikes the same tree twice, no conjurer need hope to

---

* i.e. when he was killed by Ramsden.
† It is an axiom that neither man nor any of the gods can prevent the fulfillment of the law of Karma.

mystify again the same audience in the same place with the selfsame trick.

Grim struck another match and lit the lamp. The corpse looked more dead than even Ali's brother did, who lay face-downward with the thin, round end of a brass dart just protruding from the base of his shaved skull. The dead thing's head lolled sidewise and rolled with each bump of the two-wheeled cart, amid a chorus of quick, low-breathed exclamations of:

"Allah! Lord of Mercies! Nay, there is no God but Allah! Allah! Allah!"

Then came Chullunder Ghose, near-naked and beside himself, charging by King, not recognizing him, distracted, slippery with sweat. King's fingers slipped off his arm and failed to bring him to a halt. He ran straight at the big oxen, that will gore a white man but permit the vegetarian Hindu almost any liberties. Setting a foot on the how of the yoke between them he leaped along it and collapsed in Ramsden's lap—a mound of hot flesh on a fellow every inch of whose anatomy was sore.

"Oh terrible! Most awful happenings! Rammy sahib—"

Ramsden, saying nothing, bundled him over the rump of the near ox to the street, where he lay for a minute calling on a pantheon of gods and devils. It was luck that preserved the wheel from passing over him. King turned back; Grim and Jeremy emerged; Chullunder Ghose was hauled clear of hoofs and wheels. Ali of Sikunderam suggested drastic remedies.

"A Hindu thinks fire is a god.* Burn him then with latches! Let the god wring speech from him!"

"Oh, terrible! Oh, awful happenings!" moaned the Babu.

They could not wait there in mid-street while Chullunder Ghose rambled of uncertainties. Nor was there room for the babu in the covered cart without removing guards or corpses. Corpses had it. One corpse at least.

"Out with him! Into the shadow! In with the babu! That's it—drive on, Rammy!"

Noises that only oxen understand emerged from Jeff's aching throat, and with a tail in each hand again he sent the conveyance forward, only to bring it to a halt a moment later.

---

* Agni—the principle of fire.

TALBOT MUNDY

Now another apparition raged up-street, as nearly naked as the babu had been—bearded, this one—swift—enormous—with a turban still in place and shaking what looked like a club in his right hand.

"*Sahibs!*"

"Quick, Narayan Singh! What's happened?"

He could hardly speak for gasping. There was spittle on his black beard—smoke, and its stinging red-rimmed traces in his eyes—a cut across his knuckles where le had guarded a blow—and a bloody, wet mess where a knife of some kind had passed between arm and ribs.

"They got my pistol!"

"Who? How? When? Where?"

"They did! Now! From behind!"

"Where, man? Where?"

"Her house! Gauri's!"

"Where's Cyprian?"

"*Sahibs! Sahibs!*" Narayan Singh was wilder-eyed than ever. The thing in his hand was no club, but a broken section of a bed-rail. He shook it like a clansman summoning the border-watch.

"They have burned the house!"

"And Cyprian?"

"My sons! My sons!" yelled Ali of Sikunderam. "I left four of them at Gauri's!"

He waited for no ceremony of permission—charged down-street with the remaining sons, waving his Khyber knife, beside Habibullah, bidding him make good his newly won fame as a smiter of three in three blows. And in the nick of time Jeremy pounced on the prisoner, who was seizing the obvious advantage; they fought under the wheels, rolling over and over, hardly noticed until Jeremy found breath to shout for help—a shout that saved Chullunder Ghose.

For while the babu lay in something like hysterics, grateful for the darkness in the covered cart, three men in yellow crept from the rear and groped over the cart-tail, seizing Ali's brother's corpse by both the feet and dragging it out in such light as there was for inspection.

"Dead! Nay, he is not the boaster!" said a voice in Punjabi.

"Look!" said another. "They fight under the cart! Our *guru* is alive!"

"Nay, we found the *guru's* body! Those are others! Slay!"

It was then that Jeremy shouted—then that King, Grim and Ramsden darted around the cart—then that one of the men in yellow answered:

"Nay, I say I *saw* the boaster run!"

So whether they fled from Grim and Jeremy, or whether Jeff's appearance was too terrifying, or whether they dared all in lust for vengeance on the man who "slew three Kali-wallahs with three smites," did not transpire. They fled, dodging the blows aimed left and right at them—dodging even the terrific swipe of Narayan Singh's broken bed-rail—leaving behind neither explanation nor the corpse of the guru with the bronze face—although where they had cached that was another mystery.

King tied the prisoner, Ramsden superintending. They roped him into the cart by arm and legs, while Grim kept watch and Chullunder Ghose gasped up his bad news, sentence about with the Sikh.

"They killed the Gauri with a cord!"

"*Sahibs*, they fired the house and—"

"They seized me, and—"

"*Sahibs*, I went for Cyprian, but they had him already. The bed was empty, and I broke it for a club to—"

"Hell, you men!" said Ramsden. "Why not go to the house and see."

XIII

"I FELT THE TINGLE OF THE MAGIC AND FELL UNRESISTING"

They went. They saw. There was not a trace of Cyprian—only the Gauri's house in flames and a belated fire-engine in charge of a weary man who said:

"These women's houses are a bad risk—jealousy, you know— carousal—anything may happen—lamp upset arson maybe—you police—"

But the policeman had his hands full and, being a white officer, in a land where they say the white man's bolt is shot, sought excuses for not interfering too much.

"Native prejudices, don't you know."

There lay a man in mid-street, belly-downward, with a great wound in his back such as ten lives could have sped through—a northerner— Hillman by the look of him—perhaps Sikunderam. Quarrelsome lot, those tribesmen. Probably he set the fire and died for it.

But what should a wretched policeman do, with the certainty that a Hindu lawyer would he hired by somebody to accuse him of stirring racial passions? He ordered the corpse carried to the morgue, to await identification.

Around a corner hardly a hundred yards away stood Ali of Sikunderam, most bitterly reviling fate between the bouts of explanation that he brandished, as it were, in the teeth of friends:

"*Sahibs*, they slew him as a beast is slain—my Habibullah! They ran from behind and hit him with a butcher's cleaver! What can I do? How can I claim the body? The police—"

"But how—listen, Ali! How did they come to pick Habibullah?"

"*Sahibs*—have I not said? The house was burning and no *ishteamer** yet. And no police. One stood by the corner and asked me as I ran, 'Who is the great one who can slay three men with three blows?' Who am I that I should swallow pride? I answered: 'Lo! My son, my Habibullah! He slew three with three blows! Will you see him try the feat again?'

---

* Ishteamer: fire-engine. Anything that goes by steam.

said I. And with that the fellow shouted, 'Him first!' pointing. Whereat about a dozen men ran forth from a doorway, and one of them smote my son with the cleaver!"

"What did you do?" asked Narayan Singh, standing in the shadow of the ox-cart for concealment's sake; for he looked like a man who had come hot from fighting.

"What *could* I do? *Ishteamers* came—two of them—and the police. May Allah blast the lives of the police! I ran—I and my two sons. What else?"

"No sign of Father Cyprian?"

"None! Nor of my four sons!" answered Ali, running the fingers of both hands through his gray-shot beard. "If my sons lie in the ashes yonder, burned by Hindus, may Allah so do to me and more likewise unless I burn half of Delhi to the ground! I will lay India waste! I will raise a *lashkar** in the Hills and raid and rape this land until a Hindu won't dare show himself! I—"

"Hs-s-sh!" said King. "We can't wait here. What next?"

"What next is where to hide ox-cart!" sighed Chullunder Ghose. "Characteristic of ox-carts being tractability! Requirements of this party, self included, being absence from the flesh at present! Even the police could trace us by the corpses—like a lot of bottles! Debauch of bloodshed! Self am drunk with blood—inebriated—very! I say office! That is advice of blood-drunk babu! Go to office. Subsequently I lose ox-cart in Chandni Chowk, being goat as usual!"

"But the prisoner?"

"I said 'subsequently,'" sighed Chullunder Ghose, oppressed in spirit by the world's obtuseness and its too material demands. "To the office with the prisoner; to hell with me. Your servant, *sahibs*! *Vae victis*! Caught with stolen ox-cart, trying to conceal same under garbage—no friends—no attorney—ten years—*verb. sap.*—are we going? Yes?"

They went, but Ali and one son backed off, promising to turn up at the office by another route. Ramsden, with Jeremy to lend him aid and countenance, sought an Eurasian apothecary, to whom Jeremy told fabulously interesting tales of dark intrigue while Ramsden was sluiced out, salved and bandaged—"à la queen's taste," as the man of drugs described it. Thereafter Jeremy and Ramsden chose a round-about route, using every trick in Jeremy's compendium for throwing off

---

* Army.

TALBOT MUNDY

pursuit—which brought them, subject to the quirks of Destiny, beneath the window of a building, whence policemen issued—five—that minute freed from extra duty—arguing.

"It was a hundred-rupee note!" said one of them. "Nay, fifty!"

"I saw!"

"I likewise!"

"I say it was fifty!"

"I saw you take it from his clothes. It was in a leather purse. You threw the purse away. It was a hundred!"

"Fifty!"

"Show us then!"

They all stood in a group beneath a street light, and the man who had emerged first drew a fifty-rupee note from his pants pocket, carefully unfolded it, and held it in the pale rays.

"Good that we were all dismissed together, or it would have been but ten by now!" said one of them, and they all laughed.

"Who can change it? Ten for each of us!"

They laughed again. Not one of them had change. Ramsden and Jeremy were within five paces when the laugh was cut short—turned into the blasphemy of spitting cats—and like the blast that whoops along the valleys of his homeland Ali of Sikunderam with one son swept into the middle of the group, snatched the fifty-rupee note, spat in the face of the man who had held it, and vanished!

"Hell!" exclaimed Ramsden. "Now we're it!"

He was right, or he would have been, but for Jeremy. Failing the right victim, pick the easiest and "shake him down!"

The five policemen turned on two who might have money, and who looked easy to convict of almost anything.

"*Sahibs!*" said Jeremy; and the very title flattered them. "This is the servant of the *Burra-wallah* High Commissioner Dipty *sahib*. He and I recognized those rascals!"

The police closed in around them.

"This bandaged bear? The Dipty-*sahib's* butler maybe? A fine tale!"

"Aye! And an end to it, unless ye use discretion!"

Jeremy fell back on dignity of the assumed kind—something that he lacks unless by way of mimicry. To a man those five police were Moslems. Jeremy was robed in the hated garb of a Hindu sect notorious as more fanatical than even the most bigoted "True-believers." But the police of most of the cities of the world have experienced the fruits of interference with entrenched ecclesiastics. However lawless, they let them alone if they may, occasionally envying, no doubt, the opportunities for "honest increment" so hugely greater—so immensely safer than their own.

This follower of Kali doubtless had his own way of exerting influence. It *might* be true that the "Dipty-sahib" kept a strong man in his pay for private reasons. If it were a lie, the man in bandages seemed none the less to be befriended by a member of a dangerous cult.

"Dogs!" snarled Jeremy. "Will ye snoot among the garbage, or be laid on a true scent?"

He was giving them no option really. No policeman, not the most cantankerous Mahommedan, would dare refuse a clew from a religious personage. None might wear those orange-yellow robes except the recognized initiates of a dreaded mystery. That much was notorious. Surely no initiate would play a trick on the police.

"You know where we may find those robbers?" one asked with as much deference in his voice and manner as he found compatible with True-believing.

"I know," answered Jeremy. But he knew, no more than they, as he recounted afterward, the sheer, stark impudence of the trick he was going to play on them. He was simply "spieling," as he called it— "talking to encourage the ideas to come;" and whenever Jeremy does that the unexpected happens.

"Show us, *sahib*."

Jeremy's whole facial expression changed. The idea had come to him, smiling from the blue. He wore now the look of rapt intensity with which he holds an audience, while his subtle fingers achieve impossibilities of legerdemain. That look of itself alone would have been sufficient, but for Ramsden; he had to explain away Ramsden satisfactorily, or else to extricate him brazenly, and the difficulty only added to the zest.

"You know *our* house?" he asked, selecting his words to avoid a compromising wrong phrase. (He did not even know at that time whether or not the followers of Kali had a temple, or even a meeting-place in Delhi.)

"The temple of Kali? Surely," said one of the police. "Well—go to that, and—"

They looked disappointed, and the air of deference waned visibly, as Jeremy noticed; but they did not know he noticed it.

"Nay, better; I go with you. Lead on. We will follow to attract less notice."

The police agreed to go four in front, provided one of them might follow behind for "discretionary purposes."

They were not capable of quite trusting a Hindu stranger in the circumstances, any more than Jeremy was really sure they could guide him to the enemy's headquarters. But the police know scores of things of which they do not comprehend the significance. They led Jeremy and Ramsden to the very door of a temple, on whose front the image of the Dreadful Bride of Siva scowled through her regalia of snakes and skulls.

It was a battered image. Moslem rule and riot each had taken toll of it. The nose was missing. Not a snake or skull of all her ornaments was whole. The dirt of a generation and the tireless energy of time had joined their forces, so that Kali's face was ground like that of the poor—into unrecognition; part of the disguise, that, like the necklaces and snakes. None cared. None visited that temple to ask unpleasant questions. Though the purlieus of the door were clean enough to appease the municipal inspectors, the gloom within was unattractive. He who lurked in a yellow smock in the shadows beyond the threshold was no showman, but a guardian of sacred privacy, whose very glance was a rebuff.

"Do ye dare enter?" Jeremy asked of the about-to-be-confused police.

They naturally did not dare. It dawned on them that they were fooled, and helpless.

"You should look for your Hillmen in a coffee-shop, three streets to your right and straight along for half a, mile," he told them, smiling.

So they smiled back, dejectedly, as victims of a practical joke who do not care to admit they are annoyed. They saw him thrust Ramsden toward the inner temple gloom, and turned away with a grim jest about Hindus and holy places that would have done credit to the Prophet of Allah himself.

"Let's sit," suggested Jeremy.

Ramsden sat down, almost on the threshold, almost absolutely invisible in the deep night that precedes dawn; and Jeremy beside him, next the street.

"We'll give them time to lose sight of us, and then hoof it," said Jeremy. "Meanwhile, we know now where the yellow-jackets' nest is. If a yellow-belly sees us he'll mistake me for a member of the gang."

"Not so!" said a voice in the dark within a yard of him, in English.

He looked into the eyes of death—of Kali!—of the Goddess of Annihilation!—into the eyes of Siva's awful Bride! Her arm reached out toward him from the darkness. Living snakes, encircling her hair like tresses of Medusa, writhed as in torment. Skulls that might have been of monkeys or of men—that was no telling in that light—rattled like dry gourds on a rope about her shoulders. There was a faint smell, not of a charnel-house, but of herbs that suggested prophylaxis, and by inference the reason for it—blood!

"Catch hold of me!" gasped Ramsden, reaching for Jeremy's hand. But he was fixing his attention elsewhere.

The goddess was young, as with a youth eternal. Full lips, cheeks, breasts—burning eyes aflow with something else than greed—a plump arm, shapely as a serpent—grace of movement—snakes—and dry skulls!

And the smell—the word "smell," Jeremy remembered, had brought that yellow-robed prisoner to his senses—the penetrating, subtle smell of herbs did more than offset things. It banished them! They faded out.

Ramsden had lost consciousness, huge and heavy, with his shoulders across Jeremy's thighs, until someone took him by both feet and drew him into the temple. Jeremy felt himself going. The gloom swam—full of Kali's glowing eyes—she seemed to have scores of them that everlastingly reduced themselves to two.

"I felt the tingle of the magic and fell unresisting."

He remembered Ali's boast. He let himself go—lay back in the arms of someone whom he could not see—Kali's arms and her snakes for aught he knew!—and let them drag him unresisting head-first into the darkness that was cool and echoing and dry.

So he was conscious when they slammed a door on him. Nor would he have been Jeremy if he had lain still, uninquisitive. He set to work to grope about a great room, stumbling over Ramsden's inert bulk, until his hand rested on a truckle-bed and his ears heard breathing. He produced matches from the belt in which he kept cigarettes and money under his smock—struck one—saw a face he knew, and burned his fingers while he stared at it.

"By God! Pop Cyprian!"

XIV

"We've got your chief!"

Rammy, old top!"

Jeff Ramsden had moved, and Jeremy's voice in the womb of blackness greeted his return to consciousness. But he had to repeat the words several times before there was any answer; Jeff had forgotten where he left off, and lay cautious like the centipede "considering how to run."

"Listen, it's me, Jeremy. We're under Kali's temple, and Pop Cyprian's here sleeping like a baby on a full meal. I've struck matches—seven left—can't find lamp or candle. I'll strike one more, and keep the last six for emergency. Wake up!"

It dawned on Jeff that Jeremy did not consider this was an emergency. He laughed.

"Good enough!" said Jeremy. "Don't stare at the match. It's the last, remember."

There are those who don't believe in miracles, but accept the turning on of light as commonplace. Moreover, they may vote, and some are known as educators.

This happened: where nothing was, and no light, suddenly a vaulted crypt developed, glowing with the color of warm gold wherever rays from a mean, imported Japanese match shone on a projection. Agni, leaping from the womb of wood, had wrought another wonder, that was all. (The age of miracles is done.)

Between two shadows of carved pillars lay Cyprian face-upward, like a corpse laid out for burial, but breathing rhythmically, smiling like a man who sees beyond the veil and is agreeably surprised. He lay on army blankets on a bed that could be carried easily, and was covered up to the armpits with a white sheet. The shadows all around him leaped like things alive. Arches appeared and vanished. Jeff tried to guess the height of the vaulted roof above him.

"Blast!" remarked Jeremy. "That's the fifth time! My fingers are cooked through."

Light vanished, but the momentary picture left its impression on the retina. For seconds, though his eyes were shut, Jeff saw the golden masonry, and Cyprian in an aura that the shadows were closing in like floods to overwhelm.

"I've tried to wake him," said Jeremy. "I've pinched him. He don't move. But his respiration, temperature and pulse all seem about normal. Do you suppose he's hypnotized?"

"I know I've been poisoned," Jeff answered. "You'll have to pardon my bad French."

He vomited enormously; but even so, with that necessity off his mind, he could not remember what had happened.

"You were knocked over by a smell," said Jeremy. "It didn't get me."

That was swank unshriven—Jeremy, not long ago a victim of the hypnotist whom Ramsden slew, reasserting his equality. Subsequently, from beneath, as memory always works, the salient points of recent history emerged into Jeff's consciousness, developed by the acid understanding that Jeremy had some need to assert himself.

"Wasn't I in a fight?" asked Jeff.

"No, old top. The other Johnny was. You won. Listen: King, Grim and the rest of 'em are prob'ly in our office in the Chandni Chowk, waiting for us. We're under the floor, and maybe under the cellar of Kali's temple. A lady runs the place whose hair needs combing—no, not cooties—snakes! She wears men's skulls for ornaments. Vamped 'em possibly. Our crowd hold one yellow-belly prisoner, and what with Narayan Singh and you we've killed a bag-full. Contrariwise, they've got us. My guess is we're safe enough as long as our crowd is alive and alert. But if they should burn half of Delhi in order to roast our folks alive, why then—"

"Why then you would be *spoorlos*,* wouldn't you!" said a voice in the dark, that was a man's, but for all the money in the world not Cyprian's.

Jeremy accepted that as an emergency and struck match one of the remaining six. A breath blew it out before it finished sputtering. He struck another, sheltering it between his hands. Eyes laughed at him, but a breath blew the match out before he could see the face that framed them. Nevertheless, he was nearly sure that breath and eyes belonged to different individuals. He struck a third match and Jeff prospected in his own way. Jeff's fist, launched not quite at random in the dark, hit someone hard and sent whoever it might be crashing backward against Cyprian's cot, upsetting man and cot together—waking Cyprian.

---

* Without a trace.

"Mercy, where am I? Light! Turn on the light!" said the old priest querulously. Memory failed him, too.

But a voice spoke like the resonances of a bronze bell, in a tongue that neither Jeremy nor Ramsden knew, and slowly—almost like aurora borealis—soft light beginning dimly in a dozen places filled the crypt. It seemed to commence among corners and slowly to collect itself into a whole, until at last it framed nine individuals, the chief of whom in the center out-frowned all the others as a mountain dwarfs the hills. He was motionless, immense, a man who had attained the stark simplicity of elemental knowledge and a kind of power that goes with it. Except for one thing he could have passed for a Mahatma—one of those pure embodiments of spirituality, who set the whole world first and themselves last, thus conquering the world. In his eyes there glared the cold fire of ambition. He was proud with the pride of Lucifer, who fell. Pride is the first of all foes that the Mahatma vanquishes, and so this individual's attainment, if prodigious, none-the-less was not good.

Compared to the man whom Jeff fought in the yard of the minaret he was as two to one. Even his physical strength seemed twice that of the former. In poise, calm, majesty of brow, and magnetism he more resembled one of those temple images that sit in the gloom and stare through eyes of amethyst, than any ordinary being. He looked aloof from human standards; yet—the hunger for human power burned in him, and could be felt.

His coppery skin shone, well groomed, although hardly clothed at all, and his muscles were like bronze castings. His smile was thick-lipped, but as static as the rest of him, as if it had been cast in place. On his forehead, under an orange-yellow turban, was the crimson caste-mark of the cruel goddess whom he chose to serve, but he wore no other ornament, nor any clothes except the yellow cloth twisted scantly on his loins. His feet were bare, and he sat with their soles turned upward in the attitude impossible, or at best a torture, to the western races.

"Bong!"

The word, if it was one, sounded like a hammer on bell-metal, producing overtones that hummed away into infinity. The eight who were with him hurried like supers betrayed by a rising curtain to straighten themselves into rigid attitudes on either hand—all except one, the woman. Jeremy knew her again, although the snakes and skulls were missing. Alone of all of them she sat irregular—apart from the exact arc of a circle that the others kept—like a picture of Herodias, lacking John Baptist's head just yet a while. Lovely, if you love that kind of thing. Rich, ripe, full-lipped, with eyes of a challenging candor that had looked with curiosity and some amusement—but no pity—into more and worse evil than the rest of the world suspects there is. Sex-insolence robed in a leopard-skin.

She had jewels on most of her fingers, and on one toe what looked like a wedding-ring set with diamonds; but her nostril had not been pierced for the jeweled stud so much affected by Hindu women, and her earrings were not the usual drooping things but emeralds cut table-shape and set so that even the claws of the setting were invisible.

The others were seven men in yellow smocks, not remarkably different from those who had conducted the offensive hitherto, but possibly a mite more sure of themselves and a shade less anxious, consequently, to create impressions. Seven men so much alike in motive and self-discipline that a kind of graceless unity had settled on them, making of men of varying height and weight one pattern molded by unanimous desire.

"Who are these people? Where am I?" Cyprian demanded, sitting up.

Instead of answering, the bronze man in the midst pointed a finger at Jeremy and spoke in English: "You and he, pick up that bed and set it down between you!"

By "he" he meant Ramsden. By giving a command that would probably not be disobeyed he intended to impose his will. The most imperial control must have beginning, and the hypnotist does not live—nor ever did—who can exert authority without by some means gaining first the victim's own consent.

Jeremy was done with being hypnotized.

"You go to hell!" he answered civilly in English.

"Ditto!"

Ramsden reenforced him with a gruff voice and a gesture like a gladiator's. He feared poison-gas much more than any mental trickery.

"Come over here, Pop!" Jeremy said to Cyprian. "Try to walk."

Cyprian made the attempt, getting his feet to the floor and then thrusting himself up with both hands. He did not do badly. Jeff caught him before he tripped and fell, and set him down like a child between himself and Jeremy, where the old man, leaning against Jeff's shoulder, shut his eyes after one hard look at the nine who faced him. He was conscious, for his lips were moving. He might have been memorizing a formula.

"Can you do this?" said Jeremy, smiling impudently into the face of the enemy's spokesman.

He avoided the woman's eyes. She had a long silk handkerchief that she plied between her fingers restlessly. He snatched it without looking at her, and went through the motions of the Thug-assassin, tossing the handkerchief at last into the lap of the immense man in the midst. It was the essence of disrespect—irreverence.

"Beat that if you can!"

The woman giggled. He who should have been respected spoke in an unknown language.

"*Bong!*" or so it sounded, and about eight other syllables. It was as startling as the gong that checks ten thousand horsepower in mid-turn.

Four of the nine got up and passed behind the pillars to their rear, returning in a minute with a wooden stretcher and a great weight on it. The woman giggled again.

"Look!" said the man in the midst, again in English.

But Jeremy had looked. His cue was disobedience. It did not interest him to con again the features of the man whom Jeff had fought and killed—whom he had made to sit up and seem to speak in the ox-cart.

"I get you!" he answered, laughing. "Who killed Cock-Robin? That it? Want to bet? I'll bet the man who took his number down can do the same to you! Come! Put your money up!"

Disobedience increasing into disrespect, was rising to Jeremy's head like wine. His voice and the little curt laugh betrayed it. Cyprian's old, lashless eyes opened a trifle—hardly wider than walnuts at a winter's end—and his lips ceased moving. When he spoke at last he had pulled himself together and there was the strength in his voice that is the accumulation of half a century's conceded deference. He spoke as one having authority:

"Peace in the presence of death!"

"I'm not joking, Pop," said Jeremy; but the fumes were no longer rising. "Rammy can lick that blighter!"

"Peace!" commanded Cyprian.

He was still leaning against Ramsden's shoulder. Jeff's right arm was around his waist as if it had been a girl's. Depending on Jeff's grip the old man leaned forward—raised one finger—pointed at the bronze face opposite—opened his eyes wide at last. He seemed to be drawing deep on his reserves of strength.

"Peace! Do you hear me!" He was speaking English just as Jeremy had done. "As long as we are unaccounted for—"

It was the bronze man's turn to laugh. He and the woman rang a carillon like bells in tune. The other seven smiled, as if the abyss in which their thoughts dwelt swallowed any sound they might have made.

"My brother!" said the bronze man simply, making a gesture toward the bier. The two words explained the whole of his attitude, although the word did not necessarily imply blood-relationship.

"Watch out you don't join him in Hell!" sneered Jeremy, bridling, repeating his curt, dry laugh—the danger signal.

So Cyprian reentered the lists, raising his head off Ramsden's shoulder.

"You do not dare!" he said, pointing a lean forefinger. And again he spoke English. "You have no occult power! You can harm no men who are awake. You are a weak thing—a poor thing—helpless—human flesh and blood! You are as helpless in the face of honesty as that!"

He pointed at the corpse. Wise, wise old Cyprian! Nine out of any ten religionists would have voiced some tenet of their creed, and so have given the enemy an opening into which to thrust the barbed darts of religious rivalry.

"You will never get my library," he went on. "Trustees have orders what to do with it. And if you harm me, can you pick the knowledge from my old dead brains?"

The woman laughed aloud. The man in bronze smiled triumphantly. Jeff Ramsden's arm closed around Cyprian, and Jeremy leaned forward, as if to interpose his own body between the old man and the shock that was trembling on cruel lips to be launched. News of the burning of his books was likelier than not to unhinge Cyprian. It was a bomb reserved to batter his defenses. Jeff forestalled it—drew the fuse.

"Your books are up in smoke," he said. "Rather than let them carry even one away we—"

No need to finish the friendly lie. Cyprian understood that friends had been forehanded with the torch.

"All?" he demanded.

"Every last one," said Jeff.

"You *know* that?"

"Yes."

Cyprian stiffened himself, almost as if ten years were taken off his age.

"I am content. I have deserved it. It was pride that prevented me from burning them long ago. You are certain they are all gone?"

Then the old man bowed his head, and the enemy understood there was no more chance in that direction. There is little you can do in that way with a man who owns nothing and asks no more favors of the world. But you may threaten. He tried that next: "At your age death without water—"

"Is easier than for you!" said Cyprian.

"At the mercy of ants—"

"God's creatures!" answered Cyprian. "I am old. I can face my end."

Or you may tempt—perhaps.

"We know much. You know a little. Add yours to ours, and we can track the Nine down."

Cyprian bent his head again, this time to hide a smile; but the woman saw it. She made some kind of signal to the man. Cyprian was elated. The double confession couched in ten words, that these, too, were hunting the Nine and did not even know their whereabouts, was like a breath of incense.

The man with the bronze smile read the woman's signal and appeared to be digesting it. He said nothing for about a minute. Then:

"We have a man who knows a member of the Nine by sight."

Jeff and Jeremy looked up, and down again, not daring to complete the exchange of glances. Even so, it was enough. The nine who watched all recognized the movement and interpreted it. The woman held her hands palm-downward about midway from her bosom to the floor and moved them outward in a motion that suggested leveling the earth for new erections.

"Your friends hold him prisoner!"

"You deduce that?" Cyprian asked, looking up with a swift bird-movement of the head.

Ignorant himself of whether it was trite or not, he was afraid that Jeff or Jeremy might blurt out an admission. He knew better than to give away one scrap of information. Tell the enemy nothing. Concede nothing. Yield nothing. That was next to being his religion. That was why he bought up books on occultism and the secret sciences. It was part and parcel of him.

Jeff detected Cyprian's call for discretion sooner than Jeremy did. His slower wit was working at full power, plugging as it were against obscurity; whereas Jeremy, knowing himself the quicker, was leaping from one possibility to another. Jeremy, if left to it, would have tried to strike a bargain, leaving mother-wit to solve it when the time for double-crossing came. Jeff would have used force. What his mind was pondering, deliberately rather than obtusely, was: Why had he not been searched? The comfortable weights disposed beneath the ragged costume he was wearing were enough proof of the fact. Did these men, knowing not a shot had been fired in the long night's hurly-burly, simply deduce from that a lack of firearms? Were they so careless?

Jeff doubted it. There was another reason. Figuring the probabilities he guessed that only two or three had captured him and Jeremy with the aid of gas, and had been glad enough to get them under lock and key until the others came. But they would hardly dare use gas again with their own unprotected persons in the crypt. Not very swiftly, but as surely as he sets his feet when walking, Jeff reviewed the argument, and then, as if the wound beneath a bandage hurt him, shifted his position.

Jeremy was on another track. He wanted to know what they knew, unlike Jeff, who did not care and only wanted to be out of it. A jest died still-born on Jeremy's lips. It would have suited his sense of fitness to make that dead man speak again, and Cyprian, aware of indiscretion in the air, shook nervously.

But he with the bronze smile realized that nothing he had said or done had brought the prisoners nearer to the right subjective state in which he could impose his will on them. And he lost patience. Time seemed to be an element in his immediate affairs, and the woman kept making signals that impressed the others, if not him. Suddenly he moved—about six inches—leaning forward and thrusting his hands in front of him as if they were serpents' heads.

"You—three—may—not—live—longer—than—you—can—endure—*Her*—agonies. Unless—you—choose—to—be—of—use!" he said.

Each word was separate—almost as if etched—spoken in English with an accent learned at one or other of the universities. And at the word "Her" his eyes met the woman's, as if she were the expert in applied torment.

"The younger shall be hurt first. The older shall look on," he said as if it were an afterthought.

"How be of use?" asked Jeremy.

"Like this!" said Jeff; and he was on his feet before the words had shaped themselves.

He could be quick when thought's slow processes had ground out a conclusion. Loosing bold of Cyprian he leaped at the woman and had thrown her into Jeremy's lap before Cyprian's shoulders hit the floor.

"Hang on to her!" he yelled.

And then, with every sinew aching from the former fight, he launched himself straight at the man in the middle, landing on his neck before a man could move to his assistance. One tenth of a second then would have been plenty for the whole of Jeff's plan to go up in smoke like Cyprian's library, but he was squandering no tenths. With a hand on the back of the neck of his enemy he hurled him forehead-forward to the stone floor—stunned him. And as the seven sprang to assist their chief Jeff dragged him out from under them, cuffing two into unconsciousness and knocking another into the discard somewhere behind the pillars. Then at last he drew his automatic pistol, and throwing his back against a pillar stood at bay, with a foot on the bronze man's stomach and the pistol muzzle threatening him.

"Are you heeled?" he called to Jeremy.

But Jeremy had his hands too full for any such issue as a gun. He had the daughter of the Ohms to wrestle with. A trapped leopard with the smell of the forest in her lungs would have been a toy compared to her. No python ever wrapped and unwrapped coiling energy so fast, nor struck so swiftly. She was strength and hate and savagery all compressed into the heart of charged springs, and a knife in each hand made her no whit easier to overcome. What was worse, Jeff had only knocked out three of the seven. Four were on their feet and fancy-free—it might be they were doubly dangerous for lack of the control the man in their midst had exercised before Jeff laid him out.

Jeremy with his knee in the woman's stomach twisted one wrist until she dropped that knife with a scream of anger. But her right wrist was stronger than his left, and her stomach muscles could resist his knee. She slipped out from under him and kicked the fallen knife. One of the seven pounced on it, and Jeff shot him dead before he could raise his hand to drive the blade into Jeremy.

But that was not Jeff's plan. Noise, that might bring help was likelier to bring more enemies. Gas was what he feared. As long as there were living followers of Kali in the crypt it was hardly likely their friends would turn the gas on. He wished the giant under his foot would show signs of life. If Jeremy should kill the woman and he should shoot all the others there would probably be a greater risk of gas than ever.

But Destiny was overturning. They were down inside the works. Like a pair of interwoven springs released Jeremy and the woman fought in spasms, she using teeth and he his fists at last—for how else should a man release his biceps from unyielding jaws? The underlings in, yellow lurked behind pillars for their opportunity, as likely as not possessed of firearms and afraid to use them yet lest Jeff should finish off their chief. The woman, for a second mastering Jeremy, writhed close to a pillar. Jeff decided he must shoot her—just as two men moved—the man under his foot and Cyprian. Both moved at once—spoke—used the same word—

"Cease!"

Then: "Don't shoot again. Put up your weapon," ordered Cyprian.

He under Jeff's foot shouted something at the woman in a tongue that not even Cyprian understood, and she, with a last dynamic dig with her knife at Jeremy's right eye, laughed and relaxed, so that Jeremy scattered his strength and she slipped away from him before he could recover. She had the knife poised for throwing, with the haft against the heel of her hand and her elbow well back, when Jeff coughed and her eye looked down the barrel of his automatic. Jeremy laughed and took the knife and thanked her for it, in return for which she spat so nearly straight into his mouth that he could neither eat nor drink for days without remembering it.

And all that while the light—the pale, cool, unexplained light that had started in a dozen places and appeared to join itself together into one—had continued steadily, casting no shadow in their midst but leaving all the outer portions of the crypt in darkness.

It began to grow dim; not at once, but gradually, as it once came, resolving into separate mysteries, each withdrawing, and each growing less. Jeremy went for the woman again, but she laughed, escaping his clutches easily, mocking him and as the light waned focussing her thought on Cyprian. It was as obvious as the increasing dimness that when darkness came Cyprian was due for her attentions.

So Jeff Ramsden, feeling that his plan was no good after all—but game until the gods should hoist his number—bent his knee rather than his shoulders and seized the man beneath him by the wrist.

"Come close, you two! Quick!"

Cyprian and Jeremy obeyed him, in a twilight so dim now that the pillars of the crypt resembled tree-trunks in a forest, and the shadows moving in among them, ghosts.

"Tie this man, Jeremy!"

So Jeremy took the girdle from Cyprian's black soutane and kneeling on the bronze man lashed his wrists behind him so that nothing less than sharp steel might set them free again.

"Let me go. I'm going to turn you out of here," the man protested.

"I know you are!" Jeff answered.

As he spoke, in front of him, somewhere among the deepening pillar-shadows, an arm moved swiftly and a knife struck the pillar behind him half an inch above his head. The woman's laugh rang ghostly like a pixie's in the forest, but the broken blade fell on Jeff's trussed prisoner and buried itself in the flesh of his arm. He cursed, and the woman left off laughing. Jeff took aim at where her laugh had seemed to have its origin, and fired. The pistol-flash, like lightning in the night, showed nothing but the pillars—and a gloom beyond—and no less than a dozen faces over yellow smocks, all waiting in the outer dark for *something* to begin.

"I've four shots left and no spares. Where's yours?" Jeff asked Jeremy.

There was no answer, but the sound of a struggle—strangling it might be—then of heavy breathing through the nose—and—

"*Bong!*"

It was the same word in an unknown tongue that had produced obedience before. But it was not the same man using it. It may be that a man with all his wits about him and no other care to subdivide attention might have detected mispronunciation: But there was much to think of. Expectation held its breath. It was pitch-dark now.

Jeremy, feeling for Jeff's hand, guided it to the prisoner's mouth, not speaking. Jeff felt a gag made of a turban end, and understood; his two immense hands closed on the victim's jaws, and the gag was tightened into place and held there by a pistol-butt. Nevertheless, the voice of the bronze man once more broke the silence—speaking English with an accent learned at one or other of the universities—each word separate.

"Good. You—have—won—this—bout. It—is—conceded. Go—free. Your—three—lives—in—exchange—for—mine. My—men—will—show—you—to—the—street—in—. Go—free."

Then Jeremy's voice—this time indubitably Jeremy's:

"All right, cocky! You come with us to the street as guarantee of good faith! And I want to understand each word you say. Feel the knife on your Adam's apple? It'll cut in halves the first word you use in any other than the English language! Now—give your orders!"

The voice changed to bell-metal.

"Lead them to the street and let them go. Let no harm touch them."

Jeremy's voice again, high-pitched and disrespectful, taking no man nor his makings seriously:

"We've ten shots and a knife to keep our end up with. We'll croak you at the first hitch!"

Bell-metal again:

"Make haste! The day increases. Lead them to the street."

"In darkness!" ordered Jeremy. "No light to see to shoot us by!"

"In darkness!" said the bell obediently.

There was movement somewhere—almost inaudible footfalls. Then a voice at a little distance, speaking in Punjabi—

"This way—come!"

Jeremy gathered up Cyprian, who leaned back in the hollow of his arm reserving all strength for emergency. Jeff, holding the gag firmly with the pistol-butt, seized the prisoner's neck in fingers like a vise and put such pressure on the jugular and carotid as answered all objections in advance. Together, in an eight-legged group like a spider treading warily, they started for the voice, each touching each—Jeff's strength as taut and alert as dynamite with fuse attached.

"All is well. Keep coming!" said the same voice.

"All 'ud better be well!" remarked Jeremy. "We've got your chief. He gets it first remember!"

Whoever controlled that mysterious light obeyed the order to keep it turned off. That made discovery impossible, but eased no nerves. A dozen times the giant whom Jeff was dragging writhed in a sudden effort to eject the gag, and many more than a dozen times between the middle of the crypt and a door set somewhere in its invisible circumference they drew in breath believing they were attacked.

"This way, *sahibs*!" the voice kept calling, too sugar-sweetly to be free from guile; and they kept following, too fearful to refuse. Time and again they cannoned into pillars, as if whoever led them was boxing the compass in a calculated effort to confuse.

"The door in less than ten steps, or I shoot!" said Jeremy at last.

The click of the slide of his automatic as he tested it confirmed the threat. But they were at the door. He tripped over a step that instant. And if Jeff had not needed his pistol-butt for forcing home the gag there would have been an all-betraying flash—and only India's gods know what next. Jeff used his fist instead—letting go his prisoner, swinging with all his weight behind a left-hand hay-maker, and hitting he never knew what. It vanished along with what might have been a feminine scream cut short. When he swung again there was nothing there.

"Come on!" said Jeremy, and:

"This way, *sahibs*!" said the voice.

They mounted invisible steps and came to a ramp sloping upward between stone walls. It seemed to curve around the circumference of three parts of a circle, and they took each step with shoulders against the wall, prospecting carefully, with a foot in advance for fear of traps. Once, when they had mounted for as many minutes as was possible without giving vent to emotion, Jeremy stopped in the lead and forced himself to breathe steadily a dozen times. Then, obtaining self-command:

"Remember! No lights!" he called out in the bell-metal voice.

"No lights! This way, *sahibs*!" came the answer.

Once or twice bats struck them in the face, but there was no other opposition until a great door creaked on heavy hinges and a darkness something less opaque announced that they were in the temple. It was still impossible to see a hand outstretched a yard before the eyes; but there was another quality to darkness, and the echo changed. The door to the street was shut. They knew it must be daylight, but there was nothing to prove it—not a crack that the faintest ray shone through.

But there was noise. Something—a man by his breathing—labored at a bolt, or it might be at a swinging bar that held the outer door shut. He muttered at his work.

"Krishna!" was perfectly distinct—not a word you would expect in Kali's temple, she having little in common with the god compassionate.

There was the sound of hoofs—in itself no startling circumstance, for they let the sacred bulls pass freely in and out of many Hindu temples. But the squeak of unoiled wheels was added to it; and if that meant anything it was that the dust of unclean streets had defiled a sacred floor. Dust on a bull's feet is one thing; on wheels another.

He who had led the way out of the crypt drew breath between his teeth and called to his chief in the secret tongue for orders. Jeff set his back against the heavy door to hold it open, Cyprian whispered something neither heard, and Jeremy took chances at a venture. He answered in Punjabi, in the bronze voice:

"I will see these to the street. Return, thou, and call the others to attend to this when these have gone!"

That certainly was vague enough. But it covered as much of the facts as anybody knew, and there was no need to explain why the chief did not answer in the sacred tongue. How should he dare be misunderstood by the men who held him as their hostage?

The guide seemed disciplined until his own will was an automatic agent of obedience. He turned with a retching of bare feet on stone and started back. Invisible, he sought the invisible door unerringly, and Jeff—invisible as either, and as ignorant of what might happen next as anyone on earth—played by ear, as a musician might, for the peak of the man's jaw as he passed. He hit it, which was a miracle. He sent him stunned down the dark ramp, spinning on his heels and falling backward; and the heavy door shut tight on him before the echo of the blow had ceased.

"My aunt!" said a voice in English. "Now is winter of a babu's discontent! *O tempora! O mores!*"

The belaboring of fists on iron was resumed as if in panic.

"To the last man and the last rupee—and then the deluge!" said the same voice.

The beating on the outer door redoubled—something like the fluttering of a moth against a window-pane, but heavier.

"Chullunder Ghose!"

"O gods whom I have mocked, am I in hell? Who knows my name?"

"Strike a match, Jeremy!"

The light, as the sound of its striking, was nearly swallowed in the blackness of a domed roof. But a few rays showed two oxen yoked to a two-wheeled covered cart, one standing and the other lying down, while a fat man humped against the temple door shielded his eyes with a forearm.

Jeff laughed, and Jeremy heaped swift conclusions into one mess to be brushed away:

"Selling out to the enemy? Double-crossing us? Got captured? What's the secret, babu-ji?"

"They greet me with an insult! Oh, my elements! A Frenchman would have fallen on my neck! This Anglo-Saxon race is—"

"—in a hurry!" Jeremy cut in. "Omit the captions—spill beans!"

"*Are* spilt! *Any one* can pick up same! Was suitably engaged in losing ox-cart—uncamouflaged and less amenable to shrinkage than well fed elephant or long-distance cannon. Very exercised in mind—*verb, sap*. Could neither sell nor give away same for obvious motives. Hyenaheaded *shroff*[*] approached clandestinely refused to lend even small sum on such security without proof of ownership. Same being *non est* in legal verbiage, sought to leave oxen straying in public thoroughfare. Brute beasts, having appetites, refused to be lost, and followed lone acquaintance—me!—presumably on off-chance. Most perplexing! Prayed. Not often efficacious, gods who are neglected in between-times continuing stand-offish in emergency as working rule. Nevertheless, bright notion burst bomb-like on imagination. Bring outfit here! Deposit same in midst of enemy, decamping forthwith. Off-shoulder burden of responsibility in lap of adversary, handicapping same! No sooner said than attempted—came here—door open—drove in—caught by curiosity was urged by inner impulses to forage, being poor babu with family in need of aliment. Shut temple-door accordingly in fear of observation from without. Immediately all was dark! Panic! Terror-stricken! Sought to open door again and failed! O God, what shall we do?"

Jeff Ramsden felt his way to the temple-door and groped for the fastenings.

"Where are our friends?" he asked.

"Presumably in office wondering what next! Oh, we are in the wrong place for solaces of friendship! O my God, what next!"

Jeremy, groping, lifted Cyprian into the ox-cart and asked him to stay in there. Ramsden discovered the trick of the door-fastening and set his strength against a spring that held a beam in place. It yielded inch by inch.

"Pull on the door!" he grunted.

Chullunder Ghose obeyed and in another second sat down hard on the stone floor, blinded by inrushing light. The street outside was bathed in the early sunshine, and a loiterer or two—the usual beggars and the usual social nondescripts—turned to observe what might he. The least commotion would have brought a crowd wondering. Whatever was to be done must be commonplace—as calm and apparently in keeping with ancient precedent as all the other unnoticed extravagances of a land of paradox.

Jeff glanced behind him, screwing his eyes up to penetrate the gloom.

"Chuck the prisoner in!"

"Leave him!" urged Jeremy.

---

[*] Money-lender.

Jeff strode into the dark, felt the prisoner with his toe, gathered him up, and hove him like a sack of potatoes in through the embroidered curtains.

"Chullunder Ghose! Get in and sit on him!"

The babu knew better than to disobey. Jeff in that mood is force in motion, not to be turned aside or made to cease.

"Jeremy! Walk in front!"

Jeremy looked once at him, no more afraid of Jeff than of the oxen, yet aware of something else. The idea that had caught Jeff Ramsden in its orbit and was using him as steam can use the locomotive, was irresistible. He grinned, saluted impudently, turned on his heel, and led the way, the rents that the woman had made in his yellow smock making him look more than ever like a member of India's great uncountered and unquestioned beggar-holymen.

Jeff, with a tail in each hand and his toes at work, tooled the ox-cart carefully out through the temple-door, leaving it gaping wide behind him, not once looking back, assuming to the best of his ability the expression of bored insolence that sits so often on the faces of men who deal with privilege. Even his voice as he cried to the oxen (that refuse to go unless they hear agony) had the tired note of second-hand sanctity. The ox-cart bumped over the cobbles. The splendid, hungry brutes helped themselves at random from frequent sacks of grain beneath the street-side awnings, and from infrequent carts—objurgated, but indifferent from long use. Jeremy reproved with time-worn proverbs someone who kicked the off-side bullock in the mouth for too bold robbery. All was well; or all seemed well, until from behind embroidered curtains at Jeff's back Chullunder Ghose piped up again.

"Not knowing plans, not offering to pass on same. Respectfully advise attention, nevertheless! In Chandni Chowk and environments this ox-cart will be as invisible as elephants in Pall Mall! Ford car might pass through unnoticed. Airplane would not cause comment. We are antique anachronism, subject to inquisitive police and mockery of youthful element. I urge judiciousness! Moreover, of two religious personages in my charge, one peeps through the curtains at the rear and the other chokes as if the gag were disagreeing with him. On which one shall I sit?"

It was Father Cyprian who solved that riddle—he who eased the gag in the prisoner's mouth in time to prevent asphyxiation, and he who whispered to Jeff through the front curtains, annoying Chullunder Ghose, who yearns to enjoy full confidence in everything.

"I have seen a friend of mine—Bhima Ghandava by name. I did not know he was in India. He must have just returned from his travels. We shall be safe in his house."

"Who is he? Will he admit us?" Jeff objected. Jeff's mind was bent on another course, and he yielded ungracefully.

"Yes, he will admit us. He will hide this cart. He is my friend."

"Which way?"

Jeff drove his toe under the tail of the near ox, crying like a sea-bird in the gale's lee, and they changed direction, leaving Jeremy to walk the middle of a street alone until he turned of his own accord and took the situation in. Thereafter he strove to follow with dignity, as he had led with grace.

They wended time-hallowed streets, avoiding the great thoroughfares and hunting quiet as the homing pigeon goes. There might have been a compass under the naked crown of Cyprian's head. And at last they reached a wide teak gate in a high wall at an alley's end, where Cyprian, reaching from the ox-cart, pulled a brass chain. Eyes scrutinized them through an iron grill.

"Can you entertain us? Have you a messenger?" asked Cyprian. And a voice with a smile in it answered in English:

"Why certainly. Welcome! Come in!"

Then someone rattled iron bars, and the great gate swung inward to admit them.

XV

"Abandon can't and cant all ye who enter here!"

W e're no good!"

Athelstan King was spokesman, on a cushion on the office floor with his shoulders wedged into the corner and Grim facing him, on another cushion, backed against the desk. King was suffering from ex-officialitis, a disease that gets men harder in proportion to their length of service. His best work had been done without the shadow of officialdom—over the border, where the longest purse, the longest wit, and the longest knife are Law—but that had not preserved him from official commendation afterward, which is a poison more subtle than cocaine.

Grim, on the other hand, had never been praised by anyone except his enemies, and by them only for ulterior purposes.

"I feel good," said Grim, yawning and keeping an eye on the prisoner, who was blindfolded and tied behind the desk.

"Phah! *Melikani!*"* remarked Ali of Sikunderam, sitting son-less and despondent with his back against the door. "Moreover, shaven and unmarried! What do *you* know of life's bitterness?"

"Nothing!" Grim agreed. "Life's sweet."

"I have lost my son—my best son!" Ali grumbled. "Allah is Lord of Mercies, but my Habibullah was a jewel too good to die."

They had heard that a dozen times at least between the night that seemed a thousand years away and morning that was just beginning to describe how villainously filthy was the office window. They spared their comments.

"I dare not claim the body, but the *Wakf*† will bury it, which is *something*."

Narayan Singh, his black beard resting on his chest, woke out of a reverie and seemed to consider Ali for the best part of a minute.

"Unless your remaining sons are more wakeful and alert than pigs that perish, they will be even as Habibullah," he said presently.

---

* American.
† Moslem charitable fund.

"Pigs?" Ali bridled at the word. Nerves were on edge that morning. "My sons are posted all about us as the eyes of angels! What do you mean by pigs?"

"I go to see how many of them sleep," the Sikh answered. "Let me pass."

Ali moved away from the door ungraciously and as slowly as he dared. If the Sikh had only weighed a little less—had only lacked an inch or so of reach—had only a shade less courage and a shorter list of dead men to his credit—there would have been a fight that minute. As it was, there was only a delay while Ali removed his mat, lest the Sikh's foot subject it to defilement. Narayan Singh strode out, and Ali slammed the door behind him with violence that made the clouded-glass pane rattle.

"We erred in demeaning our society, admitting persons without *izzat*,"* he announced to whom it might concern.

"*Chup!*" said King and Grim together—a very rude word in the circumstances.

Neither of them cared who knew that Narayan Singh might have their blood and bank accounts to back him for the asking.

"There's dust in my lungs!" announced King. "This office building is a fire-trap. If the enemy marked us down they'll burn the whole block. We'll have drawn ill fate on to the heads of a hundred people—or more. Suppose we move on."

"Where to?" Grim objected. "How will Rammy and Jeremy find us? This was the rendezvous."

"Was! If they were alive they'd be here."

"Life's longer than that," Grim objected. "Then there's Chullunder Ghose—"

King interrupted, smiling with a tired, wry face—not cynical, but sorry, because of the probabilities:

"They've caught him with the ox-cart. There must be a million ways to get into trouble with that contraption. We shouldn't have sent him."

"But we did," Grim answered. "Here's our place until someone shows up."

King knew that. Left to himself he would never have suggested any other course. Had he doubted Grim he would never have voiced his own doubts. But there is comfort in the privilege of pouring forth unwisdom

---

* Honor. (There is no exact equivalent.)

to be contradicted. He had been that kind of rebuttal-witness for many a good man in the toils of discouragement. It was his turn.

"Oh, go to hell!" he answered wearily.

For an hour after that they sat in silence, listening to the brassy ticking of the export-clock—the quarreling of birds along the roof-edge—all the noises that an Indian population makes in getting ready for the day—unpleasant noises for the most part from the western view. Alternately they slept by fits and starts, but there was always one of them awake, and all three instantly caught the rhythm of Narayan Singh's returning feet. Ali opened the door for him unbidden, forgetful already of the dawn's resentment.

"And the boys—my sons—?"

"Are awake *now!*" the Sikh assured him, and faced the others to announce his news.

"There are tales in the street of an ox-cart, driven by a god some say—some name the god—wandering all night about the city. The *bunnias* laugh, but the crowd is saying it portends events. Men say the oxen were as big as elephants, and the cart like the Car of Jaggernathi! They say it means India will rise and free herself!"

"Has the hour come for the North then?" wondered Ali, plucking at his knife.

"If six men of the North stay awake, I think none in yellow can pass them. But if the enemy should come in pink or green—above all green—" Narayan Singh went on.

"My sons are not fools!" Ali countered hotly, getting to his feet.

But Narayan Singh took little notice of him.

"If a man in green came, asking for the whereabouts of friends of Father Cyprian, I think our six would let him through unchallenged—"

"You lie! By Allah, in your beard, you lie!" said Ali with his left hand on his long knife, thrusting the hilt outward.

"I *think* the man in green is past the inner-guard already," said Narayan Singh, with his ear cocked for the outer passage but his eye on Ali's weapon.

"A man with green silk lining to his long cloak, and on his forehead a caste-mark such as I never saw—two triangles, one on the other. A man with a woman's smile—"

"My sons would gut him!" Ali swore.

But Narayan Singh opened the door. A man who answered well enough to the description walked in with the considerate deference of one who needs defer to nobody. The smile was a woman's as the Sikh had said, and the face a preserver of secrets, although sunnily handsome. Nothing that that man wanted to conceal would ever become news. He told nothing—gave away nothing, except that he was something of a dandy and comparatively well-to-do. The caste-mark on his brow—two yellow triangles one on the other—told nothing; one could not even guess whether he was Hindu or Mohammedan; his eyes were like a Parsi's, and his costume was a compromise—European shoes for instance, and imported socks showing under the green-lined old-gold cloak.

"Friends of Father Cyprian?" he asked, glancing from face to face.

There was no challenge in his glance, and no fear. He did not see a prisoner in yellow peeping at him from around the desk, but Ali did.

King got off the floor and advanced toward him.

"We're anxious for news of Cyprian," he said.

"I was told to bring three *sahibs*—Grim, King and Narayan Singh."

"By whom? To bring us where?" King asked.

"By Father Cyprian. As to where—that is—"

He hesitated, giving King full opportunity to frame whatever speech he had in mind. And King flung irresolution to the winds:

"Fact is, we're afraid to be seen on the streets," he confessed. "There were incidents last night. Arrest would be inconvenient. We—"

"I have a closed car," the newcomer announced.

But that eased no anxieties. A closed car outside an office in that narrow street would only arouse curiosity. The first inquisitive policeman would learn the car's number after which to trace its course through Delhi would not call for much ingenuity.

But the anonymous messenger told where he had left the car, which of itself was proof that he could only come from friends. Then within the minute, leaving Ali to guard their prisoner and gather the somnolent sons beneath his wings, King, Grim and Narayan Singh were in full flight by the private route, through the warehouse where men dealt in wholesale drugs and outlawed politics—out by a back-door to another street—across that to a sub-cellar gambling-den, whose lawless owner could not afford to tell tales—out by a window into a yard—across the yard into a shed where a Jew swapped camels and was hand-in-glove with all illicit traffickers—through his side-door into a blacksmith's shop, and out of that into a street where a big closed Daimler with crimson curtains waited. It looked like a Maharajah's car, but lacked the royal insignia, and there was no small platform up behind for footmen.

"If your honors please—"

The suave guide, holding his cloak to show as little of the green lining as might he, bowed them in, followed, and slammed the door—which was signal and direction; for without a word said, a driver who looked like a Gourkha but wore spectacles, started away at the highest speed conceivable in those thronged, narrow streets.

In fifteen minutes, by the grace of those who guide the comets in their wild ellipse, having hit nothing, killed nobody, he blew his horn in the throat of a *cul-de-sac*; and by the time they reached the end of it a great gate opened, admitting them without reducing speed.

They could hear the great gate slam, and the clang of iron bars that fell in place, but could only see ahead because of the crimson curtains. And ahead was nothing but the whitewashed stall the car belonged in, wide open to receive it. They came to a standstill with the front wheels on its threshold.

But their guide opened the near-side door and they stepped out into a garden of half an acre in which a fountain played. A house, that certainly had been a temple not so long ago, stood face to the fountain, and there were flowers everywhere—in hanging baskets—in niches where perhaps the images of gods had been—on steps and balconies, in windows on a score of ledges, on the roofs raised one above the other—and in masses to right and left of the driveway and the walk that curved between the fountain and the house.

They were thirty yards away from a pillared portico that shaded the house-entrance. Rioting colors, the splash of water and the sunlight on ancient masonry, the quiet, the coo of cloves, and that peace that comes from absolute proportion of design, united to make them feel in another world, or else on another plane in this one. The assurance of their guide completed the effect. Unquestionably he was confident of introducing them to wonders.

"Please feel at home," he said, smiling. "There should be a sign over this doorway adapted from the famous warning above the gate of Dante's Hell—Abandon Can't and Cant all ye who enter here! Another mystery? Ha-ha! You will understand it after breakfast."

Breakfast! They could smell new-roasted coffee and hot rolls! They were willing to abandon almost anything that instant. Only manners checked a stampede!

"I would burn a city for half such impulse!" swore Narayan Singh. "My belly yearns like a woman for her lover!"

But a man came forward in the portico to greet them, who might have checked a royal progress. Not that there was evidence of majesty about him, or of potential violence. There was nothing whatever forbidding in his whole surroundings. He might have been the spirit of the place, but his smile was compact of all the manly elements, and hate omitted.

He was middle-sized, more than middle-aged and yet so hale and well preserved that his age was difficult to guess, nor was his nationality determinable, although like his messenger he wore distinctly oriental clothes—a costume of compromises for the sake of comfort—Hindu on the whole. But he wore no caste-mark. There were no twin triangles on his brow beneath the plain white turban.

His beard, and, as presently appeared, his hair, were iron-gray, not long but affluent and carefully groomed. Hands, face, forehead were netted with tiny wrinkles that seemed to have been smoothed out rather than caused by time; the impression was that he was growing young again, after having faced the worst the world could do to him. Great hunters, great explorers, great law-givers, great sailors have such lines as his. He knew. He had looked in the jaws of infinitely worse than death and had not flinched. Fear for himself had no hold on him. Therefore he was lord of all he surveyed, and not proud, because pride is foolish, whereas he had humor. The humor shone forth from his eyes. Ease made her home with him.

"Please feel welcome," he said in English. "I am Bhima Ghandava, and this is my house. Your friends are up-stairs. Your wonderful ox-cart is in my stable, the oxen have been fed, and so have your friends and their prisoner. As soon as you have washed you will find breakfast waiting. After that I am sure you would rather talk than sleep, although the sleep would do you more good, so please come to the library."

There was nothing to do but accept his invitation and follow his green-lined *chela** into a place where marble, cool water, soap, towels, and the bathroom smell made life for the moment no longer a dream but an exquisite luxury.

The white man *thinks* the bath is a religion peculiar to himself. The English made a privileged Order of it centuries ago, and it is the only creed that the whole West can agree on. But it also is the one lone

---

* Disciple.

recognizable common denominator by which West and East may understand each other in the end—the outward and visible product of an inborn yearning to be clean. There was no difference between Grim's and King's devotion to the ritual and Narayan Singh's, except perhaps the Sikh enjoyed his most.

Then rolls and coffee on white table-linen in a chamber in which priests had kept the Mysteries before men forgot what such things are and what simplicity must go with them.

An atmosphere outlives the men who made it. It is easy to feel lawless in a smugglers' den—brave and determined 'tween-decks in a ship just home from drifting in the polar ice. It was easy to feel then and there that the hatch was off the hold of the impossible and all things waited for accomplishment by them who dared, and knew. There was a sense of being in the very womb of faultless Destiny.

"I would trade my whole accomplishment and all my medals, just to know I was worthy to sit here!" said Narayan Singh piously—then set his teeth into a buttered roll and washed a titanic mouthful down with coffee that smelt of paradise.

There were no attendants. The messenger in green-lined finery whom their host had called his *chela* vanished when he had shown them where to go. None intruded on their privacy until the food was all devoured, and even then it was an old acquaintance who burst in on them, weary-eyed and as contented as a bear among the honey-pots.

"*Sahibs!* Exquisite adventure! Luck at last! Gods whom we have long offended have forgiven us! We are in house of holy adept, whose tobacco is as perfect as his point of view! I swear, thou swearest, he swears! I drink, thou drinkest, he drinks! Rammy *sahib* consumed one quart of imported stout at seven A. M. Jeremy *sahib* had whisky-soda. Me, I have drunk cognac, contrary to caste and precedent. Am intoxicated with exuberance! Ghandava *sahib* drank gin—I am sure—I saw him! He does all things same as everybody. *Sahibs*, secret is, he doesn't *give* a damn! He knows too much! He is incorporated essence of accumulated ancient knowledge! Ask him anything—I bet he knows it! He put oil on Rammy *sahib's* injuries that has made him feel like pigs in clover. You, you incredulate—but me, I know a good thing when I see same. I want somebody to bet with!"

Chullunder Ghose sat down cross-legged where a shaft of golden sunshine quivered between the slats of a shutter, and fanned himself with a handkerchief.

"Am commanded to escort you three *sahibs* to *sanctum sanctorum* soon as gorges rise at thought of further rations. Personally I ate nine rolls and drank a gallon. Emulate me. There is lots more!"

They followed him up stone stairs worn by the tread of ancient feet—stairs set in the heart of the masonry by builders who had no need to economize in labor or material, and passed between what once had been the priests' rooms, walking on rugs whose origin was Asia from Mongolia to Damascus. At the end of one long passage was a door at least a foot thick carved with the stories of the gods; Chullunder Ghose thumped that with both fists. It opened at once, as if by a hidden mechanism.

They found themselves in what was probably the largest room in the building. It opened by means of high windows on a deep veranda banked with flowers, and its ceiling was vaulted in four sections, with one pillar in the midst to support the inner ends of all four arches. Somewhere were hidden ventilators through which fans drove cool air; the purr of the fans was dimly audible and, just as with Ghandava's costume, there was enough modernity about the place to provide comfort without sacrificing any aspect worth preserving.

The deep, long window-seats, for instance, were upholstered in brocaded cloth, and the stone floor was spread with several layers of rugs. There were books wherever shelves could be fitted between projecting portions of the masonry; and an enormous toucan, neither caged nor chained, sat perched on a bracket projecting from one wall, looking futuristic.

Bhima Ghandava himself rose out of an overstuffed leather armchair to greet them. Ramsden was sprawling in another one. Jeremy sat cross-legged on a divan in a corner near the big bird, whose phonetics he was trying at intervals to imitate. The prisoner, unbound, sat like a big bronze idol on the floor with his back to the window; and Chullunder Ghose resumed the perch he had left at one end of a window-seat. Cyprian was not in sight, but there was a sound of book-leaves quickly turning that suggested him.

"Please be at home," smiled Ghandava.

They collapsed into deep armchairs, but Narayan Singh gave up the effort to feel comfortable in his and after a minute squatted on the floor instead, with his back against it. Bhima Ghandava resumed the window-seat *vis-a-vis* to Chullunder Ghose, and then—as if he might have been watching through a peep-hole for the proper moment—the green-lined *chela* entered, addressed him as "most reverend *guru*,"* asked whether he needed anything, and was dismissed.

It was conceivable—although not certain by a thousand chances—that that little incident had been designed on purpose to suggest the proper attitude of deep respect. Perhaps the *chela* had himself conceived it to that end. Ghandava was not in need of the sort of mechanism that surrounds mere royalty. He provided his own atmosphere.

"I am trying to make this prisoner feel at home, too," he said with an air of comical regret, "but he seems to yearn for brimstone and red-hot coals! This is too tame!"

The bronze man sat immobile. Not a feature moved. His wrists were unbound but he had crossed his arms over his breast and held them so as if hypnotized. The proud smile on his thick lips seemed to have been frozen there. He hardly seemed to breathe. He did not blink. When King, Grim and Narayan Singh entered he did not so much as glance at them. He was like a dead man at a feast.

"He imprisons himself!" said Ghandava. "You see before you the embodiment of fear and not the slightest need for it. No combination of physical terrors could reduce him to that condition. He is self-hypnotized. He is afraid with a fear that is within himself—that he has cultivated in himself—that he has used to govern others. Dynamite could hardly loosen it. What shall we do with him?"

That was hard to answer.

"He's the head of their gang, and he's dangerous," said Jeff.

"To whom?" Ghandava asked. "He seems safe to us at present!"

Whereat Cyprian piped up, emerging from behind the only detached bookcase in the room, wiping spectacles and looking as if he had been cataloging all his life.

"You are right!" he said sharply. "He is only a danger to his friends. I say, release him!"

Ghandava glanced at Jeff, whose fist had done the capturing. By right of *lex non scripta*† the decision was up to him. But Jeff, though an irresistible force when his mind is made up, is no leaper at blind conclusions or interpreter of men's minds. His forte is common sense, applied.

"Stow him incommunicado, while we talk," he suggested, and that was carried by acclamation.

---

* Teacher.
† Unwritten law.

Bhima Ghandava summoned the green-lined *chela* by means of an electric bell.

"Such arrogant simplicity! How simple are the great! He who could *think* and be obeyed! To use a common bell—such meekness!" exclaimed Chullunder Ghose, rolling his eyes in an ecstasy.

Bhima Ghandava explained what was required. The *chela* addressed remarks to the prisoner, who took no more notice of them than the image of Buddha would if a fly had rested on it. King leaned over and prodded Chullunder Ghose in the stomach with a pole meant for closing windows.

"Less emotion!" he commanded.

Jeff hove himself out of his chair and seized the prisoner under the arms.

"Lead the way," he said simply.

But as if the threat of violence and the physical contact were all that were needed to resolve the prisoner's fear, he instantly began to struggle, springing upright as if Jeff's touch had released a spring, and smiting Jeff with his clenched fist three times running between the eyes. Jeff reeled backward and then, closing with him, had to fight like Samson to save his neck from breaking; for the bronze man got him by a hold below the arms and, spinning him upside-down, crashed his head against the floor and set his foot on the bent neck. It was only three layers of rugs that saved Jeff from being killed.

For once "Rammy old top" was in the hands of a stronger adversary. Though he swept the man's legs together with one arm and threw him, thereafter using every artifice he knew, sending home punch after terrific punch when opening offered, he could not pin his adversary down. His previous injuries, though rendered nearly painless by Ghandava's oils, were a handicap. Each sledge-hammer blow that his opponent landed, each volcanic wrench at Jeff's arms and legs, made matters worse.

The end could have only been postponed for seconds. The others began to rush to Jeff's assistance. Even Chullunder Ghose was on tip-toe to plunge into the fray, and Cyprian lay down his spectacles to look for something heavy. But Ghandava's out-stretched hand kept all of them, *chela* included, standing back, they not knowing what he meant to do, yet certain he could command the situation in a second when he chose. Even Cyprian expected it, and laid down the heavy brass vase he had picked up.

But for half-a-minute the pace was too quick for Ghandava, or so it seemed. Jeff and his prisoner twisted and writhed like bears at war in spring-time. The bronze man hurled Jeff clear, sprang to his feet again, seized a wrought-iron cobra meant to hold a lamp and lifted it to brain him.

The thing weighed about two hundred pounds, and Jeff's forearm, raised to intercept it, would have smashed like kindling.

Yet it was Ghandava's hand—smooth, soft palm upward—that met the full force of the blow, arresting it midway—a hand that looked as if it could not lift the bronze snake, let alone resist it! And he said one word, in Sanskrit possibly, at least in an unknown tongue, that seemed to stiffen the prisoner again from head to foot, so that he stood transfixed with the heavy bronze thing in his hands, arrested in mid-motion.

"Now take him away," he said quietly; and instead of Jeff the *chela* touched him. The giant set down the iron cobra and followed the *chela* like a man in a dream—out through a door, at the end of the room, that closed on both of them.

"If we use force in their way they can conquer us," Ghandava said almost apologetically. "It was what you know as luck, friend Ramsden, that enabled you to capture him last night. You took him by surprise, or he would have twisted you as a basket-maker twists the reeds between his hands. The same with every other force they use; if you stand up against it, it will flatten you. You saw me then? What I did was to redirect his energy. If I had turned it inward it would have destroyed him. Instead, I used it to arrest that iron weight in mid-career—used his energy, not mine. It is only a question of knowledge."

"Like riding a horse!" suggested Jeremy. "But how? Tell you what, sir, I'll swap you! Show me that trick, and I'll teach you any two you like of mine!"

Ghandava laughed merrily and got back to his place on the window-seat.

"I rather doubt my need to know your tricks," he answered, "and to learn mine, if you care to call them tricks, would take more years than you believe you have at your disposal. Besides—how should I dare to teach you, if I could?"

"Why not?" asked Jeremy. "I'm not a crook."

Ghandava smiled again.

"Few of us are what we think we are," he answered. "You—all of you—are on what Hindus call the Wheel. You are tied to Destiny, the agents of it, bound in your appointed places. Every star—planet—meteorite—each speck of dust that swings into view does so in obedience to law. Order is the first law. None can escape his destiny."

"Ah! Now we all get fortunes told! I shiver on brink of expectancy! Am I to be plutocrat? To go to jail? To travel overseas? To be distinguished personage?"

"You're going to be prodded in the belly!" King assured him.

"Ouch! *Sahib*, there should be a law against this! Cease!"

"If I could tell fortunes, do you think I would?" Ghandava asked.

Cyprian, with his thumb between the pages of a black book, came toward the window and chose a high-backed chair in which he could sit without doubling up like a rag doll. He preferred dignity to any kind of comfort.

"To be brief with you, Ghandava," he said, as if calling a meeting to order, "we are all in your debt for princely hospitality. Is there more we may expect of you? Our purpose is to expose the Nine Unknown. We want the secrets of the Nine Unknown—their books—their treasure—"

"Their treasure!" sighed Chullunder Ghose.

"Their treasure and their knowledge!" Grim agreed.

"Their books!" said Cyprian. "Can you help us?"

"Can I, do you mean, or will I?" asked Ghandava.

He smiled as if he found the situation funny.

XVI

"Sahibs, that is a true speech!"

Ghandava began to pace the floor with hands behind him.

"To begin with, nothing is impossible!" he said, with an abruptness that made Cyprian blink.

Chullunder Chose sighed like an epicure in presence of his favorite dish, deftly avoiding King's attentions with the window-pole. King was in favor of hard facts and no delirium.

"Does it strike any of you that this account of the Nine Unknown is ridiculous?" Ghandava asked.

"Not in the least!" said Jeremy promptly, and the others nodded.

"We *know*," said Cyprian.

"Da Gama told us," said Chullunder Chose.

"They've persecuted us ever since we took the field against them," said Narayan Singh.

"That is what appears to me ridiculous," Ghandava answered. "You presume a body of nine men, inheritors, as you describe them, of the scientific secrets of the ancients. You credit these nine with such wisdom that according to you they have been able to accumulate enormous quantities of gold at regular intervals for thousands of years without anyone discovering either its hiding-place or their method. Yet you say they have persecuted you without success. How do you propose to account for their alleged success along one line, and their rather clumsy series of failures along another? Do the two accounts appear to you compatible?"

"They don't," Grim said. "We decided yesterday that those who are attacking us probably belong to a different organization."

"Does it occur to you," Ghandava asked, "that these Nines who have attacked you are themselves in search of the real Nine?"

"That had occurred to this babu," Chullunder Ghose admitted self-complacently, with his hands folded across his stomach.

"Why didn't you tell us then?" King demanded.

"Belly being tender part of my anatomy, have said nothing that might provoke assault on same," the babu answered with both eyes on King's prodding pole.

Jeremy produced the three coins that remained from Da Gama's original treasure trove. He passed them to Cyprian, who handed them to Ghandava.

"Those look like evidence to me," said Jeremy.

"Don't forget," said King, "we've another prisoner in the office, who swears he was told off to kill a member of the real Nine in Benares."

Ghandava nodded, but Cyprian joined issue with him.

"Why believe what he says? The organization is a series of Nines, each member of a Nine being himself a captain of another Nine and so on. I am entirely satisfied on that point. Thus, the only means of control or of investigation is from the top. Da Gama said so. One Nine knows nothing of another. For all we know the Nine Unknown may be at war with one another. A subordinate told off to murder one of the Principals might say in honest ignorance—"

Ghandava interrupted him with a gesture.

"Doubt from the unexpected quarter! I see I must explain," he said; but he paused for almost a minute. His next words were dramatic—

"I am myself commissioned by the Nine Unknown!" For a second there was silence. Then—

"God bless my soul!" exclaimed Cyprian.

Ghandava laughed. Cyprian crossed himself unostentatiously. The others betrayed astonishment tinged with incredulity, except that Narayan Singh and Chullunder Chose, while surprised into speechlessness, looked disposed to credit almost anything.

Ghandava on the whole seemed not displeased with the reception of his statement.

"The 'Nine Unknown' are known to themselves by another name; and by yet another name to their few confidants; but they do exist, and they are the inheritors of all the scientific knowledge of the ancients," he went on.

"And the gold that has vanished in the course of centuries? Are they inheritors of that?" asked Ramsden.

"My friend, if I should know the secrets of the Nine, does it occur to you that I would tell them?"

"Their books! Their books!" Cyprian muttered, and Ghandava took that up with him.

"Others have wanted those. They who burned the library at Alexandria did so in order to secure them, and that was when men's memories were fresher than they are now. *They* failed, as all others have done. The Emperor Akbar tried to get the books. He plundered India for them. But he died in ignorance of their whereabouts, although in those days some of them were kept within an hour's walk of Akbar's palace."

"Then *you* know where they are now!" Cyprian said excitedly. He could keep neither lips nor fingers still.

"My friend, I have just returned from extensive travels. I know *nothing*, beyond that the Nine sent for me and that I have been commissioned to perform a duty."

"Where are the Nine now?" Cyprian asked him, and Ghandava laughed.

"We wander from the subject," he replied. "These spurious Nines, whose organization you describe, have existed for centuries. They seek the undiscoverable secrets of the Unknown Nine. Their own secrets are mere hypnotism, mere trickery, mere evil hidden under the mask of Kali-worship, Thuggee and what not else. In the place of Knowledge they have grafted superstition, and in place of Truth, fear. They rule by fear, over- and under-riding the law by keeping the custodians of public peace in a constant state of fear of them. They have nothing whatever in common with the Nine who have commissioned me, and who are altruists—simply."

"Nonsense!" exclaimed Cyprian. "I mean—pardon me, I beg to differ! If they were altruists, and have the knowledge you pretend, they would reveal it to the world—"

"For the world's undoing!" Ghandava added dryly.

"How can the world be undone by useful knowledge?" King objected.

"Or how can there be too much treasure?" asked Chullunder Ghose. "Let loose even the dogs of war—devouring monsters!—and give me money enough—This babu will buy the victory for either side! If your principals have all that money, why didn't they buy the best side in the late fracas of 1914 and finish the business swiftly? Ouch! King *sahib*, I beseech you, lay the pole down!"

"Why do they not now buy India's liberty?" Narayan Singh demanded. "The British tax-payer—"

"Who ever purchased liberty?" Ghandava answered. "Liberty is earned, or it ceases to exist!"

"Then what are they hoarding gold for?" Ramsden demanded.

"Altruism?" asked Cyprian with raised eyebrows and wrinkled

forehead, looking over his spectacles. "Is there no need of altruism at this moment?"

Ghandava fell back on his smile.

"You assume too much," he answered. "Altruism has nothing to do with selfishness."

"Then your people are not altruists in any recognized sense of the word!" snapped Cyprian.

The old man was getting more and more impatient, possibly because he felt the control of the situation and of the party slipping from his grasp. Yet it was he who had introduced Ghandava. There was not much he could do about it.

"You mean their altruism is not comprehensible to you?" Ghandava answered. "You assume that the gold that has disappeared for centuries is all accumulated in one place and lying useless. I think I can assure you that is not so."

"But the knowledge?" King objected.

"The books!" insisted Cyprian.

Ghandava smiled again and pointed a finger at Cyprian.

"You, my friend, would burn the books if you could find them! Akbar, if he had found them, would have used the knowledge they contain for the carving of new empires. Those who burned the library of Alexandria would have done at least that. Those whom you call 'my people' have their own interpretation of the books and their own opinion of their proper use."

"But knowledge," King objected again, "if knowledge is true it can't do harm, can it?"

"No? Of what is dynamite the product? Of no knowledge?" Ghandava retorted. "Was it ignorance that built the big guns and invented poison-gas?"

"The money! The money! Where is the money?" Chullunder Ghose exclaimed excitedly.

"Gold is not money. Gold is gold," Ghandava replied. "Tell me—is humanly comprehensible energy continuous without fuel? Energy must be released—is that not so? Water—coal—petroleum—the tides— harnessing, you call it. Did it never strike you there is more energy contained in a ton of gold than in a million tons of coal? Does that open any vistas? Do you see that to squander gold as money would be only to debauch the world, which is already too debauched, whereas gold's energy released in proper ways might change the very face of nature?

I am telling you no secrets. All the chemists know what I am hinting at. They don't know how to release the energy from gold or uranium or thorium, that's all."

"And you?" They chorused the question. He ignored it.

"These Nines, who are variously disguised as anarchists and Kali-worshipers, know very well that the day of gold *as money* is past. Paper based on gold is the present medium. Paper serves the purpose. Presently the gold will go—as money. It is then that its real potency will be discovered. *These three coins that I hold in my hand contain sufficient energy to blow the whole of Delhi instantly into smithereens.* Can you imagine what might happen if the wrong individuals should learn the secret of releasing that energy?"

"Inform the right ones then!" suggested Cyprian, with an intonation not quite innocent of sneer.

"Who are *they?*" asked Ghandava. "Governments? They would use the knowledge to annihilate defenseless nations. Scientists? They would incorporate, and then subdue the world into a new commercial slavery. The. churches?"

He turned to Cyprian.

"You—your church, my friend, would burn the books containing the secret knowledge—that is by your own admission. And tell me: which of the other churches would you be disposed to trust?"

"Well, what do you propose to do with the gold, or the energy released from it, or the secret knowledge?" Grim demanded.

"That, my friend, is fortunately not my province!" Ghandava answered, chuckling. "Have you money in your purse?"

Grim nodded.

"Do you know arithmetic?"

He nodded again.

"Some languages? A little natural science? A reputation possibly? Some skill in diplomacy perhaps? A little self acquaintance, worth more than all the rest? And the sum-total of all that is your capital?"

Grim nodded.

"What do you propose to do with it?"

Grim grinned, beginning to see the point.

"Is that my business?" asked Ghandava. "It is every man's own business what he does with the knowledge that he knows! It is the business of those who keep the ancient secrets to say what they will do with them. As long as they keep the secrets—"

"I am like a flat balloon!" Chullunder Ghose broke in. "Oh grief, why art thou part of me! I who was all optimism—how my buoyancy solidifies and bears me down! I saw a pyramid of gold. Necessitous by force of *Karma*,* how I thanked the gods! And now this holy *guru* takes the pyramid away and gives us energy! Oh energy! You jade! I love you not! My belly aches for money and a long rest! Ow! King sahib—please!"

"But if others steal the secret—" Jeremy suggested.

Ghandava hesitated. If guesswork had a chance of uncovering his thoughts, he was speculating whether it was safe to continue. He seemed most afraid on Cyprian's account. They say, with how much truth outsiders never know, that information won by any of his cloth is the property of all of his superiors on demand—and they are a goodly number.

However, Ghandava bound none of them by oath. Instead—again if guesswork's aim was true—he limited himself to explanations that would not explain, and to statements capable of more than one interpretation. That is the ancient and accepted way. All prophets and all great teachers have adopted it in self-defense.

"I, too, am on the Wheel," he said, pacing the floor between them like an old sea-captain on the poop. "I serve my little purpose in the great design, and thereafter disappear. Within my own sphere I am useful; outside it helpless. You recall? You came to me, asking advice and assistance."

"We've heard some bad advice," said Cyprian with the deliberate rudeness that old age claims to justify.

Ghandava took no notice of it. He even avoided the odious alternative of offering the other cheek self-righteously. Not even a fly, departing on the wing, could have been less recognized than Cyprian's remark.

"You have a plan, I suppose?" he suggested.

He addressed them all, but they all looked at Cyprian; for it was he who had been interrupted while laying down the lines of a plan, in his own place, previous to the holocaust of books. He seized the opportunity to resume the reins.

"I had a very good plan," he said peevishly. "I proposed just now that we let a prisoner go, but you have hidden him somewhere."

Again Bhima Ghandava refused to take offense. An old man's querulousness seemed to mean no more in his philosophy than the

---

* The law that the sins of former lives inevitably must be met in this and future ones.

barking of dogs a mile away. The absolute indifference to petulance offended Cyprian more than anger might have done and his feeble old hands fidgeted more nervously than ever on the chair-arms.

Jeremy, observing more intently than the others, crossed over and sat beside him. Cyprian laid a hand on his shoulder and ceased trembling. He was always more at ease with Jeremy to lean on.

"Suppose you tell the plan," Ghandava suggested, sitting back in one of the deep armchairs.

In that attitude you could imagine him in rooms at Oxford or on a grass-bank under a big tree taking part in a village council. In fact you could imagine him doing almost anything except starting trouble.

Cyprian, seeming to draw strength from Jeremy, obliged himself to smile; but he was plainly subduing passion.

"Had I known, Ghandava, that you are connected with the Nine Unknown, I never would have come here. You *know* that," he said, shaking his head at him.

"Yes, I know it," said Ghandava. "That is why I never told you, friends though we have been. But now that you are here and know the fact, suppose we make the best of it?"

Ghandava was talking at the others now, *through* Cyprian. It was growing clear that Cyprian had made his mind up to withdraw. Ghandava, realizing that, was equally determined not to lose the men who, by an accident, had come within his orbit.

"The best?" said Cyprian squeakily. "You tell me you are employed by the Nine—in their *confidence*—and you ask me to tell you my plan for obtaining knowledge of them, and perhaps for capturing their books!"

Ghandava continued smiling, but if he had looked superior he would have lost the good-will of every man in the room, especially Jeremy. He was not aggressive; not on the defensive. He was more like a counsel called in to pass judgment on a problem, seeking the solution as he listened.

"You speak as if you had the *right* to the Nine's books," he answered quietly. "They would dispute that. From certain knowledge I assure you there is nothing on earth more impossible than for you to discover where the books are. You cannot even prove that the books exist!"

"Have you ever seen them?" Cyprian asked him dryly, suddenly motionless, watching under lowered, wrinkled lids.

Ghandava laughed.

"I have seen *some* books. How shall I know to which of them you refer?"

"*All* of them!" snapped Cyprian.

"My friend, I will tell you something," said Ghandava. "There are hundreds of thousands of books, each one of which would come within your definition. There are libraries in crypts beneath the desert sands, that represent the knowledge of nations that disappeared before Atlantis took shape. There are books whose very alphabet *fewer* than nine men know, written in a language compared to which Sanskrit is a *modern* tongue. There are individual books among those that contain more true scientific knowledge than all the works of all the modern chemists and metallurgists put together. If you had all the books you would have no building big enough to contain a *tenth* of them. And if you were twenty years old you would not have time to learn the wisdom contained in one book—which book, however, it is not within your power to find."

He spoke as one having authority. But he said no more than is commonly said in the East among men who look deeper than the daily press for fact, and who listen to the real news of the hemispheres that susurrates below or else above the bleatings and bull-boastings of such as sell what they call learning in the market-place. Cyprian, King and Grim, for instance, were not in the least surprised. Narayan Singh nodded. Chullunder Ghose assented less silently:

"I have prayed to the gods; I have even bestowed expensive presents on the gods, depriving unfortunate family of necessaries to that end. I have promised the gods, so often and so suppliantly that they cannot help having heard—if there are any gods! I have even told the priests the gist of my intentions, same being probable secret of failure down to date. If I can find *one* such said ancient book and sell same to American Museum, U. S. A., I will found orphanage with half of proceeds, and no questions asked as to orphans' pedigree. Our Ali of Sikunderam may—Ouch! King *sahib*, please apply pole to proper purposes!"

"So it amounts to this," Ghandava said. "If your purpose is to rid the world of an evil, I am at your services in so far as I agree with you what evil is. If you hope to intrude on those who have commissioned me, I must merely look on. I may possibly prevent you."

"Let's make a bargain then," suggested Jeremy.

But Bhima Ghandava had no appetite for bargains.

He made a grimace more suggestive of contempt than anything he had said or done since they entered his house.

"I will do what I *can* do, freely," he answered.

"We're your guests. Outline what you will do," Ramsden suggested.

Cyprian agreed to that. There was nothing to lose by listening to what Ghandava might intend. But the trouble was that he intended not to give away his hand.

"Father Cyprian had a plan," he said, and folded his arms, leaning back to listen.

"Go on, Pop!" urged Jeremy. "Lead what you've got! Make him play higher or pass!"

Cyprian yielded, not as the men of the world yield, but with a sort of dry, implied assertion that surrender is a victory.

"We all discussed a plan—we had agreed—hadn't we?—Jeremy to visit Benares—disguised—Chullunder Ghose to talk for him—Jeremy to be dumb *fakir*—do tricks—Take the coins of course—Display them—By their means attract attention of these rascals—"

"Attention of the *rascals*—excellent!" Ghandava commented.

"The others," Cyprian continued, "Ramsden, King, Grim, Ali of Sikunderam and all his sons—go to Benares, too—disguised as Hindus, naturally. Watch. When Jeremy attracts attention of the enemy, they watch—they watch. You understand me? Very well then. That was the plan: To watch, and then track down the enemy."

"I will help you to watch and track down the enemy," Ghandava said, as a man might who is promising to vote the party ticket.

He was firm, and enthusiastic. Everyone in the room believed him, even Cyprian. But to believe is not perforce to consent.

"You understand? For my part, I have made no promises," said Cyprian.

"I have asked none," said Ghandava. "What I have to give, I give. When do you propose to start? How will you travel? Where will you stay when you reach Benares? I will do this for you," he said, unfolding his arms and sitting forward. When he opened his mouth suddenly in that way the outlines of his jaw and chin showed distinctly through the gray beard and altered his whole appearance. He seemed to age enormously—to be as old as Cyprian—to know, from having suffered it, the whole of earth's iniquity—and yet to have retained (perhaps, though, to have gained) a knowledge and assurance beyond human means of measuring. When he moved his mouth again, enumerating what he would do, the look of old-age vanished and he was almost on apparent footing with Ramsden and Narayan Singh.

"I will do these things for you; I will arrange for your protection—"

Cyprian snorted, as if he had taken snuff.

"How?" he demanded. "How?"

But Ghandava waved aside the interruption.

"I will give you permission to say you represent the Nine Unknown. That will lend authority to Mr. Jeremy's claims to be a wizard!"

"We might *say* we represented the Nine Unknown without *any one's* permission!" Cyprian objected acidly.

"You *might*. But without permission it would be *very dangerous*," Ghandava assured him; and again there was none in the room, not even Cyprian, who doubted.

Chullunder Ghose shivered and gasped like a fish out of water, and Narayan Singh, squatting on the floor, leaned forward that his eyes might look closer into Ghandava's.

Not that Ghandava minded any of those demonstrations. He seemed oblivious to praise as well as criticism of himself.

"I will provide you with means of traveling to Benares," he went on.

"Oh for the wings of the spirit! Give us but a blessing, great Mahatma, and we shall be in Benares in a minute! Put power on us! Ouch!"

King returned the window-pole to its place at rest beside him, and Ghandava continued, ignoring the babu's rhapsody:

"I will provide quarters for you in Benares. And a man shall guide you into secret places."

"What in return for all this?" Jeff demanded.

"Nothing in return. I am proposing to help you in tracking down your enemy," Ghandava answered.

"Protection? You spoke of protection," said Cyprian. "How do you propose to do that? Black art?"

Ghandava smiled at him.

"The enemy will use black art," he answered. "The enemy will destroy itself. At intervals it does. The hue and cry accumulates, and grows so great at last that the Nine protect themselves by letting ever such a little knowledge pass out into the hands of the enemy. They try to use it, and they die. There was Sennacherib—you have heard of him and his army of Assyrians? I could cite you fifty instances from history, and for every one such there are a thousand that men never heard of."

"Then you mean, your Nine masters preserve their precious secrets merely for their own protection?" Cyprian demanded.

Mention of Sennacherib's army and other Old Testament victims of imponderable forces roused him like a watch-dog guarding against trespassers. That was his field.

"No, but they protect the secrets, and the secrets them," Ghandava answered. "I will show you why. If one of you will open the big album on that small table by the door you will find in it more than ten thousand newspaper clippings in more than twenty languages, every one of which is a direct statement of what the nations are preparing to do in the next war. You will see mention of gases that will decimate whole cities in an hour; or submarines that will render the seas not navigable, and so starve peoples; of airplanes carrying two-ton bombs loaded with such poison as will penetrate all known substances and kill men in agony; of guns with a range exceeding a hundred miles; of newly discovered methods of vibration that will shake whole cities into ruins; and of many other things, some even worse than those.

"*The forces that the Nine Unknown can use are infinitely greater than any those war-devising idiots have dreamt of!* Shall they trust their secret to the daily press? And shall they not defend themselves and their secret against the ambitious rogues who stop at nothing to possess themselves of what, if they had it, would put the whole world at their mercy? And they have no mercy, you know," he added reminiscently, as if he had investigated and could bear true witness.

"Then you're asking us to track down the enemy so that you may pounce on him? It that it?" asked Ramsden.

"My friend, I ask nothing!" Ghandava answered, leaning forward, laying both hands on his thighs for emphasis. "Those who have commissioned me, forever give without exacting or accepting a return."

Narayan Singh nodded gravely.

"*Sahib*," he said, "that is a true speech. That is how a man may know that he deals with the *Buddhas** and not with rogues. They give, because they *will give*, and ask nothing because none can recompense them."

Cyprian snorted.

"How about the gold then—the gold they hoard like misers?"

---

* The word is best known as the title of the Lord Gautama or Buddha. It means "the enlightened."

"Did *you* ever part with gold to them?" Ghandava answered, with the first hint of tartness he had allowed to escape him.

Then, as if regretting that lapse, he crossed the floor and laid a hand on Cyprian's on the chair-arm.

"My old friend, I will never harm you—never!" he said quietly. "You would like to rid the world of certain knowledge—or rather of the possibility of learning it, for the world is ignorant of its very nature. Well, those who have commissioned me are just as careful to keep that knowledge hidden. The difference is that we preserve it—you would burn it—that is all. There is no chance of its becoming known. But if you will be patient you shall glimpse what might happen if even a millionth part of the knowledge were made known to men not ready for it. You shall see a wonder, and then guess, if you will, what Caesar—who crucified a million Spaniards simply because he had the power and the inclination—would have done with poison gas! Thereafter, consider what the world to-day would do with even one of the secrets kept by those whom you have heard of as The Nine Unknown!"

Cyprian's eyes were not dry, but a strong light came through the window; he pretended it was that. His lips moved silently. Then—

"I will burn all their books I can find!" he said in eighty-year falsetto.

"All you can find," Ghandava answered, smiling.

"I will not go to Benares," Cyprian announced.

He was trembling violently. He looked almost incapable of going home.

"Stay in my house. Search my library for forbidden volumes!" Ghandava urged him.

Cyprian stood up, steadying himself on Jeremy's arm, then brushing Jeremy aside.

"These shall go!" he said. "To Benares! They shall go—and shall see. And if they see books, they shall bring them—bring them back—back to me. I will burn what they bring! Ghandava says he makes no demands. These made me a promise. All the books they find are mine to do with as I please!"

He looked about him, as if expecting to be contradicted. But it was true, they had made that promise. None answered.

"Now, make whatever plans you like!" said Cyprian, sitting down.

Jeff was still pondering the same perplexity, revolving it and overturning all the possibilities to find what lay beneath, just as he would have explored a mineral prospect.

"I don't understand yet," he objected, thrusting his lower jaw forward, meaning to understand if it took all day. "You ask nothing from us? You ask us to go to Benares, don't you?"

"No," Ghandava answered. "You were going to Benares."

"What do you want us to do when we get there?" Jeff demanded.

"Nothing!" said Ghandava. "Yet your purpose was—in going there—I think—to get in touch with and to undo—will the word serve?—then to undo an organization *calling itself* the Nine Unknown. I have offered to help."

"You say that it *isn't* the Nine Unknown," Jeff objected.

"Are you less intent on that account?" Ghandava asked. "When you came this morning you were anxious for an issue with your enemy. You have felt the teeth and talons of the underlings. You asked me for help in discovering the captains. I will help."

"You propose to take advantage of us?" Jeff suggested. But his smile withdrew the sting.

"No more than you of me," Ghandava answered. "We go the same way. Let us march together. There will never be a stage of the proceedings at which you are not at liberty to withdraw."

"Accept that!" ordered Cyprian, pursing his lips up, nearly rising to his feet again, and sitting down.

They accepted, one by one, each meeting Ghandava's gaze and nodding. That was the nearest they came to a pledge at any time.

"And, now," Ghandava said, "we may as well bring in the prisoner again."

Almost before the last word left Ghandava's lips Chullunder Ghose squealed delightedly. Ghandava rang no bell. No gong announced his pleasure. Yet, exactly as he gave the wish expression the door at the end of the room opened wide and the green-lined *chela* entered, leading the prisoner as easily as a farm-hand leads a bull.

"Did you see that? *Sahibs*, did you notice—"

King prodded the babu into breathless silence. The prisoner turned with his back to the window and faced Ghandava, who observed him like a professor of entomology considering a wasp, not unkindly, almost with familiarity, wholly curious. The bronze man seemed no longer to be hypnotized.

"What shall be done with you?" Ghandava asked.

The prisoner smiled loathsomely—a brute unable to see plain motives. "You can do nothing with me! Your law is you may not shed blood," he answered.

"If I let you go, will you let these friends of mine go in peace to Benares?"

The bronze man hesitated. Then a smile of evil cunning added to the coarseness of his lips, and he drew himself up with an effort to seem princely.

"Yes," he said in Hindi—arrogant, according favors. "That is granted."

"Go then!" said Ghandava; and the green-lined *chela* led the giant out.

"Sleep now. You all need sleep," Ghandava said, and none, not even Cyprian, objected when he showed them to cool rooms within thick walls where silence and soft mattresses held promise of delight. They all slept, saving Grim, who lay awake and thought of Ali of Sikunderam alone in the office with a prisoner.

XVII

"There will be no witnesses— say that and stick to it!"

Unity is the profoundest law. Man, attempting little bush-league innovations imitates unconsciously the Infinite. So the custom is the same in Naples, or Palermo, or Chicago—Pekin—Delhi—Teheran—Jerusalem—who wages a vendetta does so on his own account, at his own risk, and he recognizes no higher law than his own will.

Police—all governments—are off-side—enemies in common, whom foes should unite to defeat. Whoso calls in the police is despicable in the eyes of friend and enemy alike.

And there is another rule, almost universal throughout nature. The unusual, the unexpected, the unconventional are fighting cues. The sparrow with white feathers, the man with new ideas, the fellow whose weapons are not *en règle*, alike must meet intense resentment. Fists in a land where daggers are the rule, are more heretical than ragtime in a synod. Heresy is provocation.

So there came to Ali of Sikunderam, in the office up the alley in the Chandni Chowk, a woman—veiled. Men say that was nothing exceptional in his experience. Seven sons by seven mothers are excuse for that witticism on which slander feeds, and scandal is self-multiplying—very breath in the nostrils of the scandalized. Nevertheless, it was nothing unusual for a veiled woman to be seen in that neighborhood. Scores—hundreds of them threaded the alley daily. None paid attention to this one as she climbed the crowded stairs, although that may have been partly because observant eyes—and in India all eyes are observant—might have noticed that several men in rather dingy yellow robes were watching her possessively from up and down the alley. No wise man insists on trouble in such circumstances.

She was veiled when she knocked at the office door. But the instant Ali opened she threw back the veil, as if she knew whom she would find in there and what means was the best for holding his attention. Certainly she seized it on the instant.

"Queen of all pearls! Pearl among queens!" he said, staring at her.

She being alone, and he well armed, there was nothing about her that he needed to fear; and there was much he found no difficulty in admiring.

She was full-lipped, heavy-breasted, and her long, black, oily hair was coiled in thick ropes that resembled snakes. She had full, bold eyes like Gauri's, whom Ali had thought of honoring with his feudal attentions until her house was burned, which made her not worthwhile. And she wore the same air of worldly wisdom and of tolerance for the world's too-little virtue that had made of Gauri such an easy lady to hold converse with. She was Gauri's size—height—so like Gauri that the floors of memory swept Ali's caution out from under him. But her golden ornaments were heavier than Gauri's. The emeralds in her ears were worth as much as all of Gauri's fortune before da Gama looted her. And in one other aspect she was noticeably different.

There was a swelling under her left jaw that looked almost like the mumps, only it was more inflamed and discolored. Someone or something had struck her, not only recently but terrifically hard.

"Queen of the queens of Paradise, who hit thee?" he demanded.

He spoke tenderly—for him; but the Asian ardor blazed behind his eyes, and no woman not on adventure bent would have faced him without blenching. Ali, however, did not consider that. Men think less alertly after going long without sleep.

"Am I in paradise?" he asked. "Art thou a houri?"

She smiled at him. It may be that the smile cost agonies, on account of the swollen jaw, but she answered in a soft, low voice that thrilled with the suggestion of mystery, speaking—marvel of all marvels!—in his own tongue, the guttural, hoarse Pushtu of Sikunderam.

"Prince of princes! Captain of the thousands!"

Perfect! That is exactly the way to speak to a Northern gentleman. Ali stroked his beard and rearranged the riding-angle of his Khyber knife.

"Djereemee-Rass *sahib*, King *sahib*, Jimgrim *sahib*, Ramsden *sahib*, all send greeting. With the sons of queens, who call thee sire, your honor's honor should follow me to a certain place."

She smiled again, and Ali stroked his beard until it shone under his hand as if from brushing.

"Who struck thee?" he demanded for the second time.

"A man in the street—a *badmash**—a man in yellow—one of those who worship Kali," she answered.

---

* Low-down scoundrel.

Ali hesitated. Natural suspicion stirred a naturally shrewd wit, and memory, on the verge of sleep, awoke with one of those starts that bring the recent panorama of events in a flash before the mind. That set him thinking. She had asked him to bring his sons; therefore they had not been waylaid yet. She had a tiny spot of crimson on her forehead, where the caste-mark of the Kali sect had been recently rubbed out. She, if one of the enemy, might know the names of all the white men in the party, because of the five-pound note in da Gama's hat-band, signed by Jeremy, and the sheet of paper in da Gama's pocket on which the Portuguese had jotted down terms—and undoubtedly names. Ali added those circumstances tip and multiplied the total into certainty: She sought to decoy him in order to force from him news of his friends' plans and present whereabouts.

"Queen of cockatrices!" he spat out suddenly, and slapped her with his flat hand over the jaw where the swelling was.

He slapped as he augured, shrewdly. Pain was so sudden and intense that for a minute she could not scream, but lay on the office floor holding both hands to her face and rocking herself. He stooped over her, according to his own account to feel for weapons, but made a commencement by twitching at an emerald ear-stud, and the speed with which she drew a dagger then was swifter than a snake's. He sprang clear, avoiding her upward stab by the width of the goose-flesh on his belly.

"Mother of corruption!"

She had had her chance and lost it. Whipping out his long knife he knocked her dagger spinning, and with his teeth showing clean as a hound's in a battle-laugh between the gray-shot black of beard and upper-lip he set one foot on her and pressed her to the floor.

"Mother of evil tidings! What ill-omen brought thee? Speak!"

But she would not speak, although he showed his swordsmanship, whirling his blade until it whistled within an inch of her defiant eyes. And from that he drew his own conclusions.

"So! Not alone? An escort waits—too far away to hear screams—but will come unless the she-decoy returns in time. Hah!"

He removed his foot from between her breasts and she raised herself with a hand on the floor, but he kicked her under the injured jaw again and with the same toe sent her floundering behind the desk, where the prisoner in yellow lay.

Suddenly then it occurred to him that she and the prisoner should not hold intercourse. It only takes a second for the East to tell the East the news. He pounced on her again and dragging her away, flung her across the room, bending then over the man in yellow to make sure his bonds were taut and cursing him for having dared to see what he could not help seeing.

"Allah! If I were a hard man I would tear thy tongue out to save talk! Luckily for thee my heart is wax. I am a man of mercy."

He repaid attention to the woman then, and it was time; she was creeping along the wall toward the door. He seized her by one foot and, she kicking like a caught fish, pulled her back to the farthest corner, where he tied her hand and foot with thin string meant for wrapping parcels, using the best part of a ball of the stuff, for Ali was no sailor.

The rest of his task was simple enough—and satisfying. He removed the emeralds from her ears, the gold from her neck, wrists and ankles, and every one of the jeweled brooches that fastened her outer garments.

She called him a pig of an Afghan for that, and he was in the act of gagging her by way of reprisal when another knock sounded on the office door.

He knew it was none of his sons. They had their own private code of signals. He picked up the only rug and heaped it over the woman to conceal her.

"Mother of a murrain!" he growled in Pushtu. "Does death tempt you? If so, make one sound, and die thus!"

In pantomime he showed how a Khyber knife goes in below the stomach and rips upward. Then he arranged the rug over her and turned to face the door.

"Open!" commanded someone—a stranger with a strange voice, speaking Hindu.

There was only one voice. He could only hear one man shifting his feet restlessly. He could not see through the frosted-glass panel of the door, nor through the keyhole for the key was in it.

"Who are you?" he demanded.

"A messenger. The *sahib's* sons have sent me."

That was an obvious lie. The sons of Ali of Sikunderam knew better than to instruct their furious sire by, deputy.

"How many of you?" he demanded.

"One."

But he suspected, and suspicion was unthinkable without its concrete consequence, with Ali's nerves in that state. He struck the glass panel with his knife-point and as the glass broke clapped his eye to it.

He could only see one man—a fellow in a yellow smock, apparently unarmed. He, too, used the broken pane to get a glimpse of Ali. He used it to good purpose. Drawing back suddenly he thrust a long stick through with such force that it drove Ali back on his heels and sent him reeling against the desk. And before he could recover a lean hand beneath a yellow sleeve inserted itself through the broken pane and turned the key. One man walked in, followed by five others, the last of whom closed the door behind him and stood with his back against the broken glass.

"Be swift!" said the first man. "Two belonging to us are here. A woman and a man. Where?"

But six to one, though odds enough, were no conclusive argument to Ali of Sikunderam. And there are few, who have not seen it, who are able to imagine the swiftness and the spring-steel savagery of the North at bay. All six drew knives from under their smocks, but all too late—Ali had laid out two of them, gutted and writhing in their own hot bowels, before he had as much as to guard himself. And as the third man advanced with a jump to engage, the sixth screamed; someone in the passage thrust a long knife through the broken glass and pierced him through the kidneys from behind.

The reserves had come! Now three men had to deal with Ali and with six of Ali's sons!

But they were three stern fighters, and they, too, had reenforcement.

She on the floor, whom Ali had struck and kicked and covered up, struggled—only ifrits or a sailor could explain how—from the tight-wound string, and seized a knife whose hilt was slippery with the blood of its erstwhile owner. With that she slashed the lashing on her ankles, and a yell from one of Ali's sons warned him in the nick of time that she was up on her feet and coming.

Rahman's pantomime saved him. Rahman, speechless with excitement, ducked as he, too, would have ducked if the knife had been swinging at the base of his on skull. And Ali imitated, hardly knowing what he did, guided more by telepathic instinct than by his reason. For the second time the woman's knife missed him by a hair's breadth. The back of his neck felt seared as if a hot iron had almost touched it, so close and so terrific was the woman's lunge.

But it was *her* last act, not his. The North's retort discourteous is quicker than the wild boar's jink and rip. The impulse brought her stumbling against his back and he threw her with the "chuck" they boast in Cornwall—over his shoulders, forward—caught her as she fell—thrust her like a shield with his left hand into an opponent, driving the long knife with his right into her body three times—and then slew the man behind her with a downward blow that split his skull midway to the mouth. The knife stuck in the tough bone. The men in yellow rushed him, taken in the rear themselves by Rahman and the other sons. Ali let go the Khyber knife and drew his dagger; and from that moment there was no more hope or thought of quarter—no hope for whichever side was weaker, unless interruption came. And the odds were five to two, for two of Ali's sons were down.

And who should trespass into other men's disputes in Delhi, in these days of non-cooperation and distrust? A man might yell for help the day long, and no more than tire his lungs. There is trouble without wooing it, and he who starts a fight may finish it counting on no interference from strangers.

Now the office was a shambles—blood and bowels on the floor—loose-limbed dead men yielding this and that way to the kicks of the frenzied living—grunts—low, explosive oaths—the sudden, sullen, lightning thrust and parry as the daggers struck or missed—no shouting now.—no breath for it—the stink of raw blood and the electric thrill of death's wings—thumping of feet growing fewer. No beasts fight as evilly as men.

Three of Ali's sons, including Rahman bled to death on the office floor while their sire raged like a typhoon over them, working with a dagger for room and time in which to free the long knife from his victim's skull. And then with a foot on the skull and a wrench he had it. So, not neatly, as Narayan Singh would have slain, but roughly like the butchers who cleave meat in a hurry as it hangs, he hacked the two remaining Kali-men to death, saving three sons—one so badly wounded that his only chance was in the hospital.

"And so what?" he demanded, questioning Allah it might be as he wiped his reeking blade on a victim's smock.

The two whole sons asked nothing, but proceeded to the looting, one stripping his dead brothers first of every valuable thing and the other naturally picking out the woman. Ali laughed at him.

"Fool! Am I brainless? Should I tie her and not scratch?"

He had no more breath for words. Disgust at losing three, it might be four sons in such a mean fight half-unmanned him. With a gesture he ordered the woman thrown under the rug again where he himself had hidden her, and the son obeyed. He did not really know why he ordered that. He was hardly thinking. Rather he was looking about him for a bandage for his son's wounds. Suddenly he thought that if he left the wounded son there, as he must, the presence of the woman's body might make lying difficult; and Ahmed would have to lie like history or else say nothing when relief should come. Lying is much the easier of those alternatives, to a man born north of where the Jumna bends by Dera Ghazi Khan.

"Take her out! Cover her in that!" he ordered; and the prisoner behind the desk, hearing but not seeing, made a mental note of it.

He heard, too, the grunting and heavy footsteps as the two uninjured sons picked up the rug with the woman's body and carried it out to be dumped in the unused cellar where rats would eat it, and whoever found bones might conjecture what he pleased.

Then Ali, bandaging his wounded son as carefully as circumstance permitted, gave him water and forbidden whisky from the office gallon jar, and bade him sit there with his back propped in a corner until someone should come from the Moslem hospital—to whom he should lie like a gentleman.

"These men in yellow came—broke in—found me and my brothers—attacked us murderously—and were slain by me, Ahmed son of Ali ben Ali of Sikunderam. I know not why they came, nor who they are."

That was the lie, and surely good enough for a man at death's door, in a land where a trial may take a year awaiting.

"There will be no witnesses: Say that and stick to it!" said Ali. "Beg of the *Wakf* for proper burial for thy brothers and, it may be, also for thyself!"

Then he gagged and blindfolded his prisoner, released his legs and hurried him out between the two uninjured sons through the door at the end of the passage into the warehouse, where all was gloom among the bales and none asked questions in any event. Thence he sent one son running to find a man, whose word was good with the Moslem hospital, and sat down on a bale of aloes to consider.

The problem was how now to get in touch with King, Grim, Jeremy and Ramsden. He was not afraid of being caught, because only his friends had keys to the warehouse door, nor afraid of consequences if he should be caught, since in a land of lies, who lies the best is king. Dead men are not efficient witnesses, and Ahmed had been well trained. But the prisoner was an embarrassment, and he did not care to dispose of him without instructions.

He removed the stuffy blindfold from the prisoner, not from merciful but mercenary reasons. The drugs in the bales all about them were pungent and exceeding dry. He had a thought, that became him as soldier of fortune.

"Are you thirsty?" it occurred to him to ask.

Unwilling to admit it, for he guessed the motive, the prisoner shook his head. Ali gravely doubted him. He sought a bale of capsicum, and pulling loose a handful crushed the stuff to powder under the prisoner's nose. If he had not been thirsty previous to that, his condition now was indisputable.

"You shall drink when you tell me where my friends are!" he said bluntly.

"I don't know that," the prisoner answered.

"By Allah, but you do! You saw the fellow with the green-lined cloak, who took my friends the *sahibs* and the Sikh away with him. You recognized him, for I saw your eyes. Tell me where he lives."

The prisoner coughed up most of the torturing dust.

"I will tell you when you tell me what you did with Her," he answered, the water running from his eyes. "Where have you hidden her?"

"I killed her," Ali answered, so promptly and frankly, that the prisoner was sure he lied.

"Let me speak with Her, and I will tell you anything you want to know," he answered.

"Answer my question. Moreover write an order for a thousand rupees payable to my son, who will collect the money and bring water back with him. Then you shall drink," said Ali; and having thrown more dust of capsicum into the prisoner's lips and nostrils, he settled down to bide his time and meditate.

Sleep was overtaking him again. He had to wrestle with his senses. Thoughts shaded into one another, and the outlines blurred until a half-dream and a fact were indistinguishable. He could not guess what capital to make of the prisoner's belief that She—whoever *she* was— was still living. He had slain her, that was sure.

The prisoner wished to speak with her, that was also sure. Ergo, she meant something to the prisoner; but what? And what might it all mean to his friends the *sahibs*? Ali was forever thoughtful for his friends, when his own immediate and perhaps prospective needs had had attention. How he wished he had brains like Jimgrim *sahib*, or King *sahib's* experienced wisdom, or Jeremy *sahib's* swift intuition, or even the ability to grind an answer out as Rammy *sahib* did, seeming to compel his intellect to work by brute force! He tried that, but solutions would not come.

He heard his son return and listened dully to the account of how the ambulance was coming presently. He heard the ambulance arrive, as in a dream, and heard the tramping and excited comments of the men, who found all those corpses and one unconscious Hillman in the office, and were suitably impressed. He heard the tramping and the voices die away, and later, as the heat increased, sent one of his two sons for water, which he drank in the prisoner's presence. Then, giving orders to his sons to increase the prisoner's thirst by all means possible, he fell asleep and dreamed, according to his own account of it, of emeralds and wild-eyed women and of a great high-priest who came and blessed him, making signs in the air as he did so with an unsheathed Khyber knife.

He awoke with a start, and stared into a strange face!

"Is this he?" a quiet voice asked, and then he heard a voice he would have known in any crowd as Jimgrim's:

"Sure. Say, Ali? What did you keep the prisoner dry for? And what does the locked-up office and broken glass mean? Bhima Ghandava *sahib* and I have had to come the back way because of a police guard on the stairs and in the passage. Why?"

Ali explained and, drawing the two aside, told partly why he gave the prisoner no drink.

"He believes SHE still lives," he added, wondering what Grim would make of it.

Grim glanced at Ghandava.

"Loose him and let him go!" advised Ghandava, almost instantly.

"By gad, sir—by the Big Jim Hill—I do believe you're right!" Grim answered.

"Ye are mad!—both mad!" said Ali, staring stupidly. "Good enough. Let the prisoner go!" commanded Grim.

XVIII

"He has whatever she had!"

It was Grim, returning from the Chandni Chowk that afternoon, awaking them one by one, who summoned another conference in Ghandava's great, cool library. Ghandava had disappeared, but the smell of artful cookery ascended from below-stairs, and the green-lined *chela* kept himself in evidence at intervals, incurious and yet alert. He never seemed to listen, nor to keep from listening, but hovered in and out like a house-mouse busy with affairs behind the scenes. Once he was gone for a whole hour.

"Giving my imagination utmost creeps!" as Chullunder Ghose remarked.

"Ghandava fears only this," said Grim: "The prisoner may be too incensed by Ali's ill-treatment. He was a wabbler to start with. You remember, when we caught him in the minaret he was flinching from doing murder in Benares. He'll return to his superiors, because there's nowhere else for him and he may flop hack altogether. He'll say the snake-woman is alive and that we've hidden her. His murderous instincts may have been so stirred up by Ali that he'll volunteer to identify and kill us all as opportunity permits."

"Why should Ghandava worry about our getting killed?" asked Jeremy, unimpressed.

"He's in with us," said Grim.

"Where is he?"

"Gone. Benares!"

Jeremy whistled. Again he saw adventure coming to him on the wing down-wind, and liked it.

"You see," said Grim, "they won't rest while they think we've got that woman. They'll not look for her corpse while they think she's alive, and they'll probably try to kill us one by one until we give her up."

"Tell 'em she's dead then, and where to find the body," Jeff suggested. "Where's Ali and where did he hide it?"

"No!" Grim answered instantly. "Let's get a woman to represent her! Keep them tracking us—you get me? Let them think their woman has swapped horses—joined us. One man we've let go will give them ground for that idea. The other—the big one—will tell 'em we're cahooting with the Nine Unknown—"

"How'll he know that?" Jeff objected.

Grim signified the green-lined *chela*, who had come in through one door, apparently to set a book in place, and walked out through the other at the rear.

"He showed him the way out. He told him that," said Grim.

"Oh glorious! Oh exquisite! What ignorant West would call 'Telepathy'!" Chullunder Ghose exclaimed. "Mahatma, knowing what outcome of conference will be, *wills* that *chela* shall say thisly and do thusly! Krishna! This is—"

"Billiards!" said King, and prodded him in the stomach with the window-pole.

"I forsee fortune!" Narayan Singh announced. But what *he* means by fortune is the opportunity to use his faculties, including swordsmanship.

"Thou second-sighted butcher!" said the babu.

"*Chup!*"* commanded King.

"You see, it's this way," Grim resumed. "Ghandava knows how we hit this trail, considers we're honest, and says we're useful to his employers. We're helping to put the hat on these criminal Nines, whose hour, by his account of it, has come. He plans to reciprocate. He'll let us see what we started after."

"The gold?" demanded Ramsden.

"So I understand him."

"Books! Tut-tut! The books!" said Cyprian, emerging with a big book in his hands from behind the detached case.

But Grim shook his head. Ghandava had said nothing about showing where the secret books were kept. Cyprian shrugged his shoulders, losing interest, and if he cared that men had died he did not show it. Probably he wanted not to seem to know too much.

"Where's Ali?" Ramsden asked again.

"Gone with two sons in search of Gauri. She looks enough like the woman of the snakes to pass for her in a pinch with the lights turned low. At any rate, she's our lone chance," Grim answered.

"Pooh!" said King. "She'll funk it."

"Broke. House burned. Past the bloom of youth. Funk nothing!" Grim retorted. "She'll jump at the hope of a *lakh* of rupees."

---

* Shut up!

"Who'll pay her the *lakh?*" wondered Jeremy.

"That was the bargain we made—a *lakh* in return for her help if we find the money."

"And if we can't collect?"

"Grim, Ramsden and Ross must pay her a solatium."

"And if Ali can't find her?"

"Then the plan's down the wind."

But it was not, although Ali came within the hour and swore that neither he nor either of his sons could find the woman.

"She is doubtless already in the household of a priest," he swore resentfully. "I could have scared the fool! By Allah! She would have obeyed if I had found her!"

"Oh, my God! *Hinc illae lacrimae!*" remarked the babu, voicing the collective gloom. "We get a mental glimpse of gold and lo, it vanishes physically with the veil of an immodest woman!"

But they were reckoning again without the green-lined *chela*. Fastidious, ascetic, handsome, one would have selected him no more than a church verger to know Gauri's whereabouts. Yet he came in smiling—said they should be getting ready—and offered to find Gauri soon enough.

"For I have means within means," he explained, without explaining.

"Get me a carriage. Send me home!" commanded Cyprian.

But that was vetoed instantly. The battle in the office was as sure to cause investigation as a fire does heat. Cyprian might have been seen passing in and out on several occasions, and if inquiry should lead to his house there were the furnace and the ashes of burned books to excite suspicion further.

"Stay here, Pop, until we come back from Benares, or our bargain's off!" said Jeremy.

"You mean—you mean?"

"If you leave this house before we return, and we find books, we'll keep 'em!"

"Take the padre-*sahib* with us!" urged Narayan Singh. "He is old and little. Somewhere we can hide him."

Behind the old priest's back the green-lined *chela* shook his head, disparagingly. But there was no need. Cyprian, loaded down with more than weight for age, would have refused that anyhow. Nor did his empty nest, with its secret squirrel-horde of books gone, attract him any more than the prospect of answering awkward questions. There would be no servant—no tidings—none of the associations that had made the place worthwhile.

"I will stay here," he said simply, and returned, black book in hand, behind the bookcase.

Then came the game of getting ready. Little, little details are the nemesis of dams, designs and men. They had to think of all the details of manner and habit, and they ended up by lamp-light, weary, with the green-lined *chela* looking on. Then, after supper in the room below, it was all to do over, for Gauri came with her maid and drilled them, while Ali snored and dreamed of vengeance on every man in India who had worn, did wear, or ever should wear a yellow smock; and it happened thus that their edifice of make-believe was crowned—pluperfect.

For Gauri was a pauper. Shabby clothes were all she had, so she and the maid, whose lack of fortune was involved in hers, were as sharp-eyed and hungry for a chance as adjutants* at dawn.

"How did you come here?" Ramsden wondered, when they paused between rehearsals.

Gauri glanced at the snoring Ali, shuddered at his long knife, and explained:

"They said he—that one—looked for me. I was afraid. His knife is his god. Better trust one who worships his belly. Better trust Chullunder Ghose! I ran and hid. But another in a green-lined cloak came, saying Ali wanted me in behalf of a *sahib* in the Street of Shah Jihan. One who overheard him told me, and I went to see. There a man with a caste-mark such as I never saw met me and brought me hither. That is how I came. Now—ye say Ali slew that woman whom ye wish me to resemble? Slew her without witnesses?"

They nodded, waiting. Something was in the wind, for her eyes shone.

"Pay me for my services whatever jewelry she had!"

"But—" Jeff Ramsden's thoughts were a bar behind the rest as usual. She interrupted him.

"*He* has whatever *she* had," she said simply.

She had cast her die, and she was a gambler heart and soul. Nothing—no argument could change her once the stakes were down; and she had named the stakes—her neck against whatever Ali's loot amounted to!

---

* An enormous bird protected in India as a scavenger.

TALBOT MUNDY

So Ali had to wake up, she protesting that the best way would have been to loot him while he slept. Grim did the explaining, taking all for granted, to save time.

"Ali, there is an argument. You settle it. One says, whoever finds this gold should have the whole of it; the others, that all should share and share in any case. What say you?"

And if the North loves one thing it is playing Solomon, pronouncing wise decisions, justice in the abstract being one thing and according it another.

"We being friends," said he, "what injures one is injury to all; and by Allah, what profits one should profit all of us. So we should share and share alike."

Grim looked disappointed—subtlest flattery!

"Then if I alone should of my own skill win a treasure, should you share that?" he demanded.

"By the Prophet of Allah, why not?" Ali answered, delighted to have Jimgrim on the hip. "Whatever any of us finds while our agreement lasts belongs to all, to be shared between us."

Grim might have jumped him then, but Grim was wise.

"Then could the vote of all of us dispose of the discovery of one?"

"Why certainly, by Allah, yes!" said Ali. "Was that not agreed in the beginning?"

"Then let us vote on this," said Grim: "Gauri offers her service for the jewels you took from the woman you slew in the office! Someone should propose a motion! Let us see the jewels anyhow."

Trapped—aware that he was trapped, and on the horns of his own verdict—Ali looked about him; for the East may not be made to hurry even in dilemma, having earned that right by studying dignity for thirty thousand years. He had two sons. Conceivably he might tempt Chullunder Ghose, or threaten him, and cast four votes. Omitting Cyprian, who might, or might not vote, that left the odds five to four against hint, for he knew Narayan Singh would side with his Western friends, and there was no doubt in his mind whatever what they would do.

He might refuse to show the loot. He might walk out, explaining he would think the matter over, and naturally not return. He who had lost so many sons had a right to consider himself—to recompense himself as best he could. Yet he was not quite sure of the value of his loot. The gold was heavy enough, but the ear-studs might be glass. In the long, long pause that followed Grim's question he even considered the thought of betrayal—for he was born north of Peshawar, where treason and a joke are one. But he knew that if he went to the police, then he would have to do his own explaining of perplexing matters that were best let lie. Moreover, the police might—nay, *would* search him.

And the men he faced were men. In his own storm-tempered, hillman way he loved them.

"It was knowing that myself must first comply with the decision, that I answered as I did," he said with dignity, hitching to the front beneath his shirt the leather-pouch in which he carried his own secrets. "Lo, I set example. Look! By Allah, let none say Ali of Sikunderam fell short of an agreement!"

Handful after handful he pulled out the necklace—little golden human skulls on a string of golden human hair—the bracelets—the anklets—the brooches—and the earrings last. He tossed the earrings into the midst of the heap, half-hoping none would notice them; but by the light he saw in Gauri's eyes he knew that whether they were glass or not they, too, were gone for just so much of the forever as a woman could withstand his siege.

"Lo, I have given five sons and now this!" he said with dignity. "As Allah is my witness, I give, knowing there is recompense."

"Someone should make a motion," Grim repeated.

"What I give is given," said Ali, gesturing magnificently. "I will not vote."

Ramsden picked the necklace up and weighed it in his hand.

"This ought to be enough alone," he said. "It's worth about—at least—"

"No! No! All or nothing!" Gauri screamed, and her eyes looked nearly as infernal as the woman's in the temple had done. "See! Look! The ear-studs—Kali emeralds!—none like them!" Then her voice dropped. "I must wear those—all those," she added, confidently, knowing her case was won. "The priestess' insignia! Mine! Keep your *lakh* of rupees! I choose these!"

They agreed, for they had to. Even Ali agreed to it. But his wintry eyes met hers, and she breathed uneasily as she put her head through the ugly golden necklace and the maid set the studs through the holes in the lobes of her ears.

"Each emerald a fortune!" the maid whispered. But Ali heard it.

"Aye, a fortune!" he said nodding. "Who should grudge a dowry to the queen of cows?" Which was a Hindu compliment, intentional, so understood and shuddered at. She knew the North, or rather the freebooting blades who came thence.

"Wear them! Wear them! They become thee!" Ali urged her.

So, with the jewels on and her hair arranged in heavy coils, the lady of delights—as Ali called her—looked not so unlike the priestess. All she lacked was, as Chullunder Ghose assessed it, "just a year or two of education."

The worst was that she thought a course of visiting from shrine to shrine and making little offerings to gods and goddesses in turn, along with favors to the priests, entitled her to know it all. Of men she was a shrewd enough judge. She could weigh the chance of wrath and pick a living in the trough of evil. But of women—save such women as herself—she knew scarce anything, and that distorted.

"Self, knowing women too well, can attempt conversion," said Chullunder Ghose and set to work to try to teach her how a priestess, used to the public eye and awe, would sit, and stand, and move about, and be.

Time and again she flung herself to the floor in tantrums, cursing the fat babu in the names of the whole Hindu Pantheon. Repeatedly he coaxed her back to patience, helped by the maid, who kept reciting what the emeralds were worth—pure music!—music that had charms to soothe the Gauri's breast.

"Even so they tell me chorus girls are taught to act as duchesses!" said the babu. "Failing all else shall escape to London and start academy of female manners! Watch me, Gauri—beautiful Gauri—goddess among women, watch me—walk like this!"

And in spite of stomach big enough for two men, hams that would have graced a Yorkshire hog, and a costume not intended for solemnities—his turban was pink—he walked across the room with perfect grace—Falstaff playing Ophelia, surpassing good.

She imitated him. He sighed.

"Thus, *sahiba*." None had ever called her that. The title is for wives of honest husbands, and she softened, even to the brink of tears. "You are a queen—a goddess. All know it. That is not enough, though. You, you the goddess, know it! You are not afraid of what they think. You do not *want* them thus to think. They *do* so think. You *know* they think. You are a goddess! Now, Bride of the Mountains, walk across the room again."

"Aye, Bride of the Mountains!" murmured Ali.

Chullunder Ghose had meant a pious compliment, for one of the names of the Daughter of Himavat, the Bride of Siva, Him who sits upon the peaks, is Gauri. But Ali misinterpreted, and Gauri understood. The jewelry was hers; and she was Ali's—no escape! She burst into tears again, beat on the floor with her fists, had hysterics, and obliged the poor babu to start again at the beginning.

Then the road! Old India by night in yellow smocks beneath an amber moon, with an ox-cart following, in which the women lay—a two-wheeled, painted cart with curtains, driven by the green-lined *chela* and drawn by the same two splendid Guzarati beasts well fed and rested in Ghandava's stable! The ancient gate—the guard, too sleepy to make trouble, too respectful to draw curtains, and aware of the weight of silver in shut palms—then the wide way flowing on forever between shadows so silent and drunk with color that the creaking of a wheel alone recalled a solid world.

And Jeremy—drunker than the shadows were! Full—flooded—flowing over with delight; the memory of wild Arabia awake within him and a whole unknown horizon beckoning in moonlight to adventure such as Sinbad knew! He danced. He sang wild Arab songs—as suitable as any, since an unknown tongue was all conditions called for. He flicked a long silk handkerchief with imitative skill. And the few, afraid night-farers drew aside to let the short procession pass.

Jeff Ramsden, striding like a Viking with a rod across his shoulder, meant ostensibly for vicious dogs, a calf like Samson's showing under the yellow smock, and an air of ownership. He owned the earth he trod on. Good to see.

Then King and Grim together, yellow-smocked and striding just as silently, more modern, more in keeping with the picture and matched, as it were, in the setting by Chullunder Ghose, who walked after them without enthusiasm, not needing to pretend, except to creed; pink turban gone, he, too, was in orange-yellow.

Then Narayan Singh, in yellow like the rest, a little too ostensibly unarmed. The hilt of something swinging as he strode was exaggerated by the smock that covered it, and his shadow resembled a monster's.

Then the cart. Then Ali and his two sons, not pleased with playing Hindu, looking like dark spirits of the night whom men might well avoid. Wayfarers beg rides in India even as in the West, but none did that night. None stole a ride. And the multitude, who make it their profession to extort alms by the ancient processes—who watch the highways and by day or dark flock forth like bugs to pester—not recognizing innocence, desisted.

All one night they trudged the highway with the geometrical designs of irrigation ditches glinting in the moonlight all about them; and at dawn they were offered bed and board by a Brahman, who called the green-lined *chela* "holy one." At one end of the garden-compound, of which his house formed the front, was a long shelter subdivided into stalls, in which he said it was his privilege to acquire merit by entertaining pilgrims. He asked no questions—only offered food and asked a blessing in return—so there they slept on string-cots, three to a stall, the women-folk remaining in the closed cart, angrily complaining of the heat.

Then night again and another march, the women, too, on foot; for they left the ox-cart with the Brahman—six or eight miles' walk in mellow moonlight to a wayside station, where a Hindu station-master said they honored his poor roof, and where, by dint of lies along the wire, he finally secured a whole reserved compartment for them on a through train for Benares.

XIX

"Once, when they who keep
the secrets—"

Benares! Mother Gunga, who if she would, could tell of the birth of half-a-world, lapping the steps below the *ghats*. Crimson fire and leaping flame where they cremate the dead. Moonlight on a hundred thousand heads and shoulders, as the "heathen" stand breast-deep reflected in the stream and pray for blessedness. Built on Benares! For the temples that have stood a thousand years are crumbling above foundations that were ancient cities before Hermes was Hierophant of Mysteries. Troy seven times rebuilt on Troy is but a new thing to Benares.

The train rolled in, panting at the end of awful night; and it was no more to Benares than a new bird added to the hordes of feathered scavengers.

Under the hot iron roof the train disgorged its crowd, itself impersonal, they seeking abstract bliss—an iron-age implement subserving Manu and His laws. It was no more to Benares than the flies that drone around the *ghats* at dawn.

The green-lined *chela* led, threading the swarm that checked and gathered itself, bleating for its females and its young like sheep, demanding neither food nor sleep but the view of Mother Gunga and the privilege of plunging in at sunrise.

Gauri and her maid walked beside Chullunder Ghose, both veiled.

"One sees us!" said the babu. "Let the veil fall open."

On the journey they had labored over it, cutting and stitching until if loosed it fell so perfectly that her face could be seen in profile—which was best—and be covered again instantly. Gauri saw a man in yellow staring at her, and snatched the veil together.

"He is big, and I am afraid of him!"

"Good," said the babu.

"But he saw I am afraid!"

"Better! He knows you are not a goddess! You *should* be afraid of him! Now, not knowing, he will go and say he knows, same being excellent in politics but no good when up against Jimgrim and the green-lined *chela*—latter being devil very likely, though I think not. Woman, behave fearfully! He turns again and looks."

So Gauri hid behind Chullunder Ghose's bulk, as if she were a merchant's wife out for the first time far from home. And the very tall man who had turned and looked beckoned another, shorter, nearly naked one, who came and followed the party, presently beckoning others to keep him company.

So, though they threaded a score of streets not wider than an ox-cart, turning this and that way almost incomprehensibly like ants, and entered at last a high door in a wall, which slammed behind them and was bolted and barred by someone in a cabin like a sentry-box, who performed his task unseen, they knew they were not lost to knowledge. They could hear the footsteps of the spies, who ran to tell their whereabouts to whom it might concern.

And here—in a quiet clean oasis—the green-lined *chela* seemed no longer in authority. He accepted orders from a man in white, whose bald, bare head was fleshless—skin on bone, as if it had died but still was needed by the body. Only his eyes lived, burning, down deep in the sockets. It seemed he was host.

"Introduce us. What's his name?" Grim asked.

"No name," the *chela* answered.

Only then they all remembered that the green-lined *chela*, too, had given no name, then or at any time.

"What's yours?" Grim asked him, but he laughed and shook his head.

So, failing introduction, Grim lined up the party, named them, and began to speak about Ghandava. That name, too apparently meant nothing here. The living skeleton in white took no account of it. He turned on his heel and led them indoors, into an ancient palace, nowadays as plainly furnished as a monastery, and up-stairs to the first floor. There, saying nothing, he made a gesture, signifying that the floor was theirs and, turning to the *chela*, who had followed, dismissed him with a monosyllable. The *chela* neither spoke nor displayed the least emotion, but turned and went.

Nevertheless there was an atmosphere of comfort, and even of friendliness. The man in white stood waiting by the door until silent servants brought water and a heap of clean sheets. Others brought food—bread, vegetables, milk—and then, but not till then, the man in white left them, not having said one word except to the *chela* to dismiss him, yet contriving to convey the thought that they were welcome.

"And why not welcome?" wondered Jeremy. "Bemares looks to me to need jazzing."

"My God!" Chullunder Ghose exploded.

All the long front of that floor was a veranda, cool and deep, facing the Mother of Rivers above ancient roofs. They had five separate vistas between temple domes, and down one lane of ancientry could see the granite steps, and thousands of naked men, and women veiled in lightest muslin, descending to bathe and pray; for sunrise is the holiest hour of all.

Rafts on the river's bosom swarmed with Brahmins sitting rigid in the act of meditation. Between the rafts the stream flowed spread with flowers, because none of the thousands had come empty-handed, but with garlands, loose blossoms and plaited strings of buds by way of offering:

The cooing of doves was all about them, and the music of temple-bells. The breath of Mother Gunga, who gives life and takes it, pervaded all—miasmic say the scientists, ignoring truth of a millennium. (They drink the water where the ashes of the dead are strewn, and take no hurt.) Birds everywhere, especially crows lining the ridges of temple roofs with jet black; and down the granite steps to the river's brink, between the men's bare legs and over the gaudy garments laid aside, monkeys scampering to drink, unfearful and unnoticed.

"Good!" said Jeremy, sniffing and filling his lungs.

Along a street below them caste-less bearers were carrying the dead on litters, to be bathed a last time at the river brink before being laid out on their funeral pyres. None noticed. In Benares it is life that counts, not death, and life is of the spirit not the senses. When a pilgrim shuffles off his mortal coil they make away with it and burn it swiftly, lest it hamper his efforts to climb higher.

Down another vista lay the ruins of a temple like an island in the stream; for centuries ago, when Gunga rose in spate, she underswept the walls and rooted in among them till the whole enormous building tumbled into the flood. Now a naked *fakir* stood on the highest stone of its ruins—young, with long hair on his shoulders—poised against the blue sky—

"Fancy free!" suggested Jeremy. "That lad looks happy. Nothing to wear, nor do but stand still! How many meals a day, I wonder?"

"One," said a voice; and there Ghandava stood, among them, unannounced!

"I have creeps!" remarked Chullunder Ghose.

He glanced at the door. It was locked on the inside, but Ghandava might have done that—only the lock squeaked badly, and nobody had heard it.

"There are three of them. The three are one," Ghandava went on, taking no notice of the babu's nervousness. "They stand on that stone all day and all night, taking turns, relieving one another."

"Why?" demanded Jeremy.

"It always was so," he answered. "But their vigil is nearly ended."

Ghandava was bright-eyed; not from opium, that is a feverish glow, but with the light of the ecstasy men earn, who by denying self attain self-knowledge. Harder work than laying bricks!

"Why?" demanded Jeremy a second time.

"Seek, and to every question you shall know the answer, if you seek well enough, my friend," Ghandava replied. "There are others who seek answers," he added cryptically.

Whereat Chullunder Ghose recounted how a man in yellow had set spies to follow them through the streets. Ghandava smiled.

"You are protected," he said quietly. "You shall decoy them to another place."

"For that they may attack us in the other place?" Chullunder Ghose asked in consternation.

"Because their time is come."

But Ali of Sikunderam grew angry at answers in the shape of conundrums. The Hindu garb and his losses fretted him. He paced the floor like a Hillman, which is a wholly different stride from any Hindu's, and rounded on Ghandava at the end of a turn—head and shoulders over him—his fingers on the hilt of something underneath the smock.

"By Allah, I have paid already more than all these! Five sons I have given!" he exclaimed. "Shall my life follow theirs without a reason? Name thy intentions step by step, *Mahatma-ji*!"

He used the word Mahatma as soldiers of fortune of the Middle Ages used the word monk—insultingly, and Ghandava, it seemed, knew better than to smile at him. An air of patronage night have been a spark to fire the tinder of the Hillman's wrath.

"Sit down then. I will tell you," said Ghandava, choosing a stool for himself and pausing until all were seated on chairs and mats.

He let it appear that Ali's protest was what moved him, and Ali made sly grimaces at his sons to signify that they should learn a lesson in deportment from their sire.

"Lo, we listen. By Allah, we have ears," said Ali at last importantly.

"You were seen to arrive in Benares," Ghandava began, "because the prisoner you let go from my house in Delhi forewarned those who are interested. You were seen to have this woman with you, and they are saying now that their priestess has wormed her way into your confidence, as otherwise she would surely have escaped and returned to them. Now, if one of you were to meet with one of them, and were not afraid, and should confirm that theory, taking an actual message perhaps from Gauri to them, using the formula, '*She says*'—"

"I am not afraid!" Narayan Singh said, interrupting. He stood up, and all who saw him knew he told the truth. He was afraid of neither death nor devils.

Ghandava nodded.

"I spoke to you all of the Wheel," he said quietly. "The Wheel turns and unless we are alert an opportunity is snatched or taken, for us or against us. In a place, which you shall see, the Nine have preserved for centuries a truth—knowledge of a truth, that is; for truth is like skill, unless used constantly it disappears. The time will cone, but is not yet, when that truth may be given to the world with safety. Those in whose hands the ancient secrets are, being human, have made mistakes. Knowledge in the hands of criminals and fools is worse than ignorance. Let me illustrate:

"You have heard of the scientist who, seeking without wisdom for the knowledge he could neither weigh nor measure, introduced into America a moth that killed the trees? So. Once, when they who keep the secrets thought the time had come, they entrusted to some chosen individuals instruction concerning the scope of man's mind. But the time was not ripe. They who learned were faithless and self-seeking, so that from that one secret that escaped there sprang the whole evil of witchcraft, sorcery, necromancy, black magic, hypnotism, what is now called 'mob psychology,' the black art of propaganda, and inventions that are even worse.

"Again: Surgeons and doctors know no more anatomy than a mechanic knows of alchemy. They who keep the secrets once taught certain men the rudiments of what was common knowledge long before Aesculapius. Those, though, turned the knowledge to their own account, so that it died again of selfishness—which is all-destroying; and all that remains of the art, that it was sought to heal the world with, is the trick by which practitioners of Thuggee kill their victims with a silken handkerchief!

"Chemical dyes mean poison gas. The art of flying, which was understood in India ten thousand years ago, means bombing of defenseless cities. Alcohol means drunkenness. Morphia, which is an anodyne, means vice. Only very rarely do the men appear in whose hands knowledge may be trusted. Then, and not until then, the world goes forward.

"But those who seek knowledge for selfish ends persist. In that way they are faithful! They seek it like prospectors—at times alone, at times in hordes. And because of the Wheel and the Law, as men unearth gold so these lawless seekers after knowledge draw near at times to the discovery. They *would* discover. They *would* possess themselves of secrets and destroy the world, unless they who keep the secrets were alert.

"Through alertness it is possible to see that they destroy themselves, as the hosts of Korah, Dathan and Abiram did in your Bible days—as Babylon destroyed itself, from too much wealth—as he who discovered gunpowder destroyed himself; only swiftly, and secretly, lest the world learn too much and inquire for more.

"The lawless Nines who hide under the mask of Kali-worship, by elimination and persistence have come near to discovering the place where the secret of gold is kept. The place must be changed— nay *is* changed; but lest they learn that, they shall be allowed to find the former place and to take the consequences. It is there that the Wheel turns and *you* enter in."

"How so?" demanded Ali truculently; but none took any notice of him, which seemed to set him thinking on his own account. He listened attentively, but with a changed expression, while Ghandava went on with his story.

Suddenly Chullunder Ghose threw up his hands in consternation.

"Holy one!" he exclaimed. "Emolument is more than pleasing, same is necessary on this plane on which we function! Is profit barred? Is all excluded but the risk? Myself am text-book of scientific ignorance and not proud, but—family and dependents—impoverished babu—*verb. sap.*, Most Holy One!"

Ghandava chuckled.

"You shall see, and may help yourself," he answered.

"When shall I go with my message to these people?" Narayan Singh asked, standing up again.

Ramsden rose, too, stretching himself, nearly as tall as the Sikh and half-again as heavy—a man to count on in tight places.

"I'll go with you," he said quietly, meeting the Sikh's eyes.

Narayan Singh bowed, smiling a little. It was just the smallest inclination of the head, but a whole song set to music could never have answered half as much. He said no word. They understood each other.

"When shall we go?" asked Ramsden.

"When you have seen," Ghandava answered. "You must see; and every word you subsequently say to them the woman must say first to you. It is essential that these criminals destroy themselves. All you are asked to do is to make that simple for them!"

They ate breakfast all together on the deep veranda, Gauri and her maid as anxious as Chullunder Ghose about the rules of caste they broke, yet none of the three willing to pose as holier than Ghandava, who ate with them and had been a "heaven-born" until he abandoned caste altogether. Gauri consoled herself with the sight of the plundered emeralds.

"I shall have enough to pay the priests," she said aloud, as if answering the voice of conscience.

She did not see Ali's flint eyes blazing, nor the sly, secretive acquiescence of his sons; nor did she know why, when the meal was done, the sons threw dice on the veranda floor. No money passed between them, but they threw three times, watching each main breathlessly, and he who lost swore acridly in the name of Allah.

Ghandava watched it all but made no comment, unless, about five minutes later as he faced the Ganges, an adaptation of two of the Apostle Paul's most wholesome axioms that he let fall had bearing on Ali's attitude:

"Since all things work together for our good, and now is the appointed time, why not? Shall we be going?"

He did not say where they were going. They followed curiously, both women keeping close to him and Ali bringing up the rear with his two sons. It was as plain as clay that the North was in the mood of those old Highlanders who followed Prince Charlie once as far as Preston Pans. The rear, where they can do least demoralizing, is the right place for those gentry.

Ghandava led up-stairs—the last way anyone expected—out on to a roof, and up by a winding flight of steps that circled about a tower, with a stone curtain on their right that rendered them invisible from anywhere unless so distant that their heads would be unrecognizable. And then down—through a door at the summit of the tower—round and round a circular stairway in the tower's core, with ample air to breathe, but in darkness so deep that Ghandava's reassuring voice seemed to come from another world:

"This way! This way!"

And the echoes rumbled down into infinity like the voice of an underground stream. Ghandava's spirits seemed to rise as they descended.

Both women screamed at intervals, but there was always somebody for them to cling to, and the voice of Ali behind them proving his own fearlessness—to himself at least—by lecturing his sons.

"A man is a man in the dark! A man is a man in the devil's face! A man dies fighting, and Allah receives him into Paradise! Fear is a fool's religion, sons of Ali!"

"Aye, and the world is full of fools!" Chullunder Ghose confessed. "Self being one! Are there snakes?"

"No snakes!" Ghandava answered.

"Insects?"

"None!"

"Lost souls?"

"No. They would find no rest here!"

"We are going down—down!" The babu's voice boomed hollow. "We are surely in Gunga's womb!"

"Not yet!"

"Oh—, where are we then? I hear the rushing of waters!"

"Only air—good air," Ghandava called back.

"I hear water boiling!"

"No, for there is none."

The babu's trepidation served to keep the women from hysterics, since he voiced another fear than theirs and the two disputed mastery instead of blending into panic and hysteria. Guided by Ghandava's voice and the feel of cool, smooth masonry now on one hand, now the other, they hurried in single file along a tunnel whose floor felt polished under-foot as if a hundred generations has passed over it.

"No bats!" Chullunder Ghose complained. "So there must be devils!"

"No, no devils," said Ghandava.

"Krishna! What then? Look! See! I am blind! I saw another world! I cannot see! I am blinded! I swim in fire! Why do I not burn?"

They stopped. They had all seen one flash, and then nothing but its aching image in the retina—light to which a blow-pipe flame would have been gloaming!

"Watch! Wait!" called Ghandava.

"Not again! Not again!" cried the babu, and his cry re-echoed in imprisoned space—"Again, again, again, again, again!" Then the light—three flashes.

"God!"

That was King, clapping both hands to eyes that had been overstrained on active service.

"Allah! I saw devils!" (That was Ali.)

"Holy One, where are we?" (That was the babu.)

"Under the bed of Ganges!"

"The fire? Is it Agni?*"

"Electricity!" said Ramsden, speaking from memory of fuses blown out in the wilderness.

"No." Ghandava was about to explain, but three more blinding flashes interrupted.

"What then?" asked Ramsden, positive, from memory.

"Gold!" fell the answer on breathless silence, in which they could all hear Ali and his two sons loosening their Khyber knives.

---

* The Spirit of Fire.

XX

"Nevertheless, I will take my sword with me!"

A Pale-Green astral-looking light developed gradually, turning the heart of darkness into twilight. They discerned the shadowy outlines of a cave buttressed with titanic masonry. There were no images, no carvings on walls, nor anything to mar simplicity. The proportions expressed restful, pure and final peace.

There was no smell of dampness, although Ghandava said they were under the bed of Ganges. There were no bats, no filth, no occupants. There was nothing in there—in an acre of earth's foundations—but one square altar set against a wall; and thence the light came, seemingly.

Ghandava led to the altar with no more outward reverence than the vergers use who show the crowds around cathedrals. It was of some green substance so like jade to the eye that Ramsden, advancing an incautious finger, touched it. He drew it back with an oath.

"Pardon! I should have warned you. Are you hurt?" Ghandava examined Jeff's finger. "It burns like radium."

"Oh, buncombe!" said Jeremy, breaking an hour's silence. "I've carried gold in my belt for years. My belly hasn't got a mark on it!"

Everyone laughed, even Ali, and the women who knew no English. But Ghandava continued as much at ease as if he stood before a blackboard.

"You see?" he said, and pointed to where the wall arched over the altar in the shape of a shovel, base to the ground, with the apex leaning out above the center of the green stone. Exactly in the middle of the arch emerged what might have been a pipe of some unrecognizable substance, and for a space of two or three feet around it the stone wall seemed to have the consistency of pumice, as if its life had been burned out.

"Hot gold drips from that opening, drops on the stone below, and dissipates into electrons!"

"Hell!" said Jeremy.

"Men could raise hell with it, couldn't they!" Ghandava answered. "There is more force in one drop than in a box of dynamite—more in a ton of it than in Vesuvius!"

"Who tends it?" asked Jeremy.

"Those whose turn it is," Ghandava answered. "They are beyond that wall."

"Where is the store of gold?" demanded Ali hoarsely.

"Gone! Removed!"

"There can never have been much gold, or who could have moved it in haste?" the Hillman sneered, nudging his two sons.

"Never more than enough at one time in this place than to keep the drops dripping," Ghandava answered. "It has been dripping since long before Atlantis disappeared. Calculate it! There is enough in store to continue the process for as long again. But it must continue elsewhere. We must find another way of purging Gunga."

"Riddles! Forever riddles!" Ali grumbled. "Who believes a word of all this? Allah—"

Ghandava interrupted him:

"Have you ever thought how many thousands bathe in Gunga daily? How many dead, who died of sickness, are laid on the banks for the stream to wash them? How many drink as they stand waist-deep in Gunga? And how few die?"

"They say it's the sunlight," King objected. "I've read that germs of sickness can't live in Ganges water because of the strong sun."

"And you believe it?" asked Ghandava. "If so, why does the sun not kill germs in the Amazon, or the Congo River, or the Jumna or the Irrawaddy?"

"Damned if I know!" said Grim. "Go on, Ghandava. Tell."

"Billions of people have drunk Ganges water, since the pilgrimages began so long ago that there is no record of them. None ever died of drinking it. They have come with cholera, and plague, and small-pox. For lack of fuel for the pyres they have thrown their dead unburned into the stream. And beside the dead they have drunk the Ganges water, taking no harm. That is because of this."

He signified the altar-stone and paused:

"Gold is the greatest purifying agent in the universe. In the words of the Hermetic Mystery: 'As ABOVE, So BELOW.' Gold is thus also the root of every evil. Gold, resolved into electrons, is the greatest force available to men. It is also by the same law men's greatest weakness. Released it could abolish labor, lack, necessity for digging coal—or it could obliterate! There is gold enough in the world to usher in the golden age, or to wipe out civilization!"

He paused again dramatically, then added:

"Nine men know the secret!"

"The devil they do!" said Jeremy.

"Many have sought for the secret until a few of them know nearly where to look. A week—a month—a year and they would find this place. It is wisdom to let them find it now. So say those who have commissioned me."

"By Allah, I weary of words!" shouted Ali, all his patience vanishing into its elements as gold had done. His voice reverberated overhead. "Show me as much gold as I can bear away, I and my sons, or—"

In the dim green light he met Narayan Singh's eyes—could not avoid them. The big Sikh leaned and shoved a shoulder under his chin, shoving him backward so that he could use his right eye only with difficulty; and his sons could not have helped their sire without first passing King and Grim, with Ramsden on King's left-hand and Grim against the wall.

"Friend Ali, peace, I pray thee!" said the Sikh.

There was no alternative. The hilt of something underneath the Sikh's long smock made that fact clear.

Ghandava looked up at the spout above the green altar, listening. He said nothing, but started to walk away, and they followed in a frightened group, the women hurrying past him and the men, especially Ali, trying to disguise fear by striding measuredly. Chullunder Ghose gave up that effort.

"Lo! I claim merit! My share of the gold is a gift to Mother Gunga!" he blustered, struggling to the last to make a joke of it, and ran. Shoving the women in front of him he disappeared into the dark and they could hear his heavy footsteps stampeding until the echoing noise was swallowed in a tunnel-gurgle sounding like a laugh.

"The gold is uncontrollable when it begins to drip," Ghandava explained. "The process can be started but not stopped. It has been so for a hundred centuries. Not even they who keep the secrets could exist inside the cavern when the drops fall."

As they left the cave a blinding flash burst behind them, casting their shadows forward into the tunnel like the fragments of shelled infantry. Even so, facing away from it, their eyes were hurt. Intellect itself seemed stupefied, and was restored by a breath of indrawn air that reeked of hot Benares, all decaying flowers, humanity and grease.

"It ventilates the tunnel," said Ghandava. "That air, drawn in, will be burned up in the next explosion."

"Where does the product go?" Grim asked him.

"It is used."

"Why doesn't the explosion burst the cave?"

"It would, but the quantity is measured."

That was all they could extract from hint by way of information. When they asked more questions he reminded them that these were ancient secrets and himself no more than a man commissioned for a task.

"Already you have seen more than uninitiated individuals ever saw *and lived to tell about*," he assured them. "And this is only one of very many wonders that are done with gold. This is only a trifling matter compared to what can be—what *is*—done daily."

"Then you are an initiate?" asked Grim. But he did not answer that.

Another flash behind them that sent tattered shadows leaping into the dark ahead showed an opening in the right-hand wall, set at such an angle and so narrow that they had passed it on their way down without being aware of its existence. Ghandava led through it now, ignoring the babu and the women, who by then were ascending the circular stair in the panic that will yield to nothing less than daylight.

"You shall see, because you must say you have seen," he explained, taking Ramsden and Narayan Singh each by the arm, as the passage widened and turned back nearly in the same direction they had just cone. Evidently they had only made a circuit to pass through the end wall of the cave. "Say nothing that is not true, even to the enemy!" he added.

And now it felt like entering the workshop where the gloaming is woven of green and golden ether. They approached a cavern—not too close, for he restrained them—in which three men watched as if attending looms, only that these looms were invisible and the shuttles resembled fish that darted to and fro forever on the sane course, each swallowing the other as they met. The pale green light resembled water—the men, great hooded seals—and the silence finished the illusion, so that the ears strained for a sound of waves on some imaginary beach.

But there was no sound—not even a foot-fall; and of gold they saw no more than one bar that a man in a hood brought down steps from a gallery hewn overhead. Even the steps resembled submarine rocks, and the whole illusion was so perfect that they caught themselves not breathing, and wondering how long they could stay submerged.

When Grim started to speak Ghandava held a hand up and restrained him. Silence, it seemed, was part of the twilight mystery. There was no heat, it was cooler there than in the other cave; no light but the dim opalescence in which shuttles made of other light swam. Nothing to understand. It stripped incomprehension naked and left it aware of itself.

"Come!" said Ghandava. "You have seen a workshop older than Benares! You have seen enough!"

Ali had seen enough to stir cupidity, and it controlled him. He brushed by with his hand on his knife-hilt and was for plunging into the cavern with his left arm hiding his face. The illusion of green water was too real to be faced without subconscious precaution of some sort. He walked forward with the sidewise pendulum motion of one who wades into the surf—threw up both hands suddenly—turned—and came hurrying back with eyes and tongue protruding. "No air!" he gasped.

But something else had terrified him—something he could not, and never tried to explain. Followed by his two sons he took to his heels, pursuing Chullunder Ghose and the women up toward daylight; and was first out on the summit of the tower with a view of all Benares, in spite of the others' long start, thanks to the legs and the wind of a mountaineer.

"Behold, who would worship Allah?" asked Narayan Singh; and there being no more Moslems there, none answered.

Slowly, with Ghandava in the lead, they returned by the tunnel and the steps within the tower, none saying much because of breathlessness, nor any climbing better than Ghandava, much the eldest, who waited at least a dozen times for them to overtake him. Up near the summit of the tower he opened a door that admitted to a gallery with a pierced stone screen around it; and there in full sunlight, with eyes aching, and with the sound of Ali's voice arguing above, they squatted down facing the Ganges to learn what more Ghandava had in store for them. He sat meditating for ten minutes before he spoke. Then:

"Only Truth persists. All *things* are relative, and pass when they have seen their day. Truth is and all phenomena are Maya.* It is nothing, then, that what you have just seen must vanish. Benares has vanished ten times. The river below you has swallowed city on top of city, and the

---

* Delusion.

cavern we were in lies under the foundations of a temple whose steps the Ganges laved long before Egypt grew beside the Nile. This was the Temple of the Mysteries before the Pyramids were built. And now it perishes. But Truth remains."

"Were the men we saw below there any of the Nine Unknown?" demanded Ramsden.

"None of them," Ghandava answered, looking him full in the face. "The men you saw are *chelas*. You will never see the Nine Unknown."

He was growing restless, for Ghandava. There was still the air of contact with eternity that made him so courteous and earned respect for him without his claiming it. But there was a subtle change, nevertheless, though he waited to speak again until he had their absolute attention. Then:

"The appointed time is now. I will instruct Mr. Jeremy and those who are to work with him. Are you two ready?"

Ramsden and Narayan Singh met each other's eyes and nodded gravely.

"There is a *chela* below, who will lead you to the place where the Kali-worshipers make ready. He will leave you there. Gauri, in a minute, taking words from my mouth, will give you a message to deliver. They will believe the message, but will keep you with them unless they are more mad than there is reason to believe. There are grades of madness. Theirs is familiar, and understood. All then that will remain for you to do will be to persuade them to watch Mr. Jeremy, and to follow him to the woman. You will be cared for. Play your parts, tell only truth, say no more than you must, and remember you are rendering a service to humanity."

"Nevertheless, I will take my sword with me," announced Narayan Singh.

XXI

"MY HOUSE IS CLEAN AGAIN!"

It was noon when Narayan Singh and Ramsden, following a *chela* fifty years of age, chose what shadows were available in streets that baked like ovens between the stifling walls. The *chela* led them past an opening in a carved wall and gave the agreed signal, passing on as if unconscious of them. They turned and walked boldly into a ruinous temple, whose floor was deep with the dung of sacred bulls and whose only light was from little oil-dishes swung by wires from a roof invisible in gloom.

As the eyes grew used to the dark they were aware of the big bronze man in yellow who had been their prisoner, standing with his back to an inner-door with arms folded over his breast. They could see the white teeth glistening between thick lips, and the whites of his eyes with a glow behind them.

He in no way resembled a spider, yet Jeff thought of him as one. Imagination painted in the web. He looked as if he expected them and, saying nothing, beckoned, with his other hand behind him on the handle of the wooden door. When they were near enough he threw the door open and stood aside to let them pass in.

Jeff led the way with the nerves of his neck all tingling in expectation of a silken handkerchief from ambush. The only thought in his head just then was whether his neck-muscles might not be strong enough to resist the handkerchief for the necessary fraction of a second until his fists could come in play. Imagination! For in step behind him strode the Sikh, who, if nothing more, would have given the alarm in time.

They were in a round room lighted by kerosene lanterns and scant rays filtered through old sacking stretched across openings in the gloom overhead. The walls were the base of a dome, whose arch was dimly visible, and around the walls not less than seventy men in yellow sat facing the center, where a plain stone platform a yard high stood in the midst of pillars that rose up in the form of a pentagon into the dark—a pillar to the apex of each angle.

They wore no masks, but the faces of all alike were stamped with evil and it would have been next to impossible to memorize the varying features. Proud, confident, deliberate crime was the key-note according unity, and it might have been four-score reflections of one face for all that a man could remember otherwise. The enormous bronze man leered at Jeff, thrusting his face so close that it was all that Jeff could do to refrain from punching him again; but all he did was to lead Jeff and Narayan Singh to the platform, where he left them to face whichever way they chose.

"You may sit down!" said a voice in English.

But they continued standing. To have sat or squatted would have betrayed the long sword under the Sikh's smock—their only weapon. Jeff had left his automatic behind on Ghandava's advice, since—as Ghandava phrased it—"it is easier not to kill when the means are absent. He who interferes with no man's *karma* is wisest."

They turned around, peering through the pillars to discover from which face the voice had come. He who had spoken waited until they both faced him, then spoke again—

"Where is SHE?"

He was a little man—the smallest in the room, and his voice was as tiny and mean as his English accent was ludicrous, stressing each syllable, querulous, excited, full of a kind of schoolmaster authority.

"*She* sent us," Jeff answered, and there was silence for the space of half a minute while they all considered the reply. Then:

"That may be so," a voice said from across the room. "How else should they know this place?"

"Why did *she* send you?" asked the little man.

He appeared to be in haste for information. Jeff obliged him.

"*She* said to me and to this other man: 'Obey me, and be rewarded. Tell those whom you will find in the place I name to follow you to where a *fakir* in the robe of Kali is performing feats. Follow the *fakir* to wherever *he* goes. *He* will lead to the place of the secrets you two men have seen.'"

"You have seen? What have you seen? They say they have seen!"

He translated the information into another tongue, and there was a chorus of exclamations. Then the little man said again—

"What have you seen?"

Jeff told him: "We saw the gold turn liquid and drop on the green anvil. We saw it turn to blinding light with a great explosion. We saw the place behind the wall, where the secret is and the men prepare it. But we only saw one bar of gold."

"Bah! Bah! Who cares for the bars of gold if we have the secret! Where is this place?"

"The gold-light blinded us," Jeff answered. "We were led. But the *fakir* knows the way."

"How should *he* know?"

"He can make the dead talk," Jeff answered with perfect irrelevance, and there was another pause while they considered that.

Narayan Singh nudged Jeff. A man who had risen from the wall was walking toward them. He came close and looked into their faces, all unconscious of the sword that trembled on the Sikh's thigh. They recognized their first prisoner whom Grim had let go. Without a word he returned to his place by the wall and then, standing:

"That is so," he said. "These are the same men. Their *fakir* makes the dead speak, having stolen that secret from the Nine or learned it from the books of Cyprian. One of them slew Kansa, our leader in Delhi, and they brought the corpse a distance in the cart with me. In the presence of all who were in the cart, Kansa spoke to me, being dead, bidding me obey these people."

He sat down. His speech, too, was received in silence.

"Why does *she* not come to *us*?" asked the man with the squeaky voice at last. And Jeff, primed an hour before by Gauri picking words from Ghandava's lips, was ready with the answer:

"She said if we would help her, we may become as you, members of your order, sharing in all things. So we help. It was *she* who went before us into the place where gold becomes light. She said she will be there waiting, only we must come soon."

"What sign did she give?" the big, bronze man demanded with a sneer.

And for answer to that Jeff threw into the lap of the little man with the squeaky voice a golden skull twisted from the end of a necklace that morning in spite of Gauri's protests. The little man considered it a minute. Then:

"This is trite," he said at last. "*She* would not have told the secret signs. See, all of you!"

And he sent the gold skull passing around the circle from hand to hand, until it returned to his again.

It was as clear as twice two, even to Jeff's ponderous intellect, that these men were not being taken by surprise. Someone had been there already—someone at Ghandava's instigation probably—warning what they could expect. They were like men strained to the start of a race, so keyed up by expectation that caution was irksome and at most perfunctory.

However, there followed a debate, because some maintained that one of the messengers ought to be kept prisoner while individuals should be sent with the other to investigate the *fakir* and report. The majority were for obeying the summons immediately. They said She was a seeress and they said other things about her, that would not look well between the covers of a book, but that explained a great deal of their ritual and superstition. And at last the prisoner whom Ali had kept without water got tip on his feet.

Jeff broke into a sweat, and Narayan Singh drew in breath sharply between his teeth, for on this man's temper—so Ghandava said—more depended than was good to contemplate.

But it seemed he was not so revengeful against Ali as to offset that against success: he spoke fluently in a tongue that not even Narayan Singh knew, apparently urging them to obey the summons and make haste—touching his own breast, as a man might who argues that his judgment of a situation was more trustworthy than others. They appeared to yield. Then the big bronze man who had acted janitor raised another point.

He, too, used the secret language but his argument was plain enough. He demanded that Jeff and Narayan Singh be tied and put in his charge. That was agreed to. He had copper-wire in his hand in readiness to tie their wrists together, but the other man who had been prisoner forestalled him with thick twine. He refused to tie their bands behind their backs, as the other wanted to, arguing that that would attract attention passing through the streets, but lashed Jeff's right wrist to Narayan Singh's left. Then someone gave them a basket to carry between them with a cloth thrown over it so that their wrists were hidden.

There was no more said. The man who had tied them lost apparent interest and mingled with the others. The big bronze man leered threateningly in Jeff's face and pointed toward the door, following about one stride behind with the evident intention of killing at the first suspicion of trickery, and the others filed out one by one in solemn procession led by the smallest man of all, who had spoken first.

Seventy men in single file, headed by two stalwarts carrying a basket between them, would arouse comment anywhere but in Benares. There, there are fifty more astonishing processions on almost any day of the year, and all are so absorbed about the business of their own escape from *Maya* that none disturbs himself about the other man's affairs.

They were not even noticed. If one thing about them were remarkable it was that they excited no remarks, despite the yellow smocks and the caste-mark of their dreadful goddess; and when they filed through a gate into a temple-yard and vanished they passed from the mind of the crowd as well.

It was a yard like any of a hundred in that city of clustered shrines. Four walls, carved deep with the forgotten stories of a thousand gods, enclosed an oblong space paved with heavy blocks in front of a temple whose every inch was carved in high relief—and all so black with age and dirt that none might read what legend it embodied. It was hidden lore, as safe from public knowledge as the books whose ashes lay in Cyprian's kiln, or as the Mysteries of the Nine themselves.

But on the temple steps in front of the portico a part was being enacted that anyone might interpret how he chose.

A *fakir* smeared with ashes, and as nearly naked as the law permits, with more meat on his well-ribbed frame than the ordinary run of *fakirs* boast, was doing tricks with three skulls before a spell-bound gathering of nondescripts. It was amusing stuff, and the effect on the audience was like champagne, laughter being ten times welcome in a place where all else is so serious as in Benares.

For a while he would keep the three skulls circling in the air in the way that any common juggler can contrive; but then, with both arms suddenly extended to their limit, he would cause the game to cease and the skulls came to a dead rest facing the audience, one on the palm of each extended hand and the third on his plain black turban.

Then each skull talked to each, or tossed amusing scraps of wisdom to the audience.

It was perfect foolery, so masterfully done that folly seemed no part of it. To an audience asking only to believe, and dreading more than anything to criticize, it was inspired—miraculous—in keeping with the place—undoubtedly contrived by unseen Powers.

The advent of the seventy in yellow, with two stalwarts bearing a basket at their head, was so plainly a religious portent that the audience, already enraptured, now gave double credence—a condition that reverted on the seventy, causing them, if not to believe in the *fakir's* occult powers, at least to credit his authority.

The *fakir* set the jawless skulls again in motion and the seventy sat down to see. Then a fat man with a naked stomach, his sanctity expressed by ashes, and a pink silk turban crowning all, came and sat in front of the *fakir*, below him on the paving stones, facing both him and the audience. And while the three skulls bobbed and circled in air the fat man spoke in Hindustance, which was the only language likely to be understood by more than a handful of any Benares audience.

"Hear what *she* says!" he whined in a nasal singsong. "Who is *she*? Let any ask who dares! Where is *she*? Let him tell, who can find her! What says *she*? The skulls will tell! Now listen!"

They ceased from circling in air and rested as before on the *fakir's* head and his extended hands. The *fakir's* ashen face was motionless, and no breath seemed to come and go now through his slightly-parted lips. Only his head jerked suddenly from side to side from one skull to the other, so that all eyes followed his. He appeared to be wondering as much as they did at the dead things' hollow voices.

Hollow they were—maybe to cover mispronunciation and croaking, as may be forgiven dead things. And as each one spoke, it moved, not much, but enough to suggest an unseen lower jaw—although if the *fakir's* hands moved too no one observed it. Not even his head seemed to nod, to account for the movement of the skull that rested on it. The *fakir* said never a word.

"I am the skull of Akbar!" said the left-hand skull.

"I am the skull of Iskander!" replied the right-hand one.

"And ye were two fools!" croaked the upper, all eyes watching it as the *fakir* turned his upward.

"I had gold in my day!" announced the Akbar skull.

"I had more! I had more!" the thing that named itself Iskander answered. And the audience thrilled. They were Hindus. Neither of those famous kings had been of their faith.

"Where is the gold now?" croaked the upper skull. "I buried mine!" said Akbar.

"I buried mine!" Iskander answered.

"Where?" demanded the skull on top.

"I forget!" said the right-hand skull.

"I lost the secret!" said the one on the left.

"I keep the secret!" croaked the upper one.

"Who art thou?" asked the Akbar skull.

"I am a woman in a leopard-skin! I am *she* who knows the secret! They who have the right should follow me!"

"Yes! Whoever is not afraid of the spirits that guard the secret, follow!" piped the fat man; and the greater part of the audience trembled, glancing sidewise at one another and remaining seated. They were no such fools as to trespass into ancient secrets. Some began to run away, fearing sorcery.

Tossing the skulls from hand to hand the *fakir* disappeared into the temple. The courtyard emptied. The men in yellow, led by Jeff and Narayan Singh carrying the basket, followed the *fakir* one by one. Another of India's every-day marvels was a thing gone by, to be discussed and magnified and finally forgotten or else woven into the fabric of religious legend.

Jeff and Narayan Singh walked swiftly. They wanted to speak, but did not dare, for they could not outdistance the bronze man at their heels; and the others came equally fast, breaking into a run as the *fakir* disappeared down an opening in the hollow-shaped floor of a dark chamber.

The *fakir* was all alone, and seemed in haste. (No sign of the fat impresario.) In darkness they could hear the *fakir's* naked feet shuffling along an echoing tunnel, and the big bronze man urged Jeff and Narayan Singh to run. Jeff kicked something, and a hollow rattle announced a skull bouncing away in the dark ahead of him. The bronze giant's toes struck another one, and a man somewhere behind them kicked the third. The *fakir* had abandoned his dead oracles! He appeared to be in full flight.

That was too much for the giant. He thrust Narayan Singh aside and rushed by, following by ear, bellowing back to the crowd to hurry after him. And as the first half-dozen forced themselves between Narayan Singh and the right-hand wall the blade of a knife passed between his wrist and Ramsden's. The thongs that held them together parted, and a voice said:

"Wisely, *sahibs*! Hold the basket as before!"

They turned to look, but could not see. The tunnel was alive with men who hurried by them, until every man of the seventy had passed, excepting one. He tugged at them.

"Now turn back!" he urged excitedly.

"Who are you Jeff asked, but he could not answer. The Sikh had him by the throat and was burning the darkness with his eyes, trying to recognize him.

"Quick! Who are you?" Jeff repeated.

As he spoke the faint reflection of a far-off flash of light lifted the darkness, like summer-lightning. Simultaneously Jeff and the Sikh recognized the prisoner whom Ali had kept dry. He was scared—in pain because of fingers clutching at his throat—but unmistakable. The Sikh let go.

"Quick! Come away!" he gasped, pulling at them,

(Pages 346-347 missing from the paper book used to create this ebook.)

. . . wads down a gun-barrel, until it ceased in what seemed vacuum. Lungs ached, and they retched; but a blast of air ice-cold by contrast, came whistling back, providing breath, but no other surcease, for they heard like a flood at war with fire the seething roar of water, and the earth's foundations seemed to shake beneath them.

"Are you there?" yelled Jeremy, groping wildly for his friends.

Narayan Singh gripped him by the shoulder, and the two turned back for Jeff. They stumbled on him, wrapped in death-grip with his adversary. The Sikh's foot struck home into the bronze giant's stomach. Jeff's fist, breaking from a python-hold, descended like a poleax on the giant's neck, and in a second the three were careering headlong for the tunnel's end with the pressure of a full gale and the roar of a boiling flood so near behind them that in their spines they knew the very feel of death. By the arms the two dragged Jeff waist-deep out of surging water that followed and swamped the hollow temple floor, and the three fell all together gasping in the sunshine on the portico.

There presently Chullunder Ghose, still smeared with ashes and half-naked, came to them with the erstwhile prisoner in yellow trying not to appear to walk with him. The babu was triumphant, the man in yellow sheepish, hiding fear under a veneer of pride.

"Where is Ali?" gasped Narayan Singh.

"Gone!" said Chullunder Ghose. "*Sahibs*, all is lost but honor!" Nonchalantly he toyed with one great emerald ear-stud. "Am unfortunate babu, but there are compensations. Devil, being slow on foot presumably, takes hindermost fugitive who is too fat to run—sometimes! There *are* exceptions. Am same. Exceptional this time—very!"

"*Where* has Ali gone?"

"Where does flame go when *any* person blows out candle? To where it came from, I *suspect*. *Verb. sap.* Ali *did* come from Sikunderam, same being suitable environment for gent of his kidney. Ali said to me: 'May Allah do so to this son of my mother, and more likewise, if those *sahibs* are not asking for destruction. I have lost too many sons. What shall I do about it? There will be police investigation and many corpses to explain.'—And this babu, being abject individual, had access of enlightenment, plus memory of much experience with legal luminaries. Am known to the police. Same is reciprocal. Police are also known to me. Nice, isn't it" he asked, turning the emerald toward the sunlight.

He was ordered bluntly to explain himself, and to cut the explanation short.

"Am not explainable," he answered. "Am portion of riddle of universe, but capable of genius on occasion. It occurred to this babu that you are very ballistic *sahibs*—oh yes, very—likely to be spat forth same as bullets from throat of any cataclysm. Yes—am optimist. Having assisted Jeremy *sahib* to juggle with skulls in temple compound, am henceforth capable of believing anything—even that Jeremy *sahib* will survive underworld explosions. Ergo—*sahibs*, there is no hurry; I tell you Ali has vanished; so has everybody!—ergo, it occurred to this babu *most* opportunely that scapegoat is needed to obsess intellect of seriously exercised police, who will be spurred to indiscreet enquiries by higher-ups in club armchairs. Who better than Ali? What solution better than elopement to Sikunderam? No sooner thought than said— for a price! Good counsel in emergency is surely worth two emeralds, but an Afghan is more thrifty than Scotchman, Jew, Armenian and Greek combined, plus Yankee trader thrown in. He would only part with one! Pretty, isn't it? Worth, what would you say? How much?"

"Come now, come—what happened?" Ramsden demanded.

"Solution happened, *sahib*, this babu advising, Ali making much haste to elope with lady. Thus. The Gauri knew too much. Too much knowledge, in brain of lady of her mode of living, leading to blackmail sooner than later always, same leading to inveiglement in nets of the police,—distance should therefore lend enchantment to otherwise somewhat faded charms of said enchantress. *Nicht wahr?* She has dowry—less one emerald, surrendered as extremely meagre fee to this babu, who explained to her that unless she shall hide her charms in Sikunderam with Ali, who will make her, perhaps and perhaps not, queen of many cutthroats, the police will inevitably capture her and take the jewelry. And to Ali this babu remarked that unless he shall take the Gauri with him, she will most certainly betray to the police his weakness for butchering inoffensive members of Hindu religious sect. And as for the maid, let Ali's son take her, she also knowing too much. Advice was accepted—on spot—instantly. Three-fold solution—very excellent. Ali has a wife, who has a dowry. One son has a wife, who has youth and good looks. The other surviving son has an example. They are gone—northward. Can you beat it? as Jimgrim would remark."

"Where are King and Grim?" demanded Jeff.

"Hunting for me, *sahib*. They are very angry. I cannot imagine why. They suspect me of complicity in flight of Ali. Most unreasonable. I am here to beg your honors' confidence—and *some* additional emolument, not as inducement—oh, no, most unnecessary!—but by way of reward in advance for holding my tongue! Am not altruist," he added significantly.

"What do *you* want here?" demanded Jeremy, looking straight into the face of the erstwhile prisoner.

"Protection!" he answered, rather humbly. "Bhima Ghandava has disappeared."

"What of it?" asked Jeremy.

"He is that member of the Nine Unknown whom I was to have killed! I betrayed my party to him, thinking it better that they should all perish. But now Ghandava *sahib* has disappeared, and I have no friends!"

Chullunder Ghose tapped him on the shoulder.

"Have you money?" he demanded. "No? Jewelry? No? Well—am charitable. This babu will give advice in *forma pauperis*. Go and be a hermit, which is proper course for individual with aching conscience and no friends! Go! Be off! In words of Hamlet, stay not—"

But the man in yellow was already gone; perhaps he was afraid of King and Grim, angry, sweating, baffled, who came hurrying across the temple courtyard.

"Bhima Ghandava has disappeared!" King announced out of breath, and then listened while Ramsden related what had happened.

They went and pounded on the door of the house where they had been lodged, but none answered, and they desisted at last in fear of the police. However, the police were all busy on the waterfront, where an ancient ruin on which *fakirs* used to stand in turns, had vanished into the river—by earthquake, as the newspapers asserted afterward— although no seismographs recorded any earthquake in Benares.

There was nothing to be done but to return to Delhi, and no man but Cyprian to whom they dared to go. To have asked anybody else to obtain European clothing for them would have led too surely to enquiry. They searched for him first at Ghandava's house, but found that empty and deserted. Cyprian was back in his own home, being nursed by Manoel, who looked ashamed—repentant.

"The rascal!" said Cyprian. "The rogue! The impudent, incorrigible sinner! You remember, there was a front page missing from one of my occult books that be had hidden under a blanket in the pantry? Well, he, Manoel had torn it out. I found him—where do you think? I found him in a rear room in a back-street starting a new religion with the aid of that page of symbols! Rascal! But he is not altogether bad. He has been a comfort. See, my sons—my house is clean again!"

"But why did you leave Ghandava's house?" asked Jeremy.

"They came and took all the furniture away!"

"Who did?"

"I don't know. People I had never seen before. They provided me with a carriage to come home in, but gave no explanations. I hope Ghandava is not in difficulties. He was always a courteous host and a considerate friend, but there is only one possible result of dabbling in occultism and the black arts."

"We heard," said Jeremy, "that he is one of the NINE—one of the actual NINE UNKNOWN."

"Oh, no," said Cyprian. "Oh, no! I don't believe it. Whoever the Nine Unknown are, they are devils—men without souls! Bhima Ghandava is a gentleman. No, no, he can't be one of them."

"Nevertheless, Pop, I believe he is!" said Jeremy.

"So do I," said King and Grim together.

"I'm pretty nearly sure of it," said Ramsden cautiously. "Remember: he said that what *we* saw was merely a trifle—nothing compared to all the other knowledge of the Nine Unknown."

"My son, it is easy to say things," said Cyprian.

"Aye," exclaimed Narayan Singh, "and difficult to know things. But I *know*. And no man can persuade me I do not know. Bhima Ghandava is one of them."

"Knowledge," said Chullunder Ghose, rubbing his fat stomach, "what is knowledge for, if not for use? Myself, am pragmatist. Myself, am satisfied that *sahibs* wisely trusting this babu to hold his tongue will provide same abject individual with continuous employment at a generous remuneration. No, *sahibs*, no! Am good sport! No—no threat intended! Blackmail not included in my compendium of ways and means! Am gentleman, accepting sportsmanlike standard of West and looking forward to reward—"

"In hell, I'm afraid, unless you mend your ways, my, friend!" said Cyprian.

A Note About the Author

Born in London in 1879, Talbot Mundy (1879–1940) was an American based author popular in the adventure fiction genre. Mundy was a well-traveled man, residing in multiple different countries in his lifetime. After being raised in London, Mundy first moved to British India, where he worked as a reporter. Then, he switched professions, moving to East Africa to become an ivory poacher. Finally, in 1909, Mundy moved to New York, where he began his literary career. First publishing short stories, Mundy became known for writing tales based on places that he traveled. After becoming an American citizen, Mundy joined the Christian science religious movement, which prompted him to move to Jerusalem. There he founded and established the first newspaper in the city to be published primarily in the English language. By the time of his death in 1940, Mundy had rose to fame as a best-selling author, and left behind a prolific legacy that influenced the work of many other notable writers.

A Note from the Publisher

Discover more of your favorite classics with Bookfinity™.

- Track your reading with custom book lists.
- Get great book recommendations for your personalized Reader Type.
- Add reviews for your favorite books.
- AND MUCH MORE!

Visit **bookfinity.com** and take the fun Reader Type quiz to get started.

Enjoy our classic and modern companion pairings!

Printed in the USA
CPSIA information can be obtained
at www.ICGtesting.com
JSHW022323140824
68134JS00019B/1254

9 781513 280790